The Friendship of Mortals

The Herbert West Series

The Friendship of Mortals
Islands of the Gulf Volume 1, The Journey
Islands of the Gulf Volume 2, The Treasure
Hunting the Phoenix

THE FRIENDSHIP OF MORTALS

⌗

Audrey Driscoll

Cover design by Alisha at Damonza.com
Author photo by Glenn Driscoll

Driscoll, Audrey.
    The friendship of mortals / Audrey Driscoll.
    554 pages ; 23 cm.
    (Book 1 of the Herbert West series)
    1. West, Herbert (Fictitious character)—Fiction. 2. Physicians—Fiction. 3. Librarians—Fiction. 4. Human experimentation in medicine—Fiction. 5. Miskatonic University (Imaginary organization)—Fiction. 6. Arkham (Mass. : Imaginary place)—Fiction. I. Title. II. Series: Driscoll, Audrey. Herbert West series ; book 1.

Dedication
To Howard Phillips Lovecraft

PROLOGUE

What do I remember?

I could say, "Everything I need to, and nothing more." But if I am being truthful (and tonight I must be truthful, for *in vino veritas*), I will admit that certain of my memories have been too heavy to carry around with me. I have entrusted them to a mental root cellar – dark, cold and difficult of access. The key to this place, unlike most keys, permits itself to be found only on nights such as this, when I have drunk deeply enough to set aside daytime scruples.

Here it is, small and ornate, a subtle thing. And here is the little door. Insert the key with trembling fingers, and turn. The latch clicks and the door opens, revealing a thin slice of darkness.

Let me pause a moment before venturing inward. Intentions straight? Resolution in place?

All right, Charles Milburn, what is it that you remember?

Darkness and light; the inherent darkness of that town – ancient Arkham, on the Miskatonic – and the darkness of secrets. Alma's bright hair, shining like rippled silk. Her silvery laughter, the touch of her hand warm like amber or October sunshine.

But these are only *feuilles mortes*, escapees from the blue dusk of dead days. They were not what drew me to Arkham and kept me there, unreasoning, unarguing, until the end. Herbert West... What was it about *him* – the steely glance of his grey eyes, with the accompanying flash from his gold-rimmed spectacles? His voice, soft but compelling, saying, "Don't be an idiot, Charles, just get on with it." And I generally did, breaking laws and the conventions of my upbringing for reasons that I have never yet been able to define. At first there was the certainty that what he said was the truth, despite the doubts thrown up by my slower mind.

But it wasn't always the truth, was it?

And so, Herbert, finally, to the end – your hand in mine, suddenly lifeless. The blank stare of your eyes. The weight of your body as I carried you to the cellar. It was dead weight; I was sure of that then, and I am now. Almost sure.

The cellar... what happened there? I was exhausted after a sleepless night and by my grief at your death, desperate for visions and wonders. *And I saw your eyes open. I heard you speak.* But before I could be sure of anything, you were gone.

I have no answers, only doubts and questions. They are my legacy from you, Herbert. Because of you, I have become a man who holds conversations with himself, with his old ghosts or with no one at all. Would it help if I remembered everything, in order, from the beginning? Would the end look different then? Probably not; I have tried to take this journey before and failed, but this night will be long and I do not think I shall sleep.

Part 1

THE UNDERTAKER'S SON

◆ 1 ◆

"Charles, my boy," old Crawford said, "I can't imagine why you would want to bother with a benighted backwater like Miskatonic University."

"It's only fifty miles from Boston," I said. "Hardly the back of beyond."

"That's not what I meant. A university is a place of higher learning, not a jumped-up lunatic asylum."

"Oh surely it isn't that bad, Mr. Crawford," I said. "After all, it's been there since 1738."

"So has Bedlam. At least that long, and it's still full of lunatics. Persistence is no guarantee of quality."

"But what is it about Miskatonic that makes you say that?" Crawford was a Harvard man through and through. I had heard him say similar (if less venomous) things about Yale and Princeton. But he'd stopped short of calling them lunatic asylums.

"Well, just look at some of the faculty – there's one fellow there, now what's his name? Quidlington, Quizzington, something like that. He's supposed to be a professor of philosophy, but I've read some of the drivel he's published. It has nothing to do with philosophy, for one thing, and no grounding in scientific or logical principles of any sort. I wouldn't be surprised to find that they have a School of Alchemy at Miskatonic. Or that the Medical School teaches divination by entrails, as though it's the Dark Ages, not 1910! Believe me, you don't want to get mixed up with a place like that. They do seem to have a lot of money, though," he added. "Lots of wealthy alumni, eager to keep the place going for some reason."

11

Audrey Driscoll

"Well, if there are that many graduates with money to spare for their *alma mater*, it must be doing something right," I said.

Crawford snorted. "You can't assume they made their money as a result of what they learned at Miskatonic."

When I said my goodbyes, I reassured Mr. Crawford I would think long and hard before I accepted any offer of employment from Miskatonic. He was an old friend of my late father's and a man worthy of my respect. But of course I did no such thing, even though I found out afterward that there was some basis for his misgivings.

For Miskatonic was the university that sent a team of professors and students to the Antarctic in a search for extraterrestrial life forms. The search was successful, but its results had to be suppressed because of developments that were too sensational even for a sensation-loving public. Then there was Walter Gilman, a student of mathematics who seemed to have found a way to transcend the strictures of time and space, but who met his end in a bizarre attack by rats. These things happened after I left Arkham, but I took care to keep myself informed of its doings. I left Arkham but it never left me.

How can I describe my first impressions of Arkham? Old it was, certainly, and dark. A dark city, even in the bright daylight of a September afternoon. As a Bostonian, I was used to narrow streets and gambrel roofs. But it was not architecture alone that created the darkness of Arkham, although the sepia and garnet-coloured bricks of which many of the buildings were made certainly contributed to it. Its situation in the river valley caused mists to gather and the air to seem heavier than in the surrounding countryside. Change was slow in Arkham, much slower than elsewhere, even in this century of spectacular change. Whatever the reason, people sometimes spoke of the 'Arkham malaise.' Some could not abide it and left, never to return. Others, artists mainly, throve on it, until it sickened them. I found it strangely congenial, until the end.

When I first saw the town, in the late afternoon, with its buildings reflected in the dark mirror of the Miskatonic River, I knew that I had come to a place where something waited for me. At that moment, before I had even seen the University or the Library, before I had been interviewed, I knew I had come home.

Two weeks later, in the autumn of 1910, I moved my few possessions into a couple of furnished rooms in a house on Peabody Street and took up my duties as Cataloguer of Greek and Latin in the Library of Miskatonic University.

Cataloguers are the invisible librarians. People who use libraries rarely consider why the books are arranged as they are, although many believe they should be arranged differently. They flip through the catalogue cards with varying degrees of excitement, impatience, even rage, never thinking that someone must have written the descriptions, selected the classification numbers and assigned the subject headings. Cataloguers do this, weaving the web of words and numbers in unvisited rooms. Mine is very much a profession in which the work is its own reward.

At the time I came to Miskatonic, handwritten cards were being replaced by typewritten ones. The studious sound of pens scraping along on card stock had been replaced by the rather more lively one of typewriter keys. The fine 'library hand' I had taken such pains to learn was nearly obsolete.

Many thousands of these cards, in their ordered arrangement within specially constructed wooden cabinets, constituted the public card catalogue, which occupied the echoing main hall of the Library with its tessellated floor, dark beams and high, arched windows. We who ministered to it were solemn and concentrated as we worked, for we knew ourselves to be gathering the shards of knowledge, ordering them for posterity and fixing them in place with rods of brass.

I have seen many cataloguing departments in my time, but Miskatonic's was the first one I grew to know intimately. It was typical, a maze of desks and book carts and cabinets. If I were led there blindfold, I would instantly know where I was from the smell of the place – a compound of dust, printer's ink, old leather, new buckram, mingled aromas of bag lunches from the staff room, and a suspicion of pipe smoke from Runcible's office. My desk was in an alcove, along with two wooden cabinets containing the few dozen shelflist drawers given over to the area of Greek and Latin literature.

I was fortunate in that I had to myself a window. It overlooked a small bricked square where the Library adjoined the Arts Building. I rarely saw anyone walk through it. Nothing grew there except mosses and golden lichens, which patterned the garnet-coloured bricks of the wall like strange flowers.

The University Librarian was Dr. Henry Armitage, a scholar of great repute, who at this time was at the midpoint of a long and distinguished career (which, nearly twenty years later, would culminate in something very like an exorcism). My immediate superior was Peter Runcible, a perpetually disgruntled man, at once ashamed to be a mere librarian and resentful of those who did not respect his title of Principal Cataloguer and Head of the Cataloguing Department.

One day, a few months after I took up my post, I was in the book stacks, engaged in tracking down some old volumes of Cicero. I had found the information I needed and was on my way back to the Cataloguing Department, when I noticed several large books slumped on their shelf like victims of a street accident. They were victims indeed, I thought, as I bent down to straighten them, of a careless shelver who really should be taken to task.

As I rose to my feet, someone spoke behind me. "Young Mr. Milburn," said Dr. Armitage. "So Runcible has you shelf-reading now?"

"No sir," I replied. "I had an errand in the Roman literature section – a cataloguing matter. I noticed that these books were falling over and stopped to straighten them. I hate to see books in pain." I stopped, blushing, when I realized what I had said.

"Books in pain!" repeated Dr. Armitage, with a laugh. "Spoken like a true bibliophile. Do you collect?"

"No sir, but I feel for books. They're like us in some ways."

"Well, I can't reproach you for looking out for the welfare of the collection," said Dr. Armitage. He hesitated. "You're a classicist, aren't you? Of course you are – honours in Greek and Latin from Amherst. How would you like to be the keeper of the *Necronomicon*?"

"I don't know, sir. What is it that I would be doing?" And what, I wondered, is the *Necronomicon*?

"Dealing with a bunch of confounded nuisances," Armitage replied. "Or, to be serious, with researchers into the obscure and the occult. Come to my office, if you can spare a few minutes. I'll describe the job and you can decide if you want it."

The Library's Administration Office occupied a spacious set of rooms on the second floor. I had been there only a few times, enough to have developed a healthy respect for Miss Edith Hardy, personal secretary to the University Librarian.

She gave me a sharp look as I followed Dr. Armitage into his office. She must have thought that the new cataloguer was being called on the carpet for some misdemeanour. I saw a flicker of amusement pass over her face as she returned to her typewriter.

"What do you know about the *Necronomicon*?" asked Dr. Armitage.

"Not a great deal," I said, carefully.

"It's a work of medieval... mysticism, I suppose you could call it," said Dr. Armitage. "Miskatonic's copy is a relatively late edition, printed in the 17ᵗʰ century, in Spain. But its origins certainly are much older than that – 8ᵗʰ century, I am told. The author was an Arab of Yemen, Abdul Alhazred."

"Is it in Arabic?" I asked. "Because that's a language I do not know at all."

"No, ours is a Latin translation, by one Olaus Wormius. It was bequeathed to Miskatonic by an alumnus. Scholars write to me from all over the country, pleading to be permitted a sight of it. I'm too busy to deal with all that correspondence. I thought I had solved the problem when I appointed John Bowen to the task. He was the obvious choice, being the Rare Books Librarian. But now that he's on sabbatical at the Bodleian, I have to find someone else."

"What about Miss Dodge?" I asked. "She's Mr. Bowen's replacement as Rare Books Librarian, isn't she?"

Dr. Armitage sighed. "Yes she is," he said. "But there's a... tradition, I suppose you could call it, here at Miskatonic, that the *Necronomicon* is not fit to be viewed by respectable women. Some of the illustrations are thought to be... excessive. And the book is considered to be 'evil,' for some reason. It's probably nonsense, but altogether it seems politic to appoint a man to the job. Well, Milburn, what do you say?"

"I'd like to do it, sir," I said. "It might be an interesting experience."

"Oh it'll be interesting all right. You can't imagine some of the characters you'll have to deal with. Well, shall I introduce you to the tome?" He took a key from his desk drawer and led me to a formidable steel door at the end of a short hallway. Inside the vault, a table occupied most of the small space between ranks of drawers. He unlocked one and carefully lifted out a volume bound in black leather and fastened with tarnished silver clasps.

"This is it," he said, placing it on the table.

I have heard people say, in late years, that the *Necronomicon* does not exist, has never existed, that it was the creation of a pulp fiction writer from Providence. This is not true. It exists. I have held a copy in my hands, have turned its pages, have read sections of it. It did not corrupt me or strike me blind, although some of the illustrations were disturbing. Eventually, it did something to me, but of a more subtle nature.

It was a quarto-sized volume, printed on a fine grade of laid paper, in a type which to my eye seemed archaic for the 17ᵗʰ century. The binding was black cowhide, rather coarse in texture but well made. The heavy silver clasps were, like the typeface, archaic, making the book appear older than it was. (It is not true, by the way, that it is bound in human skin; this is another foolish notion that its notoriety has generated).

Dr. Armitage described the procedure for examining prospective researchers, finishing with, "Well, I must hurry along now. Let me put the book away and ask Miss Hardy to give you the keys you will need."

Miss Hardy was less than impressed by this request. She looked me up and down as though she doubted I was clean enough to enter her well-ordered realm. She turned a questioning eye toward Dr. Armitage.

"Are you certain this young man can deal properly with the researchers?" she asked. "Some of them are very persistent, you know."

"I have every confidence in Mr. Milburn's abilities to distinguish a sincere researcher from a fraudulent one," replied Dr. Armitage. "Please give him the keys to the vault and show him the small interview room." Then he was gone.

Miss Hardy turned back to me. "I trust that Dr. Armitage has described the procedures you are to follow," she said, and proceeded to describe them all over again, in great detail. "You realize, of course, that you must not admit anyone to the vault. Researchers must remain in the interview room. You bring them the books they need, one at a time, but only after you are satisfied as to their motives and qualifications. And you must under no circumstances leave any of them alone with a book, especially *that* one." At the end of her lecture she removed a set of keys from a cupboard and gave them to me.

I was profuse in my reassurances that I would observe every precaution in discharging my new duties, and beat a retreat to the Cataloguing Department, from which I had been absent for at least an hour. As luck would have it, Peter Runcible was the first person I met on my return.

"So you've returned to us, have you, Mr. Milburn?" he said. "I understand you had to do some stack research. You must have done enough by now to write a book, not just catalogue one."

"I'm sorry, sir," I replied. "I met Dr. Armitage in the stacks, and he asked me to do something."

"And what might that be?"

"Look after the *Necronomicon* while Mr. Bowen is away."

Runcible's face darkened with anger. "Why should you do that? You're a cataloguer, not a rare book specialist. And you're a member of my staff, moreover. I must have a word with him about this."

He strode out of the department and I returned to my desk. I do not know if Runcible ever did protest to Dr. Armitage, but he kept a close account of the time I spent on 'extradepartmental business,' and required me to make it up in additional work.

I found it a worthwhile exchange. For one thing, I had access to the other books in the vault. Also of interest to scholars of the *Necronomicon* was *The Summoning of Demons,* by someone who styled him- or herself only as The Initiated One. It was a repellent little volume, duodecimo, the pages badly stained, bound in an overly smooth leather which, for all I knew, may very well have been human skin. There was a beautiful 16th century compilation of alchemical writings, the *Liber Arcana Vitae,* printed in France, with engravings so fiendishly detailed and lively, that they rivalled anything by Durer. And there was a fully illustrated copy of Sir Richard Burton's *Ananga-ranga, or, The Hindu Art of Love,* which I assumed was kept in the vault for reasons besides its rarity and intrinsic value. I admit I consulted it a little more often than was strictly necessary.

Over the next several months I dealt with eight researchers. I felt it necessary to exclude only one of them. This individual, whose name I have forgotten, did not inspire levity; indeed, he was rather frightening. When I told him that I could not allow him access to the work he sought because of a lack of academic credentials, he cursed me before he left the room. At least, I think the words he uttered were a curse, judging only by their tone, because the language was unknown to me.

Several months after my encounter with Dr. Armitage, one of the junior clerks arrived in my alcove to announce that a gentleman wanted to see me about obtaining access to the *Necronomicon.*

Expecting someone elderly and bearded, as my previous clients had been, I was surprised to see a young man, my own age or a few years older. He was short and slight, elegantly dressed in a long navy-blue coat. With his blond hair and gold-rimmed spectacles he looked in complete contrast to the homely, indeed shabby, surroundings of the Cataloguing Department. He came toward me, hand extended.

"Mr. Milburn, I believe? I'm Herbert West, Miskatonic University Medical School. Someone in your Administration Office said you're the person to ask about getting a look at the *Necronomicon.* I wonder if you could spare a few minutes now."

"How do you do, Mr. West," I replied, taking his hand and trying to collect my wits. I felt as though I had been buffeted by a sudden gust of cold wind. The sensation was bracing, but startling. His hand was thin and cold, but his grip was firm. The air around him seemed cold too, as though part of the chilly March day had come inside with him.

"I'm sorry," I said. "It's not possible for me to let you see the *Necronomicon* immediately. There are procedures that must be carried out first."

"Procedures," he repeated, with a slight emphasis, as though he thought I was a child who had used a word too big for me. "Yes, of course, Miskatonic is full of procedures. What do you require? Three signatures in blood? Or an oath sworn – but not on the Bible, surely?" He smiled then, and I felt that a gift of rarity and value had been bestowed upon me.

"That will not be necessary," I said. "Endorsements from two or three of your professors, written in ink, will suffice. The usual... procedure is to make an appointment with me for an interview. Would three days be enough time for you to obtain the necessary letters? I can see you on Thursday at three o'clock, in the Administration Office."

In the face of his lightness and what I can describe only as brilliance, I felt heavy and plodding, devoid of humour, parroting stodgy rules. But he did not seem particularly annoyed by the small bureaucratic obstacle I had put in his way.

"Very well, I suppose I can wait another seventy-two hours. Three o'clock Thursday, then." I could hear his steps, light and rapid, receding along the corridor, and imagined him walking quickly toward the bright day beyond the Library's doors. I returned to my desk, suddenly tired.

Herbert West's visit to the Cataloguing Department had not gone unnoticed by my colleagues. Peter Runcible, fortunately, was absent, but when I went into the staff room for afternoon tea, Alma Halsey, the sciences cataloguer, looked up from the newspaper she had been reading.

Alma and I were both graduates of the School of Librarianship at Columbia University, but she had left a year before I arrived there.

"Good thing for you old Runcible wasn't there when West came in, " she said now. "He would have called you on the carpet for neglect of duties, or at least hung around coughing suggestively. But what on earth would a medical student want with the *Necronomicon?*"

"Is he a medical student? Come to think of it, he did mention the Medical School. Do you know him?"

"Herbert West is notorious at the Med. School. I'm surprised you haven't heard of him. Papa told me he was nearly kicked out last year, for some very strange shenanigans involving dissecting room cadavers. You'd better watch your step. He's probably trying on a stunt of some kind."

I expressed surprise at her suggestion that West had been mixed up in mischief involving cadavers. I could not reconcile such repulsive doings with the elegant young man I had met that afternoon. On the other hand, Alma's information could not be discounted either, since her father was the Dean of Medicine.

"Ha! Medical students have been known to do all sorts of disgusting things. They're inured to gore and grossness. That's one of the objectives of medical training, you know. But Herbert West has even more experience with corpses than the others."

"What do you mean?"

"He used to be an undertaker, or at least an undertaker's assistant," said Alma. "His father owns several funeral homes and young Herbert worked in one of them a few summers. Got his hands dirty, you might say."

I did not know what to make of this. West and I had exchanged perhaps a dozen sentences, and yet I realized that I had formed a very definite impression about him, an impression that may have been wrong.

"Well," I said, "I'll be interviewing him on Thursday. All he needs to do is satisfy me that his hands are clean, his motives are pure and he isn't carrying a razor, or a scalpel, for that matter. I probably will let him have a look at the *Necronomicon*. After all, it isn't a cadaver."

On the day appointed I was in the Administration Office a few minutes early. West arrived while I was reviewing my list of questions for the third time.

As we took our places at the table I had an opportunity to study his appearance more closely. His was a thin face, but saved from narrowness by a certain breadth across the cheekbones. His nose was straight and rather long, and faint lines on either side of his mouth suggested frequent smiles. But his most remarkable features were his eyes. They were of a curious clear grey with darker flecks, like splintered crystals. Combined with long lashes and finely drawn eyebrows, they gave his face a startling, disturbing beauty, impossible to forget.

After the usual preliminaries, I began the formal questions. They were quite simple – academic credentials and affiliations, and the specifics of the research that made it necessary to consult the *Necronomicon*.

He was in his final year of studies at Miskatonic University Medical School, West explained. Next year he would start his internship at St. Mary's Hospital, but right now he was doing research for a paper he was writing, a wide-ranging inquiry into the history of certain medical practices. "And that's what led me here," he finished. "And, I hope, to the *Necronomicon*."

"I need a little more detail as to the information you are looking for," I said. "Why the *Necronomicon*, exactly?"

"That," said West, getting up from his chair and pacing around the room, "is a tortuous tale, and not one you really need to know." He stopped and gave me a hard look with those ice-grey eyes. "Let me say only that I am following hints gleaned from other works. All those roads led me to the *Necronomicon*. It seems that Alhazred wrote much on the transition from life to death. The actual process, I mean. You can understand that this is a subject of interest to physicians. So I was delighted to discover that there is a copy right here at Miskatonic."

His letters of endorsement, from two professors of medicine, and one, surprisingly, of philosophy, were entirely in order. But what about the scandal Alma Halsey had mentioned? Neither of the letters from the Medical School so much as hinted at that. Yet surely that was exactly the sort of thing this screening process was meant to reveal.

"Mr. West," I said, "I have been given some information, informally, I admit, to the effect that you were involved in a rather unsavoury business at the Medical School – something to do with... cadavers, I believe?"

He waved a hand dismissively and sat down again. "Oh that! It was a typical medical student stunt that I got mixed up with in my first year. You know the sort of thing – a bunch of students kidnaps a corpse from the dissecting lab and takes it on a tour of the town. Unfortunately, after the festivities were over we were in no state to smuggle the thing back into the lab, so it ended up in my rooms. The authorities were not amused, of course. They subjected me to more rigorous procedures than this one, I can tell you." He smiled again, but something in his eyes told me he was lying, and, moreover, that he meant for me to know it. "Look, the way I understand it, you'll be in the room with me while I consult the book. I have no concealed weapons. What could possibly happen?"

He was obviously impatient for my verdict, but I was instinctively certain that the Library's managers, even Dr.

Armitage, whose attitude toward the *Necronomicon* seemed surprisingly casual, would deny this request. There were sufficient grounds for me to give "lack of academic sincerity," or something of the sort as a reason for refusal. In some obscure way I felt that showing this man the *Necronomicon*, being present as he turned its leaves and scanned its ancient type with his cold gaze, would create a strange complicity. I felt that I was being presented with a challenge whose nature I could not understand.

I made a final note, put down my pen and stood up. "Well, Mr. West," I heard myself say, "I will now bring you the *Necronomicon*. After all, even if you intend to steal it, I'm quite certain you will not be able to get past our Miss Hardy in the outer office." I had a vision of Herbert West, the *Necronomicon* tucked under one arm like a football, the other arm extended, sprinting through the Administration Office, coattails flying, with Miss Hardy preparing to tackle him, and started to laugh.

West must have been surprised at my unexpected capitulation, but he began to laugh too, and the two of us guffawed together as though we shared some enormously funny secret.

I went to the vault and lifted the *Necronomicon* from its drawer. It was heavier than I remembered, and I nearly let it slip. As I adjusted my grip on the book, I became aware of a faint scent which I had not noticed on previous occasions, like that of earth, and of ancient incense. But by the time I left the vault with the tome cradled in my arms, it was gone.

My usual procedure was to place the book on the table, with instructions for the researcher to take care when turning the pages, to make no marks on them, to refrain from folding or creasing the corners. But this time, I found myself handing the book to West directly. "It's all yours," I said, as I let its weight pass from my hands to his. "Within the confines of this room, anyway."

He stood with the book in his arms, regarding me with his cool, steady gaze. "I thank you, Charles Milburn," he said. He turned away from me and laid it on the table. He stood looking at it for a moment, removed his spectacles and polished them, took a notebook and pen from his pockets and sat down. He opened the notebook and looked at something written in it. Only then did he turn to the *Necronomicon*.

West leafed through the book, obviously seeking a specific passage. Having apparently found it, he read intently for a while. His lips moved as he read, and once he muttered something.

Audrey Driscoll

Suddenly he motioned me over. "Look here, Milburn, my Latin leaves much to be desired. You're a classicist, I understand. Come and translate something for me, will you? What does this say?"

I went over and looked at the passage he indicated, and read it while he watched. I still do not understand what happened then. The literal meaning of the words I read was clear enough. I wrote down a translation quite easily. But immediately afterward, I forgot it completely. It was like the sensation of speaking while in the throes of a head cold – one knows what words one is saying, but cannot hear them. It was as though the part of my brain that read was disconnected from the part that comprehended.

Later, trying to remember what I had read and written, the best I could come up with was a few disconnected phrases, portentous and scriptural. I had forgotten the words, but I retained an impression that what I had read went beyond life and death to the ultimate foundations of existence.

When I had finished translating the section he wanted, I waited until West found another and repeated the process, with the same strange result. An hour went by, then another. By now it was nearly six o'clock, and I was not surprised when Miss Hardy tapped on the door and opened it. "I'm sorry, gentlemen," she said, "but I must ask you to leave soon. I will be locking up the Office, and you cannot remain here."

"Certainly, Miss Hardy," I said. "If you need more time, Mr. West, we can meet again tomorrow, or some other day."

He looked up, seeming rather dazed, as though he too had forgotten where he was. Then he dropped his pen and sprang to his feet. "Actually, I'm finished now. Your timing is impeccable, Miss Hardy." He turned such a charming smile on the woman that she quite melted, an astonishing sight.

"Oh Mr. West," she said, "don't hurry yourself on my account. There are one or two small things I can do here yet, if you need more time."

"No, really, I'm finished. This has been most valuable. I thank you sincerely for the opportunity. And you too, Mr. Milburn," he said, turning to me. Quickly, he gathered up his materials and put on his coat, while I locked the *Necronomicon* away once more.

The three of us left the Administration Office together. West appeared to have taken a shine to Miss Hardy, for he went down the corridor with her, speaking animatedly of I don't know what.

22

I went back to the Cataloguing Department, which was now dark and deserted. My nerves jangled with anticlimax, even though nothing much had happened. A man had looked at an old book and made some notes with my help. He would go off and write a paper on some obscure topic, citing the fabled *Necronomicon* as a source, as many others had done before him. Or he would not. It made no difference to me. And surely, now that he had achieved whatever his objective was, nothing I said or did could make any difference to him.

In the weeks that followed, I saw Herbert West several times – behind the wheel of a sporty Pierce-Arrow roadster, or with a group of other young men, probably fellow medical students, or talking intently with a man who looked like a professor. On yet another occasion, I saw him in the town with two men who wore suits but did not look like academics.

Once only did I meet him face to face, in a narrow thoroughfare known as Howard's Alley, a popular short cut from town to campus. West was walking quickly toward me, head down, seemingly thinking hard. As we passed he glanced up and I prepared to greet him, but my words remained unsaid. On his face was no look of recognition. His grey eyes, the colour of a winter sky, stared straight through me, seeing something known to Herbert West alone.

♦ **2** ♦

In early May of 1911, I asked Alma Halsey if she would care to accompany me to a concert of chamber music to be performed by students at the Peabody Recital Hall. I had given this matter a great deal of thought in the previous weeks. To most young men, my deliberation might seem amusing, but I was very unsophisticated for my age. Due to family misfortunes I had been cut off from the social milieu in which a young person learns the social graces.

Moreover, I have always known that I do not belong among the fortunate few who are blessed with beauty. The first person to inform me of this fact was my cousin Alice, at seven years old a golden-haired princess who was, now that I come to think of it, the only other person I have ever known with eyes the same colour as Herbert West's. In all innocence, she had once compared me to the Dormouse in *Alice in Wonderland*, kindly adding, "But you're a very sweet little mouse, Charlie." I was only four at the time, but I knew that mice, however sweet, were a different species. This was before I fell out of a tree a few years later and broke my leg in three places. It had not healed properly, leaving me with a discernable limp. Added a little later was a pair of thick glasses to combat my short-sightedness.

By the time I was in my early twenties I had learned how to avoid situations in which I should be imposing myself on those who did not care for my company or appearance. So finely could I judge my possible effect on someone that by simple avoidance I managed to elude rejection altogether. This of necessity had limited my social contacts even further, especially with young women.

But Alma was different. She had an easy friendliness that dissolved my protective veneer. I had begun to think that there was a genuine warmth between us, and was certain that even if she declined my invitation she would do so with kindness. Of course, I also considered whether this would result in a lingering awkwardness which might impair our collegial relationship, but decided that it was worth the risk.

I was surprised when she accepted with alacrity. "That would be very pleasant, Charles. I had been intending to go anyway, alone, since none of my friends cares much for chamber music. But it's much better to have company at a concert."

We agreed to meet in the main quadrangle of the campus, not far from Peabody Hall. I offered to escort Alma from her lodgings, but she refused, saying, "It makes no sense for you to go all that way, then back to campus again. It's quite in the opposite direction from where you live. Much more efficient to meet in the Square." I agreed, but privately resolved to see her home afterwards.

Spring comes late and hard to the Miskatonic Valley, but by May, even Arkham had begun to show signs of approaching summer. The evening of the concert was mild and still, flushed with the golden light of sunset.

I felt a lightening of the spirit as I walked along the tree-shaded avenues of the college district. The past few weeks had not been altogether pleasant. The odd emotional upheavals I had experienced as the result of my two encounters with Herbert West, along with a certain unease in my place of work and the dithering I had gone through before asking Alma to go out with me had been something of a strain.

No one had reprimanded or even questioned my permitting West to consult the *Necronomicon*. Dr. Armitage had said something about the young man's reputation, but did not appear otherwise concerned. Peter Runcible had said only that he expected me to make up the three hours I had been away from my duties, which I was happy to do. My report, finally completed after three drafts, was filed along with all the others under Book Vault – Researchers' Interviews, and the matter seemed forgotten.

I kept my ears open for any news of strange doings at the Medical School, cautiously sounding out Alma, but without results. Except for my distant sightings of West, and that enigmatic and disconcerting meeting in Howard's Alley, it was as though he had never existed.

When I met Alma in the Square, I was pleasantly surprised to see that she was wearing a pretty summer dress, quite unlike her usual practical yet unconventional attire. I was glad I had worn my best suit, rather than one of the second-bests she was familiar with from the office.

"Good evening, Alma," I said. "You are looking very pretty."

"Thank you, Charles. It's such a lovely evening I decided to do it the honour of gilding the lily." She twirled around so that her skirts swung around her ankles. Laughing, she took my arm and we went into the hall.

The place was sparsely populated as yet, and we selected a pair of seats near the front. As we chatted of nothing in particular I could hear the room filling up behind us. According to the program, the opening piece would be Beethoven's Sonata for violin and piano no. 5 in F major, known as the *Spring Sonata*, followed by six of Paganini's twenty-four *Caprices*. I remarked to Alma that the latter were fiendishly difficult to play.

"Yes," she said, tapping her program. "This fellow, Alvaro Castelo-Branco, apparently is something of a prodigy. He comes from Kingsport, from the Portuguese people there. But look, how unusual – selections from J.S. Bach's *Goldberg Variations* arranged for string trio."

"Why unusual?" I asked. "I seem to recall that it's a fairly well known piece."

"Yes, but it's usually performed on the piano," she explained. "This version is something of a novelty. The arrangement is by a Russian violinist. It should be an interesting concert." Her eyes sparkled. Quite suddenly, I felt a corresponding lightness, as though the air itself had become effervescent.

Just as the Beethoven began, my glance was drawn to the far side of the hall by a late arrival. It was Herbert West. He was alone, and took a seat at the far end of a row, near the wall.

The Paganini *Caprices* were indeed spectacular. Alma was right about young Castelo-Branco, the violinist. Now, of course, he is internationally known, his humble Kingsport origins almost forgotten. Unschooled though I was, I could discern his brilliance, contrasted with the more pedestrian talents of his fellow performers.

I watched as well as listened with pleasure, becoming truly conscious for the first time of the physical act of playing the violin. Castelo-Branco was exerting the same intense yet controlled effort as someone engaged in a fencing match, except that he stood in one place. His breathing was rapid, and I could see a sheen of sweat on his brow. It was fascinating, as though the music he played had become incarnate, no longer merely notes in the aether, but a living body which took up space and had weight. When he had done I joined the rest of the audience in rapturous applause.

But it is the Bach I will remember forever. The first grave, deliberate notes of the aria struck me deeply, with their promise of something wonderful to come. I was content to wait for it without impatience, because of the inherent completeness of the simple melody.

For some reason I looked just then toward Herbert West. He was leaning forward, his fingers on his brow so that his eyes were covered, in an attitude of profound concentration. A few moments later, he leaned back in his seat, eyes closed, as though giving himself up to the music.

The aria ended and the first variation began; with its quicker tempo, I felt a deep gladness run through me, as though I was at the start of some glorious enterprise. Impulsively, I reached for Alma's hand and pressed it hard. She looked at me, startled, then smiled and returned the pressure.

The intermission came all too soon. While the music lasted I had felt myself swung in a magical net of stars. The magic was compounded of the music, the nearness of Alma and a kind of thrilling of the nerves that seemed to come from another source altogether. As we strolled around the lobby I had little to say, but Alma commented on the performance with typical succinctness: "The Beethoven was good, the Paganini amazing, the Bach – I don't know. Maybe if the cellist and violist had been up to Castelo-Branco's calibre."

"I loved the *Goldbergs*," I said. "It was passion contained within a structure, an adventure of the spirit."

Alma was amused by my enthusiasm. "I'll bet Bach would be surprised to hear that! What a romantic you are, Charles," she said, laughing, and launched into something about counterpoint. I was happy enough to listen to her while I sipped sherry and watched people engage in their social minuets around us. Several of them were acquaintances of Alma's. She dutifully introduced me, adding some brief but trenchant details after the persons in question had moved on.

Then Herbert West was before me, shaking my hand vigorously. "Milburn! I hoped it was you. Good evening, Miss Halsey."

I thought I detected a distinct lack of enthusiasm in Alma's response. "Hello Mr. West. How are you? I would have thought you would be too taken up with examinations to bother with music."

"I have had a bellyful of examinations, all right," West replied, laughing. "But I'm happy to say they're over. This is something of a celebration." He went on to make some remarks about the performance, saying that he was certain that the music of Bach was so mathematical that it must have a measurable effect on the brain, could there only be a means of making the correct measurements. Alma responded with a little more warmth than she had shown initially. I watched them, noting, in my rather bemused state, that they resembled one another. Both were lightly built, with blond hair and light-coloured eyes. But beyond this, there was an element of contrast. Alma radiated warmth, West coolness. I was trying to figure out how this could be when I realized that he had asked me something. I roused myself from my reverie with an effort.

"...would you and Miss Halsey care to join me?"

"Excuse me," I said. "I wasn't listening, I'm afraid."

"He's still afloat on the *Goldberg Variations*," laughed Alma. "Mr. West has asked us to accompany him to supper. I'm afraid I must decline, but perhaps you are available?"

"Well, Milburn? I'd like to prolong this pleasant evening, so how about some post-concert festivities?"

"That sounds delightful," I said, without thinking. "But Alma, you must allow me to take you home first. I hope that will be all right with you," I said to West. I felt that I had committed some sort of *faux pas* with respect to one or both of them, and was not certain what I should do to remedy it.

"Of course," he replied. "I am entirely at your disposal. We'll form an honour guard for Miss Halsey." He bowed rather mockingly toward Alma, who responded in a similar vein.

"Nonsense! It's only a few blocks. I have no need for knights-errant to safeguard me home."

I insisted, however, so following the rest of the concert, which featured a Mozart piano trio of which I have no memory at all, although I normally enjoy his music, West and I accompanied Alma to the door of her house. Along the way, it occurred to me that this was an odd way to conclude an evening with a young lady. West did not seem in the least disconcerted at having created a 'three's a crowd' situation. He participated eagerly in the conversation, discoursing on a number of topics, from violin making in 18th century Italy to the latest political scandals in Boston. As on the other occasions I had met him he seemed to bring with him his own charged atmosphere. Again, I felt it affecting me, adding a spring to my step and a kind of devil-may-care attitude which was entirely foreign to me.

Alma must have sensed something of this, for she looked at me sharply as we shook hands on her doorstep. "Good night, Charles. Thank you for the concert. Enjoy yourself, but don't forget that excellent precept, 'Nothing in excess.' Good night, Mr. West."

"*Quantum sufficit,*" I replied, smartly. "*Vale.*"

"Ah the independent Miss Halsey," said West, as we turned our steps toward Arkham's commercial center on River Street. "There's a good deal of her father, the venerable Allan, in her, whether she admits it or not."

"What do you mean?" I asked, a little nettled that he should be making what seemed to be a less than complimentary remark about a young woman who had obviously been my chosen companion for the evening.

"Merely that both of them are rather given to laying down the law to everyone around them. I suppose it comes with the territory for him, but..."

I remembered Alma saying that West had been nearly expelled from the Medical School, and assumed that this incident, necessarily involving the Dean, would have coloured his attitude toward the Halsey family. But surely that was rather unjust? I was spared the need to reply, however, for he dropped the subject.

"Well, where shall we dine?" he asked. On my expressing no preference, he suggested Da Vinci's Grill, a place I had heard of but never patronized. It was not a restaurant frequented by the academic set, but rather a wood-panelled, leather and brass establishment of the sort beloved by men of business. I felt as we entered that we had somehow been transported to the financial district of New York City.

West, it appeared, was known here. A brief word to the head waiter secured for us a table in a remote corner, bathed in its own pool of yellow light.

"Do you come here often?" I asked, curious. "You seem to be what they call a 'regular.'"

"My father," he replied, looking a little embarrassed, "is the regular. I am merely a hanger-on, not even a crony, but the food is good, the service discreet, and it's not Miskatonic. There are times when it's refreshing to get away from the atmosphere of academia."

"Your father is in business, I believe?" I said, carefully avoiding any mention of funeral parlours.

"God yes, he's in business. Bakeries, breweries, real estate – you name it, Hiram West owns a piece of it. And his mortuaries, of course. A dozen of those – he's the king of the death business in Massachusetts. One time I suggested that he adopt as a slogan 'Go west with West's,' but he was not amused."

He looked at me seriously, but I caught a glimpse of mischief lurking in his eyes, and let loose the laughter his words had provoked. After this we were easier with one another. In answer to my tentative questions he told me that he was the youngest of three brothers, of whom the other two were businessmen like their father. Like me, he had grown up in Boston, not so very far from my home in Beacon Hill, except that I had been taught that the mansions of Back Bay were haunts of the *nouveau riche*, to be regarded with disdain. On my asking about his mother, he replied, "I have been motherless since the age of eight." There was a finality about this statement that discouraged further questions on the subject.

Whatever West thought of his father (and I detected a mixture of emotions, among them shame, exasperation and a grudging respect), he had certainly not rejected the benefits of the elder West's positive cash flow. Now, as on the two previous occasions I had met him, he was immaculately dressed. My best suit didn't begin to come close. He looked less like a student than a successful young professional man. Yet underneath and above and around all this was what really interested me about him – a kind of barely suppressed hidden laughter, as though he was saying: "I know a great secret, and if you are the kind of fellow I think you are I might let you in on it."

He dealt briskly with the waiter after making a few unobtrusive suggestions that prevented me from dithering over the menu, which was quite lengthy.

"Well, Milburn," he said, once we were settled with drinks, our orders placed. "*Quid pro quo,* now – what of your domestic origins?"

"My parents are both dead," I said, realizing too late how stark that sounded, but wishing to avoid the particulars of their deaths, especially my father's. "I grew up in Boston. My father was a banker. It was a fairly ordinary life, really, but now I'm alone. I have a bachelor's degree in classics and my librarian's degree, of course. Since last fall I have been a cataloguer at Miskatonic University Library."

"Oh, so you do something besides guard the *Necronomicon?*" He was teasing me, but I detected something else in his voice. "Come to think of it, I've never thought much about what you librarians do all day, besides fuss with books and tell people where things are. What's a cataloguer?"

"Well, you know the card catalogue – all those cabinets full of drawers in the main hall of the Library – my colleagues and I have made all that. No, not the cabinets, of course, but the contents. The descriptions and index terms on the cards. It's an index to all the books in the Library. You can find any book described there, and from the description and the call number you can tell whether it might be of use to you, and where to find it. You can look under authors, or subjects or titles, whatever suits you. All the books, however different from one another, fit into this structure, so once you know how it works, you can follow a thread from your starting point to the thing you need. It's all quite logical."

"I'm a great believer in logic. But how do you cataloguers make sure you're all describing and classifying the same way? Surely you don't have one system for your Greeks and Romans, and Alma Halsey quite another for the sciences?"

"There are rules for description, quite complex ones. A new version was published just three years ago. And we use a classification system developed here at Miskatonic in the 1880s. But surely you must have used the card catalogue at some point? How could you get three-fourths of the way through medical school without doing that?"

He looked a little uncomfortable. "We medical fellows have our methods and short cuts. It's considered weak, actually, to use the Library. Occasionally one of us will slip in when desperate, if we can be sure of not meeting any of the others. And we borrow books from our professors, of course."

"So you didn't get desperate until you needed the *Necronomicon?*" I asked.

"Well, not desperate, exactly. Only certain that it would have the answers I needed. And it did, too." But he would say no more about that. "So there are rules? All you have to do is look them up and you can catalogue anything? Or, for that matter, anyone could?"

I was a little disconcerted. I felt as though I was being interviewed, for what I could not imagine.

"It's not that simple. The rules have to be applied in context. There's a lot of room for interpretation. Cataloguing is more art than science. The best cataloguers try to think like the researchers who use the catalogue, to see it the way they do. Not everyone can do that."

"But you can?"

"Yes, I think so. That's one of the things that makes my work interesting."

By this time our meals had come and we were making short work of them. West had ordered a couple of bottles of wine as well, and I was finding myself more voluble than is my habit as a result.

"We cataloguers are not moles, as some of my colleagues think," I said. "I think of us as... weavers. Spiders, perhaps."

To my surprise, West immediately saw what I was getting at. "Spiders? Of course, the catalogue is a kind of web, isn't it? At least, that's what your description made me think of. I suppose you have to be fairly versatile, don't you – to understand what all those books are about? And then there are different languages... I have more respect for you librarians now, I can tell you," he said, raising his glass. "To cataloguers."

"Yes!" I said, my enthusiasm for my obscure field breaking out in response to his understanding. "But enough about me. What led you to the study of medicine?"

"Death," said Herbert West.

My surprise must have shown on my face, but after a moment he continued. "When I was eight, my mother died, and my twin brother. They got sick and never got better, despite all the doctors and treatments my father called in. I watched it all, as a child will, even though they tried to stop me. It seemed to go on forever, but I suppose it was only a couple of weeks. Every time another doctor left, I would go to my mother and ask her if she would get better. Until she couldn't speak any more. And my brother – well, it was like watching myself die.

"Their deaths left me virtually alone, since my two remaining brothers were five and eight years older than I. I got angry instead of sad, because I was certain there was something that could have been done to save them. Everyone was just too stupid to see it. So I read everything I could find about death, which wasn't much, in the Pater's library. Yes, he actually has one, bought lock, stock and barrel – if you can say that about a library – in the true Hiram West manner. Once I was in school I found more – scientific stuff, but also philosophy. My teachers suggested I study medicine, so here I am."

While he was speaking I found myself touched with pity by the vision he had conjured up – the little boy, frightened at what was happening to his mother and brother. Twin brother, no less. But it was too glib. And there was no passion in his eyes to match the words.

Still, I could not very well express doubts about a story like this. Instead I asked, "And what area of medicine will you specialize in, or do you know?"

"I think so," he replied. "It's something I'm developing myself, and altogether unprecedented. Would you like me to tell you? It's quite a story."

Here it is, I thought. Aloud I said, "Tell me."

Over coffee and brandy he told me a great deal. Some of it, perhaps most, was the truth, or nearly.

"You know, of course, that my father owns several funeral parlours. He no longer works as an undertaker; as I mentioned earlier, he has expanded his business interests and now is concerned primarily with managing all his enterprises. But at one time he was a funeral director. He apprenticed under my grandfather and great-uncle, who started the business." He laughed. "Father would rather soil his hands metaphorically and achieve greater profits. But I have always been aware that some of our livelihood came from dealing with the dead.

"Anyway, a few years ago when I was considering medicine as a profession, I did my own apprenticeship. I thought exposure to corpses would be practical, if only as preparation for the dissecting room.

"At the same time I was taking courses in biology and philosophy at the University. Have you ever read Haeckel?" On my expressing only a passing familiarity with the name, he explained. "Ernst Heinrich Haeckel is a German who has worked in both these fields. He developed a theory of the mechanism of life, based on the work of Darwin.

"The key word here is *mechanism.* All living things can be reduced to pure matter. You may have heard that most of the human body consists of water. Water and carbon, and a few other elements. Put them all together, precisely, and you have that violinist who entertained us so superbly tonight. Or Bach himself, for that matter. Change the chemistry, even slightly, and you have an idiot, or a lump of dead flesh. The thing that makes the difference between those two states, that's what I am looking for."

"Death, you mean? The moment the soul leaves the body, or – ?"

West waved a hand dismissively. "I'm not concerned with the soul. I've never seen one or heard of anyone who has – not anyone credible, anyway. And I've seen several people die – oh yes, they don't spare our delicate feelings at the Med. School! – and many others who were already dead, of course. Not a soul among them. It's all chemistry and electricity, from respiration to digestion and the activity of the brain. I leave the soul to dreamers and clerics.

"The thing that really interested me was the way in which the physical mechanism changes to produce the ultimate change we call death. I felt that if I could understand that I could come up with some way to delay, or even reverse it."

"So you're a student of Thanatos," I said. On his inquiring look I explained. "A personification of death in ancient Greece."

"If you say so," West said. "Anyway, one summer there was a minor plague here in Arkham, one of those sudden things that comes and goes within a few weeks. We undertakers were uncommonly busy, as you may imagine. I was probably working too hard, and such work too! Like the Black Death of the 14th century. Well, one night I had a dream – they're all brain chemistry, don't deceive yourself! – it's your own mind sending you messages, but sometimes they're useful. I dreamt I could see the chemical composition of a dead body – the very essence, I mean, as though it had been exploded into fundamental particles. I could see that there was an imbalance, and I knew that I could re-start the engine of life by the application of an appropriate chemical stimulus.

"When I began at the Medical School, I tried discussing my idea with some of my professors. They agreed in theory, but did not seem in the least interested in any practical experimentation. So I went ahead anyway, on my own.

"You know how embalming works, don't you?" I shook my head, surprised by the question. "No? Well, it was developed by physicians. William Harvey used the injection technique in his study of blood circulation. A Scottish anatomist called William Hunter was the first to apply it to preservation of corpses. It became a profession in its own right during the Civil War, when people wanted their sons' bodies shipped home for burial. Now I have found a medical use for the technique once more. You see, in embalming, the corpse's blood is drained and replaced with a preservative fluid. There is a special apparatus for injecting the chemical and aspirating the body fluids. It occurred to me that with a few modifications this could be a means to inject a revivifying fluid into a body without circulation, a body whose heart had stopped. The chief problem, of course, was what would such a fluid consist of, and how could it be made? This became my obsession.

"First I had to develop a substance enough like blood to substitute for it, but which had also the necessary galvanizing effect. It wasn't easy. A hundred times I felt like giving up. Many rabbits, guinea pigs, cats, dogs and monkeys met their ends at my hands. Several times I obtained signs of life, but since each species requires a unique formulation, there was no point in wasting my time on formulae that could be used on animals only. I approached the college authorities again, to give me authorization to use human subjects.

"You know, Milburn, these professor-doctors, they make all kinds of sanctimonious noises about working for the good of mankind, doing no harm and all sorts of mumbo-jumbo, but when someone comes along ready to make them a gift of something truly revolutionary, they retreat into a pathetic Puritanism. Not only did they refuse me, they threatened to take away my laboratory privileges if I persisted.

"Well, you can guess what happened next. In desperation, I availed myself of a human subject from the only source readily open to me – one of my father's mortuaries. I had to transport the body to a lab at the Medical School, where I had the necessary equipment and chemicals. It had to be done discreetly, of course, which meant I had to do it in the middle of the night. Even then, there was a night watchman who had to be negotiated with. Unfortunately, the experiment failed, probably because the corpse was too old by then, the delicate mechanisms of life stalled beyond repair. And worst of all, I was discovered by some busybody who reported me to the college authorities. The learned and benevolent Dr. Halsey himself threatened me with expulsion should I so much as hoist a guinea pig in the laboratory again. And my father, though no saint, was not pleased at my unorthodox proceedings with one of his clients. But he did help to work things out with Halsey in the end."

As West spoke, I watched his hands. They were strong hands, beautifully shaped, the nails cut short and immaculately clean. I watched them pick up and lay down items of cutlery, raise his glass to his lips, make an eloquent gesture to emphasize a point. I had difficulty imagining that these hands had done the things that he described, had touched many corpses, had intimately probed their cold flesh and opened their arteries. These hands had been stained, perhaps, with blood grown thick and viscous with death. They had handled shining knives and hollow needles, poisons and secret substances. He must have looked with his grey eyes into blank, glazed ones in which death had extinguished the spark, and thought, "It need not be forever," as he calculated the forces required to accomplish the unthinkable.

I remembered the few dead people I had seen – my grandmother, when I was nine, and my mother. My father too, but he was alone in the category of the self-murdered. To me they had seemed like spent flowers, drawn in upon themselves, sealed shut from life, stilled forever. I could not imagine wanting to animate them. Surely the very desire to open these closed beings, to force life back into them, was a blasphemy. I realized I was sliding into bemusement, and spoke to bring myself back.

"So it wasn't dissecting room cadavers after all," I said.

"No, of course not. Such things would be of no use to my work. They're pretty much pickled by the time we students get our hands on them. Mind you, that little adventure I described to you some weeks ago did happen, but it was routine medical student stuff – tradition, really. Even Halsey probably did something like that, centuries ago."

"So you're telling me that you are able to bring the dead back to life."

"Yes," he answered simply. "Under certain conditions I believe I can do just that."

"And what might those conditions be?" I asked. So reasonable had he sounded until now that I hesitated to express disbelief without further details.

"That's exactly what I'm trying to find out. I know that there's a limit of time after death beyond which my method will not work. But I don't know as yet whether there's a gradation of effectiveness within the limit. In other words, I suspect that a corpse can be restored to full and effective life within only a short time after death. Beyond that time, a kind of life is possible, but the individual may no longer be recognizable as the person they were before death, due to loss of cognitive functions. Such a being may still serve a purpose, however."

"What sort of purpose?"

"Well, as an experimental subject, for example. What you would have is a body with physiological functions, but no mind. A perfect thing on which to perform certain experimental procedures, don't you think? Consider how that would prolong the useful life of the citizen."

I could not tell whether he was joking. I thought not. I wondered if the horror I felt showed in my face. "Have you actually done that? Carried out experiments on one of these... mindless things?"

"No, for the simple reason that I have not yet achieved a successful revivification. I must do some more fundamental work first, but that's difficult, now that I'm under scrutiny by the Medical School."

"But West, I'm not sure I understand. You're saying that you might be able to restore a dead person to full life, is that right?"

"Exactly. I'm certain of it. But within certain parameters only."

"All right," I said. I was trying hard to get my mind around the idea. "All right, but a person who is dead usually dies of something. Something harmful, I mean, that has done damage to the body. That's why they're dead. So even if you manage to restore life, wouldn't you just have someone who's on the point of death again?"

"Ah, but it would give you a chance to heal them, wouldn't it? How often do you hear it said that someone might have lived if only help had arrived sooner? If we had been able to try this or that technique? Once the body is functioning again, measures could be taken to counteract the injury or disease, just as though death had not intervened. Obviously, it would make no sense to revivify bodies that were seriously damaged or deteriorated. And even if a person is revivified for only a short time it could make a great difference, in certain situations."

"Like what?"

"Well, let's consider a few. Unfinished business, for example. People who die before they can make a will, confess to a crime or make some other revelation, such as the identity of a murderer. Wouldn't that be useful?"

"I suppose so, but it conjures up some rather macabre scenarios. A dead person being dragged back over the threshold and interrogated by greedy relatives or the police."

He seemed a little annoyed. "Perhaps, but it's unlikely that the greedy relatives or police would be capable of or equipped to carry out the procedure. For me, all those worthy reasons are beside the point, actually. The real reason I have devoted myself to this problem is to introduce the element of choice. When I perfect my discovery there will be a choice even to return from death, however briefly."

"But it won't be the dead person's choice, but someone else's. Yours, I suppose. A corpse would have no idea that it might be brought back to life. What if it didn't want to be?"

"Corpses don't have a choice. They simply don't care. But once alive again, he would have the choice to end his life once more. That choice is always available, to all of us."

A lot you know about that, I thought, remembering again the scene in my father's study the day after the collapse of the Western Massachusetts Bank. But I didn't want to talk about that with Herbert West.

"So who would such a person be?" I asked.

"What do you mean?"

"Well, this... thing you would have after you administer your formula – who would it be? If he died as John Smith of Arkham, is that who he would be when he comes back to life? Someone with all the attributes of the living John Smith – oh, I don't know – his speech habits, food preferences, sense of humour. You know, things that aren't necessarily dependent on intelligence, but which certainly are part of someone's personality."

"Personality... I don't know, Milburn. I haven't given that much thought. I suppose there might be some changes. That's something else that would be revealed only by experimentation."

I could not let go of the matter so easily. "This John Smith, would he still love his wife? His children? Would he keep his friendships? Because those things are as important as cognitive functions, surely?"

He stared at me for a second or two, as though he had discovered a new life form sitting in the chair across from him. "Are they as important?" he asked. "I'm not certain about that. And I have no idea how one would test such notions scientifically." After another short silence, he appeared to have dismissed the subject.

"There could be another reason for this research." He gave me a mischievous look. "With your concern about the soul, I would have expected you to have thought of it already. Wouldn't you like to have a chance to speak with someone who had actually crossed the threshold, as you put it? Surely he would have a tale worth listening to. Why, even a materialist like myself might be interested, if only as a means of exploring the effect of oxygen deprivation on the brain."

"Is that how the *Necronomicon* comes into it?"

"Ah, the *Necronomicon*. As a matter of fact it does, very much so. But look, I think they're getting ready to close here. How about if we go back to my rooms, and I can tell you the rest?"

West insisted on settling the bill. "After all, I invited you and have been bending your ear for hours. The least I can do is supply the grub."

We walked rather slowly back to the college district, West showing consideration for both my limp and unaccustomed state of tipsiness. He, on the other hand, did not seem in the least affected by the lateness of the hour or the amount of wine he had drunk.

West's rooms occupied the entire ground floor of a Georgian house on College Street, near Miskatonic and St. Mary's Hospital. The apartment was spacious and comfortably furnished with what he described as castoffs from the paternal attics. He made us some coffee and resumed his narrative.

"Curiously, I found the beginning of the thread that led me to the *Necronomicon* in my father's library," West began. "Truly! Remember, I told you that he had bought the collection intact. Well, whoever put it together had wide-ranging interests, as well as good taste in bindings, which was what mattered to Father. But I found it quite valuable. In a way, my entire career began with those books. You see, among them were some writings on alchemy. Fortunately, I made the leap to chemistry before I absorbed too much of the mystical mumbo-jumbo. In college I couldn't choose between chemistry and biology, so looked for something in common between the two, which led me to my present interests."

I remembered what he had told me in the restaurant, that it had been the deaths of his mother and brother that had led him to study medicine. I nearly asked him about this apparent contradiction, but he was clearly in full flight, pacing back and forth with a glass of whiskey in his hand.

"Anyway, to get back to Father's library, it was in one of those books that I found an oblique reference to 'the principle of life in death as articulated by Alhazred.' Well, that phrase 'life in death,' struck me as worth following up, but I had no idea who Alhazred might be, until I asked one of my professors – Quarrington, it was. He wrote one of my endorsements for you back in the spring. He's a professor *emeritus* of philosophy. An interesting fellow – knows something about everything. Anyway, he told me about Abdul Alhazred, of San'aa in Yemen, who wrote a book called *Al Azif* in the 8th century. Some time later the *Al Azif* was translated into Greek, under the title *Necronomicon*, which it retained in other translations, into Latin and even English."

"That would be the uniform title for it, then, with *Al Azif* as a cross-reference. And *The Book of Dead Names*, too, of course." I said this before I had realized it.

"Uniform title?" repeated West. "What's that?"

"Oh, it's something we use in cataloguing, to bring together works that have been issued under different titles. I'm sorry; I spoke without thinking. Please go on."

"Well, anyway, *Al Azif* is the *Necronomicon*, or rather, the *Necronomicon* is a translation of a translation of *Al Azif*. Imagine my delight when I found we had a copy, right here in Arkham! In Latin, fortunately, not Arabic. But as you know, my Latin is only just functional, so I was extremely lucky that you were there to translate for me."

"But I couldn't understand any of it!" I exclaimed. "The words, yes, but not their significance."

"I understood them quite well," said West, a strange look in his eyes. "They inspired me, in fact. After those hours with the *Necronomicon*, I did my best work so far. It wasn't facts I found there, you understand, but something that turned my thinking about the nature of cells and how they function as living entities. It made all the difference. I was in the laboratory every night for weeks, and now I think I have a revivifying fluid that will be effective on a human subject. What I need now is a subject. And an assistant."

"Surely one of your fellow students – " I began, but West cut me off with his characteristic wave of the hand.

"They're a bunch of sheep," he said with contempt. "They won't get involved in anything even slightly unorthodox, for fear of jeopardizing the all-important diploma. In fact, I'm fairly certain it was one of these fellow students of mine that tipped off Halsey the night I made that one attempt I told you about."

He began pacing again. "I'm so close!" he exclaimed. "But now it's more risky than ever. I have a laboratory of sorts here, but it's barely adequate. So I'll have to break some more rules, I guess. Any amount of them. And even more, I need a trustworthy assistant. How about it, Milburn?"

"Me?" I cried, astonished. "Why on earth would you want me? I'm a librarian, not a doctor or a scientist of any sort. And in case you haven't noticed, I limp."

Again that wave of the hand. "So what, I'm not planning on doing any running. It's quite simple, Milburn. You're a romantic, and despite all those rules you live by, you obviously know it's necessary to break them sometimes. Look at that *Necronomicon* business. I was certain you would find some reason to keep me from it. My reputation had preceded me, I knew. So I was pleasantly surprised when you let me go ahead. Believe me, anyone at Miskatonic who breaks a rule, however small, has my vote." He smiled. "And now that my professors think I've gone in for reading dusty old tomes they figure I'm not as dangerous."

"So what would this... assistant of yours do?" I asked.

"Simply be an extra pair of hands, eyes and ears. One pair of each, I mean." Again that smile. "Say you'll consider it, at least."

"I'll consider, but not tonight," I said, starting to get up from the sofa. "I'm about ready to collapse."

"Of course," said West, extending his hand and hauling me to my feet. "I've kept you entirely too late. Look, suppose we meet here in three days, at six o'clock? You're finished work by then? Good. Well, good night, Milburn. It's been a delightful evening."

I walked slowly home under a sky full of stars. It had been a long evening – Alma, the music, and now the revelations of Herbert West. I had never known anyone like him. His brilliance and coldness, combined with a worldly air, produced in me an impression of ineffable glamour. Having been on the sidelines for most of my life, I was immensely flattered that one of the players at the centre of things had noticed me, even wanted my help. Oh, I realized even then that West was probably not all he seemed. There were disturbing hints of unsavoury connections and a love of deception for its own sake. But what of it? Why should I not, for once in my life, avoid the well-trodden path of duty and seek adventure in wilder realms?

Did I really believe that Herbert West could raise the dead? I did not, then, but I believed he was a man who could do extraordinary things, and that by associating with him I might become a little less ordinary myself.

♦ 3 ♦

The next day I was heavy-eyed and heavy-headed. When I entered the Cataloguing Department, Peter Runcible grinned at me knowingly.

"Well, well, Milburn! Overindulged a little last night, did we? I didn't think you were that sort." Chuckling, he walked away. Alma Halsey looked at me sympathetically, but later, when I was sipping tea in the staff room and starting to feel a little better, she said,

"Evidently classicists are as reluctant as most men to practice what they preach."

"It wasn't I that was preaching, it was you," I replied grumpily. "And anyway, as excesses go this was minor."

"Oh, now he's a man of the world! Forgive me, but I think for you this was a major debauch." Curiosity got the better of her then, for she asked, "So where did you go, some saloon on Water Street?" This was where Arkham's seedier drinking establishments were located.

I tried to give her a withering look, but that's hard to do when your head is still pounding, and anyway, it was always hard to wither Alma.

"We went to Da Vinci's Grill, if you must know. And had quite a good meal, too."

Alma whistled. "Da Vinci's, eh? I'm almost sorry I didn't go with you. It would have been quite the field trip, seeing the *arrivistes* of Arkham in their own milieu."

"Oh don't get all hoity toity and intellectual with me, Alma," I said. "You're just jealous. It was quite an interesting evening."

"I'll bet it was," she answered. "Look, Charles, there's something I'd like to talk to you about. How about if you come to my place for afternoon tea tomorrow?"

West had not sworn me to secrecy, or even asked for my discretion, but it didn't take much imagination to realize that if I wanted to throw in my lot with him, the true nature of his research must be kept absolutely secret. I resolved to maintain a close watch on my tongue the next afternoon.

Alma lived in a curious little apartment at the top of a house on French Hill Street. Although only a short distance from Arkham's best neighbourhoods, the area was showing signs of decline. Many of the houses had been turned into apartment buildings. Paint had faded and peeled, and efforts to conceal small blights such as ash cans and laundry lines were flagging. It was as though the waterfront slum to the north had thrown out a tentacle and induced a subtle decay.

Alma's place was furnished in a style which could be described only as eclectic, but the atmosphere was warm and welcoming. No less so was Alma herself, wearing a kind of smock over her skirt and blouse, her hair tied back with a ribbon.

She motioned me to a cushion-laden sofa and went to make tea while I admired the way she had accommodated the comforts of life in the small space at her disposal. Her home resembled a ship's cabin, afloat on the sea of leaves visible through the windows.

Once she had furnished me with a cup of tea fragrant with honey, Alma lost no time in pressing me for more details about my dinner with Herbert West.

"What did he want from you, anyway?"

"What makes you so sure he wanted something? Besides someone to share a meal with, I mean. He'd just finished exams, he said, and wanted to celebrate."

"Hmm. From what I know of Mr. West he is not usually given to such spontaneous conviviality."

"He didn't seem to want anything much, really, just to talk about... well, his studies and that sort of thing."

Alma looked unconvinced. "I wouldn't be surprised if he's softening you up for something."

"What do you have against Herbert West, anyway?" I asked. "It was quite plain to me from the moment we met him at the concert that you don't care for him."

"You're quite right there. I don't like him. I think he's unscrupulous and devious. And a real manipulator. Look at the effect he's had on you, for example."

"What effect?"

"Well, I think you're quite impressed. I do admit he is very attractive. But make no mistake, he's entirely self-centred. And cold as ice."

I was beginning to think that Alma's aversion to West was rooted in nothing more than some sort of romantic connection gone wrong. She quickly dispelled this notion, however.

"Oh, don't think I dislike him because he rejected my charms, or something silly like that. He's not my type, for one thing. I've had very little to do with him, but I've heard quite a lot, from Papa and others at the Med. School."

"So what is it you've heard?" I asked.

She looked serious. "That's why I asked you here, actually, Charles. To tell you what I know about Herbert West so you have something to counterbalance your romantic notions. Because I still think he sought you out with some purpose in mind."

"Sought me out? But he just happened to be at that concert – "

"Never mind all that. Just listen."

I listened.

Herbert West had gained admission to the Miskatonic University Medical School some three years previously, Alma said, having first obtained a Bachelor of Science degree in chemistry. In short order he began to make a nuisance of himself by proposing wild theories about the reversibility of death, and worse, carrying out bizarre and unauthorized experiments on animals in the Medical School's laboratories. It was this latter habit that had caused the college authorities to step in and threaten to restrict his laboratory privileges.

"Why?" I interjected. "Was he breaking the law – stealing people's pet dogs and cats, for example?"

"Well, no," Alma answered, "but there was something undisciplined and unstructured about his carryings on. They weren't part of a program of rational study, which is what first and second year medical students are supposed to be engaged in. They aren't expected to do original research at that stage, for God's sake."

I reflected that for whosoever sake West did his experiments, it wasn't God's. Aloud I said,

"It sounds to me as though they were out of their depth with him. Did it ever occur to anyone that he might be the medical equivalent of a prodigy? Like that young fellow we heard playing the violin the other night."

"Oh Charles," Alma said, shaking her head, "it's quite obvious that West did a good job of impressing you. I'm probably wasting my breath. But he didn't stop at cats and dogs, however legitimately acquired.

"He got a dead human body from somewhere. Probably one of his father's mortuaries. This would have been the fall before last – October or thereabouts. He'd been told to stop his animal experiments by a certain date, or else. So I guess he got desperate and decided to try a human being." She shook her head again. "Such a waste of his talents. Papa says he's really very competent at his normal studies."

I refrained from pointing out that this could be another indication that the good professor-doctors of the Medical School simply didn't know what to do with the cuckoo in their nest.

"Anyway," Alma continued, "he got this corpse into the lab somehow, late at night, of course. He'd bribed the night watchman not to report him. First and second year students aren't allowed into the labs at night, you see."

West had also smuggled into the lab some sort of apparatus which he had connected to the corpse. He was engaged in pumping a fluid into it when he was discovered.

"It was bizarre and horrible to see, apparently," said Alma. "It looked as though he'd had an accident with the equipment. A tube had burst, or something. When Papa and Dr. Hobson got there the place looked like a slaughterhouse – blood everywhere – the 'patient's' blood, of course, and all over West too. There he was, blood all over that pretty face of his, but cool as can be, and laughing! That's what really bothered them."

I nearly laughed myself, realizing that this description of the scene neither surprised nor shocked me. In fact, it was exactly what I would have expected of the Herbert West I had begun to know. I wondered what had prompted his laughter. The experiment had failed, of course, so it must have been ironic amusement at the outrage of those whom he believed to be willfully ignorant.

"How did your father happen to know that West was in the laboratory that night?" I asked.

She looked uneasy. "I think someone tipped him off. Another student, maybe." She didn't go so far as to suggest that West had been watched, but I remembered what he had said about betrayal.

"Anyway, the next day Papa called West on the carpet and told him he had one chance to redeem himself. And he was forbidden to use any laboratory at the Medical School except under close supervision, for his course work only, for the remainder of the year." She paused. "That seems pretty lenient to me, considering that he was already under threat of suspension. I wouldn't be surprised if West senior weighed in with the senior college administration to smooth things over for his boy."

"Yes, what about Hiram West?" I asked. "His son seemed rather ambivalent about him."

"Really? A point in his favour, there. Hiram's a typical businessman, in most ways. Into every kind of enterprise, and filthy rich. But none too scrupulous, if what I've heard is true. The thing is, he's the sort of person that could be persuaded to be a major benefactor of Miskatonic. So it's not really in the interests of the college to discipline his son too harshly. And in your case it's another reason to be careful."

"I hardly think I'll ever pose any threat to Hiram West," I said. "Really, Alma, you're taking all this much too seriously. I admit I find West a rather interesting type, but our paths aren't likely to cross very often, after all."

"I hope not, for your sake. I have a bad feeling about that young man."

"And this young man?" I asked, feeling suddenly playful. "What sort of feeling do you have about him?"

She regarded me with her head tilted to one side, a little smile on her lips. "Oh, I think he's a very nice young man. I quite enjoy his company. Seriously, Charles, I do. I'm glad you came to Miskatonic."

We went on then to talk about other things, including Alma's ideas about the 'new woman.' She felt very strongly that young women should be encouraged to leave their parents' homes and support themselves for a while before they married.

"Otherwise the poor things are perfectly helpless, aside from housekeeping and looking after children. And so dull, too."

"You are surely an example of the other kind of woman, then, Alma. There's nothing dull about you."

"I hope not," she said, looking pleased.

We parted in this mood of friendly bantering. But walking homeward, I knew that my mind was operating on two levels. On one, I was developing a closeness with Alma that I found pleasing and gratifying. On the other, I was ready to throw myself heart and soul into whatever adventures I could find in the proximity of Herbert West. It was as though I stood in a house looking out through two different windows. From one I saw a warm and sunlit meadow, humming with bees, from the other a black sky blazing with unknown stars.

The next morning I decided to go to church. I was not a regular churchgoer, and when I went it was not for the conventional reasons. I went to honour the memory of my mother, Helen Devereaux Milburn, and to hear the music. I did not consider myself a practicing Catholic, but my mother had been one, and for her sake I maintained a tenuous link with the Roman Church.

There was no Catholic church in Arkham. That town had not gone so far from its Puritan roots as to permit such a thing. It was necessary to go to neighbouring Bolton, where a large population of Irish and Italian immigrants attended the Cathedral of the Immaculate Conception.

It had rained in the night, but the sky had cleared by the time I set out. The sun was swimming up from a sea of mist which gave ordinary things an otherworldly air. The venerable buildings of Arkham were softened in outline, yet sparkled as sun-shot raindrops fell from eaves and cornices. The air was sweetly fragrant and birds sang loudly. A short walk took me to River Street, where I boarded the old, rattling bus that shuttled between Arkham and Bolton twice a day.

Bolton is situated on a small hill, and so escapes the fogs and mists that plague Arkham. The hill falls sharply to the river on one side. At its summit is the Cathedral, a neo-Gothic building of the late 19th century, built large to accommodate the sizeable congregation of Bolton and the surrounding districts. No restraint had been exercised in the frescoes, which depicted various scenes from the Bible and the lives of the saints in vivid, almost lurid detail.

And yet, I found it peaceful. The effect of the frescoes was softened by the scale of the building and the way the light fell through the tall windows. There was an atmosphere of stillness which is common to all places of worship, from a Quaker meeting house to St. Peter's Basilica itself.

The Catholic service must be admired for its universality. One may attend a church in any city, with a congregation that speaks who knows what language, and experience the same Mass as in one's own church at home. I enjoyed hearing the Latin words spoken too, even though it was ecclesiastical Latin with the singsong accents of Italy.

The Cathedral was blessed with an enthusiastic choir and a choir director who was a true musician – Franz Marcello, an Austrian-Italian. He was a skilled organist, composer and choir director. The congregation was regularly treated to very fine singing, and occasionally to miracles of Renaissance polyphony. To hear the Mass sung, rather than spoken is a true pleasure, when the singers know their work and do it well. Today, to my delight, it was Palestrina's *Missa Papae Marcelli*, which strikes such a fine balance between ornateness and simplicity.

I lost myself in the overlapping waves of pure sound, unfolding and unfolding around me until I felt myself to be in the middle of a crystal globe suspended in a gulf of sunlight. From the first notes, I was borne upward by the voices, clear sopranos and deep baritones, floating on the sunlit air charged with dust motes. I was more than usually moved, probably because of the strangeness and potential dangers of the things about which West had told me, and the need to come up with an answer for him the next day.

During the sermon, which was a long one, I thought again of West's ideas about death and its possible reversal. Did I believe him? What did I myself think about death? Both my parents had died prematurely, my father by his own hand. I could not see that revivification such as West proposed would have served either of them – had my father returned to life he would still have been a failed banker. And my mother would have been the widow of a suicide, who had lost her home, her social position and her garden.

My mother's garden! I think it was the great joy of her life, more than my father, certainly, or me, or even music. It was when she no longer had it that she sickened and died.

We must have had several gardeners, over the years, but I remember only one. Michael O'Connor had been something else before taking up horticulture, perhaps a teacher, probably a poet. He did more than dig and prune and cut the grass to order. He advised my mother as to what to plant and how to achieve perfection in the perennial borders and shrubberies. The two of them would have long conversations while walking among the beds and borders, comparing the merits of one rose versus another, or debating whether lilies would do better with a southern or an eastern exposure. The garden was their joint enterprise. I realized that, even though my father did not. Michael left us when I was ten or so. I did not know the reason for his going and I never saw him again.

One fall when I was perhaps seven years old, I found a dead bird in the garden. Distressed, I demanded that the creature be given a funeral. A cigar box was found for a coffin, and Michael O'Connor fetched a spade and dug a grave beneath some shrubs. After we had deposited the little coffin and refilled the hole I asked,

"What about birds that don't have people to bury them, Michael? What happens to them?"

"Most birds, most critters, really, don't get buried by people, Charlie. Funerals are something only people do."

"So what happens to them? Birds and critters, I mean."

"They go back to the earth. To the place of life and death. Come over here. I'll show you something."

Near the potting shed, fallen leaves had been raked into great heaps. Michael pointed to one of them and said, "Here's one of those places. You see all these leaves? They'll rot here over the winter and next spring and summer. And next fall I'll take the black stuff they'll have turned into and spread it around the garden. The plants will use that black stuff to grow better. So you get life coming from death. It's the same with that bird. When it was alive it ate seeds and bugs and worms. They died, and the bird lived. Now the bird's dead, and a lot of critters will use up that bird, use it to keep themselves going, until they die and turn into food for something else. This is what happens to just about all animals. But people, now, they try like hell to keep themselves from going back into the earth. They have coffins and vaults, and all sorts of things to keep that from happening."

"Why do they do that?" I had never heard about any of this before, and found it intensely interesting.

"I guess because they figure they might need their bodies again, later. Some people think our bodies will get up again and join with our souls in Heaven."

"Do you believe that, Michael?"

"No I don't. I think our bodies come from the earth, and go back to the earth. I think that's the way God wants it to be. Maybe he takes our souls back to himself. I don't know about that. But you only have to be a gardener to see how life and death are parts of the same thing."

Some of the piled-up leaves were still brightly coloured, red and yellow. Others had faded to a dull brown, and still others were nearly black. A rich odour of over-ripeness hung in the warm air, from plums that had fallen from a nearby tree and lay with juice oozing from their split skins. Wasps buzzed and crawled around them, feeding on the sweet stuff. Here was life in death, indeed.

Now, in the church in Bolton, years later, sitting on the hard wooden bench, with the voice of Father Duranti droning in my ear, I remembered the rotting leaves and rotting plums and Michael O'Connor telling me of the place of life and death. Where, I wondered, did Herbert West's researches belong in this cycle? Why should I involve myself in his wild enterprise? Did it matter that I personally had no desire to vanquish death in the way he had described? For me there was something repugnant about the idea of a body that had been dead, however briefly, being forced into some grotesque semblance of life. Repugnant and unlikely too. I could more readily believe in the eternal life of the soul.

Shortly after my father killed himself, I had consulted a medium in an effort to communicate with his spirit. I thought if I could speak with him for only a few minutes I could ask him if he had found peace, and I could tell him I loved him, something I had not done for years. But the medium (Madame Zsa Zsa was the name she used), festooned in veils and scarves, painted eyes peering at me rapaciously, had filled me with distaste. How could this woman, with her false name and false accent, breach the mystery of death? Rather than insult the memory of my father, I abandoned the idea.

But now, perhaps, I would have an opportunity to speak with someone who had crossed the mystical barrier between life and death. Even to know that consciousness survived the process of dissolution would be a revelation indeed. Would such knowledge increase my faith, I wondered, or erode it further? The experiment, I thought, would be carried out on more than one subject.

The sermon ended and the measured ceremony of the Mass resumed. For the first time in years I prayed – for the souls of my parents, for Michael O'Connor, wherever he might be, for myself. But it never occurred to me to pray for Herbert West.

The bus was considerably fuller on the return trip to Arkham. This time, I had a seatmate – a tall old fellow, somewhat stooped in the shoulders.

"I like going to church," he said, sitting down with a sigh. "Sometimes I go two or three times on a Sunday. Doesn't matter which one – R.C., Baptist, Episcopalian – I go to all of 'em. I suppose it comes of spending so much time in churches when I was working." He held out a hand. "My name is Philip Howard, by the way."

I looked more closely at my companion as I shook his hand. He was dressed in a somber black suit, old but well cared for. Something about it, and his rather formal manner, made me curious.

"What sort of work did you do, Mr. Howard?" I asked.

"I was in the undertaking trade, worked for West's Funeral Home for thirty years. I know most of the folks in town, dead and alive, but I don't believe I've seen you before."

"I've lived in Arkham for less than a year, and I have not yet attended a funeral here. Were you a funeral director?"

"For my last ten years I was. Before that I did whatever needed doing, drove the hearse, built coffins and so forth."

"Did you see much of Mr. West?"

"Which one?" He laughed a little. "I worked mostly for Mr. Joshua West and his brother Henry. They were real undertakers, now. When Hiram took over the funeral business was only a sideline. He hired managers to oversee it. Had better things to do himself, I guess."

"Did Hiram West live in Arkham, then? I thought he was from Boston."

"Right you are. Wests are from Boston. The connection to Arkham was the funeral homes. Joshua and Henry bought up all the homes in the smaller cities around here back in the early '80s. And the other connection was Mrs. Hiram. She was from Arkham and couldn't bear to leave it, seemingly. Some folks figure that's why she left him, but I think there must have been more to it than that. In '94 or '95, that was. Now it might be true she came back to Arkham, all right. Her people, the Derbys, have been here for generations, you see."

"Left him!" I exclaimed. "But I was under the impression that she died many years ago." I did a quick calculation. West had said that his mother had died when he was eight. He must be about twenty-five now, I reckoned. "At least fifteen."

"Well, you heard wrong. It was fifteen years ago, all right, but she didn't die. She left Hiram and the boys and probably came back to Arkham. She might still be living here, for all I know."

I had suspected that West's poignant tale of his mother's death was not altogether true, and I could now understand why he might prefer to think of her as dead, but it seemed odd that he could live in the same not very large city as she and continue to deny her existence. Perhaps he had no idea that she might be in Arkham.

"There were only three sons, then?" I asked, remembering West's mention of a twin brother who had died at the same time as his mother.

"Only the three, and the two older ones were in their teens when she left, so they probably didn't feel it too much. But the little one, Herbert, he was only seven or eight, and I can imagine it would have hit him pretty hard. He had her looks, too, unlike his brothers, who take after Hiram, too bad for them."

He laughed shortly. "That little Herbert, though, he was a tough one. Maybe her going didn't do him that much harm after all, or maybe he just didn't show it. Not much scared that boy. I remember him going along with his Grandpa Joshua when he took Mrs. Beazley around to show the country folks what a well-preserved lady she was."

"Who was Mrs. Beazley?" I asked.

"She was a corpse! Yes indeed, before embalming became popular, undertakers had to advertise it somehow, to get people wanting to have it done to their dear departeds, you know. Someone hit on the idea of fitting up a body – one that would have gone to the potter's field, of course – no sense in taking a chance on running into its relatives somewhere – and showing it around as a kind of sample. A picture's worth a thousand words, and all that.

"So Wests got this poor woman, some lady of the evening, probably, and gave her the treatment, dressed her up nice and drove around all the little burgs back in the hills, there." He waved a hand vaguely westwards. "Dunwich and Aylesbury and Dean's Corners. Godforsaken little places, all of them. I don't know how much business they drummed up there. One of our embalmers, George Price, a real joker, he named her Mrs. Beazley after his old aunt. Looked just like her, he said, but didn't talk as much. Anyway, young Herbert, later on he worked in the trade, too. Did the embalming. That was before he went to be a doctor, of course."

I did not trouble to inform the old fellow about my acquaintance with West. I was too occupied with digesting his bizarre tale. My impressions of West had led me to believe that he perfectly fit the type of the young dilettante son of the *nouveau riche* tycoon – privileged, a little dandified, but with something besides, an iconoclasm bordering on wildness.

But this! Mrs. Beazley, and long drives along narrow winding roads to primitive villages so his grandfather could hawk embalming to their benighted inhabitants. Perhaps this explained something of West's apparent deviousness. Clearly, his had been no ordinary childhood.

By now we had reached the Arkham terminus. I said goodbye to Philip Howard, thanking him for his interesting stories.

"Not at all, young fellow. People tell me I run on too much, and maybe they're right. It's nice to find someone who hasn't heard it all before. Good day to you!"

The next day, immediately after work, I went directly to West's rooms, as we had agreed. West ushered me into a spacious room he used as a study. The desk was littered with books and papers. West himself appeared remote and distracted, not inclined to small talk.

"I have made up my mind," I said. "I would be honoured to assist you with your experiments."

"Would you, now?" he said, with what can be described only as a private smile, looking at something unguessable and distant in a corner of the room. I was disconcerted. Had I perhaps misunderstood him the other night, and was now being presumptuous?

After this uncomfortable moment he turned his remarkable eyes fully on me.

"I'm glad to hear that, Charles, " he said, springing to his feet and holding out his hand. I got up and took it. We stood there for a moment, hands clasped, and I felt a most extraordinary elation rush through me. Then he said, "This calls for a toast." He left the room briefly and returned with a bottle of whiskey. As we raised our glasses he said, "To our enterprise! Death be vanquished!"

After this he became businesslike.

"I want to make sure you know exactly what it is we will be doing," he began. "Securing a suitable body is the most difficult problem. The obituaries are no good these days. People who put obituary notices in the newspapers generally get their deceased relatives embalmed. And even though embalming was one of the things that showed me how revivification might be accomplished, it's entirely fatal to my process, which depends on the interaction of the introduced fluid with the natural blood. An embalmed body no longer has any natural blood. Bodies buried in the potter's field are therefore superior for my purposes to the worthies in Christ Church Cemetery. A kind of social reversal, you might say." He smiled.

"The thing about burials in the potter's field is finding out about them in time. Obviously, we can't hang about in the burial ground on the chance. I figure accident victims would be the best specimens, provided they're not too mangled by whatever killed them."

"Excuse me... Herbert," I interrupted, using his first name, as he had used mine. "Where are we going to do the experiment?"

He looked annoyed. "Haven't you been listening? The logical place would be one of the labs in the Med. School, but since logic doesn't operate there, the only other possibility is here, in my rooms. Even that will be risky enough. We'll have to get the apparatus in place with only the shortest notice, since I dare not set it up ahead of time and risk its existence being discovered.

"Another thing, Charles – the revivifying solution is quite unstable. I'm certain, based on my animal experiments, that it loses its effectiveness after a few hours. So you see, as soon as I hear of a suitable body, we must formulate the solution, set up the equipment, and transport the subject in short order. That's why I need your help."

"What will you want me to do, exactly?"

"Well, that depends on the precise circumstances. You'll set up the apparatus, I think. I'll show you how it works in a few minutes. I'll cook the solution. But the trickiest thing will be getting the body into the house. Don't imagine that we'll carry it on a stretcher. That would be as sure a way as any to tell anyone who happens by that something unorthodox is going on. No, I've decided that the best approach would be for the two of us to act like gentlemen returning home from a jolly evening, holding up our even more inebriated companion. Think you're equal to that, Charles?"

I was momentarily horrified. Of course I had realized that West's experiments of necessity involved corpses, but in my naïveté I had not imagined that my role would require me to handle them in any intimate way. I had imagined myself standing at West's side, handing him things and watching enthralled as he performed his scientific miracles. Suddenly I remembered what Philip Howard had told me about West and 'Mrs. Beazley.' I shuddered. What was I getting myself into?

But it was too late to back out. "I hope I can do it," I said, as steadily as I could. "Do you have the equipment here? Perhaps you could show me how it works now." I was determined to forge ahead, hoping that my misgivings did not show on my face.

"Not so fast, Charles. There's one more thing I have to tell you. Then I'll give you a minute to think about the whole business again before you really decide. I realize this must seem pretty drastic to someone who hasn't had my experience.

"You must understand," he said, looking at me seriously, "that I have no idea what a revivified body might do. Without a doubt, brain cells will have been lost during the interval of death. The brain chemistry may have changed too, in some subtle way. That's why freshness is so important. We may find ourselves dealing with a quasi-vegetable idiot, or with a person who appears to be entirely normal, but with some loss of cognition. On the other hand, we may get violent reactions of the most extreme sort. I found this to be quite common in my animal experiments. After a while I routinely used restraints and kept a syringe full of a deadly alkaloid on hand to dispatch any subjects of the violent sort. This is a dangerous business," he said slowly and emphatically. "Think about it for five minutes. If you decide you want out I'll not blame you."

He returned to his writing, completely ignoring me. I watched him as he made some notes, shuffled through papers, got up to take a book from a nearby shelf, consulted it, wrote some more. My mind was completely blank. For me it really was too late to back out, and had been so ever since I had made my declaration upon my arrival. But I let the five minutes elapse, just the same.

When the allotted time had passed he directed his gaze back to me and asked, "Well, Charles, are you in or out?"

"I'm in," I said, relieved that the period of limbo was over.

"Good. Actually, I knew you would be. But I wanted to make sure it was a considered decision on your part. Now come with me and I'll show you the apparatus."

He led me to a small room at the back of the house, ostensibly used for storage. There was a large table by one wall, which could be moved to the centre of the room. Inside a crate was the apparatus for creating and administering the critical fluid.

"The idea is that everything can be dismantled and packed away quickly, should the need arise. That would be fine in case of a superficial search, by police or others. It would not, of course, be proof against a more systematic investigation, which is why I'm so anxious to achieve success quickly. Once I get some documented positive results, those fools at the Med. School will have to acknowledge the value of my work. Besides, after this summer I'll be neck-deep in clinical work. Sixteen hour days won't give me much time for this."

Assembling the apparatus was not overly complicated, although I could see that care was needed to make certain that all the connections were properly made and tightly secured. West spent less time showing me the laboratory equipment he would use for preparing the solution – balances, beakers, flasks, pipettes, a long glass cylinder he called a burette, and a host of other things. I found it all rather bewildering, but reflected that I would not, after all, be required to use it.

Once we had finished with these practical matters, West cooked us a supper, for it was growing late. He was as quick and neat-handed in the kitchen as among his test tubes and retorts. "I cook quite well, actually" he said. "It saves a lot of time, not to be forever running out to taverns and restaurants and getting distracted. This *frittata*, now, will have taken less than half an hour from start to finish. And that includes eating it."

"*Frittata?*" I asked. "I thought that was an omelet." It was very good but with flavourings new to me. I was no hand at cooking, which made me a ready victim of my landlady's miserly meals.

"So it is, but an Italian one."

"Where did you learn to cook Italian omelets, Herbert?"

"From an Italian lady. What did you think?" He gave me a look of amusement combined with something else which made me desist from further questioning. I had a sudden vision of West in a kitchen with a fascinating dark-haired woman. The process of digesting this idea as well as the meal left me rather bemused.

Before we parted, West stressed once more the need for prompt action should a suitable corpse become available. "I'll send you a message," he said. "Either at the Library or at your rooms. Come here immediately and be prepared for a long night." He handed me some books. "I don't expect you to become either a chemist or a physician's assistant," he said, "but it wouldn't hurt you to get acquainted with some of the fundamentals of anatomy and laboratory work."

That evening, I had a look through the anatomy book. I found it hard going, and the illustrations were rather loathsome. It occurred to me once more that West may not have found the best possible assistant in me. Ironically, Alma Halsey, with her scientific background and quick wit, would have been a more suitable choice. But I did not think she would be at all sympathetic to his cause, and her general dislike and suspicion of him would preclude such sympathy from developing.

I awoke with a jolt at three in the morning, a bizarre dream fuming its way through my waking brain. I had been frantically trying to connect West's revivifying apparatus to a red-haired, painted-faced hag who could only have been the infamous Mrs. Beazley. All the while, West was impatiently tugging at my sleeve and saying, "Hurry up, Charles. Freshness is absolutely critical if you want to save her."

♦ 4 ♦

I asked Alma Halsey to go out with me several times that summer, to a lecture, a play and a band concert in the park by the river. On none of these occasions did I speak of West to her, and she did not ask me whether I had any dealings with him.

One July evening, as we walked slowly along French Hill Street toward the house where Alma lived, I asked about her father, Dr. Allan Halsey. I was curious to find out more about West's nemesis, even though Alma was hardly an unbiased source.

"Papa? Oh, he's the original solid citizen. Too solid, I think. No new ideas can penetrate that cranium, not if they come from me, anyway. He was dead set against my going to medical school, but thought librarianship was a suitable profession for a young lady. And at least he and Mama have been good about my working at a job. And I managed to move out of their house. The wife of one of Papa's colleagues needed a companion when her husband died. She keeps afloat by renting out rooms, you see, so the parents agreed that I should live with her and help her out. I think it's because they're sure it's only temporary. Until the right young man comes along, you know."

"And is it?" I asked.

"Not at all. I intend to go on working, whether I get married or not. And I have no plans for that at present," she said, laughing.

I did something else during those weeks of waiting. I went once more to look at the *Necronomicon*, this time for my own reasons.

The more I read about the medical and scientific topics recommended to me by West, the less I understood his reasons for consulting the ancient tome. I could not fathom how a medical researcher in the 20th century could find anything even remotely relevant in the writings of an Arab of Yemen who had lived more than a thousand years before.

There was also the disturbing memory of the hours I had spent poring over the book at West's side, translating, supposedly, but I knew not what. Again and again I had tried to relive that experience, to wring memories from my brain. Had I been the victim of a hallucination? I am a competent Latinist, but had found the language of the *Necronomicon* dense and impenetrable. I had translated word by word, not comprehending any unified meaning. So late one day, I went again to the Library's Administration Office.

It was a hot, still afternoon. The formidable Miss Hardy was on her annual vacation, leaving the office staffed only by her assistant, a browbeaten young woman by name of Miss Reid. She had no objection to my brief explanation that I needed to check a reference in one of the rare books in the vault.

I unlocked the heavy door and entered. It was a little cooler there but the air seemed dead. Because I expected my visit to be a brief one I did not bother to carry the book out to the consultation room. When I lifted it from its drawer, it felt extraordinarily heavy, even more than it had when I handed it to

West. And again, I was conscious of an odour – cold earth, as on that other occasion, but also a faint scent of narcissus. When I laid the volume on the table at the back of the vault I felt as though I relinquished a heavy burden.

I certainly did not expect to be able to find the exact passages I had translated for West. I remembered that he had brought some references with him, which he had used to find the paragraphs that interested him. He had never told me how he could have navigated with such precision in a book he had never seen before, an ancient book which lacked such modern features as a table of contents or index, written in a language with which he was only just conversant.

I opened the book at random and read the first text I saw. The black type was so sharp and bright that the letters seemed almost alive. It was as though the *Necronomicon* spoke to me, confidentially, in a barely audible murmur. As nearly as I can remember, this is what it said (the translation my own, of course):

The wind of the world blows equally through the living and the dead. He that fears not the night nor the Worm that gnaws, he that looks into the microcosm and the macrocosm, he that dares to follow the spiralling of the blood into the abyss, may cleave the lesser from the greater, the immortal from the mortal, and find life in the place of death. But one that ventures therein should have at his side a good companion as his doorkeeper and warden, for it is written that none shall tarry over-long in the nether deeps, lest he cede himself entirely to the Worm.

Surely this was the passage I had vaguely remembered! Profoundly astonished, I read it again. Comprehension brushed at my consciousness, then departed on dark wings. The perfume of narcissus was suddenly intolerable. Blackness enfolded me, and I fainted, sliding to the floor while grasping at the table for support.

I came to myself to find Miss Reid grasping my shoulder and whispering anxiously. "Mr. Milburn, wake up! Mr. Milburn, are you all right? Should I fetch a doctor? Oh dear, oh dear!"

"I'm all right," I said, although I wasn't. My head ached and I felt embarrassed and confused. It had been a mistake to stay in the airless vault, especially on such a hot day. "Really, Miss Reid, I'm fine. It's quite hot and stuffy in here, and I must have... nodded off. I think I had better go home now."

With her rather ineffectual help, I managed to get to my feet and close the *Necronomicon*, taking care to avoid looking at the page I had been reading. The strange perfume had vanished as though it had never been. It was only as I was leaving the Library that I remembered I had not made a note of my visit in the vault log, contrary to regulations.

By the following afternoon I was feeling better, although I had a lingering headache. I was leafing through an unbelievably dull treatise on Greek philosophy that I was cataloguing when one of the library pages came puffing up to my desk with a note for me. I thanked the boy and waited until he had gone before I opened it.

It was from West. *Come immediately*, it said.

Now? I had never been less inclined to engage in something both illegal and dangerous. And what the devil were we going to do at four in the afternoon? Even at my slowest and clumsiest it could not take more than an hour to prepare the laboratory and assemble the equipment. Surely West did not intend to transport a corpse through the streets of Arkham during the afternoon rush hour? But perhaps he had managed somehow to smuggle the thing into his rooms already. In my fragile state I found only scant comfort in this possibility.

And yet I never even considered not going. I grabbed my jacket and ran for the door, only to encounter Peter Runcible.

"And where are you off to, Mr. Milburn?" he asked. The hot weather was not kind to him. He looked damp and wrinkled. I imagined a miasma of sweat hanging about him, and felt sick again.

"I'm... not well, sir," I answered, wildly. This was true. My headache was worse, and I felt hot and cold by turns. "I must go, now!"

My desperation must have suggested to him that I was about to be sick on the floor. "All right, all right, go home if you must. But I hope to see you here tomorrow morning, alive and well."

I waved a hand toward him and ran.

It was only three blocks to West's quarters. Five minutes after I had escaped from Runcible, I pounded up the front steps, crossed the porch and hammered on the door.

After a moment, West opened it. He looked as cool and calm as I was hot and frantic. He motioned me into the hall, closed the door and looked me up and down.

"You get good marks for speed, but a failure for discretion," he said. "Next time you must try to arrive with less of a flurry. We don't want to attract attention, you know."

"What do you mean, 'good marks,' 'next time'?" I asked, breathing hard and getting angry. "Do you mean to say this was some sort of test?"

"Yes, of course," he answered. "My apologies, Charles, but you must admit that I couldn't very well give you prior notice. It's crucial that there be no slip-ups when the time comes."

"Herbert," I said, "this is unreasonable. I left work early, saying I was ill. There'll be the devil to pay for that tomorrow. I'm hot, I'm tired and I'm... disgusted."

He looked astonished. "Really, Charles, I shouldn't think that a three-block walk would be such an inconvenience. And anyway, it isn't really a test." He produced once more that charming smile that had disarmed Miss Hardy, and me, too. "We have a body."

I flopped into a chair. "This is too much," I said. "Give me a minute. You mean this is really it? We're going ahead?"

"We're going ahead. Tonight."

While we fortified ourselves with a plate of sandwiches and some lemonade, West outlined his strategy.

"First we'll set up the lab and prepare the solution. Then we'll have a rest. This is going to be an all-night enterprise, so we need to be reasonably fresh going into it. It doesn't get really dark until after ten, unfortunately, but that can't be helped. As soon as it's dim enough to blur details we'll dress as workmen and carry our equipment to the site."

"What equipment, what site?" I asked. "I thought we were doing it here." My headache had faded, but I still felt foggy.

"The site is the graveyard by Hangman's Hill, the potter's field," said West. "And the equipment is a couple of spades, some rope and a pry-bar. Is that clear?"

"Graveyard, spades?" I knew I sounded like a babbling idiot, but I couldn't help it. "We're going to dig up a grave?"

He gave me a look that dropped the temperature in my immediate vicinity by several degrees. "Charles, did you actually think that the body would be delivered to the door by Acme Corpse Specialists? I thought I explained all that. Yesterday I heard that a young fellow named John Hocks had drowned in Summer's Pond and was to be buried today in the potter's field. So tonight is our earliest opportunity. I thought I was giving us plenty of time to get ready, but it seems I'm wrong. Now, do you think you can pull yourself together by nightfall? If not, say so now and go home. In your present state you'll be no help at all, quite the contrary."

"I'm sorry, Herbert. I've felt a little shaky all day. It's the heat, maybe. But about this body, I thought you said we could get one from the morgue."

"In theory, yes. It would certainly be quicker and neater, except for two things. One: I don't have access to the morgue. I'm not yet a doctor, and I'm under a cloud at the Med. School, as you know, so I would have to bribe the attendant just to get in. Getting out with a body would be next to impossible. Two: what do you think will happen if the experiment is a failure? I don't think we can assume that the subject will leave here on his own feet. If it's impossible to get a body out of the morgue, it's utterly beyond the realm of imagination to get one back in.

"Now this fellow Hocks is already buried. The world is finished with him. He doesn't have to be accounted for. No one is going to come looking for him. He was from Maine or somewhere. He has no known relatives here and was buried at public expense. No one will know that he's going to leave his resting place at Hangman's Hill and spend some time with us. If we don't attract the wrong sort of attention, that is." He gave me a hard look as he said this, obviously regretting his choice of accomplice.

"It's going to be a bit of a job, getting him out," West continued. "The old body-snatchers, the resurrection men, didn't bother with finesse. They just dug a narrow shaft down to the head end of the coffin, smashed a hole in it and hauled out the corpse. So what if it got a little scuffed in the process? The customer was going to cut the thing up, after all. That would be fine for us if we were certain we wouldn't need to put him back in, but since we might, we must expose the whole thing and open the lid. And it's best not to cause additional injuries."

"Put him back in?" I asked, feeling slow and stupid once more. "Why would we have to do that? I thought the idea was to bring him back to life."

West gave me another chilly look. "It is, but in an experiment one must always be prepared for results different from those one expects. He may very well remain dead. We must be ready for that. Now, if you're clear on that part of the business, let's set up the lab."

The by now familiar task of assembling the equipment calmed me a little. Over the table which was to hold the body, I set up a collapsible framework . On it I mounted a reservoir for the liquid, another for the blood which would be removed from the subject, and an array of tubes, valves and pressure meters.

While I was engaged with this, West was weighing and measuring chemicals and reagents, mixing, heating, filtering and titrating. I watched the conclusion of the process with fascination.

Into a flask containing a clear fluid, he added, drop by drop, another clear fluid from the glass cylinder he had called a burette. He was absolutely concentrated on what he was doing. I suspected that I could have left the room, danced a jig, or done anything but interfere with him, and he would not have noticed.

Suddenly, a transformation occurred. The liquid in the flask appeared to ripple and became a violet colour. There was no gradual transition; the change was instantaneous and complete. Looking more closely, I could see a strange iridescence within the fluid. West stoppered the flask and sighed with relief.

"That's done, then," he said. "Sometimes it fails to react if the proportions aren't exactly right."

Our preparations were complete by early evening. West showed me to a sofa in the parlour, saying that I should get some rest. We would prepare to leave the house after ten o'clock.

I found it impossible to sleep, or even to relax. As soon as I closed my eyes a welter of images, real and imagined, churned through my brain. What if we were seen digging up the grave? How could we possibly carry the body to the house as West had proposed? How far was it to the graveyard, anyway? I wondered if I was physically equal to the task before me. And what would the outcome of the experiment be?

Lying on the sofa in the unfamiliar room, I felt suddenly lonely for my own ordinary life. What was I doing here, preparing to help this peculiar stranger perform an act which was both illegal and repugnant? Just about this time, I thought, I would normally be reading a little before going to bed, or perhaps enjoying a pleasant stroll, possibly with Alma. What she would think of this stunt – for so it seemed to me now – I could only imagine. Emancipated she might be, but I was certain that her world-view did not include nice young men who engaged in a little body snatching on the side.

Eventually I fell into an uneasy doze which must have become a sound sleep from which West had to shake me. "How are you feeling, Charles? Do you think you can do this?"

"I hope so," I replied, thinking immediately that I was too hesitant. "Yes, I can do it."

By ten-thirty we were ready to go. We had changed into some dark shabby clothes West had produced, and carried our spades and other implements muffled in a couple of sacks.

"Don't hurry," West admonished me as we left his rooms by way of the back door. "We're just a couple of tired fellows making our way home, not a pair of resurrection men." And indeed, his whole aspect had changed. The battered hat he wore concealed his bright hair, and the slouching walk he had assumed made him look the very picture of a workman going homeward after a hard day.

Despite my anxiety, I emitted a muffled laugh at the *double entendre.* It wasn't only resurrection men I thought of, but ghouls.

It certainly was a perfect night for ghoulish doings. The moon was waning and cast little light. The stars were bright in the gaps between occasional clouds. I remembered my vision of the sunlit meadow and the black starlit sky. *I guess I'm flying now,* I thought absurdly.

Twenty minutes of steady walking brought us to a belt of trees between the graveyard and the fields beyond the town. It was dense enough to conceal our presence from passers-by until we could be about our real business.

We made ourselves comfortable in a little hollow, laying our burdens down carefully and propping our backs against the trunk of a large maple. Now that the adventure was really under way I felt almost calm and began to get sleepy.

Suddenly, West grasped my arm. I looked in the direction he was pointing. Some way to the north was Aylesbury Street, which a little further west became the Aylesbury Pike. Shadowy figures were moving along it, in the direction of Arkham. I heard the tramp of feet and some muffled conversation. Eventually these wayfarers passed out of sight, going toward River Street and the town.

"We'd better give it another hour," West whispered. "I didn't think there would be so many people about."

Conversation was obviously out of the question. I leaned back against the tree trunk and closed my eyes. I could hear the small sounds of night creatures going about their business, and a faint rustle of wind in the leaves. I could smell the freshness of growing plants and the musky earthiness of dead ones. Beside me, West was still as a stone.

I must have nodded off, because suddenly I was awake, aware of a new sound. A stealthy sound, yet distinct. I listened, trying not to breathe. There it was – a faint, irregular crackling or scraping that seemed to come from nowhere and everywhere.

I remembered where I was. Beneath me lay the dead, dozens of corpses in varying states of decay, their skulls grinning mirthless grins. The roots of the tree I was leaning against were entwined among bones, drawing nourishment from them. Worms and insects burrowed through the mould, revelling in unspeakable feasts.

Straining my ears, I detected yet another layer of sound. Not the rustling of vermin, nor the slow disintegration of matter, but a toneless hum that registered on some sense beyond the aural, vibrating the filaments of my nerves and making me at once hyper-alert and paralyzed. It was as though I had become a receiver for an incomprehensible telegraph message from some inconceivably distant place.

I began to think I could discern individual voices. If I listened long enough I would understand what they said, except I wasn't sure I wanted to. Than West nudged me and I nearly screamed. "Come on, Charles, wake up," he whispered. "Time to get on with it."

"Wait, Herbert," I said. "Can't you hear it? Listen."

"Hear what?" He paused for less than a second and stood up, reaching out a hand to help me up. "There's nothing to hear, now that you've stopped snoring. I nearly woke you up a few times, it was so loud."

I decided not to argue and got to my feet, cautiously stretching out the stiffness in my limbs. I could no longer hear the sound, much to my relief. West picked up our tools and led the way into the burying ground.

A mist lay over Hangman's Brook and the distant Miskatonic. It must have been close to midnight.

Unlike the orderly plots of Christ Church Cemetery, with their marble and granite monuments and wrought iron fences, the graveyard at Hangman's Hill was informal and unkempt. Once or twice a year the grass was scythed and underbrush cut back, but most of the time the place was left to itself, except when a new grave had to be made.

It was not difficult to find the newest grave. A mound of fresh soil and trampled grass made it clear that this was our goal.

"We'll pile all the earth here," West said, indicating one side of the grave. "That will leave the other side clear for lifting him out, and it'll be easier to shovel the dirt back in. Yes, we must fill it up again, over the empty coffin. We may not be in a position to return him tonight, and we don't want to leave an open hole."

I was annoyed at West's insistence on assuming that the experiment would be a failure, leaving us with a corpse on our hands again in the end. If success was so unlikely, I thought mutinously, why were we even bothering? But I knew better than to voice these thoughts.

The digging was a tiresome business, especially for me, unused as I was to physical labour, and lacking West's stamina and sense of purpose. It occurred to me as I toiled that this aspect of grave-robbing would be a sufficient deterrent for most would-be ghouls. It was neither thrilling nor aesthetic.

After nearly an hour of steady labour, West struck the coffin lid with his spade. "We're nearly in business now, Charles!" he said, as we scraped away the remaining soil and exposed the wooden box. I felt relief mingled with apprehension as I straightened my tired back and leaned on my spade to rest. I was bathed in unaccustomed perspiration. The air in the grave seemed suddenly thick and fetid, and I longed to be somewhere else.

"Where did you put the pry-bar?" West asked, impatiently.

"It's here somewhere," I muttered, feeling around behind me. I had stuck the tool into the side of the pit, for fear of losing it.

"Well, find it, will you! We have to get on with this."

Just then, my hand struck the bar, which fell onto the coffin lid with a thud.

"Give it here!" West snatched it from me and began to pry up the lid. When he had loosened all the nails, I helped him lift it off and cautiously shone a light within. The dead man lay on his back in a most unremarkable way. I felt inclined to stare, but West did not let me.

"Here, let's get the rope around him," he said. I passed it to him, keeping hold of one end while he tied the other around the body, under the armpits. We climbed out of the grave and hauled the corpse to the surface. I felt a distinct reluctance to touch it, but West showed no such squeamishness.

"I want to see if there's water in the lungs," he said. "We must drain out as much as possible if there's to be any hope of success."

We hoisted the unfortunate fellow up by his legs, then lay him face down on the ground. West manipulated his arms for a while, then got up.

"They probably got most of it out trying to resuscitate him" he said. "I think it's all right. Now we just have to fill in the grave." He jumped back into the hole and replaced the lid of the coffin. Hurriedly, we shoveled the excavated soil back into the opening and mounded it up as it had been previously. At West's suggestion I concealed our spades and other tools in the woods. A feeling of utter unreality possessed me, born of weariness and my sudden recognition of the outsideness of our doings. I found the thought of re-excavating the grave almost insupportable. For this reason alone I hoped West's revivifying fluid would be a roaring success.

With the grave restored to something resembling its former state, we turned our attention to its recent occupant. We put the body into a large sack we had brought with us. This mode of transportation would suffice until we reached the first houses on College Street.

Our homeward progress was slow. The body in its sack was heavy and awkward. I found it difficult to maintain a good grip on the thing while I traversed the narrow path along Hangman's Brook. Several times I nearly fell, and soon felt a childish resentment toward West for selecting as unfit a creature as myself to be his assistant. But he said nothing beyond the minimal instructions needed to direct my steps. His apparent patience only made me feel more wretched.

At a vacant lot at the corner of Hill Street and College, we changed our mode of transport. I was glad to lay down the burden, if only for a few minutes. We divested the corpse of its sack and stood up with it slumped between us. Clumsily, I slung the dead left arm over my shoulders and reached around its back. This put most of its weight on the side away from my bad leg, which was starting to throb. I could feel the coldness of the dead flesh through the layers of clothing between it and myself. Only the living warmth of West's arm where it touched mine behind the corpse's back kept me from giving in to my revulsion, dropping the thing and running away.

Our unwieldy six-legged ménage lurched slowly along College Street. No acting was necessary on my part to simulate the unsteady gait of the inebriated. As I grew accustomed to the weight, something caused me to visualize our passage as an observer might have seen it. And with this occurred one of those odd doublings of consciousness – at one and the same time I was carrying a dead man and watching one being carried, disguised as a drunkard. I seemed to discover within myself a kinship with men of darkness, body snatchers, ghouls, resurrection men, an unholy lineage harking back to the despoilers of the royal tombs of Egypt.

Since the distance to West's lodgings was now a mere three blocks, I hoped we could reach our goal without encountering anyone, but our luck failed as we were passing St. Mary's Hospital. A lone man, who from his gait appeared to be in the state we were hoping to imitate, came toward us.

"Sing!" West commanded, and broke into a rather good rendition of *To Anacreon in Heaven*, an odd choice, and an unfortunate one for me, who did not know the words. But the tune, of course, is that of our National Anthem, so I sang that instead. Together we created a fine cacophony as we lurched the last hundred yards.

As West fumbled with the key to the back door, a window in the next house flew open and a sleepy voice growled imprecations at us, ending with, "What do you fools think you're doing, trying to wake the dead?" Fortunately, the door opened then and we fell through it, laughing like loons.

Our laughter was short lived, but at least it made me forget for a moment that the night's real business had yet to be done. And at least we were no longer on the streets with our illicit burden.

"Why on earth did you sing?" I asked. "That guy across the street wasn't going to bother us. And now whoever that was yelling through the window will remember us too."

"They'll both remember a couple of drunks singing, and another who was too soused to stand. Not two men carrying a third one, who could have been sick, or dead. Window-dressing, Charles. A diversion. At least I hope so. Now let's get on with it, for God's sake."

We lugged the body into our improvised laboratory and hoisted it onto the table. "I'm going to wash up and change my clothes," said West. "I suggest you do the same. We're in no state to conduct an experiment." I was surprised at this seeming frivolity in one who was so keen to 'get on with it,' but did as I was told. Ten minutes later, we returned to the laboratory, West in a completely fresh set of clothes, I in the sweaty items I had been wearing when I left the Cataloguing Department an eternity ago.

West put on a white lab coat and tossed me another one. "Put that on," he said. "That's better. Now, let's get him undressed."

I looked unhappily at our guest. Now that we were in a well-lit place I could not ignore the still, waxy face, its eyes slightly open, giving it a suspicious, moronic look. The fellow was wearing a dirty checked shirt and a pair of overalls.

"Must we? Can't you inject the stuff into him with his clothes on? After all, if he gets up and goes out we don't want him to be indecent."

West ignored this attempt at humour. "We have to take his clothes off, Charles. No arguments. What's the problem, anyway – haven't you ever seen a naked man?"

"Not often," I replied, trying to be truthful without admitting the extent of my naïveté. "And never a dead one."

West laughed. "I've seen many dead ones. And believe me," he said, taking a scalpel and slitting the overalls down the front, "nothing we do to a corpse troubles it in the least. Corpses simply don't care."

I did not bother to point out that if all went as he wished, this one would no longer be a corpse in an hour or two, and might very well object to how we treated it. Instead, I removed the fellow's shoes. They were old and broken, obviously the ones he had been wearing when he drowned, because they were still damp. I wondered that they had not slipped off. He had no socks. West lifted the corpse's shoulders and asked me to remove the shirt. Then he lifted the body at the waist while I pulled off the legs of the overalls.

The corpse lay naked on the table. In life it had been an ordinary-looking young man of perhaps twenty years, brown-haired, thin but not scrawny, the muscles of the chest and arms developed from physical labour. There was a partly healed cut on his right arm. The skin was a strange yellowish colour, suggesting wax rather than flesh, with purple patches here and there. I was reminded obscenely of something on display in a butcher shop. Despite West's casual attitude, I studiously avoided looking at what one commonly called the private parts. Although death had stolen this man's right to privacy, I did not have to comply. I thought I could smell the beginnings of corruption, and a cold smell of earth.

West was moving about rapidly, collecting equipment from the crate which had been converted into a kind of laboratory bench. He was completely absorbed, and appeared utterly comfortable with the situation, in contrast to myself, who wanted nothing so much as an excuse to leave the room.

He stood for what seemed like a long time with a stethoscope pressed to the corpse's chest. "Purely for the record," he said, making some notes. "I have to certify beyond a doubt that he's dead before we begin. And he is.

"At this point," West continued, in what I was coming to think of as his lecturing mode, "the problem is to introduce fluid into a body without a pulse, in sufficient quantity to be effective. In theory it should be possible to inject it directly into the heart, but in practice this has too much potential to cause damage to that organ and negate the revivifying effect. So it's necessary to use a mechanical pump to substitute for the action of the heart, introducing the fluid into a major vein and withdrawing excess blood through a major artery. This is the reverse of what is done in embalming. The revivifying fluid must enter the heart in order to cause it to contract, which is why I shall introduce it through the jugular vein. And the excess blood will be drawn out through the femoral artery, which is sufficiently distant from both the heart and the brain not to interfere with the balance of things. The apparatus becomes, in effect, a temporary extension of the body's circulatory system."

He picked up another scalpel. "As an embalmer I would just slit open a number of blood vessels to ensure maximum blood flow. But there, of course, the objective is to drain out all the blood and replace it with embalming fluid. Here we want to remove only a portion of the blood, and add the new fluid. So we must follow this more exact process, because we don't want to do any further damage."

He made a careful cut into the flesh of the neck, exposing a blood vessel. Then he picked up a long hollow needle, which he called a cannula, and carefully inserted it into the vein, then repeated the process on the upper part of the corpse's left leg. He attached to each needle a length of rubber tubing which dangled from the apparatus.

I watched, fascinated yet horrified, imagining the needles, which suddenly seemed very large, piercing the walls of the blood vessels and sliding inside. I wondered how that would feel, and thought I was going to be sick. That wouldn't do. I became aware that West was speaking once more.

"Now we're ready to introduce the fluid, but it must be done carefully, making sure that the pressures are in balance and not excessive. That's the purpose of these meters and valves. I want you to watch this constantly and let me know the instant this one reaches 200."

I took my place by the meter he had indicated, glad to have something to divert my attention from the thought of those dreadful needles. West picked up the flask of violet coloured liquid he had prepared earlier, and poured the contents into the reservoir of the apparatus. Then he opened the main valve and the drainage valve and began to work the pump.

At first nothing happened, except that the tube leading from the reservoir swelled and grew rigid. Suddenly, I became aware that a dark fluid was dripping into the empty flask. I realized with a jolt that it was blood, the dead man's blood, and began to feel sick again. I concentrated on the pressure meter to steady myself. Slowly, the level of the violet fluid in the reservoir declined. The indicator held at a steady 160, then began to climb: 170, 180, 185, 190. "It's at 195, Herbert," I said. He grasped the knob controlling the main valve. A few seconds later, I said, "Two hundred!" The reservoir was nearly empty. Turning off the flow, West sighed audibly.

"Well, that's it. That's as much as he can take. Now we just have to wait."

He turned away, checking his watch, and made some more notes. I, with nothing to do, watched the corpse. It looked as dead as ever. West glanced at me sharply.

"If you want to be useful, Charles, perhaps you could take some of the blood in that flask and put it in a couple of test tubes. No, not like that. Use this pipette. Like this. Then pour the rest down the drain."

I did not greet this suggestion with eagerness, but did as I was told. Returning to the room with the empty flask, I found West in a more affable mood.

"I think we should see something within an hour," he said.

It was now after three in the morning. Dawn comes early in summer, so it would be impossible to return the corpse to its grave under cover of darkness. My heart sank at the prospect of repeating our macabre adventure in reverse order the following night.

West, on the other hand, did not show the least anxiety. "People think of undertakers as only one remove from ghouls," he said, "but in my experience most of them are artisans of a sort, and try sincerely to deal with their clients in a respectful way. Except that with all the new tools and techniques, it's easy to get carried away. My great-uncle Henry had a tendency to do that. He would order all the latest preservative fluids, pumps, injectors, tilting tables and other innovations advertised in the trade magazines. Not to mention things like makeup, cheek-stuffers, eyelid forms, and wigs." He laughed. "I think Henry's aim was to send the corpses on their way looking better than they ever had in life. But it drove his brother – my grandfather,

69

you know – wild. 'We're undertakers, damn it, not taxidermists!' he'd roar. 'And what's more, we have enough junked equipment to fill a warehouse, so don't even think of buying any more!' They were a pair, those two."

I listened to him, but could not ignore the body on the table. It looked as dead as ever, and I wondered how long we would have to wait before we gave up.

"Do people often get buried alive?" I asked.

"Charles, you ghoul! No. Not any more. Not since we've had decent stethoscopes. But at one time it was quite possible for someone who showed no obvious signs of life to be buried. I suppose that's why some customs specified so many days between death and burial. If he's beginning to rot, the reasoning went, he must be dead. And it's normally true."

He was amused at the revulsion that I must have shown on my face. "And of course, there were all sorts of inventions in the last century to forestall the consequences of premature burial – bells or other alarms that could be activated from within a coffin, and devices that would assure a supply of air to the occupant. A fellow called Fearnought – yes, that really was his name, Albert Fearnought, of Indianapolis – patented something especially elaborate. A flag would pop up at the foot of a grave, should its occupant make the slightest movement. I suppose it would be incumbent on passers-by who saw it to salute and run for a spade."

"I wonder if that would happen very often," I said. "That someone would actually wake up in their coffin. What a horrible thought!"

"It happened all the time, if you believe some of the stories I've heard the older fellows tell," said West. "You can imagine – a grave exhumed for some reason years later, and the body inside it with hands worn to tatters, and bloodstains on the inside of the coffin lid. Of course, a lot of those stories are mere legends of the trade, a kind of currency passed around as fellows try to do each other one better. But I was present at one case in which a corpse actually came back to life.

"It happened during that plague I told you about before. Everyone, doctors, embalmers, clergymen and funeral directors, had been run off their feet for weeks, as people became sick, died and became corpses needing burial. It's very likely that proper attention wasn't given in all cases, if you know what I mean. A woman was brought in, a lady from the High and Walnut Street district – where the best of Arkham society lives, of course. The family wanted the body embalmed, and were willing to pay twice the going rate for fast service, so a couple of us were diverted from dealing with the plebian corpses to handle that one.

"I was assisting Harry Logan, our senior embalmer. We had the body on the table and Harry was getting ready to cut the arteries, in order to drain the blood. There he was, scalpel in hand, ready to cut, when I decided to say something that had been bothering me for a while.

"'Isn't she a little too pink, Mr. Logan?' I asked. 'What do you mean, pink?' said he. You see, Harry and the others weren't all that happy to have the big boss's son working with them. Oh, by the time the epidemic was over they knew me to be a reliable worker, a good pair of hands, but they weren't really welcoming, all the same. Embalmers are one of the most secretive occupational groups of all, as you may imagine. A real secret brotherhood." He smiled strangely. "I could tell you things... But I won't.

"Anyway, to get back to the lady on the table. 'I think she looks too pink to be dead,' I said, deciding to get right to the point. 'Perhaps we should check her over.' Normally in such a case a doctor would be summoned, but we knew they were all busy with people who were sick but still unquestionably alive. As a would-be doctor, I offered my services.

"Harry wasn't interested. 'I don't really think that's necessary, Mr. West,' he said. 'She was brought in yesterday, after all.' He accused me of impure motives. 'You just want to get a feel of her,' was how he put it. 'I know you young fellows.' Then he proceeded to cut. Fortunately, he was a little more hesitant than usual, and at the first prick of the blade the woman shot up and shrieked. It was quite amazing – from a lifeless (though pink) corpse to a hysterical female in less than a second. Harry jerked so violently that his scalpel went flying. I found it stuck in the ceiling the next day."

"So what happened then?" I asked, fascinated.

"What do you think? A happy reunion, rather than a funeral. As far as I know, she's still alive today. Fortunately they didn't sue."

As he talked, West had been checking the dead man periodically. Now he bent over the body once more. Suddenly he grew tense and listened intently for a long time. Then he slowly straightened up. His eyes were shining, his face full of exaltation.

"He is not dead, but only sleeps," quoted Herbert West.

For a moment I could only gape. Then I hurried over to West's side. He clamped the earpieces of the stethoscope into my ears. It took me a moment to adjust, then I listened hard. I heard a faint pulsing. It's only my own blood throbbing in my head, I thought, but as I continued to listen I found that the sound was distinctive and outside myself. The dead man was dead no longer.

A few minutes after West had detected a pulse, the man began to gasp and cough. West asked me to help support the patient (for that was what he had become) and prepared some sort of injection. "This should help him snap out of it," he said, as he shot the stuff into the fellow's arm.

The coughing lessened, then stopped. With a groan, the man lay down once more on the table. I could see that a faint trace of colour had returned to his skin, but he still appeared to be not far from death. Discreetly, I tried to peer into his eyes, to see if some spark of intelligence remained, but he had closed them.

West hovered over his patient for the next hour. He spoke little, only to ask me to hand him things or hold things. I noticed that he drew blood from the man's arm and put it carefully into some labelled test tubes. During this time the condition of the revivified man did not change much, to my ignorant eye, except that his colour may have improved a little. He coughed at intervals, but did not speak.

Early light was now visible around the edges of the heavy curtains that covered the room's single window. It reminded me that there was a world outside this room in which I felt I had passed the greater part of my life.

Suddenly, the man on the table let out a shriek. His eyes rolled in their sockets and fixed on West. Before either of us could move, he leaped to his feet and let out a string of incomprehensible words, although West declared later that they sounded to him like, "Jesus, Mary! Help me!" Pushing me aside, he dashed toward the curtained window, smashed the glass, bringing down the curtain in the process, and escaped.

It took us a few moments to get through the back door, which was locked. By the time we were outside we could see nothing of the fleeing figure. College Street was deserted. We split up and searched the area, looking behind fences and hedges, peering down side yards and into porches. Then we circled around both alleys which paralleled College Street and repeated the process with back yards. We searched an ever-widening area, until we had covered several blocks each way, before we gave up. By this time daylight had come and people were beginning to move about.

We walked back to West's rooms, our inappropriate laboratory garments rolled up under our arms, still looking for our escaped patient.

"He must have blundered in among the hospital buildings," West said suddenly. "Or maybe even onto the campus. You may see him in the Library later today."

Back at West's lodgings, we dismantled the laboratory and returned it as far as possible to its appearance of a storage room. West declared that we should resume our normal activities, keeping our eyes open for any sign of the escapee.

"He's bound to be noticed in short order," said West. "Naked men do not abound on the streets of Arkham, even in hot weather such as this."

"But what if he comes back here?" I asked. Now that we had begun to deal with practicalities, my anxiety had returned. "He could bring the police right to your door."

"Yes, in theory," West replied. "But somehow I don't think that will happen. The prognosis for that fellow isn't good." He seemed about to say something more, but thought better of it.

I went home to wash and change my clothes before going to work. I managed to function that day, despite my exhaustion, but avoided protracted conversations with my colleagues, including Alma and Peter Runcible. The latter went out of his way to make sure that I was at my desk. Alma said only, "You look exhausted, Charles! What have you been doing?"

I nearly started to laugh, but stopped myself. "I felt ill yesterday. It was the heat, perhaps. I... didn't sleep very well, but I think I'm feeling better."

She looked skeptical, but did not persist in questioning me.

The previous night's adventure seemed incredible now, especially the resurrection and disappearance of the dead man. Had he been patient, victim or experimental subject? My inability to settle on a suitable epithet was indicative of my ambivalent feelings about the whole episode. "The corpse doesn't care," West had said. But our man had not been squarely in the corpse category, had he? When he began to breathe and cough, when he had broken the window and run out into the street, he had been a corpse no longer, but West's patient. Or had he? My tired mind went around and around these questions, without finding any satisfactory answers.

I did not get much work done that day. As soon as I arrived home I fell into bed and slept, if I can be permitted the simile, like the dead.

I was awakened by a steady knocking on my door. Startled and disoriented, I struggled out of bed and into a bathrobe. I opened the door to find West there, beautifully dressed and cool as the proverbial cucumber. He came in, waving a newspaper.

"Have you seen this, Charles? No, I don't suppose you have," he said, looking me over. "Well, read it now, while I make some coffee. I trust you have some in this bachelor establishment." He was already rummaging in my minimally equipped kitchen, finding the coffee pot, beans and grinder and firing up the gas ring.

I turned my attention to the newspaper, folded open to a page near the front.

Curious Incident Near Hospital

A peculiar event occurred at about seven o'clock this morning near St. Mary's Hospital. Two orderlies reporting for work were attacked by a man who had been lurking in the shrubbery near the service entrance to the main building. Both were beaten about the head and one man was stripped of his outer clothing and shoes while unconscious.

Police were summoned to the scene but no trace of the assailant was found. The weapon was thought to have been a piece of lumber picked up from a nearby building site.

One of the victims stated that the attacker was a medium-sized individual who appeared to be naked except for a burlap sack tied around his waist. He was barefoot, but no trace of footprints was found because the attack occurred in a paved area bordered by lawns.

Both orderlies are expected to recover from their injuries. Investigations continue.

By the time I had read and absorbed this, West was pacing around impatiently in my sitting-room.

"You see?" he said triumphantly. "I told you it would be all right. No connection to us, but I have the experiment fully documented, including tests on those blood samples. There were differences between them indicating that vital processes had definitely begun. But I need more results before I can publish."

"Wait, Herbert," I said. "What do you mean, no connection to us? Hocks is at large, running around loose. He knows what we look like and where you live, or at least where he was when he came back to life. They're still investigating, it says here. You may get a visit from the police. At least two people saw us going into your place with the fellow the other night. And we don't know who might have seen him this morning, or us, for that matter, running around the streets like idiots. And what about his clothes? What did we do with them? Wouldn't whoever put Hocks in his coffin remember what he was wearing at the time?" My mind raced. There seemed to be so many details to this business.

"His clothes are dust and ashes, so you need not worry yourself on that point. And I've had the window repaired. I've been busy today, unlike some people I could mention. But never mind that," he continued, handing me a cup of coffee. "Drink this up and listen. I'm certain that Hocks wants to avoid the police as strenuously as you and I. In fact, I suspect he wants to avoid anyone and everyone. The only reason he attacked those fellows was to get some clothes. He's left the scene, you can be sure of that. I don't think this case will go much further. Now, I propose we make some plans for our next experiment while this one is still fresh in our minds."

"But Herbert," I interjected, "surely we can't just... forget about him? He's our responsibility, isn't he?"

West looked at me coldly. "Why? He chose to run away. I certainly don't feel obligated to run after him. Now, next time – "

"*Next* time?" I said, aghast. "We're not finished with this time, if you ask me. Aside from the moral aspects of the thing, aren't you interested in Hocks as a... a subject? Don't you want to study him? I thought that was the point of all this."

West stopped his pacing and stood with his back to me. "Charles," he said, and his voice had an edge to it I had not heard before, "this is *my* experiment. I thought you understood that. I'm finished with Hocks. Is that clear?"

He turned around and looked at me. I made myself meet his eyes, startled for an instant to see in them a flicker of uncertainty, quickly suppressed. Then he went on, as though the interruption had not occurred.

"For one thing, I think I had better rig up some sort of restraints on the table. We can't have subjects running amuck. I should have done it before, considering the violence I saw in some of the animals. We're lucky he just ran away and didn't attack one of us. I'm sure if we could just get a fresher corpse we'd have even better results..."

He went on and on, speaking ostensibly to me, but in reality using me as an object toward which to direct his thoughts, which at times ran too quickly for me to follow. I watched him and listened with an odd mixture of dismay, irritation and fascination. He was in full flight, and had been all day, that was obvious. I wondered whether he had slept at all.

"...so I think we must try it again as soon as a suitable subject becomes available. Are you game, Charles?"

He spun around and faced me, smiling, those remarkable eyes full of certainty that my answer would be yes.

"Yes," I said, despite my misgivings. "But I have to admit, Herbert, I hope it won't be for at least a week. I don't have as much stamina for these goings-on as you. And I still think we should try to find Hocks."

"Nonsense," he said, laying a hand briefly on my shoulder. "You did well. I couldn't have managed without your help. As for Hocks, I won't bore you with technicalities, but I'm certain we've seen the last of him. And now, what do you say to some dinner? My treat, but it will have to be Da Vinci's again, since it's so late."

In Da Vinci's Grill, we were shown to the same private corner table as before.

Our conversation during the meal was general, as though West had put the topic of his research into a box. Every now and then I caught myself wondering where John Hocks was, and what he might be doing, but I said nothing.

As we walked homeward through the deserted streets, I noticed that West looked behind him several times. I nearly asked him why, but doubted that he would admit that he was still nervous about Hocks.

Before we parted, I surprised myself by asking, "Why do you want to revivify dead bodies, Herbert? I know you've explained it before, but what's your real reason? Is it immortality you're looking for?"

"Yes, ultimately. But if it is ever to become possible, it will be only because someone dared to learn more about death – what it really is. That's the ultimate secret, isn't it? But I think it will take me the rest of my life to fathom it."

It had become my custom, two or three days a week, to accompany Alma to French Hill Street after work before making my way back to my own lodgings on Peabody Avenue.

The day after Hocks's disappearance, she seemed somewhat preoccupied. As we went down the granite steps of the Library and across the main campus quadrangle she said,

"I couldn't help overhearing what Runcible wanted to talk to you about – "

"'Couldn't help overhearing?'" I mocked. By now I was aware of the fact that, due to some quirk of acoustics, there was a spot by a certain section of the shelflist that allowed one to hear most of what was said in the Department Head's office, as long as the door was open. "I wondered why you had so much shelflisting to do in the history section."

"I was diversifying my areas of expertise," said Alma. "But seriously, I thought I heard him say he saw you roaming around the streets at dawn yesterday."

"He did, but so what? He's an interfering busybody."

"I thought you looked like death warmed over yesterday. Wait a minute – it has something to do with Herbert West, doesn't it? That grave at Hangman's Hill – "

"What grave?" I asked. I knew I had spoken too quickly and urgently, but I could not help myself.

Alma looked at me strangely. "Haven't you heard? It was in this morning's *Advertiser*. Someone's been digging in a grave in the potter's field, the one where that fellow who drowned was buried the other day." Her eyes widened. "Oh Charles, don't tell me you're mixed up in some sort of insane body-snatching operation of West's!"

I kept my voice calm. "Alma, you're making some big assumptions here. Yes, I was out early yesterday, or late, if you prefer. Herbert and I made a night of it and I slept on his sofa for a while. I was sick earlier, but by the time he turned up that night I was feeling better, so... And yes, this time we did go to Water Street. Runcible must have seen me when I was on my way home. I don't know anything about any grave. You seem to think that West does nothing but collect corpses. Actually, he has many interests."

"Interests on Water Street," Alma said. "I don't know that I would be too proud of sharing those, if I were you. Really, Charles, I still think you should avoid him."

I did not want to fabricate untruths in order to reassure her, and I could not tell her the truth. Instead, I took her hand and said,

"Don't worry, Alma. When it comes to a choice between Herbert West and Water Street, or you and French Hill Street, you're the winner."

"Oh, you – you're just trying to divert me with sweet talk." But she looked pleased, and did not question me further about West. It was only later that I realized I had lied to her after all.

West was right, in a way. Our involvement with the corpse of John Hocks was never brought home to us by any of the conventional authorities, although we had (I thought) left such a trail of evidence that any competent investigator should have found it necessary to question one or both of us. Our grave-digging tools, for example, stayed in the woods near Hangman's Brook for several days before I remembered them. West retrieved them that night, but anyone could have found them in the meantime.

Fortunately for us, the authorities did not think it necessary to exhume Hocks's coffin to make sure he was still in it. They must have assumed that the disturbed earth on the grave was the doing of pranksters or amateur ghouls who had done no more than scuffle the surface to elicit 'thrills.' This was Arkham, after all. Up to a point the usual laws were enforced, but beyond it was a shadowy region in which wandering corpses, abducted infants and unorthodox ceremonies were ignored by the authorities, as though denial negated their existence. As we would eventually discover, this official blindness had its own hidden rules and boundaries.

Both West and I kept our ears and eyes open for further news of the escapee. Ten days went by and I was beginning to feel a tentative relief when stories appeared in the papers about a furtive 'wild man' who had been sighted around farms in the region, stealing from orchards and gardens. Over the next three months, details of increasing gruesomeness emerged, of animals taken and found to have been drained of blood. As often happens in rural areas, wild tales began to circulate of a monster that fed on blood. The *Arkham Advertiser*, in a typical effort at urban sophistication, treated these rumours with a levity that was nearly offensive. *Wild Man Seen Again* read a headline in the middle of August.

The Wild Man of Arkham has apparently struck once more, this time at Summer's Farm. Mr. Summer said he spotted a shambling form among the farm's outbuildings at dusk on Wednesday, but could not see it clearly enough to furnish a description. Investigations showed that some tools were missing from a shed, specifically a mattock and a spade. The spade was subsequently located at the edge of a potato field, where someone had apparently been digging potatoes. Mr. Summer has also reported apples stolen from trees at the far end of his orchard and the theft of chickens and eggs. Evidently the Wild Man is attempting to obtain a well-rounded diet. Similar thefts have been reported from other farms between Arkham and Bolton this summer. The missing mattock has not been found.

"He was at Summer's Farm," I said to West the next time I saw him. "Do you suppose that's significant? The other sightings were all closer to Bolton."

West seemed inclined to ignore my question. "Who was at Summer's Farm?" he asked, finally. "What are you talking about?"

"John Hocks, of course," I said. "Do you think he's trying to… find his way back or something? Trying to find us?"

"No, I don't," West said, frowning. "And what's more, I wouldn't assume all these supposed thefts from farms were done by Hocks. If he's trying to get back somewhere it would be to Maine, wouldn't you think? That's where he was from. These farmers just want to stir things up; I doubt if they count their chickens every day – in the literal sense, anyway. As for Hocks, I'm certain he's either dead or gone. Most likely both."

"But dead chickens were found. And lambs too. Someone had eaten parts of them. Raw."

"No doubt something did eat them, but why should it be Hocks? Any other time dead livestock has been found, people quite reasonably assumed it was roaming dogs or other animals that were responsible. But it's much more exciting to speculate about a fiendish Wild Man, especially when the papers cater to the notion."

He refused to listen to any more about Hocks and grew angry any time I brought up his name.

♦ 5 ♦

Some years before, I had for a time read anything I could find about the experiences of persons who had nearly died but had subsequently been resuscitated or had spontaneously recovered. Their reports of what they experienced while 'dead' demonstrated a surprising degree of similarity: a feeling of floating toward a distant light, of great peace and exaltation. Some had seen their own bodies lying far beneath them. Most had been unhappy to return to life, feeling deprived of the tremendous events of which they had experienced only the beginning.

I had developed this interest after the deaths of my parents, of course, and after I had abandoned any efforts to communicate with them through a medium. I was drawn to the idea that a dying person may experience something wonderful, rather than the terror of imminent extinction.

After West's initial revivification attempt, I remembered these accounts of the near-death experience, and wondered what John Hocks might have reported to us had there been an opportunity to question him. With all the excitement, I had not considered doing this until after Hocks had vanished. I suppose it was also because I had not really believed that West's treatment would be successful. After all, my participation in the business had been prompted not by scientific motives but by personal ones – namely, a fascination with the investigator, rather than with the subject being investigated.

But now I had an opportunity to pursue this area of interest, as well as assisting West with his. I drew up a list of questions to ask: What did you see? How did you feel? Were you afraid? Could you hear sounds? Were there any others in that place? And so on. I became quite enthusiastic and finally discussed the matter with West.

"I have no objections, Charles. If you want to interview the subjects, feel free, as long as you are prepared to quit immediately should it become necessary. In fact, it would be useful for me to observe their responses to your questions – oh, not what they say, but how well they understand and articulate. As an indication of cognitive function, you know."

"Why not what they say? It might be interesting."

"To a romantic like you, because these are romantically inspired questions. I can give you the real answer now: the glorious visions result from brain cells starved of oxygen. It's like the fall colours of the leaves, which are also products of breakdown. That's why you find all those similarities among the different accounts – the visions are the results of the same chemical processes."

"Well, but has it ever occurred to you that these brain processes might be the means by which the consciousness finds the peace of death? After all, it's not the body we're talking about here. It's the inner self, the spirit, that experiences these ecstasies. So instead of saying that the ecstasy results from the death of brain cells, one could say that the soul departs from the body in ecstasy as the brain cells die." I suspected I was on shaky ground, but persisted in my argument nonetheless.

"I think that's what the logicians would call an argument *a posteriori*, Charles. And anyway, you can talk all you like about the soul and what might be happening to it, but until you can scientifically demonstrate the existence of a soul there is no point in speculating about when it leaves the body or where it goes. I am not concerned about anyone's soul."

I was disappointed by West's mechanistic outlook, and resolved to prove a thing or two to him, just as he was determined to prove to the Miskatonic professors that the ideas they had mocked had a basis in fact.

By the time the fall semester began, West was fully reinstated at the Medical School and started his internship at St. Mary's Hospital. On the few occasions we met he warned me that he had every intention of carrying out another revivification experiment as soon as the opportunity arose.

"Now that I have full laboratory access and am working in the hospital too, it will be much easier, although still risky," he said. "At least the matter of transport will be simpler. No more grave robbing and getting overly friendly with corpses on the street, Charles."

I had to admit that this was a relief. There had been no more reports of the supposed 'wild man,' and when I thought of John Hocks at all, I assumed he had left the district.

Early in October Miskatonic threw open its doors to alumni, supporters and the interested public for its quadrennial Open House. This event was intended to promote the institution as a worthwhile cause for philanthropists, and to attract promising students and faculty.

As a junior member of the Library staff I took my turn at presiding over an exhibit of informative materials and answering questions from passers-by. I led tour groups around the building, giving a set speech about collections and services.

The tour did not include the vault in the Administration Office. I was asked several times about the *Necronomicon* and the other rare volumes. The idly curious had to be satisfied when I told them that these books were kept in a secure place due to their rarity, and that a special application was required to see them. One immensely aged individual, however, was so insistent, and in such a whispery voice, difficult to comprehend, that in the end I approached Dr. Armitage to obtain special permission for a viewing. To my surprise, he recognized the old fellow, and introduced him to me as Dr. Augustus Quarrington, Professor emeritus of philosophy. After a moment, I recognized the name. He had written one of West's letters in support of his application to see the ancient book. And he had been one of West's professors, too.

I escorted Quarrington, who walked very fast for a man of his age, to the consultation room. It was my first visit to the *Necronomicon* since that disconcerting one in July. It was also my last, since John Bowen returned to Miskatonic shortly after this and resumed responsibility for the books in the vault.

I picked up the black-bound volume with its silver clasps and placed it in front of the old man. This time it weighed no more than it should have, and there were no strange odours. Quarrington did not open it immediately, but put both hands on it and ran them over the leather, in a way that reminded me of a blind person trying to determine the identity of an object. Then he opened the book and leafed through it, seemingly at random. At intervals he bent so closely to the page he was looking at that he seemed about to kiss it. More than once, he muttered words incomprehensible to me, words which did not sound like any language with which I was acquainted.

At length he closed the book and laid his hands on the cover again. Then he looked up at me. To my surprise, he was grinning.

"You've looked in it. Oh yes, my boy, I can tell. I can tell that someone has looked. Not just you, but another, and he's taken something away, too. It's out in the world again, doing the Work. I can tell."

I tried to reassure him that no one had taken anything from the book; that would not be allowed. But old Quarrington merely chuckled to himself and repeated, "It's out there, working." He said nothing more, except just as we were leaving the Administration Office he looked at me hard with eyes of a startling blue and said, "Be careful, young fellow, and tell your friend the same. Him especially. He's not as tough as I once thought. You're the tough one."

On the final evening of the Open House, there was a reception in the Library's main hall, hosted by Dr. Armitage. All members of the professional staff were expected to put in an appearance, circulate among the guests and "represent the Library in a favourable way."

During a lull, I joined Alma near the refreshment tables. Like naughty children, we exchanged acerbic comments about the people with whom we had been chatting so earnestly a short time before.

Over Alma's shoulder I could see a fairly large group arriving. "I think we must return to our labours," I said.

"Bear up, Charles, only an hour more," she replied, hurrying off toward a European-looking man who was greeting her as "My dear Miss Halsey."

I might have paid more attention to this had I not heard my own name. It was West, accompanied by several men whom I had never seen before. The foremost of them was a sixtyish individual who gave an impression of largeness, although it was a matter of breadth rather than height. He looked at me with rather prominent eyes, which, along with his wide, thin-lipped mouth, made me think of a toad.

"This must be young Mr. Milburn," he said, advancing upon me.

"Yes, Father," said West. "This is Charles Milburn. Charles, I would like you to meet my father, Hiram West."

I murmured the appropriate words, allowing my hand to be crushed in the large bony one of West senior. In his father's presence Herbert seemed curiously quelled, his mercurial quality unaccountably absent. Though as elegantly dressed as ever, beside his father he appeared younger and thinner than I remembered him. If I had not known otherwise I would have found it hard to believe that this pale, delicate young man had exhumed a corpse and returned it to life.

Hiram West, on the other hand, had an inexorable quality that assigned a place to everyone within conversational range and absorbed them into his entourage, willy-nilly. I could feel myself being swept along to an unknown destination, like a leaf which has landed in a swiftly flowing stream.

"It's good to know that Herbert is making some friends and getting out a bit," said West senior. "A young fellow like him shouldn't shut himself up with a bunch of test tubes and chemicals all the time. I'm always telling him, 'Herbert, you have to circulate!' A doctor is just another kind of businessman, you know, and in business it's who you know, not what you know, that counts. Now you're a librarian, I hear..."

Without giving me time to reply he kept talking, until I found myself trying to explain to him what a cataloguer does, just as I had to his youngest son, months earlier. But this time I knew it was a lost cause. Hiram West cheerfully voiced opinions to the effect that the catalogue was a great thing, the Library was great, and Miskatonic U. was a great place. From time to time he would ask one of the other men in the group for affirmation, which would be promptly expressed by the individual addressed.

These men were of a type unknown to me. They were not working men, nor academics, nor businessmen in any sense of the word that I recognized. Perhaps they were lawyers, or perhaps only what Herbert had cryptically referred to as 'cronies' the first time we had gone to Da Vinci's. West senior obviously preferred to travel with a shoal of these individuals in his wake, although their function was not immediately apparent to me. Apart from saying "Yes, Mr. West," when required to, they were silent.

I was intrigued, and so had few objections when I was caught up in the West entourage as Hiram, expressing thanks and good will to Dr. Armitage, swept us all out of the Library. I managed to get close to Herbert, who looked at me apologetically.

"Sorry, Charles," he said. "This wasn't my idea. The Pater's in one of his expansive moods. He's decided to become a patron of higher learning, and has been getting acquainted with Miskatonic all week. Sometimes I think he doesn't realize it's not for sale. When I heard he was coming to the Library reception I thought I had better come along. He's rather overwhelming when he's onto something new."

I was spared a reply by West senior issuing orders.

"All right, everyone! Supper time! They'll be expecting us at Da Vinci's. They'd better." He laughed loudly. "Charles, you'll join us, of course. Come along."

He led us to a large black car. A chauffeur stood by holding the door for him. I slid into the other side with Herbert. The entourage climbed into two other cars parked nearby. One preceded us and the other followed as we set out.

While Herbert had been given a certain deference and a secluded corner table at Da Vinci's, Hiram got the red carpet treatment, almost literally. The head waiter and some of his subordinates were lined up at the door as we filed in. He showed us to a group of tables, at which the cronies disposed themselves in some predetermined pattern. Hiram took a place at the centre, commanding Herbert to sit at his left, me at his right. I was the guest of honour, apparently, which made me nervous.

Drinks appeared as though by magic, followed by what could be described only as a feast, liberally accompanied by more drinks. My host exhorted me to partake freely.

My recent experience with elaborate dinners was limited, but those I had been invited to had generally included ladies. This one was unique in being an all-male event, which, to me, seemed unfinished, even crude. No one became disorderly, but it lacked grace.

Hiram West set the conversational topics and tone. While I knew that the matters talked about could be broadly described as 'business,' it was surprisingly difficult to determine just what the business was. Names and numbers were frequently mentioned, along with cryptic phrases.

Every now and then Hiram remembered my existence and made efforts to include me in the conversation. For the most part, these efforts were short lived and unsuccessful. Once, however, he asked me about my father.

"Milburn... That reminds me of something," he said, looking at me closely. "Was your dad George Milburn?" On my replying that yes, he had been, Hiram said, "I knew your dad, boy, not well, but enough to say I'm sorry about what happened to him. A fellow can take only so much trouble at once, I guess."

Soon after this, I lost the conversational thread once more. West senior and the cronies were engaged in an animated discussion about the fortunes of someone called Muggsy, or possibly Buggsy. I disengaged from the words, and fell to observing the men as they talked, gestured, lit cigars, drank. I could not see much of Herbert, seated as he was on the other side of his father, but I did not think he was taking part in the conversation either. In fact, at one point I was certain he was writing something or doing calculations in a notebook.

I began to wonder what it must have been like for him, growing up in his father's house. It may have been rather like this dinner, womanless, rough-edged, with conversations made up of short, staccato sentences, like bursts of gunfire. And in the midst of the hurly-burly was the slight blond boy, going about his business with cool self-possession – reading the books in his father's library, following a path that led to science, to medicine, finally to the *Necronomicon* and grave-robbing and a corpse stirring to life in a makeshift laboratory. I was growing tired, and already more than a little tipsy. I wondered whether it was pity I felt, or admiration.

My musings came to an end when I became aware that Hiram West was once more addressing me, "...should be a good one! What do you say, Charles?"

"I'm sorry, Mr. West, I wasn't paying attention."

"Falling asleep, eh?" said Hiram. "You young fellows just don't have any stamina! When I was your age I would have just been getting going. What I was asking you is if you're interested in some sport tomorrow night."

"Sport?" I asked. What could he mean? A football game, or hunting, or something else? Impatiently, he explained,

"Boxing! The fights! We're bringing in some imported talent, all the way from New York City. It's a chance for you college boys to see some real life for a change."

I was about to make some excuse. Boxing, wrestling and all pugilistic sports had absolutely no interest for me. Just then, however, I saw Herbert looking at me from behind his father's shoulder. Gone was the dim, bored look he had worn most of the evening. His face was animated, his eyes shining. Silently, his lips formed the words, "Say yes."

"Well, Mr. West," I said. "I've never seen a boxing match. It might be interesting. Thank you for inviting me."

"'Might be interesting!'" roared Hiram, clapping me on the back. "Oh, it'll be interesting, all right! Now, Herbert, what about you? I know you always say you don't like the fights, but if Charlie here is going, how about it?" He turned to his son, who, I noticed, had quickly readjusted the expression on his face.

"All right, Father," he said. "Just this once I'll come, if only to make sure you don't corrupt Charles. I don't think he knows what he's in for."

"Good!" said Hiram. "Let's meet at the Mermaid, on Water Street. We'll go from there."

Soon after this, Hiram called for the bill and his chauffeur, signalling that the evening was over. Herbert refused a ride for both of us, saying, "Charles and I will walk. It's only a short way, and we young fellows need the exercise, to build up our stamina."

When we were walking through the misty autumn night, West said, "Well, that's the Pater. What do you think of him?"

"He seems very... convivial," I said. "I suppose it's being in business. All those deals to work out..."

"Convivial, nothing! He's an old blowhard. All right, he does have a talent for deals, as you call them, but his veneer certainly is a coarse one. I don't mind it, really; I'm used to it. But this has all worked out splendidly. I can feel it."

He leaped up suddenly, laughing, caught at a branch overhead and broke off a twig. Landing, he ran ahead a few steps, executed a kind of pirouette and waited for me to catch up. Then he walked backwards for a while, facing me.

"You mean this boxing match?" I was feeling slow and stupid once more.

"Yes, of course!" said West. "Not that I give a damn for boxing. A complete waste of time, I figure. But it's a violent sport, and sometimes people get badly hurt. Quite often, in fact. And sometimes they die."

I was beginning to see what he was getting at. "You mean – a fresh corpse?"

"Exactly! As fresh as can be, barring I create one by killing someone – which would be absurd, don't you think?" He was half-laughing, half-serious. This was the Herbert West I was used to, all right.

"But if someone gets hurt at one of these fights, don't they just get taken to the hospital?"

"Not at all! The fights are illegal, you see. The city fathers of both Arkham and Bolton have decided to ban the practice of men getting together to bash at each other with bare fists, while other men watch them and lay bets on who gets beaten to a pulp first. It promotes decadence and disorder, they say, and maybe they're right. In any case, the fights haven't stopped, just gone underground – into someone's old barn or similar place."

"But your father talked as though he'd had something to do with organizing this one."

"Oh, I think that's quite likely," said West. "Father's moral code is a very practical one. If he can get away with a profit, it's the right thing to do. He thinks of the law as a kind of obstacle course which only proves what a clever guy he is in the end."

It occurred to me that in the way they regarded rules and authorities, at least, father and son were not so very different.

"So there's a chance we'll be doing another experiment tomorrow night?" I asked.

"There's a chance. I would advise that you be prepared for it."

Alma belonged to a small literary circle, comprised of younger faculty members and senior students at Miskatonic, mostly women. She had at one time suggested that I might like to join, so as to even up the gender imbalance a little. I had not been eager, being a determined non-joiner, but had not refused outright. As we descended the front steps of the Library, I remembered, too late, that this evening it was Alma's turn to host a meeting of the circle, and that I had half-promised to attend.

"Just come and meet them," she had cajoled me some weeks before. "You'll find them a congenial group, I think. Serious, but not too highbrow."

I had not wanted to refuse. At the very least, it would mean an evening in Alma's company, which I found most congenial. I could let the literary discussion wash over me while I watched her bustle about, handing out tea cups and pithy comments. Now, of course, I had to tell her I could not come.

"You didn't say anything about a prior commitment when I asked you, at least two weeks ago."

"That's because it isn't prior. It's just that I met West and his father at our reception last night, and West senior bullied me into coming along to some sort of dinner tonight. He's very hard

to resist." I hoped that she would not ask me what I had done the previous night.

"Yes, I saw you being hustled along by him and his henchmen," she said. "Well, Charles, you know what I think of the Wests. You don't really know what you're getting into."

A part of me agreed entirely with this sentiment. But another part was full of a nervous excitement. Also, I was grateful that Alma seemed relatively unconcerned about my absence from her literary evening. I felt a sudden rush of confused tenderness toward her.

"Look, Alma," I said, placing a hand briefly on her forearm. "I feel like a cad for missing your meeting. I know you wanted me there, and I appreciate that."

She smiled, a little sadly, I thought. "It's all right, Charles. Maybe next time."

West and I had agreed to meet at his rooms early that evening, then to join the rest of the party at the Water Street tavern. On the way, he told me of the preparations he had made earlier that day, should we be in a position to do an experiment later that night.

"This time our venue will be one of the Medical School's laboratories. I have free access now, as you know. It'll be easier to deliver the goods there undetected than to my rooms. I think this time we shall be able to count on motor transport. Acme Corpse Specialists will be at our service," he said, smiling. "You see, in the event that one of the participants is killed, the organizers are quite efficient in disposing of the corpse. There is always a vehicle of some sort available.

"There is one problem, however. Obviously, I couldn't very well rig up restraints in the lab without someone noticing and reporting it to Halsey. So we'll have to do without. That's a little worrying, because men of the type we may be dealing with are given to violence, and would be more likely than most to react violently upon revivification. But it's a risk we have to take."

West certainly did not look anxious. He was as buoyant as I had ever seen him. Something of this mood communicated itself to me, and I felt an extra spring in my step and a quickening of the heart. As we bent our steps toward Water Street, we must have truly looked like what we were, and yet were not – two young men heading out for a night on the town, except that West carried a black bag of the type favoured by physicians on house calls. "Tools of the trade," was his terse reply to my question about it.

I had never been to Water Street before, although I had heard quite a lot about it, much of it colourful, little of it good. After crossing the Miskatonic River we entered a different world. On one side of the street were the piers, docks and warehouses which were a product of Arkham's seagoing mercantile history. On the far side were the railroad tracks. At the west end of Water Street was a cluster of taverns, bars and cheap eateries, most of which were already doing a roaring business on this Saturday evening. We could hear the tinkle of a piano being played in one establishment, hearty singing in another.

The Mermaid was one of the oldest taverns, harking back to Arkham's earliest times. Part of it was built right over the river, on pilings. I had heard rumours that more than a few bodies had been given a quick exit by way of a trap-door in the floor.

As we entered the dimly-lit interior, which smelled of tobacco smoke, beer, ancient wood and tar, we found that Hiram West had preceded us. He was accompanied by only two men tonight, silent muscular individuals introduced as Jerry and Mike. It appeared that the three of them had already partaken of refreshment. Herbert and I declined, so when the others had emptied their glasses we were on our way.

Hiram led the way to a vehicle parked behind a nearby outbuilding. It was not the luxurious automobile we had used the previous night, but an odd-looking, boxy contraption, the rear of which seemed disproportionately tall.

"Ah, you brought the Clodhopper," said Herbert, laughing. "Think it might come in handy?"

"Well, you never know," replied his father. "The Clodhopper can handle anything we might have to deal with, and it doesn't have 'I'm a hearse' written all over it."

"This is a vehicle used for economy-priced rural funerals," explained Herbert. "Father had it made up specially some years ago. He needed something that could travel faster than horses and not get bogged down in the country roads." He motioned me to climb into the rear seat. Hiram and Mike got in the front. Jerry drove.

The Clodhopper was surprisingly comfortable, despite its gloomy associations and bizarre appearance. "Extra springs," Herbert explained. The seat he and I occupied was immediately in front of a space large enough to accommodate two old-fashioned coffins, or a single casket of the modern type.

We drove a long way through the night. I was never certain just where we went, but I think our direction was roughly north and west. Herbert and I did not speak; Hiram and the others carried on an intermittent conversation in low voices. Once or twice I glanced at my companion. He sat upright, staring straight ahead, his clear profile as though carved in silver. I could not begin to guess what he was thinking about.

After a longish interval, at least half an hour, and probably closer to forty-five minutes, we turned off on a narrow, bumpy road. Five minutes later the vehicle slowed and stopped. On getting out I could see the characteristic shape of a barn silhouetted against the starlit sky. Light leaked out through the open doors. A dozen or more vehicles of various types were parked around the open space before it. I could hear a murmur of many voices.

A couple of formidable looking men flanked the door. They appeared to recognize Hiram and his two companions, and ignored Herbert and me as we followed in their wake.

Inside, a surprisingly large and motley crowd was gathered. Most of the men were working-class types, both rural and urban, disposed in groups and knots on some crudely built bleachers which lined three sides of the building. Although the barn's original tenants had been absent for a long time, there was a faint aroma of hay and manure, overlaid with tobacco smoke, beer and unwashed bodies. I could hear English spoken with a number of different accents, as well as Italian and what I assumed was Polish.

Hiram West led us toward some bleachers to the left of the roped-off area that occupied the middle of the barn. Here was a group of rather more prosperous looking men. Most were of the same type as Hiram and his cronies, dressed in good suits, but with neckties a little wider and cigars a little fatter than good taste dictated. There were also some who looked as though they might be members of Arkham's or Bolton's professional and business class. Farther back in the shadows I thought I saw a couple of professors from Miskatonic, behind a boisterous cluster of students.

Hiram engaged in loud conversation with some of the others. Two of the younger men in his group looked toward Herbert and me and nodded in apparent greeting. He acknowledged this, but made no move to go over to them. To my inquiring glance he said only, "My brothers." I looked curiously at the pair. Now that I knew of their relationship, I could see a family resemblance to Hiram. The three projected an aura of self-confidence and control, tinged slightly with menace. I looked away before I could seem to be staring.

Herbert and I found seats in the third row from the front, near an aisle. I looked about me with interest. Herbert remained silent, still wearing the same closed, concentrated look I had observed on the drive from Arkham.

Finally there was a general move to find seats. By now the barn was full. Latecomers stood in a crowd just inside the doors, which had been pulled shut. Several beer barrels had been broached, and the contents were being distributed to customers by panting boys.

Suddenly a fellow in shirt sleeves, with a handlebar moustache, shouted, "All right, everyone, we're ready to start! Last chance to place your bets!"

There was a flurry of last minute betting. Then, from the narrow aisle which divided the middle range of bleachers, the first pair of contestants emerged.

They were a couple of young working men, stripped down for the occasion to short pants. They were introduced as Stan Wozniak and Tony Abruzzo, to the roars of their compatriots and supporters in the crowd. With no further preliminaries the match began.

I was too naïve to recognize the vast difference between a properly conducted boxing match and this illegal, bare-knuckled fight. But it did not take long before I began to suspect that a wide gulf lay between the Marquis of Queensberry's rules (of which I had heard a vague rumour) and the spectacle which unfolded before me.

After some preliminary circling and tentative jabs, the first blow was landed, I think by Abruzzo. I was surprised at the solid, meaty sound it made, and even more surprised by the visceral response in myself. Wozniak responded with a well-aimed punch of his own, and soon the combatants were exchanging volleys of blows. When blood began to flow the yells from the crowd grew louder, acquiring a certain savagery. The atmosphere thickened and grew faintly red before my eyes. Then the shouting seemed to recede and become fainter, until I could hear only the grunts and gasps of the combatants and the thunk of flesh-encased bone on bone. I realized I was shouting too, I know not what.

A light touch on my arm brought me to my senses. Of all the men in the place, only Herbert West retained a calm demeanour. Looking at his pale, composed features, I felt a rush of shame.

In the ring, a heavy blow to the side of the head by Wozniak had felled the Italian, Abruzzo. He lay on the floor, his head in a widening pool of blood. Wozniak was declared the victor, and raised his fists in a gesture that struck me as gratuitous. I could hear a clinking of coins as bets were paid up. Two men arrived with a stretcher and hauled away the unconscious Abruzzo. Fresh sawdust was spread over the bloody spot on the floor. Suddenly, I realized that West was no longer beside me. Looking around, I caught a glimpse of him vanishing down the aisle in the wake of the stretcher. I wanted to follow, but the next fight (between Johnny "Boomer" Smith and Rocky McHenry) was about to begin, and the narrow passageway was full of tough-looking men I did not want to try to displace.

Distracted by thoughts of what West might be doing, I paid little attention to the bout. Instead, I had a sudden vivid mental image of Alma's sitting room, afloat on its sea of golden leaves. Alma, wearing a dress of sherry-coloured velvet, was leaning earnestly toward someone I could not see. Her lips moved, but I could not hear what she was saying. I thought it might have been, "Only now..."

West, bag in hand, emerged from the passageway. He returned to his seat, saying, "Abruzzo will be all right. It looked worse than it was. He's regained consciousness. I sponged him off and stitched him up. Insane business, isn't it?"

His manner was so disconcertingly cheerful in the raw atmosphere of the place that I could only stare at him. In the ring the second bout was coming to an end, "Boomer" Smith having conceded to his opponent before too much damage had been inflicted on his person.

Two or three more of these amateur engagements between local pugilists took place. None was as spectacularly violent as the first had been, and none affected me in that unsettling way. West began to look bored.

An intermission followed, the main purpose of which seemed to be to allow more time for bets to be placed and more beer to be sold. I bought some, since the heat of the place had made me thirsty. West declined. From the excitement around us I suspected the *pièce de résistance* was about to take place.

I was right. The next bout featured the 'imported talent' Hiram West had mentioned the previous night. One was Buck Robinson, the "Harlem Smoke," a large black man, and the other was "Kid" O'Brien, a hulking blond fellow with a nose so altered from its original shape by repeated abuse that it had assumed a most un-Hibernian hook.

I could see immediately that these two were professionals, if such a word can be used to describe individuals whose business was bare-fisted fighting. Their demeanour lacked the feverishness displayed by the amateurs. There was no rush to land blows helter-skelter.

From the first, I suspected that Robinson was the better of the two. He was faster, his footwork better, his feints more deceiving. O'Brien seemed always to be a shade late, and was soon in a defensive position. Robinson began to make contact. Again I heard that unmistakable and somewhat disgusting meaty sound of flesh striking flesh, like something being beaten with a padded club.

Like the first, this became a bloody fight. Long after a regulated bout would have been stopped, this one went on and on, Robinson delivering blows all around O'Brien's head. Again, I felt that involuntary savage response within myself, but it passed away quickly when O'Brien dropped to the blood-spattered sawdust and lay still.

This time, West did not wait until the man had been carried away, but leaped into the ring and bent over O'Brien. Despite a growing sickness inside me, I made myself push my way to the ropes. West was running his hands rapidly over the fighter's head and chest, raising an eyelid to peer at the pupil, checking for respiration and pulse. To my astonishment, I heard him speak to one of the hangers-on in what sounded like Italian. He beckoned me over, saying, "Stay close by, Charles. We'll be leaving soon."

O'Brien was loaded onto the stretcher and carried out of the ring. "That one's a goner," someone said, and several times I heard the word *morto*. The one close look I had had at O'Brien's face, pulped under the blood that covered most of it, had sickened me. I followed behind the stretcher as best I could, afraid of being left behind in this alien environment of blood and sawdust.

We left the barn by way of a rear door. The Wests' hearse was parked outside. Jerry and Mike slid O'Brien's lifeless form into the vehicle and closed the doors. Mike climbed into the driver's seat, Jerry beside him, and I resumed my place in the back. West was the last to get in. A man who had been talking to him thrust his head into the door, speaking in rapid Italian, incomprehensible to me except for *Dottore West*. West said something to him and laughed. He pulled the door shut and we were off.

"Where's your father?" I asked.

"Some of his associates are here. He'll go back with them, or with my brothers."

The return trip to Arkham was not nearly so long as the drive out had been. This puzzled me until I realized that on the outward way we must have followed a circuitous route to prevent us from finding the place again.

Once we were in Arkham, the driver turned off the headlights. Hiram West's economy hearse ghosted along the streets to the Miskatonic campus. Following West's directions, we came to a stop by a building I recognized as part of the Medical School. West jumped out of the vehicle and busied himself with unlocking a nearby door. I heard him giving instructions to Jerry and Mike. Soon they had O'Brien's corpse loaded onto a kind of trolley that West must have had ready inside the door.

"Wait at the place I told you about, at Hangman's Hill," West said to the two men. "If I need you again tonight, I'll send word."

We went inside and West closed the door behind us. I heard the click of the mechanism and knew it had locked itself. As quietly as we could, we wheeled the gurney down a long corridor. West unlocked another door, marked Pathology Laboratory, and we entered.

West locked the door behind us and made sure the window blinds were closed before he turned on the lights. The room contained several laboratory benches equipped with microscopes and other apparatus. Shelves held glassware, and at one end of the room were ranks of cabinets. The most prominent features, however, were three large slab-like tables, faced with porcelain, whose surfaces were slightly depressed below a rim. They resembled very shallow sinks, complete with water taps and drains.

There was a plaque on the wall with words in Latin. *Hic est locus ubi mors gaudet succurso vitae* (This is the place where death rejoices to come to the aid of life). "What's that about?" I asked West.

"Oh, all pathology labs and autopsy rooms have those," he replied. "I suppose it's meant to reassure those who must deal with corpses that there is a good reason for it. And in our case it's entirely appropriate, isn't it?

"Let's put him on this table," he continued. "You know the routine by now. Get his clothes off while I set up the equipment. Here, you'll need this." He tossed me a white coat. "Ready, Charles?"

We hoisted O'Brien onto the table. He was quite heavy; I knew I never would have been able to carry him as we had done

Hocks, but his clothing, being minimal, was far easier to remove than Hocks's had been. I could not help but note the extent of the man's injuries. His nose was almost certainly broken again. There were numerous gashes on his cheeks and forehead, and his lips were completely lacerated. The flesh of his face was not blackened and swollen as I would have expected, possibly because death had occurred before this process could take place. His knuckles were split and a couple of his fingers stuck out at unnatural angles.

"Broken, of course," said West, coming over with his apparatus and noticing my scrutiny of these injuries. "Bare-knuckle fighting is a brutal sport. That's why it's illegal. But in this case we're the beneficiaries. Here, hang onto these tubes while I clamp this thing on. Notice how I've adapted it to this table. A little extracurricular project I've been engaged on these past few weeks."

West polished his spectacles and began a detailed examination of the corpse, to make sure that no vital signs were present, he explained. He also collected blood samples, as he had with Hocks. While he was doing this, I asked if I could clean the blood from O'Brien's face.

"Go ahead, if you like. Doesn't bother me," said West, with a shrug.

I fetched a basin of water and a cloth and wiped off most of the blood. Why did I do this, I wonder? For our former subject, Hocks, I had felt only repugnance. Certainly, I had no reason to regard this prizefighter with any sort of affection beyond the recognition of our common humanity. Perhaps it was because I had watched him receive the blows that had killed him, and had, despite myself, derived a certain dark pleasure from that spectacle. Perhaps it was simply that he, unlike Hocks, had not lain in the earth. Or perhaps it was because I considered him to be my experimental subject, as well as West's. I fully intended to ask him my list of questions, should circumstances allow it. I had given this some thought on the dark roads to Arkham.

West straightened up from the notes he had been making and went to an inconspicuous cabinet in a corner. Finding yet another key in a large bunch he took from his pocket, he unlocked the cabinet and removed a flask of the violet-coloured liquid, and a syringe containing a colourless one. "Charles, note carefully where I put this," he said, placing the syringe on the bench nearest the table where O'Brien lay. "If he should become uncontrollable, one of us will have to inject this. Right in the neck," he said, indicating the spot. "No hesitation. All right, let's get on with it." Looking at my watch, I was surprised to see that it was only a little after midnight.

West picked up a scalpel and began the process of locating the blood vessels. This time I watched with interest rather than repugnance.

I stood by the pressure meter as fluid began to trickle into the corpse, and blood to trickle out. The pressure had not approached 200 before the fluid reservoir was nearly empty. West turned off the tap before air could enter the vein.

"Well, here we are again," he said, smiling at me over the corpse. "Now we wait." His words were spoken lightly, but I thought he looked a little anxious.

While we waited, we disassembled the equipment, cleaned it and locked it away in the cabinet from which he had taken the fluid. "Only I have a key to this one," said West. "One of the first things I did here was change this lock."

For the next half hour we carried on an intermittent conversation while West occasionally checked the corpse. His anxiety seemed to increase as the minutes went by, and soon communicated itself to me. To divert him, I asked, "Where did you learn to speak Italian, Herbert? That was quite a surprise to me."

"Oh, it's just Boston street Italian. I learned it from the kids in the neighbourhood. No quoting Dante for me, I'm afraid. But it comes in handy sometimes." He said no more, and I wondered again about his past. I found it hard to reconcile myself to the notion that Italian immigrants abounded in Back Bay, or that the Wests had ever lived in the North End. Clearly, something in his answer did not quite add up, but his manner discouraged me from questioning him further.

Twice while we waited he directed me to turn off the lights, unlock the door of the lab and listen in the corridor, to make sure no one was about. On the second of these occasions, I had just relocked the door when I was startled beyond words by a deep groan.

"Charles, the lights!" cried West. "He's alive!"

My hand was shaking, but I managed to switch on the lights. Hurrying to the table, I could see that a change was taking place in O'Brien. Colour was flowing into his face, and a strange rapid vibration of the limbs began, growing stronger as I watched.

Muttering something about, "...spasms, must be stopped," West found another syringe in a clutter of instruments, and quickly filled it from a bottle. He injected this fluid into the man's arm, then listened intently to the heart. The trembling lessened, then stopped. Shortly afterward, O'Brien's eyes, which had been moving rapidly from side to side beneath the closed lids, opened briefly, blinked, then closed again.

West ministered to the revivified man for the next half hour. For brief periods he was almost alert, then seemed to lose consciousness again. Occasionally a frown creased his forehead, and he groaned.

"Is he in pain, do you think?" I asked.

"I imagine he is," West replied, "but I don't want to risk giving him anything that might destabilize him."

"Can I try to speak to him?"

"I don't think you'll have much luck. But we agreed that would be part of the experiment, so go ahead. Only one question, though. Pick your favourite."

I had thought about this earlier. If I had only one question to ask a man who had returned from death, what would it be? "Where have you been?" seemed like the obvious one, but what if he answered, "A barn near Arkham"? West would find this amusing, but I would be disappointed. In the end I had decided on "Tell me what you remember." This was open enough that it might elicit either trivia or great revelations. And once the subject had begun to speak, perhaps I could nudge his memories toward my area of interest.

I bent over Kid O'Brien, who was breathing heavily through his mouth. I could smell a dark foulness that I instantly thought of as the smell of death. If this was no longer a dead man, it was by only the smallest degree.

"Kid O'Brien," I said. I wished I knew his real name. 'Kid' seemed unbearably flip in the circumstances, and 'Mr. O'Brien' absurdly formal. "Kid O'Brien, can you hear me?"

He groaned again. Then, in a faint, cracked voice he said, "Thirsty." Of course he would be thirsty! I felt ashamed at not having thought of this before.

"Herbert, he wants water," I said, looking around for him.

West came over with a beaker. It did not appear that O'Brien could sit up to drink, so he trickled small amounts between the mangled lips with a pipette. After a while O'Brien raised a hand and said,

"Okay. Where am I?"

"In a hospital," West said. "Can you remember the fight?"

I was a little resentful at the way he had taken over the questioning, but listened with interest for O'Brien's reply.

"Fight?" He sounded foggy. Desperate lest he lose consciousness again, I pressed forward.

"Do you remember anything at all? Tell me what you remember."

"Robinson... 'Harlem Smoke,' hah!" He made a retching sound. "Goddamn bastard cheats... Went away... got away from Robinson. Went through that door..." He sighed, and air bubbled through his broken nose.

"What door, Kid?" I asked, excited. This sounded interesting. I looked up and met West's eyes, amused and cynical. That annoyed me, and I pressed on. "Did you go through a door after Robinson knocked you out?"

"*I went through!*" suddenly roared O'Brien, sitting up. "It was great there! Peaceful. Warm. And you bastards made me come back!" He was almost sobbing now, but reached out with a muscular arm and grabbed West around the neck. "Got you!" he grunted. Twisting his body, he turned onto his side and held West in a kind of headlock. He bore down, pressing West's neck against the edge of the table.

West clawed at the arm that held him, but with absolutely no effect. He was agile and strong for a man of his size, but no match for the prizefighter, even in the latter's weakened state. His spectacles fell off and landed on the floor. His face grew flushed and his eyes bulged.

Fighting off the paralysis that threatened to render me useless, I reached over to the laboratory bench and snatched up the deadly syringe. I turned back to the table and approached O'Brien from behind. He was too intent on strangling my friend to take any notice of me. I leaned over his back and drove the needle hard into the side of his neck, then depressed the plunger.

I had plenty of time in the moments that followed to wonder what I would do if the stuff was ineffective. I had a vision of myself smashing the empty flask that stood nearby and trying to cut O'Brien's throat with the broken glass, when he went limp. West, suddenly released, fell to the floor. For another heart-stopping moment I thought he was dead. Then he drew in a great shrieking breath, and another, and began to cough. I sat on the floor and held him while he coughed and wheezed for several minutes. Finally, he began to breathe more normally. His face was pale, except for two red patches on his cheekbones.

"Can you get up?" I asked. He seemed weak, and a huge wave of anxiety washed over me as I realized that if West was incapacitated, I was in charge of this mess.

"All right," West whispered. "I'm all right, just can't talk." I helped him to his feet. O'Brien lay slumped half off the table. The syringe was still stuck in his neck. His face wore a snarl of rage.

West paid no attention to the body. He was obviously unsteady, half leaning against me. "I owe you my life, Charles," he whispered. His eyes were wide and somehow uncomprehending. "I knew we needed restraints..." His voice trailed off, and I thought he was about to faint.

Just then I heard a door slam far away, and footsteps, faint but coming closer. Panic swept through me. Surely we were about to be discovered! One of us had to do something. No – *West* had to do something. Only he had any right to be here.

"Herbert," I said, grasping his shoulders and shaking him. "Someone's coming! You have to go out and stop whoever it is from coming in here." I knew the door was locked, but if this was a night watchman, surely he would investigate a lab with lights on at this late hour? And he would have a key. "Go out and talk to him!"

West began to move toward the door. I was relieved to see that he seemed to be making an effort to pull himself together, but he still looked very shaky. It took several seconds of fumbling before he unlocked the door. He went into the corridor, closing the door behind him. I pressed my ear to it and listened.

"Is that you, Gibbs?" I heard him ask. To my relief, his voice, though hoarse, sounded nearly normal. "I was careless cooking up a batch of chemicals in the lab here, and got a lungful of fumes. Thought I'd die coughing."

"Oh, so that was you, Mr. West," said the watchman. "I wasn't sure what I was hearing, but it sounded like trouble. You want to watch it with those chemicals, that's for sure. Why are you in here working on Saturday night, anyway?"

"Work is its own reward," said West. "Besides, I had something to do that couldn't wait. I'm finished now, I'm glad to say, even though it almost finished me! I'll be leaving in a little while, Gibbs, don't worry." I grinned with delight. This sounded more like the West I knew!

Gibbs bade West a surly goodnight and went back down the corridor, still grumbling, by the sound of it. West returned to the lab. He was still quite pale, and the flesh of his neck was bruised and swollen.

"We have to finish up here, Charles," he said. "I'm not in the best of shape. The main thing is to dispose of the body. You have to go and fetch Mike and Jerry. They should be at Hangman's Hill. Take the route we used the night we dug up

Hocks – down College, then along the brook. They should be parked behind some bushes just inside the graveyard."

I took off my lab coat and put on my dark jacket. "Are you sure you'll be all right alone, Herbert?" I asked. "You don't look well."

"I'm not, but I'll be all right." He pointed to O'Brien. "I'll get this guy ready to go and meet you at the outside door in precisely..." he paused, looking at his watch, "twenty-five minutes if you hurry but don't run. Does that sound reasonable?"

I assured him that the time would be sufficient, and set my watch to the same time as his. I was about to leave the lab when West called me back.

"Take this along." He took a pistol from his pocket and handed it to me. "Just in case."

"In case of what?" I asked. "How long have you been carrying that around?"

"I believe in being prepared," he said, avoiding my eye.

"It's Hocks, isn't it?" I said. "You do think he might be looking for us, don't you?"

"Not at all," West said. "You'd better get going."

Carefully, I slid the pistol into my pocket. "Where did you get it?" I asked.

He pushed me toward the door, not gently. "None of your business," he said. "Twenty-five minutes, don't forget."

The corridor was dark and quiet. I had a momentary jolt of anxietywhen I thought a key would be needed to open the outer door, but noticed a thumb-latch in time. The door locked behind me, and I set out into the night.

It was two o'clock on an October morning. The campus lay silent about me. I threaded my way through narrow passageways between buildings devoted to the pure and applied sciences. Soon I was on College Street, moving rapidly but without the kind of hurry that might attract attention.

I realized then that despite the lateness of the hour and the shocking events I had witnessed, I felt intensely alive and energized. Even the possibility of a lurking John Hocks did not trouble me. Tonight I had travelled in a hearse to an illegal event. I had seen men engage in brutal violence toward one another, and I had seen a man die. I had seen that same man return to life, and had spoken with him. I had saved my friend's life. I had killed a man.

At this thought, I stopped moving. Yes, I had killed O'Brien. True, he had been not far from death anyway, but he had undoubtedly been alive when I shot the drug into his neck. But what else could I have done? O'Brien had not been amenable to reason, and I knew I could not have overpowered him physically. West would have been dead if I had tried any other means but the one I had used.

By this time I had reached Hangman's Brook. As I made my way along the hummocky ground beside it, I became acutely aware of the night, its sounds and smells – the dark smell of water, the musky yet sharp odour of decaying leaves, overlaid with a faint whiff of wood smoke. Stars blazed cleanly in the black sky. I felt as though I could walk forever through this vast yet intimate darkness. But now I was approaching the graveyard. Crossing the rutted road, I passed a copse of large bushes, lilacs, I believed. On the other side of them was the Clodhopper.

I rapped at the driver's side window. It opened a crack and Mike's face looked out. By the faint light of a hooded lantern they had been playing some sort of card game. A bottle of liquor stood on the dashboard.

"Mr. West is ready for you now," I said. "The same place as before."

"And the other one too?" Mike asked, grinning.

"Yes, him too," I replied, opening the back door and climbing in without waiting for an invitation or providing any explanation.

Evidently, Mike and Jerry did not need additional details. I had been endorsed, it seemed, by Hiram West the previous night. Now, to a very limited extent, I was his agent. This thought made me uneasy, as did the unaccustomed weight of the pistol in my pocket.

Minutes later, the Clodhopper pulled up to the door of the Medical School's laboratory building. Checking my watch, I found it was just short of the twenty-five minutes West had specified.

"Wait here," I said, and climbed out. Cautiously, I approached the door and knocked. To my relief, West opened it. Behind him I could see the gurney with O'Brien's body on it. West had wrapped it in something, which on closer inspection proved to be a lab coat.

"After all, we want him to be decent for his last trip," West said, with a smile I could only just make out. He sounded tired.

Jerry and Mike emerged from the hearse, and at West's direction loaded the body back inside. "The usual treatment will be fine, Mike," I heard West say. "No, I don't need a lift. My rooms are close by here."

Mike said something that sounded like, "Is he all in one piece or did you saw off a bit, Doc?" West made some joking reply, and we turned to go.

"What will they do with him?" I asked, as the hearse departed from view.

"West's Funeral Home in Boston was the first to install a crematorium," he said shortly. "It comes in handy at times."

We said no more on the short walk to his rooms. At the door, I asked if he needed my help with anything else that night. He shook his head.

"No, Charles, I'm about done in. But come tomorrow afternoon, if you can. I'd like to review the whole situation."

I agreed, and turned homeward.

♦ 6 ♦

But I did not want to go home. I was full of unspent energy, and knew that sleep was out of the question. I was at loose ends at three in the morning. I considered going for a long walk to induce tiredness, and set off eastward along College, intending to take a cross street northward to the Miskatonic River. But no street appealed to me, until I found myself on French Hill.

I did not admit to myself that I was going to Alma Halsey's place until I was within sight of the turreted house in which her lodgings were located. In those times it would have been out of the question for a man to call on a young woman of good family unannounced and at a very late hour. Indeed, this is still a breach of courtesy, if not of morals. But somehow I had convinced myself that on this particular night, in my state of strange elation, I would be welcome.

I let myself in quietly and tiptoed up the several flights of stairs, wincing whenever one creaked. Finally, I stood before Alma's door. Only then did it occur to me that what I was doing was unwise. Alma would almost certainly be asleep and would fail to hear my knock. I would have to knock loudly and repeatedly to awaken her, also rousing other occupants of the house and ensuring for myself a justly unwelcoming reception. But so strong was my conviction that I was on a path intended, that I continued to hesitate, standing before the door with its brass knocker, caught in limbo and yet strangely content to be there.

Suddenly, I heard a sound from within – footsteps, surely? Then a light glowed faintly under the door. She was awake! It seemed to me only logical that my presence had made itself known to her, and that now it was inevitable that I take the next step. So, very gently, I knocked.

Several seconds passed, and I was wondering whether to knock again, when the door opened a crack. Recognizing me, Alma opened it the rest of the way. "Charles!" she whispered. "What are you doing here? Are you all right?"

She wore a dark blue robe. I could see the white lace of a nightdress underneath. Her feet were bare and her hair was tousled. She looked a little anxious, but not, I thought, annoyed.

"I was in the neighbourhood, so I thought I'd drop by," I said, starting to laugh at the banal absurdity of this statement.

"Well, you'd better come inside," she said. "What do you mean, 'in the neighbourhood?' Have you been wandering the streets again with that ghoul Herbert West?"

"We haven't been wandering the streets. But I was at West's place, yes. After we left his father's party we... got to debating life and death, and lost track of the time."

"'Life and death.' Well, that's certainly a meaty topic. I was just getting up to make myself some chamomile tea, since I couldn't sleep. Would you like some?"

"Alma, I think there's a reason you couldn't sleep tonight. I think part of you knew I would come. So forget about sleeping. Forget about tea. Let's enjoy each other's company." I felt an irresistible impulse to pace around the room, and gave in to it. "Tomorrow is Sunday. We have no obligations." I turned back toward her and took her hands in mine. "It's a pity there's no music, so we could dance." I slid my arm around her and whirled her around in a kind of waltz.

"Charles, what's gotten into you? You're acting very strangely. Have you been drinking?"

"Only the night air, and starlight, and intimations of immortality," I replied. It was as though I had absorbed West's peculiar energized atmosphere, borrowing it when we parted at his door, like a coat he did not need for the rest of the night. Maybe it was because of the pistol, which I had forgotten to give back to him when we parted. Whatever the reason for this state, I was enjoying it. It was like drinking wine without, as yet, any sorry consequences.

I didn't want to let her go. Through her garments I could feel her ribs as she pressed herself backward in an effort to put some distance between us. "Charles, let me go!" she said. "This isn't like you. Why are you so – ?"

"So happy. Because I am. And no, it isn't like me. Tonight, for the first time in years I'm happy, Alma."

As I spoke, I realized that the logical implication of my words was that I was happy because of her. But that was not true, rather the opposite. I had sought her out, I had come to Alma Halsey in the dead hours of the night, not seeking happiness, but bearing it with me – a strange happiness born of blood and death and unnatural life.

"I'm glad, Charles." She had relaxed a little, now, had stopped pulling away from me. "But this is so sudden."

"I know it is, Alma, but it's right. All night, all through that long dinner with Hiram West and his... associates (and what a bunch they are, let me tell you), all the time I was talking with Herbert about... well, about all sorts of things, like what it must feel like to die, and whether someone brought back from death could remember it – all the time in the back of my mind I was thinking about you. I saw you, you know – you were wearing a velvet dress, sort of golden brown velvet, and you were talking to someone, but I couldn't hear what you were saying..."

"Saw me? What do you mean?"

"It was a kind of vision – All right, I did drink quite a lot of wine at dinner, but that was a long time ago. I guess I must have fallen asleep for a few seconds, and had this wonderful dream of you."

She was laughing, her eyes a warm blue in the dim light. "Oh Charles, you're such a romantic! I do enjoy your company. Even now, even like this."

"Especially like this." I put both my arms around her, pulled her to me and kissed her. This was the first time I had really kissed her. Before this, the most I had done was discreetly brush my lips on her cheek. She made as if to pull away again, then yielded. A long moment later we moved apart a little. I tried to read the expression on her face. Bewilderment, even fear, but also curiosity and dawning passion. I loosened the robe she wore and thrust my hands under it, so there was only the thin fabric of her nightdress between us. I drew her to me again, whispering, "Alma! Let's go into your bedroom."

As I led her into the darkened room, as she let me take the robe from her shoulders, as I removed my own clothing, I felt something totally alien well up inside me and rush to my head like some marvellous drug. I wondered if this was how it would feel if Herbert West's magic fluid was pumped into my veins – as though my blood had been transformed into pure light. I did not know whether Alma resisted any further. I knew only that this was the end of the trajectory. All of myself, all of these days and months and nights of secret doings had culminated here and now. If I was a river, I had reached the sea. I spent myself in her, in the ocean that was Alma.

I awoke to bright morning light welling into an unfamiliar room through unfamiliar curtains. I was alone in the room. Alma was not there.

I sat up, feeling uncertain as to what to do. Perhaps I should leave. Just then, she came into the room. She was wearing a skirt and jacket, and looked thoroughly businesslike.

"Good morning, Charles," she said. "I'm afraid I must rush off. I'm in the choir at Christ Church, and must be at the ten o'clock service. I forgot to tell you last night. But don't you rush. In fact, I would be grateful if you were to wait a little while before leaving. Discretion, you know." She kissed me lightly and was gone.

I got up slowly, getting into the wrinkled clothes I had worn the previous night. I did some sketchy washing and tried to put my rumpled hair in order with my fingers. Looking in the mirror, I felt peculiar. The unnatural excitement of the night had passed, but not completely. I knew that I should have felt ashamed at what I had done, pressing myself upon a young woman who, though not altogether unwilling, was not unreservedly happy about what I demanded of her. I knew this, and yet, looking at my reflected image, I, the I that was present in my skin, did not feel ashamed. Lingering among the memories of the night was that feeling of completion, of rightness.

A few minutes later, I let myself cautiously out of the apartment. I met no one on the stairs, and only one person in the foyer, a man also on his way out, who did not so much as glance at me. I walked homeward, unhurried, thinking about Alma. I could not guess, from the little I had seen of her this morning, how she felt about what had passed between us. She had seemed cool and cheerful, her usual self, in fact. I did not think she could have assumed such a guise of normalcy to hide feelings of distress or anger. That was not her way. And she had kissed me…

Did I love Alma Halsey then? I did not. I felt for her a great tenderness, a deep affection born of friendship. For some time I had known that it was slowly ripening into something that might eventually become love, but it had not been that which had compelled me in the night. It had been something outside myself, or rather, something which had never been a part of me before, but now was.

Later that day, after several more hours of sleep, I made my way to West's rooms. He greeted me looking quite well, and as elegant as always. The only signs of the attack by O'Brien were some bruises on his neck.

"I'm glad to see you so well, Herbert," I said. "You seemed pretty shaken up last night."

"I was, then, but I'm all right now. But you, Charles, you look quite splendid." He smiled. "It seems that the adventures of the night agreed with you."

I felt myself blushing, and turned aside to hide it. There was no way West could know of my visit to Alma after I had left him. "Well, I slept most of the day."

"Whatever the reason, I'm glad you find these experiments no hardship. Because last night would have ended very differently had you not been there."

"I want to talk about that, actually. I killed him, didn't I? I killed a man. Oh, and I should return this." I handed him the pistol.

He took it and laid it casually aside. "Well, yes, technically you killed him. But as far as the rest of the world is concerned, he was already dead. Just ask Mike and Jerry what they brought to Arkham last night – 'a stiff,' is what they'll say. I guarantee it."

"But he wasn't dead when he just about choked you! He wasn't dead when he yelled at us for bringing him back! He wasn't *dead*. So I killed him. You can't get away from that."

"What are you saying, exactly, Charles?" His voice was quieter than usual, but with an edge.

"I don't like what these experiments are doing to me. Now I'm a murderer, as well as a grave robber. Whether anyone else knew about O'Brien coming back to life or not, he was alive and I made him dead. That makes me a murderer."

I had been facing one of the windows as I spoke. Somehow, I could not say these things to his face. I was surprised that I said them at all. West grasped my shoulder and turned me around. Looking directly into my eyes, he said,

"And if you hadn't made him dead, as you put it, I would have been dead. Would you have preferred that?"

"No, of course not. I thought about that on the way to fetch Mike and Jerry last night. I reached the same conclusions. I guess it wasn't murder, really. But where are we going with this?

So far we have revivified two corpses. We lost Hocks and had to turn O'Brien into a corpse again. So what's the point?"

West sighed. "Sit down, Charles. I thought we needed to review the situation today, but now it seems we must go back to fundamentals.

"When I first told you about my research, back in May, I said, if you recall, that it was a lifetime's work. Now, how many experiments have we done together?"

"Two," I replied. I felt like a student called on the carpet by his professor for inexcusable ignorance.

"Exactly. Two. Now, the nature of this work is such that each time a little, a very little, knowledge is gained. Surely you must have noticed the data I record each time, the blood samples I take, the measurements. It's only by building up a mass of such data that I will achieve anything. Do you understand this?"

"Yes. Well, no, I guess I don't. I didn't think it would be like that at all. I thought that after one or two successes, Dean Halsey would let you go ahead in the open, with the support of the Medical School."

"Don't be naïve. Academics don't give their belief so readily, and their support even less so. Especially when they don't want to believe in the first place. They'll find a host of reasons not to believe, even in the face of what most would consider proof."

"So what will it take to make them believe? Why would two dozen cases convince them any more than two?"

"Because after two dozen, or two hundred, I'll have enough data to publish. It won't be Halsey and his hangers-on who will judge then, but scientists everywhere."

"Two hundred!" I was aghast.

"Well, maybe not that many." That wave of the hand again. "Look, Charles, I think I know what's bothering you. Perhaps I overestimated your tolerance for going against the rules, even for a good cause. It's the business of acquiring the bodies that's the problem, isn't it? We had to dig up the first one. For the next one we had to go through that business of the prizefight. Although you rather enjoyed that, didn't you?"

For a second, I saw again, vividly, Robinson's fist connecting with O'Brien's face, and the spray of blood. I heard again that thump-crunch of flesh ground between bones. I said nothing, and West continued.

"You've been entirely reliable in the lab. And last night – you couldn't have done better. When Gibbs came around I was in a total funk. You snapped me out of it. You got Mike and Jerry pretty smartly. And that was after you dealt with O'Brien. So I can't proceed without you, Charles."

He leaned forward. Never had I seen him look more sincere. His grey eyes held mine with absolute steadiness.

"It's getting the bodies that's shaken your resolve, I'm sure of that," he said again. "Well, that'll be different from now on. This business with O'Brien was a whim, I admit, and an ill-considered one at that. I simply couldn't resist the prospect of working with a really fresh subject. But now that I'm an intern, I have access to the morgue. I'll know immediately when a subject becomes available. It'll be a simple matter of carrying out the procedure – two or three hours at most. No more grave digging, no more prizefights. And we simply return our material to the morgue when we're finished. It'll be perfectly safe."

"So you anticipate that most of them will be dead again within a few hours of revivification? But Hocks was – "

"Forget about Hocks, for God's sake! He was a... he wasn't a good specimen, I've told you that before. Yes, I'm fairly sure most of these morgue subjects will be short-lived, which is just as well. Do you imagine that I want to start a home for revivified corpses, Charles? I expect most of them will be half-wits at best. By the time they come into my hands they'll have lost too many brain cells to be fully-functioning human beings. O'Brien was something of an exception, because we got him so soon after he was killed, but I suspect that all the battering he had sustained in his career had damaged his brain. Apart from freshness, he wasn't a really good subject." He touched the bruises on his neck.

"What I saw, especially in the case of O'Brien," I said, "were men undergoing a dreadful experience – a kind of reverse birth into a broken body. I can see that they may not be fully-functioning, as you put it. But in that case, what's the point?"

"Each attempt adds to the sum total of knowledge. Remember that! Eventually mankind will understand more about death because of my work. And yours, too. Charles, what about your part? Last night you actually got O'Brien to talk about what he experienced after death."

"You don't believe in that anyway," I said, persisting in my role of devil's advocate. "You think it's just brain cells dissolving, or something. And anyway, you could interview them yourself."

"So prove me wrong!" said West. He got up and began pacing, a sure sign that he was getting wound up all over again. "Yes, when it comes to all that stuff about the death-memories of the soul, I'm every bit as skeptical as Halsey is about my ideas.

But there's nothing to stop you from gathering data to set against my skepticism. It's your project, though. And that will mean that two different kinds of research are being done using these subjects, which is practical and efficient, wouldn't you say?"

He stopped in front of me and gave me another steely look. "Because I intend to go forward, with or without you, Charles. By the *Necronomicon*, I do. Are you with me, or not?"

If I said no, if I left, having dissociated myself from his work, I would never see him again, would never experience the special electricity that seemed to surround him. Until now, a kind of under-thought had been pushing me forward – now that Alma and I were to be lovers, perhaps, what room would there be in my life for West and his doings, which so often verged on the illegal? But the brief vision I had then, as he stood before me with the question hanging in the air between us, of my world without him in it, was so flat, so bleak, that even Alma seemed like a pale wraith. No, since the night of the concert, and maybe even before that, some fundamental part of me had been linked to Herbert West.

"I'm with you," I said.

West's anticipation that the process of obtaining experimental subjects would become easier proved true. Due to a fortunate conjunction of personalities, the chief surgeon of St. Mary's Hospital, Dr. Welburn Bright, took a liking to him. West's dexterity in the operating theater and his cool, detached manner appealed to Bright, who was of the scientific, patient-as-object school of thought. Through this connection, West was assigned a small, under-equipped room in the basement of the hospital, which he furnished as a rudimentary laboratory. The reasons he gave for needing this facility were rather vague – something about a special research project in pathology – but they satisfied Dr. Bright. Dean Halsey attempted to dissuade his colleague from showing favour to West. Dr. Bright, however, felt his position of authority at St. Mary's very keenly, and made it clear to Dr. Halsey that he would not be permitted to exert his authority beyond the boundaries of the Medical School.

"The old tyrant has finally met someone he can't push around," said West, chuckling, as he recounted this episode to me.

Alma had a rather different opinion, as might be expected. "Herbert West has managed to convince that old autocrat Bright that he deserves special favours. Are you sure he doesn't have some sort of hypnotic technique? But then, how would you know? You're as enchanted by him as Bright is."

During this time, there were few things about me that Alma did not know, but the extent and nature of my involvement with West's researches was one secret that I resolutely concealed from her.

With the unexpected bonus of his own laboratory, located right in the hospital, and on the same floor as the morgue, West and I soon worked out an efficient routine for securing research material and conducting our experiments. West kept a close watch on new arrivals at the morgue, obtaining information on the age and condition of a corpse, and the causes of its death. He had to be particularly vigilant, since the Medical School had first choice of all unclaimed bodies for its dissecting rooms.

West had observed the routines of the hospital's night watchmen. They were creatures of habit, one of which was card games in the boiler room. Between the hours of eleven and three in the morning we could usually expect to work unmolested.

Only a few minutes were needed for us to get everything ready. Then, the rapid but silent dash along damp, brick-lined corridors, the quick deployment of a key, a search by penlight along the ranks of numbered drawers to find the abode of our subject. Its silent occupant would be transferred to a gurney and quickly wheeled to our laboratory.

The revivification procedure itself became so familiar, that it assumed an aspect of ritual. Laying out the corpse on the table, garbing ourselves in white, the preliminary ablutions and West's spectacle-polishing, all put me in mind (blasphemously, I thought at the time) of the Mass. As a child, I had sat through many a lengthy service where the bustlings of the priest and his attendants with vestments, chalices, ciboria, cruets and the other material implements were the only things that held my interest.

After the preparations would come the central matter, the engaging of the apparatus with the corpse, and the mechanical replacement of blood with the violet-coloured liquid. Invariably, the tension would grow at this point, the twelfth time as much as the first. West was the high priest, his attention fixed on the meters and tubes, the taps and the pump, and I, his eager acolyte, obeying his orders, following his lead.

Then the vigil. Even now I can see the dank little room, a little too dimly lit for a laboratory, the cold corpse on its cold slab, West making notes, pacing about, checking for vital signs in the subject. And I – sitting on one of the rickety chairs, I would read, or more often, think – about the purpose of what we were doing, about what might be going on inside the body and brain as West's drug did its work. I thought about rats, and whether there were any in this cellar. I thought about my parents, about Michael O'Connor and John Hocks, about decay and rebirth (rather than revivification), about the places of life and death. Was this such a place? And I thought about Alma, and the things we did in her white-curtained bedroom. I thought about these things as the minutes ticked by and water dripped somewhere in the distance, and the other corpses in the nearby morgue, lucky enough to have escaped our ministrations, went about their business of dissolution.

Not all of our subjects returned to life, but most did. Those who might think that West's successes were dubious because the subjects were not really dead in the first place would be wrong. If that were the case, the physicians of Arkham had much to answer for, in that so many of their patients went to the morgue with a spark of life flickering unattended within them. Of the twelve attempts we made between the boxer Kid O'Brien and the unfortunate Robert Leavitt of St. Louis, fully nine returned, however briefly, to a semblance of life.

My reverie would be broken – by an excited word from West, by a sigh from the form on the table, or, disturbingly, by a deep, agonized groan. I think it was the groans emitted by some of our victims that led to my instinctive but suppressed conviction that West and I were causing suffering. Whatever the value of the scientific data he was amassing, I could not help but wonder if it was justified.

For West, the moment of revivification was the goal and crown of the enterprise, whatever he may have said about data-gathering. I was engaged in another line of research during this time, a private one. While Herbert West studied death and revivification, I studied Herbert West. I watched him as the water dripped and what might have been rats scurried in the bowels of the old building. I watched as the cool scientist was transformed into something else when the first signs of returning life appeared in the clay under his hands.

Invariably, he called me over to bear witness. Even when it became evident to me that my assistance was no longer strictly necessary, even when it must have been plain to him that my enthusiasm had waned, still he wanted me at his side to see and hear and feel the evidence of returning life, life that was there at his command.

Of our four complete failures, three expired within minutes of the first signs of returning life, and nothing West did to them after this had any effect. One appeared to be stable, but when it opened its eyes, it gave us a look of such horror that I felt an answering surge of horror within myself. Then it fell back, as dead as it had been before our ministrations. On these occasions, I noted, West's face quickly lost its look of exaltation, became still and cold as he went about the business of noting the particulars and dismantling the equipment.

The five revivified beings with whom I managed to converse were poor things, plainly so impaired in their cognitive functions that my records of these sessions consisted of little more than my initial question, "What do you remember?" followed by broken and meaningless phrases, inarticulate mumblings or involuntary gargling and gagging sounds produced by the vocal apparatus as West's solution excited the broken physical mechanisms of their bodies.

A few uttered words that seemed to be in keeping with observations made in other cases of persons recovering from near death – references to a tunnel of light, perfect peace and reunion with loved ones. "I saw Mandy!" said one man, shortly before his final collapse. I remember hoping that she was still waiting for him after his second death.

None of the five lived very long after my questioning of them. Their return to life was tenuous at best, and after they had uttered their few words, or merely babbled incoherently for a while, the vital force waned rapidly. Not one of them displayed any sustained vitality, unlike Kid O'Brien, or especially our first subject, John Hocks.

"These morgue subjects certainly are disappointing, aren't they? Don't you get discouraged sometimes?" West had just finished writing up his notes on our latest failure, and I could no longer hide my doubts about our project.

"Disappointing? Say rather, unspectacular. I have learned something from almost every one of them. I suspect they may be weak because most of them died after illness, rather than quickly and violently like our first two."

West enjoyed reviewing his data and formulating theories based on them. He could go on for hours, quite unaware that he had left me in the dust long before. To forestall another monologue, I decided to ask another question, one so staggeringly elementary I wondered that I had never dared to ask it before.

"What's in it, Herbert? In your revivifying fluid, I mean. What are the ingredients?"

He looked at me for a moment, seeming a little disconcerted. Then he gave me one of his beautiful smiles. "What if I were to say... palladium infused with krypton halides, bathed in essence of iridium and bound with imperishable gold?"

"Is that really what's in it?" I was fairly certain he was making fun of me, but was in no mood to play along.

"No, of course not, but it might as well be, for all you would understand if I were to tell you. No, no, don't get upset – you just don't have the necessary background in chemistry. I can tell you that it contains organic molecules only one remove from being alive. When properly formulated for a specific organism, they bind with the existing structure and produce an excitant effect on the vital mechanism."

"Organic molecules." I said.

"Exactly. And don't ask me to draw you a picture, because you wouldn't understand it."

Unlike West, I did not have a scientist's training, or the willingness to repeat an experiment endlessly for the sake of small increments of data. It was his determination, optimism and sheer strength of will that I found compelling, even when I doubted the ultimate value of his work. I suspect it would have been the same if his goal had been to grow a blue rose, or turn base metal into gold.

If his field had been horticulture or alchemy, however, I would have found it easier to maintain my enthusiasm. West, with his peculiar, unemotional personality and his experience with handling the dead, was unaffected by the depressing nature of our subject matter. I, despite developing some facility in the handling of the corpses and apparatus, was never able to harden myself to the struggles of our victims. More than once I attempted to explain this to West, but he brushed aside my reservations as projections of my romantic temperament.

"You've tried to interview them, haven't you?" he asked. "And most of them were no more than brainless lumps of flesh, correct? So how can you imagine they are suffering? What you see and hear are nerves responding to random electrical impulses from the brain, that's all."

At length, I was forced to conclude that West had a mechanical circulating device instead of a heart, or, more accurately, that he was devoid of those emotions which are normally considered resident in the heart. Not once did he betray any sympathy for the sufferings of our experimental subjects, nor even express regret that they were a necessary if undesirable by-product of his research.

I had never had a close friend before. As a child I had been thought delicate, especially after the injury to my leg, and had therefore been carefully shielded from companions and activities which might cause further damage. Being of a nature that was happy with solitude and self-sufficient, I did not realize that I was missing anything. At school I had found my niche among the bookish, studious boys, but had not formed lasting friendships with any of them. Later on, my family's troubles had dissociated me from those among whom I should have, in the normal course of events, found friends.

Spending as much time with West as I did, it was inevitable that I learned more about him. Unlike me, he was a great believer in physical fitness, which he cultivated by masochistic practices such as fasting, cold baths and long cross-country runs.

Although he avoided smoking and most forms of overindulgence, he appreciated good wine with meals, and several times a year, not to put too fine a point on it, he liked to get drunk. He said this was a way to clear his mind and begin afresh. "Otherwise, my brain gets clogged up with details. A good debauch is like great storm that blows out the extraneous stuff. Afterward there's room for new ideas. It's a kind of death and revivification, only the fluid is different," he laughed.

He quite deliberately planned for these brain-clearing sessions, as he called them, selecting a time when he had a night and a day without obligations. He would lay in a supply of the best Scotch whiskey and invite a selection of congenial companions to his rooms, with a terse message such as *Brain clearing tonight. Join me if you like. West.*

He was always interesting, even when he was irritating. Whatever the topic, he had an opinion, usually an informed one. He could argue a point endlessly, but without rancour. He could be sarcastic, but his manners were always perfect, even when he was lying.

It soon became clear to me that he took pleasure in deception for its own sake, sometimes telling long, elaborate lies, simply to test the credulousness of his listeners. There was a kind of innocent joy in his manner as he indulged in these untruths and in the verbal parrying that followed. Once he told me that he had been home all day, when he knew quite well that I had seen him crossing the campus quadrangle several hours before. When I confronted him with this fact, he said,

"Ah, but that wasn't me you saw."

"Of course it was you! Who else could it have been?"

"My twin brother, of course."

"But you don't have a twin brother! He died – you told me so yourself."

"Did I? Well, you can't believe everything you hear, obviously."

In November, a mutilated corpse was found in a wood near Dunwich village. The dead man, evidently a tramp, had been killed by repeated blows with a sharp, heavy object. The body had also been, in the delicate phraseology of the *Arkham Advertiser*, 'tampered with,' as if the injuries that had caused death did not constitute tampering. Local rumour was more explicit: the corpse had been disembowelled and the heart removed. The crime was, of course, attributed to the elusive Wild Man.

"Now we really have to tell the authorities what we know about Hocks," I said to West.

"Why?" His eyes were as cold as the time I'd met him in Howard's Alley, and as friendly.

"Because now he's murdered someone," I said. "And we know why too."

"All *I* know is that someone killed a tramp," said West. "I don't know that John Hocks was the killer; in fact, it's extremely unlikely that he was. Telling the police – who are, generally speaking, a herd of ignorant louts – about my scientific work would only get me arrested, or locked up in Sefton Aslyum. You too, perhaps, which certainly would not help find whoever murdered this tramp."

He was very convincing, and I was quite ready to be convinced.

Even now there are things that can instantly take me back to those Arkham years before the Great War. Certain musical passages, certain phrases (I can still hear West saying "Let's get on with it, then," as he always did as we began one of our revivifications), and scents such as the autumnal odour of ripe decay, the smell of wood smoke, or the perfumes of sandalwood and narcissus, bring back to an almost intolerable degree the intensity of that time.

For in addition to Herbert West, there was Alma. Between the two of them, I existed in a charged, electrical atmosphere. In retrospect, I understand that the situation was possibly unhealthy; certainly it was not sustainable. But oh, how wonderful that time was for me! It was as though I had discovered the secret at the heart of the world and had it all to myself.

The first time I saw Alma Halsey again after my visit to her in the early hours of the day Kid O'Brien died his second death, was at work the following Monday. I had arrived early on purpose, because I felt anxious about meeting her again, now that the nature of our relationship had been radically altered. I took care to be ensconced in my alcove, apparently hard at work, at the time when she normally arrived. It was not until the mid-morning break that I saw her.

As luck would have it, the two of us were alone in the staff room. Alma came in as I was pouring myself a cup of tea. My hand jerked involuntarily, and I spilled some of the hot liquid. The resulting minor confusion dissipated the awkwardness of our initial greetings.

"Charles, how are you?" she asked, a faint blush appearing on her cheeks.

"I am quite well, Alma," I said. "I trust you sang well at Christ Church yesterday morning."

Her blush deepened slightly. "I think I did, despite not sleeping much the previous night," she said, looking me straight in the eyes. At this point we both began to laugh, and I felt a great relief wash over me. I had feared that she would have become angry at the events of that night, or worse, hurt or shamed. But that did not seem to be the case.

"Are you free this evening?" she asked me.

"Perfectly." She was still looking at me intently, but I could not read her expression.

"Come over then." Two of our colleagues entered the room then, and we said no more.

Alma opened her door to me that evening wearing a dress of golden-brown velvet, a colour that accentuated the blondness of her hair. Around her neck was a pendant of amber mounted in silver. I caught a faint scent of sandalwood. For a moment I stood silent. I had never thought Alma could look so exotic, for one thing. For another, I suddenly remembered the vision of her I had had during the boxing match.

"Alma," I said, "you look like a dream – my dream!" She grasped both my hands in hers and drew me toward her, saying,

"Come in, Charles! Are you going to stand on my doorstep all night and stare? But I'm glad you like this dress."

"Alma, I can't explain what came over me the other night. I think it was in a way the result of what West and I were doing earlier that night – talking and, well, drinking, and so on. I left his place feeling – exalted is the only word I can think of. And I had been thinking about you all evening, so it seemed logical to come here. To share my happiness with you..."

"It was a surprise. Not that the possibility hadn't occurred to me, but I hadn't thought of you as being... well, so insistent."

She stood in front of me, her blue eyes glowing. She'll tell me she never wants to see me again, I thought. I'll have to quit my job and leave Arkham... My heart beat heavily and I found it difficult to breathe.

Alma took my hands in hers. "Only now do I see clearly," she said. "I know what I want. You. I want you to be my lover, Charles."

I felt my face split open in a foolish smile. I did not know what to say, but I pressed her hands.

"This is going to be an adventure," she said, laughing. "I haven't had much practice at it, and neither have you, I think. A certain amount of discretion will be needed, but not as much as you would imagine. I'm already known as 'one of those new women.' And this is Arkham, after all." She began to pace around the room, reminding me suddenly of West.

"Is Arkham the Greenwich Village of New England?" I asked, intercepting her and putting my arms around her.

"Worse," said Alma. "The Village might have its anarchists and freethinkers, but here in Arkham we had witches, hundreds of years ago. The first practitioners of free love in America, if you believe some of the stories."

"But they paid for it." I shivered, in spite of my self.

"One always pays for one's choices," she replied, suddenly serious. "I'm ready to pay, Charles. Are you?"

In public, I was recognized as 'that young librarian friend of Alma's.' We appeared together at public functions. That winter we went ice-skating on Summer's Pond. I joined her literary group. Finally grateful for those long-ago dancing lessons I had shared with my cousin Alice, I accompanied Alma to tea dances at one of Arkham's better hotels.

But our public togetherness, although enjoyable, was merely a façade for our private relationship, which was played out in Alma's little apartment. We met there because my rooms were unwelcoming and my landlady vigilant and censorious. Hers, on the other hand, was indifferent, or perhaps merely discreet. Being a friend of the Halsey family, she had a special status and shared some of Alma's free-thinking ideas.

There was something about the inherent deceptiveness of this relationship – innocent on the surface, darkly passionate beneath – that was intensely erotic. Maintaining this duality became an end in itself.

Did I love Alma then? I thought I did, but I was young, and it is easy to mistake passion for love when one is young. Certainly, when it came to the test I failed her. But that was much later.

♦ 7 ♦

Early in January of 1912, Dean Allan Halsey held a reception at his home for the faculty of the Medical School, its benefactors and its graduating class, as well as the University administration and selected other Miskatonic faculty. I fitted into none of these categories, but Alma procured for me a special invitation.

"It's time you met my parents," she said. "And this is the ideal occasion. There will be so many people milling around that you'll be safely introduced before you know it."

"But won't that give them the wrong idea? They'll start thinking I'm a prospective son-in-law." Occasionally I said things like this to tease her, knowing her aversion to marriage.

"Not they!" said Alma, with a bitter little laugh. "Mother has given up on me, and as for Papa, he's been introducing me to hand-picked students for years. Perfect little gentlemen, all of them, and dull as pencil stubs. So that doesn't matter. But you must meet them, Charles. We've been seen together enough that Mother's friends are asking her about 'that young man I saw your Alma with.' You know the sort of thing. We have to establish a link between you and my parents, find some common ground they can be comfortable with. Once you've been safely slotted into a social niche it will be all right, but right now you're a loose end that Papa will feel obliged to follow up."

I remembered West's suspicion that someone had been watching him on Dean Halsey's orders, and agreed to attend.

On the appointed Sunday afternoon, I put in my appearance at the Halseys' Georgian mansion on Saltonstall Street. I was shown into a large bright room full of people. At one end was a table laden with food and drink. At the other, among a knot of other guests, the senior Halseys held court. I knew both of them by sight, but took the opportunity to observe them before going nearer.

Allan Halsey was a tall man who obviously wished to appear distinguished. Everything about him proclaimed this, from the precision of his iron-grey hair to the polish of his shoes. Unfortunately, the effect was a little diminished by a rather weak chin. Mrs. Halsey was very much in the mould of the society woman. Alma bore a strong resemblance to her, in terms of facial features, at least. Involuntarily, I thought of our most recent meeting, two nights before, and felt myself beginning to smile.

"There you are, Charles!" said the object of my thoughts, startling me. "How long have you been standing there with that vacant look on your face? Come along and I'll introduce you to your hosts.

"Papa, this is my colleague Charles Milburn," she said. "Charles, this is my father, Dr. Allan Halsey."

I extended my hand. "I'm pleased to meet you, Dr. Halsey." I wondered what this rather pompous man would do if he knew the true nature of the relationship between his daughter and her colleague and experienced a moment of irrational fear lest my thoughts communicate themselves to him by proximity. Then he was making the usual social noises and the moment was over.

Alma directed me toward her mother. Up close, the resemblance between them was less pronounced, due primarily to the calculating expression in Mrs. Halsey's eyes. As she looked me up and down, I could see her processing my name through her personal social index. "Milburn, you say? From Boston?"

"Yes, Mrs. Halsey. My father was George Milburn. My mother was Helen Devereaux, from New York City." I gave her these leads to save time. In her presence I felt only discomfort. Her husband had at least made a show of cordiality.

"Ah yes, I remember now," she said. "Your poor mother. It must have been most unpleasant for her."

I nearly said, "His blood and brains were splattered all over his study. Yes, it certainly was unpleasant." But I contented myself with noncommittal affirmative sounds.

Having put me into the category of people who didn't matter, Mrs. Halsey was clearly finished with me. Gratefully, Alma and I made our escape.

"There, it's done," she said. "Charles, I apologize for my mother. She's a hopeless snob. I'm sorry I had to put you through that."

I reassured her that I had survived intact. Soon after, in keeping with our code of absolute discretion in public, she left me to greet some of the other guests.

Looking around, I spied West by a distant window. The low winter sun was behind him, turning his hair into a halo of gold. I made my way over to him. "Herbert, I'm glad you're here. I feel like a fish out of water."

"Not only that but gutted and ready for the pan. You barely survived your inspection by the formidable Mrs. H.," he said with a sardonic smile. "I saw the way she raked you over, chewed you up and spat you out. Lucky for you the lovely Alma was there to pick up the pieces. Congratulations, by the way."

"Congratulations for what?"

"Your... what shall I say? Friendship isn't the right word, exactly. Damn it, why must one always resort to French for these things? Your *affaire de coeur*, Charles. Your *liaison*. I thought you've been looking especially content lately, but had supposed it was a side-effect of helping to further the cause of science. I can see now that was naïve of me."

"I don't know what you're talking about," I said.

"Charles, I'm no romantic, but I'm not unobservant. It stands out all over the two of you. It's the way you so self-consciously resist getting too close to one another. And the way she protected you from that Gorgon of a mother was touching in the extreme."

With the light behind him I could not make out his expression. His tone of voice was the same ironically bantering one with which he had greeted me.

"Well, yes, all right, Herbert. Alma and I are more than friends. I hope you'll be discreet, though."

"Perfectly. My only concern is that you don't suddenly decide to abandon our cause." He moved over to my other side, so that the light fell slantingly on his face. But its reflection from his spectacles hid his eyes, and I still could not read his expression. I reassured him that he could count on my assistance, as always.

West excused himself, having noticed someone trying to attract his attention from the other side of the room. Cut adrift, I began to feel the all too familiar sense of being an invisible visitor in a crowd of people enjoying themselves. I noticed a white-coated waiter presiding over a large punch bowl and decided to fortify myself.

After a while, I began almost to enjoy my invisibility. Sipping punch, I wandered among the guests, overhearing snatches of conversation.

"Don't you trust him! He's in the Dean's back pocket."

"I saw her myself, I tell you! Naked as the day she was born!"

"It's the chloride, not the sulphide. Makes a big difference."

"It'll kill more than half of them, you can be sure."

Suddenly, I heard someone speaking to me, and returned to earth with a small jolt. Dr. Armitage was with a group of serious-looking men, veterans of many receptions, to judge by the dexterity with which they manipulated drinks and *hors d'oeuvres*, all the while talking and nodding portentously.

"Milburn, it's good to see you here!" Dr. Armitage said, as I approached. "I've always thought that my librarians should get out more in the University. Especially you cataloguers. I daresay it was that young fellow got you an invitation – the one that asked to see the *Necronomicon* a year or so back. I saw you talking with him just now. East, is that the name?"

I had not realized that Dr. Armitage could be so chatty. "Not exactly," I said. "It's West – Herbert West." I felt a sudden surge of goodwill toward my director, so glad was I to see a familiar face.

"Actually," I continued, "it was Miss Halsey that arranged for my invitation."

"Of course! I should have realized. Miss Halsey... mm-hmm." He looked toward the Dean and Mrs. Halsey, and began to say something, but thought better of it. "She's a cataloguer too, of course," he said, finishing with a sip of his drink. He turned abruptly to the man beside him, a bald-headed, alert-looking fellow who appeared to have been listening to our conversation.

"Dr. Hobson," Dr. Armitage said, "I would like you to meet one of my librarians. This is Mr. Charles Milburn, of the Cataloguing Department. Dr. Hobson is in the Surgical Department at the Medical School."

Hobson clamped my hand in a hot paw that seemed entirely the wrong sort of equipment for a surgeon and looked at me hard, as though he suspected me of deception before I had even spoken. "So you're a cataloguer, are you?" Without waiting for a reply, he rushed on. "Any educated person should be able to put a few books in order and keep them that way. I couldn't believe it when Armitage told me there's a whole department of you librarians in his shop, just to catalogue the books. Maybe that's why I can never find anything in that place of yours. Too many cooks, eh? Do you suppose that's it?" He gestured rhetorically with a miniature sausage on a stick.

My feeling of warm conviviality drained away, quickly and completely. I was beginning to wish I had left while I was still invisible. Now there was no escape. Hobson wasn't making social small talk. He wanted an answer.

"Dr. Hobson," I began, "there's quite a difference between a departmental reading room and the University Library. The more books you have, the more diverse their subjects, the more expertise it takes to organize them. But I'm not sure I could help you, in any case. I know next to nothing about medicine. My field is classics."

"Classics! Hmph! Well, maybe that's different, but I doubt it. So what are you doing here, with all of us medical men?"

"I have a friend in the Medical School," I said. I didn't want to bring up Alma's name. The last thing she needed was for Hobson to be reminded that she catalogued in the area of medicine.

"Oh, and who might that be?" Hobson demolished the miniature sausage in a single bite. I was alarmed to realize that he was more interested in what I might say in reply to this question than to his earlier ones.

"Mr. Herbert West," I said, wondering if I was starting something I would regret.

"Oh ho! The dangerous Mr. West! I should have guessed."

"Why do you say that?" I asked. "Dangerous in what way?"

Hobson laughed, a harsh sound like a dog barking. "He's a renegade, that's what! One of those smart young whippersnappers who can't resist showing off. Those kind are always trouble. I know because I was one myself. So you're a friend of his, are you? Well, if you're a good friend, you'll advise him to play by the rules."

"But I would expect that a... questioning attitude would be welcome in an educational institution such as the Medical School. As long as it's an informed one, that is. Wouldn't you rather have students who engaged in debate, rather than supine receptacles for orthodoxy?" I noticed that my glass was empty once again and wondered if there was any punch left and whether anyone would notice my fourth trip to the punch bowl.

Hobson moved closer to me and made a gesture that looked vaguely threatening. "Supine receptacles? You can't say that about anyone at the School, young man. But your friend West, well, he's sure he knows better than anyone. And he doesn't stop at debate. Do you know that in his first year he actually wanted to do experiments with corpses? Thought he could bring them back to life or some such nonsense. Well, I have to credit Dr. Halsey with more patience than I would have had. He didn't expel West, although he could have. But I have to admit, he's got the technique. Good hands – he's lucky that way. But he has to cultivate the right attitude."

"Perhaps you're right, Dr. Hobson." I wondered what he would do if I said what I was thinking, which was, *Oh, he's got technique, all right. I've watched him use it many times, to do things you couldn't imagine.* Suddenly, I knew I had to get away from him. I fancied that West was watching me from somewhere in the room, could almost feel his eyes boring into the back of my head. And I was ravenously hungry. "Excuse me, please, I just remembered another engagement." I hoped I sounded convincing. "It was good to meet you."

"Tell your fellow librarians to stop making everything so complicated! Logic, it's all logic!" he said, turning away. I resolved at all costs to avoid a second encounter with him.

Proceeding toward the buffet table, I had to change my plans when I spotted Peter Runcible hovering over the savoury delicacies. He was not someone I would choose to seek out at a social occasion – or any other occasion, for that matter. I began to feel that I was surrounded by enemies – the senior Halseys, Dr. Hobson, Runcible. Even Dr. Armitage couldn't be trusted not to deliver me into another uncomfortable situation.

Alma was some distance away, talking with a couple of women and a professorial-looking man. I tried to catch her eye, but failed, which was probably just as well, because I was by now more than a little tipsy. It was time for me to leave. I looked around for the door, wondering if the Halseys would notice or care if I departed without formal farewells and expressions of gratitude.

Someone approached me from behind. I expected it to be West, ready to interrogate me about my conversation with Hobson, but I was surprised to see Prof. Quarrington. His diminutive, bobbing form reminded me of a bird or a small rodent.

"Good day to you, Charles Milburn!" he said. "I'm glad to see you here, yes I am. Doing your job, just as a good friend should. My commendation to you, young man."

"Thank you, Prof. Quarrington," I said. "But I'm not certain just what you mean when you say I'm doing my job."

He did not speak but grasped my sleeve and pulled me around to face in the opposite direction. Chuckling, he nodded toward a corner of the room, where West was talking to a man I did not recognize. "Keeping watch, that's your job. Look at him, over there, showing off, proving to everyone what a scientist he is! He has great gifts, that young fellow, and the pity is that he knows it too, at least about some of them. Someone has to make sure he doesn't go up in flames before his time, and it just happens that you're that someone. I knew it, and here you are, which proves I was right."

"You're referring to Herbert West? You believe I should... watch over him?"

"Yes, of course! He's an absolute phenomenon, more than anyone guesses, except me." He chuckled again. "As for why, well, think back! The *Necronomicon*! Both of you read it, I know that. You can't turn back the pages."

"Why does it matter that we both read the *Necronomicon*?" I asked.

"Because it's a catalyst, that's why! Don't you know what a catalyst is? Ask *him*; he knows." Another nod toward West. "You just have to take what comes, and keep faith. Don't worry, I'm on your side!" He gave my arm a weak slap and moved away, surprisingly fast for one with his peculiar gait, and I lost sight of him in the crowd.

I decided again that it was time to leave, propriety be damned. I scanned the room once more, and saw West not far away. He saw me at the same moment and came over.

"Fleeing the field already, Charles? I must say, you did rather have to run the gauntlet, didn't you? The formidable Mrs. H., then Hobson, then Quarrington. Well, if you want an accomplice, I'm available."

I hesitated. I had an idea that what he really wanted was to question me about what I might have said to Hobson. What *had* I said to him about West? My memory was already growing fuzzy on this point. I looked around for Alma, but could no longer see her. Escape was paramount. "All right, Herbert," I said. "Let's go."

After a flurry of brief encounters with some of West's professors and fellow students, he and I left the Halsey residence together. "I've had a bellyful of this posturing," he said. "I would suggest a brain-clearing session, except that my brain is still clear from the last one. But come along to my place, and we can kill the afternoon in some agreeable way. I think it needs killing. I go on duty at the hospital at eight, so that gives us several hours. I have some new gramophone records. And I can come up with a meal of some sort. Or did you partake of the bounty we are leaving?"

"Actually, I didn't eat a thing," I reassured him. "And yes, I am rather hungry."

"I saw you talking with Hobson," West observed as we reached the sidewalk. "He seemed excited. What was he going on about, anyway?"

"The Library," I replied. "He claims he can't find anything there, and thinks we librarians should use logic. Oh, and he says you have good hands."

He gave me an amused look. "Good hands, eh? That would be a supreme compliment, coming from that old ogre, if he weren't the most ham-fisted of a bad lot. Hobson won't admit it, of course, but he's learned a thing or two from *me*. What did Quarrington want?"

"I'm not sure what he wanted. He's certainly a character, isn't he?"

"A veritable paragon of idiosyncrasy," said West, who seemed to be in an extraordinarily good mood, for some reason. "He didn't say – or ask you – anything about me, did he?"

"You? No, not at all. Why should he?" *He really is full of himself*, I thought.

If he was disappointed, he didn't show it. "Oh, no reason," he said. "It's just that with Quarrington, you never know what might come out."

"What's a catalyst, Herbert?" I asked.

He frowned, then looked amused. "Why on earth would you need to know that?"

"No reason, I just heard someone back there use that word. It sounded like a scientific discussion, so I thought you might know."

"A catalyst is an agent that precipitates a reaction, but without taking part in it. It makes something happen, but itself remains unchanged."

I thought about this for a while. "Thank you," I said. "It's still Greek to me though, or rather, if it were Greek, which I suspect it is, I would understand it, better than chemistry, anyway."

He laughed. "I do believe you're tipsy, my friend."

On the way to West's rooms, it occurred to me that I knew next to nothing about my friend's dealings with women. Newly alive to the delights of love as I was, I wanted others to experience them too. But he had never spoken of any romantic connection, except that vague reference to an Italian lady who had taught him how to cook. And yet he was exactly the sort of young man who would be considered a good catch – intelligent, articulate, wealthy and good looking.

I pondered this matter during our meal, which consisted of a rather good soup West called *minestrone,* and cold roast beef. As we were washing up the dishes, a mischievous impulse made me say, "You'll be a blessing for some emancipated woman, Herbert, when you get married. In between patients you can cook supper for her when she comes home from her work."

He gave me a strange look. "I have no plans to marry," he said. "My brothers are entirely capable of carrying on the family name."

"But there's more to it than that," I said. "What about... companionship, and love?"

"Sentimental nonsense!" He had regained his usual ironic manner. "I would rather put my energy into my scientific work."

"All right, but what about the physiological side of things? I know how keen you are on physical fitness and health. Isn't it true that a man has certain needs that must be fulfilled if ill-health is to be avoided?"

He busied himself in the pantry, evidently finding a pressing need to reorganize its contents. "Don't you concern yourself about my health, Charles," he said indistinctly from its depths. "I know more about physiology and anatomy and all that stuff than you ever will, and I assure you I'm perfectly healthy. Now, look what I found." He emerged triumphant, holding a bottle. "A survivor from my latest brain-clearing. Not enough to do any damage, but it will nicely accompany that new gramophone record by Caruso, don't you think? Find some glasses."

"But you're going on duty in a couple of hours!"

"No matter, Charles. Moderation is my watchword. Glasses."

While the great Italian sang arias by Verdi and Puccini, we sipped Scotch and West spoke of his researches. He was growing impatient to make some progress, but had no control over the availability of suitable research material. "Ah well, winter is a good time for deaths. Corpses resulting from death by exposure might be especially suitable for our purposes. So we should keep our hopes up."

I thought as I raised my glass to this sentiment that, given his peculiar preoccupations, it was perhaps just as well that West was not romantically inclined. Not many nice young ladies would be eager to socialize with this elegant fellow if they knew what he did in his free time. But then I remembered that on a few occasions he had disappeared for several days, saying that he was going to Boston on business. Perhaps the 'business' involved female companionship he did not wish to talk about. In any case, the matter was, for the time being, closed.

Soon after this, we had news of the Wild Man that even West could not ignore. After a week of extreme cold, the absence of smoke from a farmhouse five miles from Arkham attracted the attention of neighbours. On investigating they found a scene of horror: the farmer lying dead in a pool of blood in the upstairs hallway of the house, his wife in a similar condition on their bed. A mattock, doubtless the very one stolen months before from Summers farm, lay on the floor. And in a corner of the room, cowering as though trying to push himself through the walls, was a hairy, grotesque creature with blood in his hair and beard and splashed liberally on the ragged clothing he wore. He was making inarticulate animal sounds and clutching something to his chest. It was an infant, evidently the child of the dead farmer and his wife. It too was dead, with bite marks on its neck and face. One of the ears was chewed and torn.

Sickened, the neighbours left two of their number to make sure the creature did not escape. The others returned as quickly as possible with reinforcements, including members of the Arkham police force. The man in the corner did not try to run away, but went with his captors willingly. The only time he showed any resistance at all was when they took the child's corpse away. Then he seemed inclined to grow savage once more, but was quickly subdued.

Questioning was useless, for he never spoke. If the grunts and ululations he emitted had any meanings, they remained known to him alone. He was declared insane and incarcerated in Sefton Asylum.

A week later, I had an unexpected visit from West. He looked pale and wretched. If it had been anyone else, I would have thought him unwell, but West was never sick. I prepared to broach once more the subject of John Hocks and the murders. It had been a few weeks since we had done an experiment, and I was determined to clear things up between us before I would participate in another.

I need not have bothered. "It was Hocks after all," he said, and I understood that his sickly appearance must have been the result of having to admit that he had been wrong.

"How do you know that?" I asked, more gently than the circumstances warranted.

"One of my professors consults to Sefton occasionally. He was there when they brought in the so-called Wild Man, and for some reason decided that it would be instructive for us students to see him. So we made a little field trip to the ward for hopeless cases. Each of us took a turn at peering through the little window in the door of his cell. By that time they had cleaned him up and shaved off the beard, so I recognized him. It was Hocks, all right." He stopped speaking and sat staring at the floor, chin propped on hands, elbows on knees.

I digested this information for a few moments. "Did anyone else recognize him?"

West shook his head. "No, fortunately for us. When the police arrested him at that farmhouse, I suppose he was unrecognizable. No one else made the connection between the terrible Wild Man and the late John Hocks, itinerant labourer. With luck he'll never regain the power of speech. You pray, don't you Charles? So pray that Hocks remains mute. And that the good people at Sefton don't let him escape."

"Yes, I suppose that would be – "

He continued as if I had not spoken. "He stared right at me." West looked more unsettled than I had ever seen him. "Charles, he knew me."

He got up and left without another word.

It was surprising how quickly the matter of Hocks faded from our minds once he was incarcerated. West resumed his experiments, and I continued to assist him. Hocks could do no further harm, I reasoned, and by remaining in West's confidence I could perhaps intervene to prevent another horror.

The rest of 1912 passed in a happy blur, largely due to my liaison with Alma, with its exciting mixture of openness and secrecy.

There were long periods when I saw little of West. He was entering the final stretch of his medical education, and what with upper-level classes at the Medical School and interning at St. Mary's had little time to spare. "I think they try to eliminate the weakest of us by sheer volume of work," he said once, laughing. "Fortunately I am equal to it, but only just." Indeed, he looked thinner and a little worn.

During this time, West's attitude toward Allan Halsey changed from a good-humoured contempt to something approaching hatred. His references to the man became quite vitriolic. When I asked him as to the reason for this he replied only that the Dean's unprogressive attitude toward research was increasingly galling to him, as his own knowledge of medicine increased. He could see further possibilities for scientific progress if sufficient boldness were employed. "It's not just me he has thwarted," he said. "There are one or two fellows in the School with great original ideas they haven't been able to test, all because Halsey won't let them use the resources here at Miskatonic. You may not realize it, Charles, but this college has first-class facilities for medical research, and they're being wasted because of this nincompoop Halsey and his antediluvian ideas."

I had never allowed myself to use my relationship with Alma for West's sake, but I did so now. Discreetly, I inquired as to whether she was aware of any increase in the antipathy that had always existed between her father and his most troublesome student.

"You know I don't usually discuss such things with Papa," she said, frowning a little. "But now that you mention it, I overheard him tell one of the other professors recently that "if West manages to graduate before I find it necessary to discipline him again it will be a miracle." Then he said that his hands are tied by Hiram West. Do you have any idea what he could have meant by that?"

I said I did not, but I had suspicions, which I voiced the next time I saw West. "So Father is putting pressure on Halsey," he said. "I wasn't aware of that, but I'm not surprised. You know he's been making generous donations to Miskatonic since last year. Being what he is, it's natural that he would take a proprietary attitude. I suppose Halsey thinks I've been taking advantage of the situation. Well, I suppose I have, but in ignorance." He fell silent, looking thoughtful.

I wondered if West was engaged in unorthodox activities besides those of which I was aware. When I ventured to ask him, he was cagey. "Well, it depends on what you would consider unorthodox. I do use my lab for other things besides the revivifications, you know. And Halsey thinks anything is unorthodox if he wouldn't do it himself. Which includes just about anything worth doing."

Several weeks later, I was surprised to be called into Peter Runcible's office, and even more surprised to see Dean Allan Halsey there. Despite my alarm, I managed to retain a calm exterior.

"Mr. Milburn, I understand you're acquainted with Dean Halsey," said Runcible. "He has asked me to allow him to use my office this afternoon so that he may confer with you."

He made effusive farewells to Halsey and left, giving me a look of mingled amusement and curiosity. If he had not closed the door, I would have presumed to do it myself, remembering the acoustical quirk that allowed listeners in the main office to hear what was being said in this one.

Halsey looked at me in silence for a moment without speaking. His rather muddy grey eyes were surrounded by wrinkles. I thought he looked older and wearier than the man I had been introduced to several months before.

"Mr. Milburn," he began, "I came here to talk to you, instead of summoning you to my office, because I wish to approach a delicate matter with the utmost discretion."

I said nothing. After a moment he continued, "I believe you are acquainted with Mr. Herbert West, a student at the Medical School."

"I know Mr. West, yes," I replied, wondering where this was leading.

"You may be aware, then, that he is in a rather equivocal position at the School."

"No indeed. My impression is that he is nearing the completion of his studies and hopes to qualify as a physician next year."

"Quite so, Mr. Milburn. But only if we at the School are satisfied that he does not violate the standards of conduct we demand of our students."

"I'm not sure I understand you, Dr. Halsey."

"Let me put it plainly. Herbert West is suspected of unorthodox, indeed, illegal activities in connection with some extracurricular research he has taken on. Naturally, this would prejudice his chances of qualifying as a licensed physician."

I was not sure what response he expected, so I made none, merely looked attentive and a little puzzled. Strangely, I was not nervous. After a moment, he went on.

"What we need is proof of West's involvement in these activities. At present we have only suspicions."

"I'm sorry, Dr. Halsey," I said. "I do not believe I can help you in any way. As you know, I am a cataloguer here at the Library. My field is classics. I am acquainted with Mr. West, but have no other connection to the Medical School."

He smiled. "Mrs. Halsey recently reminded me of your somewhat... unfortunate family circumstances, Mr. Milburn. I seem to recall that your father left very little after his sad demise."

"That's my private business, sir. I don't see what it has to do with this 'delicate matter' of yours."

"Now, now, Mr. Milburn. This is no time to pretend ignorance. I don't imagine that Miskatonic pays its junior librarians a very princely salary, does it? I believe you may be in a position to furnish me with information, in which case I think you would see a small but significant increase in your earnings. What do you say?"

I felt exactly as though I had been wrapped in warm dreamy sleep and was naked and shivering with cold water dripping from me. It took me a while to find my voice.

"Dr. Halsey," I said, getting to my feet. "I will not dignify your suggestion with a reply. I consider it an insult. I think this interview is at an end."

"Not so fast, young man," he said. He was grinning unpleasantly. "You're not lily-white yourself, you know."

I stopped and waited for him to continue. I could feel my entire body shake with each heartbeat, and wondered if he could see that.

"On a certain night last October, you were observed in attendance at an event which included illegal fighting and gambling. Do you deny this?"

"Yes, I do deny it." I thought quickly. There had been students from Miskatonic at the prizefight, and even some faculty members. If Halsey was trying to use information from such sources against me, he was grasping at straws. But the knowledge that someone had bothered to notice and report my presence was troubling.

It seemed that Halsey was aware of how ineffectual his half-threat was, for he did not pursue it.

"Very well, Mr. Milburn," he said, standing up. "But should you reconsider, my offer stands. I can be reached at the Medical School. And let me offer you two pieces of advice as well. First, stay away from Herbert West. He's not a good companion for a young fellow who has a long way to go if he wants to rebuild his standing in the world. And second – " he paused in the doorway, giving me a baleful look, "stay away from my daughter."

I felt an eruption of rage. I wanted to hit him, to deliver to that self-satisfied countenance just one punch of the sort that Buck Robinson had landed on Kid O'Brien. I relished the crunch of cartilage, the spurt of blood. But of course I did nothing of the kind. Instead, I said, "Dr. Halsey, I would like to make two things clear to you. First, Herbert West is my friend. Second, your daughter Alma is also my friend and colleague, and is of an age when she no longer needs your permission to choose her associates. Now I will bid you good day."

I returned to my alcove on legs that had turned to rubber. My limp had worsened and I was glad I had no farther to go before I collapsed in my chair. I did not know what I would do if Halsey followed me, but I heard the outer door of the office slam, so assumed he had gone.

I left a note in West's mailbox on my way home, asking him to come see me about an urgent matter. Several hours later he entered my door, bringing with him a wave of rain-washed air. He had just come from the hospital and looked as tired as I had ever seen him. But the weariness fell away as I began my story.

When I came to the part about the opportunity I had been given to better myself at his expense, he jumped up and exclaimed, "The devil! He tried to bribe you! This is serious, Charles. He's never been this methodical before. Go on."

He paced around the little room while I continued my narrative. When I had finished he said, "This has gone too far, by God! Until now I've treated Halsey like an obstacle to be circumvented. But this calls for something more." He fell silent, obviously deep in thought.

"Why do you suppose he's doing this? After all, you'll be finished at the School in less than a year. Then you can do whatever research you like. So why should he persecute you like this?"

"It's exactly because I'm nearly finished that he's redoubling his efforts," said West. "He knows it's his last chance to blacken my reputation."

"But why? Why should he want to blacken you?"

"Allan Halsey is revered as the Student's Friend and Mentor, a real father figure. Well, he's that only for the students who toady to him and do everything his way. For them he opens the laboratories, hands out the money, makes the introductions. But should anyone suggest that there might be another road that should be tried, one that may or may not prove to be a dead end, he tells that person not to waste his time, but to return to the well-traveled Halsey Highway. And yet it is exactly on those side paths that real scientific progress is to be made."

I had heard this, or variants of it, many times before. But it wasn't the answer to my question.

"I know that, Herbert, but what is it that he has against you specifically? You've said that there are others in your class who want to do unconventional research, but were discouraged. Does Halsey go after them like this?"

"No he doesn't. As to why he singles me out, I think there are a number of reasons. One is that he doesn't approve of the *parvenu* son of an undertaker presuming to join the ranks of the medical elite. And the fact that my father has become a benefactor of Miskatonic galls him.

"Another thing is that I got started on my revivification work early – in my first year. Halsey has this notion that first year students should speak only when spoken to and think only what they are told to think. Anyone who dares to *suggest* something – anything at all – is branded a renegade. So when I started with the animals practically the minute I got into the lab he nearly went apoplectic. Luckily for me a couple of the less fossilized professors spoke up for me – he's just a boy, there's lots of time to shape him into the correct mould, etc., etc. *ad nauseam*. Well, I didn't agree with them, but at least it got me a reprieve. Anyway, ever since then Halsey has had it in for me personally, and now he's realized that this is his last chance to squeeze me."

Again he fell silent. Some moments later he said, "I think I have it. For the next few months we'll have to avoid experiments, unless we're lucky enough to get a perfect specimen. The dubious ones aren't worth the risk. And I'll be a model of discretion, toadying to Halsey every chance I get. In the long run it will be worth the lost research time. Also seeing the old bastard's disappointment at the failure of his plot. But that's not enough..."

"What do you mean?"

"Well, to put it bluntly, I want revenge. When the Dean of the Medical School stoops to such sleazy measures to pursue a personal vendetta against one of his own students, avoidance is not enough. I have to give him something to remember me by."

He took several more turns around my room, occasionally muttering things like, "No, that's no good – too crude, for one thing," and, "That would take too long." At one point he threw out an observation, "Every man has a secret or two. Even you, Charles. So don't imagine Halsey is exempt. It's just a matter of..."

A moment later, his eyes lit up. "That's it, of course! And he owes me one, I think. Absolutely! Look, Charles, I must go now. Don't worry, I don't think he'll trouble you again. Not as long as I keep my nose clean, and for the next three months it'll be the cleanest nose in Arkham!"

I heard him laughing as he ran down the stairs.

In the next several months, West and I did only one experiment. The subject was the victim of a factory accident. His arm had been cut off by a piece of machinery and he had died of blood loss.

"We can't pass this one up," said West. "You see, the only thing wrong with him is blood loss. And the missing limb, of course. But the essential mechanism is intact. The only thing I'll have to do is tie off the blood vessels to the arm before we run in the fluid."

We were more than ordinarily cautious, reconnoitering the situation scrupulously before our every move. We blocked any cracks through which light could leak out of the laboratory with fanatical care. We not only fastened restraints on the corpse, but one of my jobs was to stand by with a carefully fashioned gag, in case of untoward vocalizations. We thought our chances of escaping undetected were better than average, since Dean Halsey was out of town that week.

The subject, Albert Whidbey, was one of our more promising cases. Under the influence of West's revivifying fluid, he readily showed signs of life. Even though I had seen the phenomenon several times before, I felt once again that jolt of the miraculous at the fact of life coming from death under the hands of my friend.

I was able nearly to have a conversation with Whidbey, although it was rather like trying to hold an intelligent dialogue in shouts with someone a hundred yards away. Much was lost in some cognitive gulf that lay between him and me. In response to my questions and promptings, he spoke of a light, of flying, of heavenly music. He spoke of seeing his mother and father, "...so lovely, they looked, all young and happy." Then his face creased and he began to cry.

Shortly after this began the drifting away that we had seen several times before. Although the vital signs had been strong and stable, an inexorable weakening began, which continued despite all of West's efforts. He had developed a substance that he had hoped would counteract this fading, but it proved utterly ineffectual in this case. I hoped Whidbey had managed to find his way back to the place of light and music, but the look of terror that came over his face in his last seconds made me shiver.

After we had returned the body to the morgue and cleared away the evidence of the experiment, West said, "I wish I knew what causes that fading away. It almost seems willed, but that can't be..."

Still thinking about Whidbey's words, I said, "Perhaps they want to go back to... whatever lies beyond. Maybe once someone has disconnected from the world he doesn't want to come back. Don't you think that suggests there's something besides the physical mechanism? You seem to be able to re-start that, but without the participation of the person's so– the will, I mean, life simply cannot be sustained. Maybe you need to find a subject with more force of will."

West gave me a look of mingled annoyance and amusement. "Certainly something interferes with the physical mechanism, but I'll bet you anything it's a physical something. The interesting thing is that it manifests the same way, regardless of the cause of the first death." He sighed. "It's too bad we have to be so damned careful these days. I'd like to gather a lot more data on this phenomenon. Oh well, just a few more months."

"You don't intend to stay in Arkham after graduation, surely?" My question sounded casual, but I was certain that he would be keen to get away from the place where his talents were undervalued. With his abilities, the field would be open to him, whatever the blots on his academic record. I tried not to think of how empty Arkham would be without him.

"Why not?" He seemed puzzled at my question. "For one thing, it would be a good place to set up a practice, for an energetic fellow like me, anyway. Bolton is growing fast and will supply no end of patients. Foreigners, of course, but so what? A body is a body. From what I've seen, they're all pretty much the same inside. Miskatonic's facilities are superb, and old Halsey can't last forever. So it will do for a start."

Herbert West graduated from Miskatonic University's Medical School in the spring of 1913. The commencement ceremonies were held at the beginning of June. Knowing West's dislike of what he called posturing, I was surprised to receive an invitation to attend the function as his guest. I was even more surprised that he had invited Alma as well, and furthermore, that she had accepted.

On a perfect June day, rare in misty, muggy Arkham, Alma and I found ourselves in Miskatonic's Convocation Hall. Alma was beautiful in a white dress of some filmy material, discreetly ruffled, with a neckline that fell just below her collarbones. With this she wore a pair of shoes of white kid leather. I can still visualize those shoes, with their squarish toes, ankle straps and louis heels. At the sight of them, and of Alma's neatly-turned ankles, encased in white silk stockings, I felt a wave of pure lust wash over me. If it had been anyone but West who was graduating that day I would have murmured to her that we must go, immediately, now. I would have taken her arm and marched her out of the hall and to my rooms. Instead, I looked studiously at the floor and told myself that anticipation would sweeten the fruits later on.

The dignitaries of the Medical School, in full academic regalia, had assembled on the stage. Also present were a number of ladies, chief among whom was Alma's mother, splendidly hatted and gowned. Her imperious glance raked over the lesser females around her, as if she was on the lookout for an excuse to banish a non-conformer from the ranks of the elect. In the audience I saw Hiram West with his two older sons and the usual entourage. At the back of the hall I caught a glimpse of Professor Quarrington.

The University Marching Band struck up one of Elgar's *Pomp and Circumstance* marches, and the graduates filed in to take their places in the front rows. Several speeches followed, full of sonorous phrases and venerable platitudes. I listened only to the rise and fall of the speakers' voices, amusing myself with the notion that it was rather like following the bass line in a piece of Baroque music. I looked at Alma's shoes, and at the firm line of her jaw, and the sweet curve of her neck and the way the little tendrils of flaxen hair had come loose from the knot at the back of her head. My thoughts were very pleasant, and later I was glad to have had this drowsy interlude, because shortly afterward, all Hell broke loose.

The graduates were called in alphabetical order, so it was some time before West's name came up. I sat watching the Cranes and the Edgars and the Fillmores and the Jacksons go up to the stage to receive their diplomas from the Dean. West had not spoken to me again of his plan for revenge on Dean Halsey, but I knew him well enough by now not to suppose that he had abandoned it.

Finally, I heard the name Herbert Francis West. I had not known what his middle name was, and while I was pondering this detail, West stepped lightly onto the stage and walked toward the Dean. His academic gown fitted him as though it had been custom made, which it probably was. The black formal drapery, and even the ridiculous 'mortar board' suited his fair colouring to perfection. Standing before Halsey and the other dignitaries, he put me in mind of some prince of Renaissance Italy, a Medici or a Borgia.

He took the diploma from Halsey with a courtly bow which was entirely proper, if a little flamboyant. But here the familiar ritual was broken, for instead of grasping the Dean's hand briefly in his own and departing, West handed something to Halsey. It was a flat rectangular object, nearly a foot square. I wondered how West had managed to conceal it so well throughout the proceedings. Was it perhaps a peace offering of some sort? That seemed unlikely.

Now he was saying something to the Dean, who was beginning to look flustered. West wore a smile as angelic as I had ever seen on his face, and was utterly at ease despite the slight disturbance he had created, that was even now escalating into something else.

For as Dean Allan Halsey looked at whatever it was that West had given him, his face turned deathly pale and seemed to crumble. One hand clutched at his chest. He looked wildly around, as though for help which did not come. Mrs. Halsey, pushing aside a gaggle of ladies, rushed to her husband's side. Moments later she let out a piercing cry and fainted. Two other ladies promptly followed suit. Several professors crowded around to see the cause of the distress. A murmur broke out among them as the object was passed from hand to hand. For a full minute, utter pandemonium reigned on the stage. Finally, one or two of the professors galvanized the others into action. Mrs. Halsey and the other prostrate ladies were carried off the stage, presumably to be revived with smelling salts. Someone took the Dean over to a chair and gave him a glass of water. West, in the meantime, had left the stage and the hall. No one had thought to stop him.

"I must go to Papa," said Alma, looking thoroughly upset. I took her arm and helped her to the stage. She bent over her father and asked him if he was all right. I could hear the man who had given him the water reassuring her. He sounded like a practicing physician. Having nothing to do for a moment, I looked around the stage where the dignified order of academic ritual had so utterly given way to chaos. I saw something lying on the lectern, among the few diplomas which had not yet been awarded. Surely this was the cause of all the distress, the thing that West had given to Halsey? I went over, but had only a fleeting glimpse of the object before some professor picked it up with a glare at me and thrust it under his gown. That glimpse was enough, however.

It was a large photograph, tastefully framed, showing, in unmistakable detail, Dean Allan Halsey, in evening dress which was seriously askew, with a laurel wreath tilted rakishly over one eye. He balanced on his knee a buxom young woman whose lacy costume left very little to the imagination. She held a glass in her hand, and he seemed to be getting ready to let her take a puff on the fat cigar he held in his – the hand that was not busy fondling one of her breasts.

Alma had finished commiserating with her father. Halsey appeared a little healthier, but not much. I heard some muttering among the professors to the effect that the show had to go on. Finally, the Dean, still in near-shock, was led away. I escorted Alma off the stage, and Professor Hobson called out the name John George Willson.

"Did you find out what happened to him?" Alma whispered to me. "It was something West gave him. Did you see it?"

"No," I lied. "Someone picked it up before I could see. I'll try to find out later."

I was torn between my responsibility to Alma and my intense curiosity as to how West had managed to get that photograph. To my relief, Alma had regained her normal decisive manner. "I'm going straight to the parents' house," she said. "They were taking them both there. No, it would be better if you didn't come. But come to my place tonight." She hurried away.

I made directly for West's rooms. His academic regalia had been flung onto the back of an armchair, and he was stretched out on the sofa, laughing.

"It worked like magic!" he cried. "Oh Charles, it was priceless! The look on that smug old bastard's face! It was one of the best moments of my life."

I threw away my nagging scruples and joined in his laughter. When it had subsided a little, I asked, "Herbert, how on earth, where on earth did you get that photograph?"

"Well," he began, clearly relishing the revelation. "I wanted to do something that would deflate the pompous old windbag, something public, so the graduation ceremony suggested itself. When I remembered that I would be wearing academic dress, I realized I could smuggle something fairly large onto the stage undetected. Really, it's a wonder there aren't more knifings or shootings among academics, given the grudges one finds. At first I thought of something in the anatomical line, an embalmed body part of some sort. But that wouldn't have redounded well on me, since what I wanted was to make him look bad but leave myself untouched. Then I remembered a rumour I had heard, that Halsey has a roving eye, and enjoys spirited entertainment on occasion. Now, there's a club in Boston, the Gai Paree Club, it's called. It caters to an exclusive clientele – businessmen, mostly. And professors too, it seems." He began to laugh again.

"But how did you get the photograph? Did you go to this club?"

"Not I," he said. "Not my scene at all. But, well, one of my brothers owns the place. I've always thought it a vulgar enterprise, but in this case it was certainly useful. Jeremy owed me a favour – don't ask why because I won't tell you. I asked him to find out if Halsey was one of his customers. It couldn't have been easier. You see what I meant when I said that every man has his secrets. Let this be a lesson to you, young fellow," he said, wagging a finger at me. "Celibacy may be dull, but it has its uses. But now it's time for a celebratory libation."

Even as I raised my glass to my lips, I remembered Alma and began to feel uneasy. She certainly had nothing to celebrate. "You really shouldn't have invited Alma," I said. "I know how you feel about Dean Halsey, but she had nothing to do with that bribe and it upset her to see her father like that."

West looked a little uncomfortable. "I have to admit I was thinking more of the effect on him of knowing she was there than the reverse. And anyway, she has you to administer comfort and commiseration."

"Yes she does, and I would suggest you keep that in mind. In fact, I really ought to be going now."

West raised his glass mockingly. "Far be it from me to deny comfort to a lady in distress."

But before I left, I could not resist asking a final question. "What did you say to Halsey when you handed him that thing?"

"I merely commented on how refreshing it was to find that he, too, was doing some extracurricular research of an unorthodox sort, except that his was in the field of anatomy."

The Commencement Incident, as it came to be called, had far-reaching consequences for many that were on the platform that day, but not for Herbert West. He had hit upon exactly the right scheme. The target of his revenge had been struck hard, in public, but nothing much could be brought home to him. Diploma in hand, he had vanished, unscathed.

Feeble attempts were made by the administration to hush up the scandal, but enough people had seen the damning photograph that it was soon general knowledge that the Dean of Medicine had been caught *in flagrante delicto*. It was not so much that he had been disporting himself in a house of ill-repute (albeit a high-class one), but that his misdemeanour had been displayed to the community. The academic world is prepared to wink at the peccadilloes of its leaders, but not when they are thrust under its collective nose in such an unmistakable way.

Allan Halsey took an extended leave of absence from his duties, and eventually retired early from the post he had held for twenty years. Mrs. Halsey suffered a long period of ill-health, during which her usually full program of social affairs was abandoned, much to the relief of matrons lower on the Arkham pecking order, over whom she had ruled with a rod of iron. In the present day a divorce would have ensued, but these were uncommon in 1913. The Halseys retreated from the public eye to deal with their troubles.

Alma took it harder than I ever would have imagined. For all her coolness and flippant remarks about both her parents, her ties to them and to the social order of Arkham, were deep. The worst part of the situation for her was that there seemed to be no one who was clearly the wronged party. As objectively as I could, I explained that her father had pursued a course of action against West that was unethical at best. I agreed that West's means of taking revenge were unsportsmanlike and demonstrated a lack of maturity on his part but, the fact remained that her father had put himself into the compromising situation shown in the photograph. She was fair-minded enough to acknowledge this, but that did not diminish her resentment toward West.

"You must tell me, Charles, did you have anything to do with this business?" She looked so downcast, so unlike her usual vivid self, that I answered as honestly as I could.

"No, Alma. West said something about revenge at one point, when he was angry with your father. But I didn't realize he was going to do anything until he actually did it."

"But surely you must have guessed! You know him better than I, and I know he doesn't make empty threats. You should have asked him, followed him, something!" She covered her face with her hands. "I just can't see beyond this thing. Everyone seems bitter and evil and uncharitable." She looked at me with sudden fierceness. "Charles, you must stop associating with Herbert West! I warned you about him from the first, and now he's shown just what sort of person he is – absolutely without scruples, who will do anything to achieve his ends, without regard for the harm he does. Consider, why did he specially invite me to that ceremony? So I could see my father and mother in distress, so Papa would know I had been there to see. And you've been very cagey when I've asked you how he got that photograph, but I'm certain it was through some unsavoury connection. I must ask you, Charles – please drop him!"

"He's my friend, Alma. He's done me no harm."

"But he's done me harm! And I'm more than your friend."

I felt a sinking of the heart. From the first, I had feared that some day I would be asked to choose between Alma and West. But I needed them both. I tried to hedge.

"Look, Alma, I know how badly you feel about all this. I can't expect you to be kindly disposed toward West after this. But I honestly cannot promise you to end my friendship with him. Please don't make me choose between you."

She laughed bitterly. "Just now I'm in no position to do that. If I drive you away, I'll be altogether friendless. I'm not strong enough for that." She sighed. "Well, enough of this for now. I'm too tired to think any more."

I saw her to her bed, but did not stay. As I left her house, I considered going back to West's, but for Alma's sake refrained and went home instead.

♦ **8** ♦

That summer West busied himself with establishing a practice in Arkham. One of the first things he did was to look for a suitable location. After some searching he purchased a large lot on Boundary Street, close to St. Mary's Hospital and incidentally not far from the potter's field at Hangman's Hill. When I asked whether this proximity was intentional, he replied, "Not really. But one never knows when it might be necessary to do a little digging."

He immediately hired workmen to build a house with suitable premises for a physician, complete with consulting room, surgery and living quarters. "I shall live over the shop, Charles," he said. "At first, anyway. It suits me perfectly to have everything in one place."

A few months later, West gave me a tour of the completed structure. "You must see the cellar first," he insisted. The cellar looked unremarkable, even a little small, I thought, until West opened a door concealed by a set of shelves and escorted me into a modern laboratory. It was every bit as well-furnished as the one at the Medical School, where we had revivified Kid O'Brien.

"Father floated me a rather generous loan," said West, "so I decided to have all this installed immediately. The workmen for this part were from Boston, and were paid extra for discretion. I expect to spend many productive hours here."

At the end of a short hall was an iron door which proved to belong to an incinerator, of the latest and most efficient model, West reassured me. "The chimney runs underground and pops up in the middle of the shrubbery at the back of the property – just where one might expect rubbish to be burned."

West's living quarters on the second floor were also something of a revelation. He had disposed of most of the furniture from his old rooms, and had made several trips to Boston in the course of outfitting his new premises, and at least one to New York City. "The old stuff belonged to my grandfather, and was relegated to the attic when the Pater felt it was no longer worthy of him," he said. "But I've kept some of the better pieces."

We began with the sitting room. Near the fireplace, two sofas and a number of chairs and small tables formed a convivial group. At the far end of the room was a piano, its dark curving shape contrasting pleasingly with the rectilinear forms of the other pieces. On the near wall an old mirror gave back the scene in a watery, wavery reflection.

With the exception of a fine cabinet of inlaid woods in geometric patterns, the furniture was nearly all dark, plain and functional, both the familiar New England pieces from West's grandfather and the more recent ones. The somberness was only slightly relieved by the white walls and ceiling, and a few touches of brilliant colour in the carpets, lamps and ornamental glass objects. On the mantel was a clock of ebony and silver, and a pair of silver candlesticks of elaborate and sinuous shape. The windows were uncurtained, but in each one hung a panel of leaded glass, clear and coloured, in graceful geometric patterns through which twined shapes of leaves and flowers, like vines on a trellis.

At first, I found it all rather oppressive, almost gloomy. Only when West moved past me into the centre of the room did I perceive that, consciously or not, he had created a perfect setting for himself. The effect, I thought then, was one of brilliance in darkness. With him as its focus the room was suddenly complete and balanced.

"It's quite... impressive," I said finally. "But I didn't know you play the piano, Herbert."

"I don't," he replied. "It was my mother's. My father had no use for it, so I relieved him of it some years ago. It's been in a warehouse since then. Now I can finally give it an appropriate home."

The dining room was a pleasant surprise. Its walls featured panels painted in an abstract pattern in cream and various shades of yellow and green, reminiscent of reeds or papyrus. Here and there were fanciful golden flowers, and insects like dragonflies. The furniture was of golden oak, light and graceful with slightly curving lines. To my exclamations of admiration, West said only, "I hired someone to design this. An artistic French lady. At least, her name was French, but I have some doubts as to its authenticity. Her accent had a way of slipping over to this side of the Atlantic. But she did quite well with this room, I think."

"She did indeed," I said. "It puts me in mind of a sunny afternoon on a river. You will have to have some splendid dinners, Herbert, to do it justice."

"First I need to hire a housekeeper."

Once the "incomparable Mrs. Fisk" (as West called her) was found and installed, he set a date for his housewarming. He invited the few friends he had made at the Medical School, including several students and one or two faculty members who had been sympathetic to some of his ideas. He also invited me, and, surprisingly, Alma. I wondered whether this was merely a diplomatic gesture, a genuine attempt to establish cordial relations, or merely a quirk of fancy on West's part. In any case, it was not put to the test, since she refused to go.

"I can't," she said to me, after writing a terse but polite note of refusal. "If things were different, I'd enjoy exchanging repartee with Mr. West. But right now, I'd either get angry and make a scene, or just feel alienated." She made no objections to my attending, but I felt guilty nevertheless.

The dinner was quite a success. The meal was excellent and the wines equal to it. West's gift for maintaining a conversation drew me into the mainly medically-oriented group. Naturally, our private research was never mentioned, but some of the things we had discussed over the years, such as the existence of the soul and the ethical aspects of research on human subjects, were thrashed out with enthusiasm.

West declared unequivocally that it was perfectly legitimate to use human beings as research material, provided that researchers adhered to standards. Individuals who are otherwise a drain on society, such as the insane and incorrigible criminals, would be ideal for the purpose, he said. I suspected that he was exaggerating for effect, and made no comment, although I did think fleetingly of John Hocks. One or two of the others responded, vigorously opposing what they called a barbaric notion.

"I hope for your sake, West, that if by some mischance you end up in the asylum or in jail, this idea of yours isn't in force. Or would you consider it an instance of justice in action?" This provocative observation was made by John Billington, a young man in his final year of studies at the Medical School, and one of whom I had heard West speak highly several times.

West considered for a moment. "If the mischance, as you call it, was that of insanity or criminal behaviour, I suppose it would be justice. The question is whether it's better for the state to keep such individuals incarcerated at public expense, in an utterly pointless existence, or to employ them for the greater good. I would rather be experimented upon for a few weeks and mercifully dispatched, than imprisoned for endless years."

Billington did not appear convinced. "I wonder if you would change your mind if it really came to that point, West," he said, looking serious. Then he smiled, saying, "But it's not likely to happen. I've never known anyone as hard-headed as you, and as for the law, I think you know how to elude it." A general laugh followed this comment, and the conversation turned to other things. But I did not laugh. A shadow had fallen over me, and it took nearly the rest of the evening for me to shake it off.

Over the next several months, West's practice attracted a rather diverse clientele, which included faculty from Miskatonic and some of the burghers of Arkham. Most of his patients were drawn from the immigrant population of neighbouring Bolton. The Arkhamites were attracted primarily by curiosity about the young man who had so discomfited the eminent Dean of Medicine. Those who found West's doctoring style congenial remained; the rest drifted away. The people from Bolton, I suspected, had heard some rumour of the young doctor who had been present at a prizefight nearly two years before, who had spoken Italian and had come to the aid of Tony Abruzzo. They were mainly farm and factory workers, and their illnesses and ailments were of the crude variety common among such folk. There were also occasional spectacular injuries such as that which had killed Albert Whidbey. Knife wounds, too, were not uncommon, incurred when passions were fueled by drink. West, as it turned out, preferred dealing with such repairs.

"I'm good at cutting and stitching," he said to me one evening when I had dropped by for a visit, "so the Bolton patients have confidence in me. The worthies of Arkham, on the other hand..." He laughed. "I suppose I lack the proper 'bedside manner.' I admit that I have little tolerance for people of privilege whose principal ailments are boredom and an inability to make up their minds.

"I'm no disciple of Drs. Freud or Jung, Charles. I do best with visible wounds and injuries. If there is nothing I can do, no treatment or drug that I can administer, I say so, and suggest that the individual try someone else. There are plenty of men, self-styled psychoanalysts, ready to listen *ad infinitum* to self-indulgent maunderings, charging a hefty hourly fee besides."

It soon appeared that West was destined for a surgical specialty. Several other Arkham doctors had called him in on difficult cases. His reputation was further enhanced by a terrible accident in which a train had struck an automobile at a crossing. One of the motorists had been killed outright, but the other two survived, largely, it appeared, through the efforts of young Dr. West.

Socially, young Dr. West was not much more available than Herbert West the medical student had been, despite the demand for his presence at social functions. He was hardly the heroic type, being rather slight and of no more than medium height, but he held himself and moved in such a way as to suggest that his was the most desirable size for a man, and that larger fellows were labouring under a handicap. He had clear-cut features, blond hair, a smile of extraordinary sweetness and remarkable grey eyes. The gold-rimmed spectacles he usually wore enhanced rather than detracted from his elegant appearance. Finally, he was known to be wealthy, and there clung to him an aura of danger and rakishness, resulting from the dubious reputations of his father and brothers, and, of course, from the Commencement Day Incident.

Whether West's practice absorbed the greater part of his energies, or whether his enthusiasm for revivification waned in the face of indifferent success, we did fewer experiments in the new premises than we had in the dank little room in the hospital. I was not particularly sorry. My doubts as to the value of our work and its ethical ramifications persisted, but I did not often voice them.

I knew he was engaged in experiments besides the revivifications. There was a room in the cellar laboratory that remained locked. When I asked him about it, West made its status clear.

"Those experiments may prove to be even more important, in the end, than my revivification work. But they are not at a stage where I am prepared to discuss them. Even with you, Charles."

He gestured toward a stack of notebooks piled on his desk. "I've gone over all the data," he said, "and I think I've reached the limit of what I can learn given my current methods. I have some ideas for improving the revivifying fluid, but they need further testing. The primary difficulty is the availability of subjects.

"I've concluded that it's possible successfully to revivify a corpse only within a limited time after death. Twelve hours or less. Less than six, really, if one expects any kind of cognitive ability to remain. As you know, in all our morgue cases, I made note of the time that had elapsed between death and the revivification attempt. This graph," he waved a sheet of paper at me, "shows a clear correlation between that and the success of the attempt, expressed in time between revivification and final death, qualified by other factors, such as ability to articulate. Our most successful case to date was O'Brien. It's too bad he was such a violently disposed individual. If you hadn't had to kill him he might have proved very interesting."

"But Herbert," I said, "what about John Hocks?"

"Ah yes, John Hocks... You know, Charles, I've thought a great deal about Hocks. All the evidence now points to the strong possibility that Hocks wasn't dead when they buried him."

"What?"

"It's the only explanation that fits. He revived beautifully. He was articulate, or at least he probably was. We didn't exactly get a chance to interview him, if you recall. Comparing him to the morgue specimens, I think he had died well within the twelve hour period. Since he was buried before noon on the day we exhumed him, he must have lain in that coffin alive for several hours, at least."

Like most people, I was horrified at the notion of premature burial. "Perhaps he wasn't dead at all, ever. Maybe he was alive when we... did the experiment, and that's why he – "

"No chance. Not at all. Charles, I know how to check for vital signs. There were none. He was dead. But it hadn't been thirty-six hours, as I first thought. Eight or ten is more likely. You may even be right – premature burial may have predisposed him to violence in some way. He must have died slowly of asphyxiation, rather than quickly by drowning. Ironic, isn't it, that our first two experiments should have been our most successful."

146

"So you think we need fresher specimens." By now I used his euphemisms without a second thought.

"Exactly. In revivification, as in cookery, freshness is all. I am sorry to conclude that the opportunity to reverse death is so limited. But at least it gives me a clear direction for future efforts."

"Well, surely that should be no trouble now. What about your patients – those who are close to death, I mean?"

If I had thought to shock West with this callous suggestion, I was disappointed. "Don't suppose I haven't thought of that," he said. "But on analysis, there are a number of reasons why patients, of the ordinary sort anyway, are no good for my purposes. You must agree that anyone who dies of a lengthy illness is not going to be a good candidate for revivification."

I did, with a shudder. These had been some of our most repulsive specimens. Only West's resolve had kept me from mutiny a couple of times.

"Second, patients rarely drop dead in their doctor's office. If they're well enough to arrive there on their own feet, they usually leave by the same means. If they need to be carried in, those who do the carrying usually stay to await results. Most often, people die at home or in the hospital. In both situations there are other people about and procedures that must be followed. By the time the body is left where we can get at it, too much time has passed. So despite my improved facilities, I am as handicapped as ever when it comes to suitable subjects. Now if I could grow them myself..." He broke off, with a laugh.

"Have you ever considered soliciting a volunteer? You know – ask someone to sign a statement that if they are ever killed in an accident, their body goes to you for scientific purposes."

"Now that is a good idea, Charles." West got up and began to pace, as he always did when excited. "A very good idea. It would have to be done carefully – the right sort of person, the right sort of approach. And there would be all sorts of noise from men like Halsey if word got out – indignation at the vulgarity of it, and so on. It would have to be someone strong-minded, too, not to be dissuaded by interfering busybodies. The trouble is, of course, that even if I were to find several prospective... donors, I couldn't count on any one of them being available at a given time, if ever. I can't expect people to kill themselves on my account." Suddenly, he struck the desk with his hand.

"Damn it, if only there was a sure way of getting the right sorts of subjects! I'm keen to start testing the improved formula, but there's no use wasting time on morgue denizens. It looks as though the only choices I have are to resign myself to taking much longer than I ever imagined, or – "

"Or what?"

"Why, engage in more illegal activities, of course." He smiled. "Don't panic, Charles. I'm not sure just what form they would take as yet. But I'll think of something.

"What we really need," he added, "is a war."

At the beginning of the new year, I took Alma to New York City. I had planned and saved for this trip since the previous summer. Since I was not prepared to give up my association with West for Alma's sake, I sought for ways to compensate for it. In no way did she expect compensation. I hoped that she would not recognize it for what it was, but I thought she was happy to be distracted.

I wanted the trip to be a memorable one. To this end I had been assiduous in my economies, and had amassed enough of a surplus to go first class. We stayed at the Waldorf-Astoria on 34th Street. Alma wanted to pay for her own room, but I overbore her. "This was my idea, and it's my treat, all the way. If you don't agree, we might as well turn around and go back to Arkham."

"All right, Charles," she laughed with some of her old lightheartedness. "Be the masterful man, if that's what you want. Just don't expect me to be putty in your hands."

The fall and early winter had been difficult for Alma. Despite her modern ideas, it is not easy in a place like Arkham to dissociate oneself from family scandals, especially for women. Several friends had dropped her outright. Others had asked questions under the guise of friendly concern that were clearly attempts to satisfy prurient curiosity. She had not spoken much of these things, but I often saw weariness and sorrow in her face, and she had grown thinner. I hoped these few days away would lift her spirits.

We were fortunate in the weather, which was cold but clear. At Alma's insistence we walked through the streets of Manhattan, looking into shops, buying food from street vendors, stopping at cafes and watching the crowds pass by. We made up stories about the people we saw. It was as though the city was a huge entertainment put on exclusively for us.

Later, in a hired carriage we toured around Central Park, watching the snow under the trees turn to that exquisite shade of blue that it assumes as a winter day changes into night. "Do you suppose this is why they call it *'l'heure bleue'* in France?" asked Alma.

"I wouldn't have thought they get enough snow there," I replied. "But it certainly fits, doesn't it?"

As the soft blueness deepened into night, I kissed her, first with tenderness, then with passion. "Let's go back to the hotel," she said.

I had arranged for a bottle of champagne to be delivered to Alma's room. We drank a toast to the New Year, and to each other. Then we went to bed.

This was the first time I had spent an entire night with Alma. In Arkham our need for discretion had caused me always to leave before dawn. Blissfully realizing this time that there was no need to go, I watched Alma sleeping beside me, a look of peace on her face, and felt a rush of tenderness. Enough of this limbo existence, I thought. Tell West to find himself another assistant. He doesn't really need you anyway. Marry Alma and get on with life. But later, this seemed only a dream I had had.

The following day we toured the Metropolitan Museum of Art, galleries and bookshops, where each of us found things to delight the other. How well I remember Alma coming over to me, eyes shining, leading me by the arm to some painting, saying, "Come here, Charles, you must see this, it's just the sort of thing you'd love..." And most of the time it was.

That evening we went to the Metropolitan Opera – Puccini's *Madama Butterfly*, with Geraldine Farrar and Giovanni Martinelli, Toscanini conducting. I had procured the tickets from my mother's New York relatives, who were subscribers. My hints became something like pleas as the weeks went by. Finally I received a letter saying that my cousins would be out of the country for part of the winter, and I could attend a performance in their place.

For a couple of provincials, Alma and I were rather well turned out. She wore a dark blue dress which clung to her figure, decorated with an intricate design in small shiny beads, a long velvet coat and matching hat. In addition to formal evening wear, I was decked out in a cape and silk top hat. These items belonged to West. He had pressed them upon me when he heard of this expedition.

"I have just what you need, Charles. Don't imagine you can get away with that shapeless tweed object you call a coat. That will only confirm what those NYC *parvenus* think of us parsimonious Yankees." He went into his bedroom and returned moments later with the cape. "I wore this to the Met. myself, once," he said, "to a performance of *Faust*."

It was, of course, black, but this was the only sober thing about it. The garment was cut so as to swirl about the wearer's ankles (calves, in my case, since I was nearly half a head taller than West). There were small lead weights sewn into the hem to exaggerate the effect of one's movements, West explained. The lining was of peacock blue silk. He made me put it on and take a turn around the room.

"No, no, no! You don't *clump* in a garment like this. Here, let me show you." He put the thing on and demonstrated the trick of the quick turn that made for a dramatic swirl and flash of blue. On West it looked entirely natural, but I resolved not to bother.

"You look magnificent, Charles!" Alma exclaimed as I met her in the lobby of our hotel. "Quite the man of the world."

I admitted that my finery was borrowed, and from whom. "Well, he does have good taste in clothes," she said. "I've never said otherwise."

Our seats were rather good ones, in the centre of the balcony. "Oh, it's like being inside a chocolate box!" said Alma, as we entered the maroon and gold splendour of the auditorium. We chatted about our surroundings and the opulently dressed people we saw entering the private boxes, but as the time neared for the performance to begin, we fell silent with anticipation.

From the first notes of the orchestral prelude, something felt wrong between us, rather like the disjoint situation in the first act of the drama, in which Butterfly's delusion about her marriage is so pathetically obvious. During the great love duet, I took Alma's hand in mine, and felt a closeness to her such as I had experienced at other concerts. But as the story darkened I felt her withdraw from me, gently yet inexorably.

During the tragic aria '*Un bel di*,' in which the heroine's confident words are belied by the agitation of the vocal line, I reached once more for Alma's hand. She acquiesced briefly, with a little pressure, then drew away. I looked at her face, expecting perhaps to see her moved to tears, and uncomfortable with it, but she sat rapt and dry-eyed. Not until near the end of the opera, when Butterfly sings the *arioso* passage beginning '*Sotto il gran parte del cielo?*' in which she agrees to give up her child, did Alma acknowledge my presence. Suddenly she turned toward me and I could see that her eyes were full of tears.

Afterward, we had a late supper at a restaurant near Times Square. Alma remained serious and a little subdued. More than once she said something about the prevalence in the opera of the idea that women must pay a heavy price for love. "It seems almost a choice between life with a man, or life itself," she mused. "Think of that aria – one fine day when he returns everything will be beautiful. Until that day she is in limbo. Nothing else is as important as him, not even her child. She postpones happiness until his return, and when he doesn't return to her, she chooses death."

"But Alma, this is opera, not a prescription for life," I protested. "You're supposed to experience the tragedy vicariously, with your emotions excited by the gorgeous music. It's meant to make you feel, not think."

"Well, I'm sorry, Charles, but I have this habit of thinking. Actually, I admit I've allowed my personal thoughts about life to colour my enjoyment of the evening. You must forgive me, and know that I am grateful to you for taking me."

After this I could see that she was making an effort to resume her old lively style of conversation, but the very fact of the effort made me unhappy. And I myself kept pushing away the nagging idea that the character I most resembled was the less than admirable B.F. Pinkerton.

Fog swirled through the streets as we made our way back to the hotel. I drew Alma close to me, and was glad that she did not resist. That part, at least, of our relationship was intact. But even in the depths of the night, as we sought one another with the passion that renews itself always, I realized that the theme of the evening had changed to one of endingness.

In the years that have passed since that time I have often thought about Alma. I think now that in my youthful ignorance I misjudged her, especially at the vulnerable time that followed the downfall of her father. I think that if I had asked her then to marry me she would have agreed, after a token refusal or two. She must have thought that the trip to New York, and my insistence on paying for everything, was preliminary to a proposal. When none materialized she must have resolved to rely only on herself.

Some weeks after this I received an urgent summons from West. Expecting that he had managed to obtain what he would no doubt call 'suitable experimental material,' I promptly made my way to his house. To my surprise, I found that I was going to be given a course in laboratory work.

"Two developments, Charles," said West, as we descended to the cellar. "First, I've come up with a way to stabilize the fluid, so it is now possible to make it in quantity for future use.

Second, I have no time right now to do that myself, so I must prevail upon you."

Everything about the situation bothered me, from the peremptory nature of the summons, to West's terse manner, to his assumption that I was available to do this work, whatever it involved.

"What makes you think I can do it at all? From what you've told me, it needs a lot of precise measuring and fiddling. I know next to nothing about chemistry. And anyway, why can't you do it, since it's so important?"

"For a good reason, and quite delightfully ironic, in fact. I'll be back at Miskatonic for a while, not as a student, but as an instructor. How things change, eh?"

West had been recommended by the influential Dr. Bright to the Acting Dean of the Medical School (replacing Allan Halsey, who was still on leave) as a possible clinical instructor, because of his growing reputation as a surgeon. When an unexpected vacancy had come up, he had been offered a temporary appointment.

"And I want to do it, Charles. I have some innovative techniques I want to pass along to the younger fellows. No, not experimental, merely improvements on the standard methods.

"But you can see how this constricts my time," he continued. "There are my regular patients, my hospital patients, my research and now this. It's probably just as well good subjects are so scarce these days. But I want to build up a stock of the fluid, so we have plenty on hand when the need arises. Also, I use it in some of my other work." He said this last in a manner that I knew well enough to interpret as, "Don't ask, because I'm not going to tell you."

"All right, Herbert, but how on earth do you expect me to manage? Do you have a recipe, like in a cooking-book? I might remind you I know almost nothing about that either."

"Oh I know that. I've set everything up for you. Here's your recipe, if you like," he said, showing me several sheets of paper covered with his spiky handwriting, and some sketches as well.

"And here are the ingredients, on this shelf. You will see that I've labelled the various components by letters and numbers, not by what they actually are. That makes it simpler for you, and should anyone come prowling around, it's just as well that everything is in code."

He explained the procedure, repeating the parts I did not understand, until I could demonstrate to his satisfaction that I could competently carry out the weighing and measuring, mixing, heating and decanting. The trickiest part of the process was at the end, when one liquid was added drop by drop to another until a reaction took place, and the fluid changed to the characteristic violet colour.

"One drop too many and it's all over," said West. "That's why I do it in this rather fiddly way, with the burette and everything. I haven't yet found a way to achieve good results by straight measurement. There are too many variables such as temperature and humidity. But I can't emphasize too much the need to keep your wits about you at that stage."

"What happens if I put in too much? Does it go a different colour? And what would be the effect – on the experiment, I mean?"

"No, you wouldn't see a colour difference. And as for the effect, it would overwhelm the mechanism. The subject would revive, all right, but in a short time the heart would start to race, and literally explode. Given the scarcity of good corpses, I wouldn't want that to happen.

"Now, how about if you make the next batch by yourself? I'll observe and let you know if you do anything wrong."

So it was that I became West's unpaid lab assistant, as well as his accomplice in grave-robbing, illegal transport of corpses and experimentation. For several months, I spent a considerable number of evenings in his laboratory. I don't know whether the chemicals I worked with had some subtle effect on me, but after cooking up two or three batches of the stuff, I felt strangely restless. Once I went to Alma in this state, but after an hour of my overstimulated company she asked me to leave, disturbed by my inability to stop talking or to stay in one place for more than five minutes. After this I made a point of avoiding her on these nights, and found other means of dealing with the strange urgency, namely long walks followed by writing reams of poetry fit only for burning the next day.

The main room of West's laboratory was about twenty feet square, containing a dissection table rather like those in the Medical School's Pathology Laboratory. In addition there were the usual fittings – lab bench, sink, bunsen burners, microscopes. Along one wall were shelves and cupboards containing glassware and other implements, as well as a variety of chemicals. Next to these was a narrow door leading to the annexe, in which West worked on his other experiments. It was always locked. I knew this because I checked.

One night I was preparing to brew up yet another batch of what I privately called Dr. West's Magic Elixir. It had been brought to my attention that the supply was running low. "How can that be?" I exclaimed, only half-jokingly. "There were three flasks just a few days ago, after you had me do that marathon session on Saturday. What do you do with the stuff, drink it?"

West had a trick of slightly widening those grey eyes of his to express varying emotions, from surprise to disbelief to a certain amusement. But it could also mean exasperation, even anger, as on this occasion. "What do you think?" he asked. "I've told you, I use it in some of my other work – important work which I shall tell you about in due time. Now I'm off to the hospital. I should be back in a couple of hours. Two litres ought to do it."

An hour later I had prepared one litre of the violet coloured fluid. I gazed at the stuff in its flask. It was a very strange colour, somehow shifting in intensity, even appearing slightly iridescent. This was very curious, because the two liquids that were combined to produce it were clear as water, until some exact proportion was attained, when the transformation occurred. "Organic molecules," West had said. I wondered for the fiftieth time how this substance worked. What did it do inside the dead arteries, the dead heart, to make a corpse breathe and move and speak again, however briefly? Knowing nothing much about physiology, and in absolute ignorance of the constituents of the liquid, I could not begin to guess. For me, the business came down to faith – faith in Herbert West. I sometimes fancied that the fluid itself actually had very little effect, that it was merely a medium for West's will, which was the force that actually brought about the transformation.

I began the process all over again for the second litre. West had explained that it was not possible simply to 'double the recipe,' because of the precision required in some of the steps. I was weighing some powders when I discovered that there was an insufficient quantity of one of them. The stock jar, carefully labelled, was on one of the higher shelves nearby.

I must have been careless in positioning the ladder, for as I reached the next to highest rung and shifted my weight in order to reach the jar I needed, it slipped. So quickly did everything happen then that I had no chance to grab at something to save myself. This was just as well, since the only possible thing I could have grabbed was the shelves, which would have brought them and the heavy glass jars they supported down on top of me. I fell, striking my head glancingly on the edge of the porcelain-topped table. I must have been unconscious before I reached the floor.

I was insensible for a long time, as such things go – half an hour at least, West thought later. But for all I knew, it might have been millennia, during which humanity died, and the sun burned away, and the earth as we know it was consumed. The universe itself may have ceased to exist and been formed anew from primordial dust. My return to consciousness was like being born, a hard and painful birth. I came to myself through a rushing blackness that was sickening in the extreme. When it was over, I knew I was lying on my back, although I could see nothing and did not know where I was. There was an awareness of I and not-I, but that was all.

Then a terrible knowledge overwhelmed me. I was in West's laboratory, on the table, and West, not knowing I was still alive, was preparing to revivify me. I could feel his quick cool fingers unfastening my collar, touching my neck. Something cold pressed against my chest and I heard a metallic clink. I struggled to cry out, to move, to open my eyes, but to no avail. In a moment, I knew, I would feel the searing pain of the scalpel opening my neck, and the hollow needle would slide into my vein. What would happen then? Had West ever injected the fluid into a living body? Would it kill me? "It excites the vital processes," he had said once when I asked him how the stuff worked. I envisioned my heart racing to the point where it burst – hemorrhage, apoplexy, death. My eyes opened suddenly, and I screamed.

Or at least, I thought I screamed, but emitted only a convulsive gasp. West was bending over me, but I saw no scalpel in his hand. He did not speak, but a curious collection of expressions passed over his features. I saw relief, yes, but only after a kind of thwarted excitement and – I was sure of it – disappointment.

"Well, Charles," he said at length, "it seems you'll live, but you have a lump the size of an egg on the back of your head. No, don't try to get up just yet. I have to do some things first."

He shone a light into my eyes and watched my pupils contract. He pinched my extremities and asked whether I could feel it. He asked me various things about myself, and, when the answers seemed to satisfy him, helped me to my feet. I felt only slightly dizzy, so West suggested we go up to his living quarters, where he settled me on a sofa.

"I came home about nine o'clock and found you on the floor," he said. "You were in quite a deep state of unconsciousness. You've had a concussion, certainly. If you had hit that table just a little differently, I think you would be dead."

"Surely no, Herbert," I said, voicing the thing that had been in my mind ever since I regained consciousness. "Surely by now I would have been on the way to my second life."

"You know me too well, Charles." He looked directly into my eyes and said, "Yes, if you had died, it would have been an almost ideal situation – a freshly dead body, as the result of an accident. Except that head cases don't make the best subjects. But already in the lab, too! Entirely the act of friendship I would have expected from you."

"But how do I know it didn't happen? Maybe I've been dead, and am now the first person to have been successfully revivified."

"Sadly, no. If that had been the case you would have found yourself on the table, not on the floor. And instead of bringing you up here and giving you tea I would have been busy gathering data and making notes."

"Coming back to consciousness was dreadful," I said, shuddering. "It really did feel like what I've imagined those corpses must go through – a kind of tearing of the fabric of reality, and utter helplessness. Like birth in reverse. But really, for a while there I was sure you thought I was dead and were getting ready to pump me full of fluid. And I had a batch all ready, too. Before I was finally able to see and speak I was certain you were going to cut my neck open and stick a needle in."

"Now, Charles, if I know nothing else I can certainly tell whether someone is dead or not. You were breathing, and I had no trouble finding a pulse."

"But you would have done it, if I had been dead," I persisted.

"Yes, I would have. It would have been criminal of me not to have made the attempt. Consider, if I had not, if I had merely done the expected thing – reported an accidental death and let the machinery take over, you would be dead now, and would stay that way. But if I had used you as a subject, there's a chance you would be, well, less than dead now."

"Less than dead. That's about how I feel, all right. I don't think I'm up to making up that second litre. I'd probably mess it up."

"That's all right. Go home and sleep. I'll make up the second batch, and maybe more. I'll be up late anyway."

I made my way homeward, still feeling shaky. I was glad to get away from him. His reasoning had been entirely logical, but its coldness repelled me. It disturbed me that I could make the transition from friend to experimental subject in the length of time it took him to do an examination for vital signs. And there was another thing. Between the look of disappointment I had seen on his face when my eyes opened and the look of relief that followed had been an expression of utterly cold calculation.

♦ 9 ♦

That spring I moved to more spacious quarters, quite close to West's old rooms on College Street. An increase in my salary permitted an escape from the two shabby rooms I had inhabited since coming to Arkham.

I was fortunate enough to rent the entire second floor of a house quite close to the Miskatonic campus. My landlord was something of a Bohemian, a poet and occasional lecturer in the English Department, by the name of Marcus Desmond. He and his wife entertained a great deal, occasionally including me in their rather casual gatherings. From time to time, Desmond himself would turn up in my quarters, eager to talk about anything and everything, and to drink whatever I had on hand. I found this arrangement generally congenial, despite occasional noise and disruptions. I was independent, yet not altogether isolated, and no one cared if my comings and goings were erratic at times.

West gave me some of his surplus furniture – a rug, some bookshelves, a couple of little tables. I have them still. Alma gave me good advice on decorating without extravagance. She and I made an expedition to Boston, to shops that sold prints and other art works at reasonable prices, as well as more practical items.

Once I was settled, I invited both of them, as well as a few other friends and colleagues, to a small celebration. I was not without trepidation, given the animosity which existed between these two closest friends of mine. However, I need not have worried. The Commencement Day Incident had faded from Arkham's collective memory. Both West and Alma behaved with exemplary politeness. In fact, I considered the evening a modest success.

Alma was the last to depart, but depart she did. By this time there was no doubt but that our affair was cooling. Strangely enough, our friendship did not seem to be affected, for which I was profoundly grateful. Indeed, the bittersweet quality of these days was a pleasure in itself, as though the slow dissolution of the bonds of passion created beauties of a different order. And every now and then the old ardour flared up anew.

One afternoon, a message from West arrived at my desk. *Brain clearing session tonight. Please come.* This was unusual; more often it said "Come if you like." And certainly "please" was most uncharacteristic. Although the prospect of serious drinking did not attract me just then, I resolved to go. The last few times I had seen West he had been rather down in the dumps, which was also uncharacteristic.

These so-called brain clearings of West's – what other people called debauches or merely drinking-parties – had become quite rare since he had taken up doctoring.

"I'm not thinking as intensely these days – getting old, I suppose," he said, with one of the sweet smiles that seemed to belie his words. He was only twenty-seven.

When I arrived at West's that evening I could see at once that it was not to be a typical drinking session. For one thing, I was the only guest. For another, there was only one bottle of Scotch on the table, along with glasses and a jug of water.

"Only the two of us tonight, Herbert?" I asked, pouring my first drink of the evening.

"Yes. As you may have guessed, this isn't a real brain clearing, only a kind of *in memoriam* for our younger days. And I have business in Boston tomorrow. But this seemed as good a time as any to... well, to talk."

"About what, Herbert?" I was mystified. West never had to set up an occasion to talk. He could hold forth on nearly anything any time, if he was so inclined.

"Oh, cabbages and kings," he said, laughing and reaching for the bottle. "Or cauliflowers and deans, if you prefer. I can't think what's come over me lately. Such seriousness! And where does it get me? Life was a good deal more entertaining in my pre-Hippocratic days, when my only patients were already dead.

"Speaking of which, unless we're blessed with a good subject for revivification soon, my new research direction will be my only one."

"So will you tell me about it now? You've been so secretive about it."

"With good reason. When something seems impossible, it's altogether best to keep it secret until it no longer seems that way. And I must admit, it does still seem that way." He gave me a speculative look. "Well, Charles, you've never blabbed to anyone, so I will tell you that the new research concerns not revivification, but... renovation. Yes, it might be called that, certainly."

"Renovation. What – you mean, of bodies? A fountain of youth? That would be something indeed."

"Not exactly. Not yet, anyway, although ultimately perhaps. Let's just say that I think I have found a way to repair or even replace parts. But that's all I'll say right now."

As we talked, I happened to notice that there were some pictures on the wall behind the piano. I had never seen them before, and assumed that they were newly acquired. I went over to look at them more closely. All three were obviously the work of a single artist. The style was vaguely reminiscent of the Symbolist painters of Europe, especially Gustav Klimt and Jan Toorop. The scenes were depthless and abstract, demonstrating a skillful use of dark and light tones. At first I thought the hieratic figures in stylized poses were mythological or literary personages, but on studying them more closely, I perceived that these works depicted scenes of surgery. Each one showed the horizontal shape of a patient being ministered to by a masked form who was surely a surgeon, but of a diabolical sort I hoped sincerely was only a figment of the artist's imagination.

In one picture this sinister individual was extracting an organ from the patient's body. In another he appeared to be attaching an appendage of grotesque shape and unknown function to the hapless creature. In the third, he held in his hand a flask containing a brilliant blue liquid, and was in the process of decanting it into the patient's mouth, which was held open by a shadowy assistant.

The longer I looked at these images, the more disturbing I found them. The relentless deliberation exhibited by the figure of the surgeon, the terrified helplessness of the patient (or victim?) made me think that what I was looking at was a personification of evil.

"Do you like them?" asked West, startling me. I had failed to notice his approach, and did not expect to find him next to me. Something in his voice made me look at him sharply. He was smiling in a way I could think of only as mischievous.

"Not altogether," I replied. "They're well executed, certainly, but I find the subjects rather macabre."

"Well yes, I agree. That describes them rather well. But I think they're appropriate. I considered hanging them in my office downstairs, but didn't think my patients would appreciate them."

"I dare say they wouldn't!" I said, laughing in spite of myself. "Who is the artist?"

"A student at the Medical School, one Walter Dixon Taylor. I think you met him here once. Former student, I should say. He decided he couldn't stand the sight of blood and dropped out a few months ago. I imagine he's happily starving in a garret and painting more things like these. He owed me money, you see, and gave me these paintings instead, a few days before he decamped. The longer I have them the more I think I've had the best of the bargain."

"Do you know what inspired these scenes?" I asked. "Or are they purely imaginary?"

"What a question, Charles! Take another look. The first one is realistic enough – obviously an ectomy of some sort – splenectomy, appendectomy, it's hard to say which, and doesn't really matter. But the other two – I can tell you unequivocally that no one I know has ever endeavoured to graft an object of this sort onto a patient. And the third is surely not an advisable way to administer a liquid. No, I think Taylor was exploring his own antipathy to the profession. He was really quite unstable."

"But why do you suppose he decided to give you these particular pictures?" I thought I remembered Taylor from West's housewarming dinner, not quite a year before – a dark young man, and rather silent. He hadn't said much, only gazed intently about him in a manner I had found disconcerting.

"They were his choice. For all I know, he might have painted even more shocking ones. Why should it matter, anyway? Sometimes I think you're growing too suspicious for your own good."

He resolutely refused to answer any more questions, but proceeded instead to analyze a recent scandal that had erupted in the School of Engineering. One of the professors there had been denied funding for the development of a portable drilling apparatus that could be used for geological research in remote regions. Instead, money had been awarded to a rival working on an improved kind of machine-gun. It seemed that the first professor was claiming that the award was not objective because one of the members of the granting committee represented a manufacturer of armaments. West saw in the situation some parallel with his old dilemma at the Medical School. I could not quite follow his reasoning, and found myself assuming my old role of devil's advocate.

By the time we had thrashed over the engineers, the bottle was nearing emptiness and the two of us were pleasantly inebriated. Suddenly West said, "Now, Charles – I have a small confession to make."

I had never heard anything like this from him. Confessions were definitely not in West's line, requiring as they did admissions of wrongdoing or error.

"You remember all that stuff I told you – now when was it? – oh yes, over that first dinner we had at Da Vinci's, after the concert by that young violinist. Castelo-Branco, that was the name. Well, all that stuff about my mother dying, and my twin brother – it wasn't exactly true, you know."

"I know. I've known for years." It was West's turn to look astonished, something else at which he did not get much practice.

"How did you – ?"

"I met an old fellow one day, shortly after that dinner, in fact. He used to work for your father, and your grandfather too. His name was Howard, Philip Howard."

"Philip Howard," West said slowly. "Oh yes, I remember him now. A chatty old fellow. So what did he tell you, exactly?"

"Just that your mother didn't die when you were eight. And that you never had a twin brother." Knowing West's enjoyment for adjusting the truth, I didn't want to make it too easy for him by revealing everything Howard had told me.

"Just that, eh?" West was laughing. "You know me too well, Charles. All right, I'll tell you what I meant to all along, and you will judge who told you the truth, Philip Howard or I. From what I recall of the fellow, he liked to spin a yarn.

"And he was right, my mother didn't die – not then, anyway. When I was eight, she left my father and us boys and disappeared. And no, I never had a twin brother. I told you that story, I suppose, because I wanted to convince you of the purity of my motives and the worthiness of my cause. At the time, of course, I underestimated your shrewdness and overdid the pathos."

"You certainly did. But Herbert, why are you telling me all this now?"

He looked uncomfortable. "I'm not certain. I suppose it's because we've been... associates, and friends too, for so long that it didn't seem right to keep up that old fiction. But of course I didn't know you had already been enlightened by Mr. Howard.

"And there's another thing. It's rather hard to explain." He stared off into space for a moment. "It has to do with some of my patients in Bolton. The Italians. You see, I think I might be related to some of them."

I was astonished until I remembered his explanation for the fact that he spoke a little Italian. It had seemed suspect at the time. "Related?"

"Through my mother's mother. She was Italian, and had relatives in Bolton. It all goes back to that prizefight we went to. Word got around in Bolton that there was a young doctor there named West who spoke Italian. Since then, a few patients, older people mostly, have been asking me about my grandmother and my mother. And of course, I have nothing to tell them. It's as though there's a great hole in my past." He fell silent, but I said nothing. After a moment he continued.

"My parents' marriage was not a happy one. Or, I should say, even less happy than most. My mother was the result of an unlikely union between an old Arkham family, the Derbys, and an Italian immigrant's daughter from Bolton. I'm sure there's a story there, but I don't know it. And how she came to marry Hiram West I'll probably never know either. I'm not sure I want to.

"My grandfather and his brother, Joshua and Henry, were the founders of the funeral business. They were typical Yankee businessmen – hardheaded, hard working, and essentially honest. They stuck to their undertaking, and made a success of it. True, they joined the vulgar rush after the Civil War trade, and some of their advertising methods were in questionable taste, but they were straightforward. But my father... he could never be content with only one business. It wasn't the fact that it was undertaking that bothered him, just that it didn't offer him enough scope. Merely to work away at a trade was too dull. He needs to buy and sell, take over, break down and build up. It goes beyond business for him, I think. It's the control he needs – the more the better, and not necessarily by gentle persuasion. Certainly, he exercised an iron control in his family.

"You've met my father, Charles. I'm sure you saw a jovial buffoon, a little loud, a little overbearing, but full of good will. Right?"

On my acknowledgment of this description, he said, "Nothing could be farther from the truth. There is no good in him, only will. Toward those who fall in line behind him he's benevolent. To those he doesn't need he's indifferent. To those who oppose him he's ruthless.

"I think my mother was rather like yours in some ways, Charles. From what you've told me of her I think there were similarities. A love of music, certainly, a romantic nature, perhaps. But all lightness of spirit must have been pretty much bullied out of her by the time I was even half aware of such things. I think she must have survived for years by suppressing her true nature. But then something happened..." There was another long silence. Then he said,

"I think she had a love affair. Or wanted to, at least. Even that would have done it. I've asked my brothers about this, carefully, you understand. Jokingly, even. They are five and eight years older than I, so Jeremy would have been nearly fourteen and Hiram Jr. sixteen. My mother was not yet thirty-five. But either they didn't know much, or they didn't want to tell me. Hiram just refused to talk. Jeremy brushed me off with an insult. So I had to fall back on my own memories.

"Our coachman at the time was a good-looking fellow called Desmond Robertson. I almost remember something – it seems like a dream and maybe it was one – but there's a picture in my mind of this Robertson helping my mother out of the carriage. She had been to a luncheon or something, and I was watching for her from my room on the second floor. There was something about the way he took her hand... Nothing improper, you understand, just a subtle thing. And the way she looked at him... I never said anything to her. What could I say? But I've never forgotten it."

It was as though his words broke a seal in my memory, and I had a sudden vivid picture of a sunny clearing in my mother's garden, with its table and chairs. I was walking toward it, down the shaded *allee* of clipped yews. I stood in their green darkness and saw my mother and Michael O'Connor as though in a cave of sunlight. In the dazzlement I saw him take her hand and kiss it. I saw her touch his face. I knew that I should not be seeing this, that I must speak of it to no one. They had not seen me. I turned around and went away.

West had begun speaking again by the time I was able to pay attention to him. "Robertson disappeared shortly afterward. I think he was fired, but I don't know for sure."

"You mean – he might have been murdered?"

West looked uneasy. "It's possible. And yes, my father is certainly capable of having done it. Or having it done. But I don't know.

"And not long after, my mother left. I don't think he realized she was capable of doing such a thing. She had been so submissive for years, you see. If he had known he would have stopped her. She must have gone to her father, here in Arkham, but not for long. My father would have known where to find them, after all. I wonder, now, if she might have gone to Bolton for a time. But that doesn't make sense either. Those elderly patients spoke of her as though she was a distant memory, just a child. They didn't seem to know anything about her after she disappeared."

"Philip Howard seemed to think she was in Arkham," I said, hesitantly. "I remember thinking at the time how strange it was that you and she would be living in the same city, given the circumstances."

"In Arkham! But how would he know?"

"I'm not sure. Maybe he was guessing. But he said her family had been here for generations. Here, not Bolton. I suppose he was referring to her father's family."

"The Derbys. Yes, that may be. We have very little to do with them, actually. The usual bad blood. Well, if that's true it would be very interesting. But I think I'll keep this bit of information to myself, Charles. Please don't tell anyone. And I must speak to Philip Howard too, if I can track him down."

"But why all this secrecy?"

"Haven't you heard anything I said? My father is not a forgiving man. Don't imagine that he would be eager to kiss and make up with his erring wife, even after more than twenty years."

"What happened to you after your mother left?" I asked.

"I got along as she had, by being quiet and no trouble to anyone. Mostly I stayed out of my father's way and did as I was told. Strangely enough, I get along with him. My brothers... well, Hiram Jr. is all right, but Jeremy... For some reason he hates me. But it's a good thing that Father has them to carry on his empire. He's had few expectations of me, so it was easy for me to go my own way. Still, he rather likes the idea of having a physician in the family."

"But who brought you up? You know, showed you how to do things, how to behave, that sort of thing?"

"Sometimes I think I brought myself up," he said with a smile. "After my mother left, the household was in disarray. I remember trying to organize a birthday party for myself when I turned nine, since there was no one else to do it. Things would have been worse without our housekeeper, Mrs. Petrucci. Talking with her helped me retain the Italian I had learned from my mother. That's how I learned to cook too, by hanging around the kitchen. At least there was order there. The rest of the house was pretty chaotic, what with my father and his cronies coming and going. The library and the kitchen – those were the places I felt most at home. But yes, that was a bad time, those first few months..."

164

He fell silent for a while, then continued. "Eventually my father hired a tutor to look after me. An Englishman. Father had an idea he would give me the right sort of polish, or something. When I was thirteen, he sent me away to an English-style boarding school. Since then, for all practical purposes, I've been on my own."

Shortly after, the evening came to an end and I went home, full of thoughts. For the first time I saw certain similarities between West and myself. We had both had odd, lonely childhoods, he more so than I. Perhaps this had worked in some subtle way to bring us together, even though the outward reasons for our association were entirely unrelated.

And despite the story of his mother, which I had mostly believed, I could not push away a thought which had recurred several times as he described his father's personality. In some ways he might have been describing himself.

Part 2

THE AMERICAN VOLUNTEER

♦ 10 ♦

The summer of 1914, the last before the Great War, was an extraordinarily beautiful one. Although not normally an outdoorsman, even I could not ignore the glorious weather. Several times Alma and I escaped Arkham and went to the seashore or to nearby Kingsport.

Kingsport is insular. There is a lively commerce between Arkham and Bolton, but Kingsport looks to itself alone, itself and outer Ocean. The narrow road that leads there from Arkham goes nowhere else and few travel it. No railroad goes to Kingsport; the sea is its only highway. Despite its remoteness and self-containment, a few outsiders find their ways there – artists, antiquarians, philosophers and seekers after curiosities. They are tolerated for the commerce they generate but are not actively encouraged.

On one occasion in late July West came with us, surprising me by accepting my invitation (for which I had prudently obtained Alma's rather unenthusiastic approval).

Some years before, Alma's father had made her a present of a Ford automobile. "I think he did it to make me feel guilty for deserting the parental home," she explained. Despite this reservation, she had learned to drive the car and did so competently. On this particular day we loaded it with the usual picnic paraphernalia, picked up West at his home and headed for Kingsport.

Just before the road took a steep descent into the town, Alma turned the car sharp left, onto a dirt road that led up to the cliffs to the north. It zigzagged up a steep slope and ended at the edge of a belt of wind-twisted trees. Beyond this was the broad grassy cliff-edge.

Audrey Driscoll

It was a strange place, but with a pleasant strangeness, a world unto itself that cared nothing for things outside, neither town nor country, human or inhuman. We could see the roofs of Kingsport huddled below; northward, even higher cliffs blotted out the sky. In the distance behind us lay Arkham, its many steeples putting me in mind of a celestial city.

As we unpacked the lunch, Alma told us how she had come here many times as a child, on picnic parties organized by her governess. "Those days were so long and so lovely," she said. "Each one seemed as long as a week, from the time we woke up in the morning, all excited because it was a picnic day, until we went home in the dusk, tired and gritty but mindlessly happy. Listen to me, reminiscing like an old lady! But it's true – time passes more quickly the older one gets. I expect for old people a year must seem like a week. I wonder why?"

"There must be a law of physics, as yet undiscovered," said West. "Someone at Miskatonic is probably doing research on it – a disciple of Professor Quarrington's, probably. It sounds like the kind of thing he would have taken up."

"Oh, you know Professor Quarrington?" asked Alma, looking interested. "I've never met him myself."

"I took some classes from him, years ago," West replied. He did not seem inclined to say any more, and soon changed the topic.

Over lunch, our talk turned to local history and legends. Alma told us that on one of the highest cliffs there was reputed to be a strange ancient house, built on the very cliff-edge, so that the front door opened out into empty space. It was said to be inhabited by a being not entirely human.

"People hereabouts say that anyone who enters the house leaves their soul behind when they leave. When they go home they are changed forever."

"In that case I should probably try to find the place," said West, smiling. "Since I profess to have no soul, I should logically emerge unscathed. What do you think, Charles?"

"If anyone emerged unscathed it would be you, Herbert. Where is this house, exactly?"

"Up there," answered Alma, pointing. "At the top of the very highest of the cliffs, and sometimes it can be seen from Kingsport. People say it's most perilous when there are lights and music. That and when the fog comes in from the sea."

We lazily finished off the picnic lunch, disinclined to go anywhere or do anything. We discussed the legend of the strange high house and other stories that clung to this haunted region.

For once our conversation did not become a debate, with West and Alma taking opposite sides of an issue, and I trying to maintain a friendly neutrality. Perhaps it was because they were both skeptics when it came to ghosts and the supernatural. I had other ideas but lacked the energy to argue them.

I lay on my back looking up at the sky and the ever-changing clouds. West was similarly disposed a few feet away. He wore white trousers and a white linen shirt, with a panama hat partly obscuring his face. From where I lay I could just see the silvery gleam of his eyes beneath his lashes. Alma, in a blue linen dress, was looking out to sea, where the horizon dissolved into pearly mist.

I treasure this memory, for this was the last time the three of us were together.

A week or so later, as Alma and I were walking homeward from the Library, she suddenly said, "I've been thinking of leaving Arkham, Charles, but I can't quite make up my mind to do it. I keep questioning my motives, for one thing."

"And what are your motives?" I asked, trying to hide the shock I felt.

"There are so many... I don't feel at home here as I used to, ever since that business with Papa, you know. And I'm not sure I want to be a librarian all my life. I'd like to earn a higher degree, in some area of science, perhaps. Or if I do keep working as a librarian, I'd rather be at one of the really big universities. Miskatonic is such a backwater. Or – I just don't know. I'm restless. Maybe it's the fall coming, and all these troubles in Europe. Somehow I feel I need a change."

"And you would like to... change our situation too." I wasn't sure whether I was making a statement or asking a question.

"Well yes, that would be one of the consequences, but it's not a primary reason." She smiled at me. "Now Charles, we agreed long ago that our 'situation,' as you so coyly term it, was never intended to be permanent. And lately – but I would miss you terribly. I can't deny that. It's another reason I keep vacillating. So don't start planning my farewell party yet."

We had reached the corner where we usually parted. A sudden rush of nostalgia flooded over me and with it something else. I laid my hand on Alma's arm. "I'll see you later. Would that be all right?"

She looked away, began to shake her head, then stopped and turned toward me, smiling. "All right, Charles," she said.

West had been considering using electricity to enhance the effect of his revivifying fluid and was now absolutely committed to finding a subject to test this. "It must be soon, Charles," he said, pacing around his study. "If not, there is another course of action I can take. But it's by no means a straightforward one. So let's hope our luck changes. Or that I can make it change," he added, in a low voice, as though speaking to himself.

The following day I was in West's cellar laboratory, compounding more of the revivifying fluid, in anticipation that a suitable subject would soon be found. I did not realize just how soon.

The final step of the procedure was the titration, which of necessity required close attention. As I watched the clear liquid fall drop by drop into the flask, ready to close the stop-cock at the precise instant the characteristic violet colour appeared, I realized that I heard sounds as of a conversation. The laboratory was nearly sound-proof, but it was possible to hear a little of what transpired on the floor immediately above. I took little notice at first. Patients and others were always coming and going during West's office hours, but they did not usually linger to converse in the hall.

Suddenly, I heard a stranger's voice speaking loudly, then a muffled yell and a thud. Moments later, West came running down the steps and into the room. "Quick, Charles! Come and give me a hand up there. Good, you're finished with that." He glanced at the apparatus, where a full flask of the violet liquid now stood.

"What do you mean?" I asked, flustered. "Who was that upstairs?" The disturbance had distracted me for a second, and I could not be certain that an extra drop or two of the activating agent had not found its way into the fluid. But West was already half way up the stairs. I resolved to mention the matter to him at the earliest opportunity.

The front hall contained only a coat rack and a table bearing a fern in a brass pot. Now, however, there was something else on the polished floor – a large sandy-haired man, lying on his back. A leather case sat next to him. He was pale and did not appear to be breathing.

"What happened to him, Herbert?" I asked. "Do you want me to telephone the hospital?" If the fellow needed medical attention, why wasn't West supplying it?

"Too late," said West, in a satisfied tone that seemed completely inappropriate. He locked the front door and said,

"Charles, I would like you to meet Mr. Robert Leavitt, our perfect subject. Now, help me get him downstairs."

"You mean he's dead?"

"No, he's having a little snooze," answered West, sarcastically. "Of course he's dead! He came to the door asking for directions. I thought he looked sick and invited him inside. I went to fetch a glass of water but when I came back he was on the floor. A heart attack, by the looks of things. He's definitely dead. Unfortunate for him, but lucky for us."

"But Herbert, we can't just... use him! Surely someone will come looking for him."

"Not any time soon. He's from St. Louis, on an extended trip. He said so before he keeled over. No one's expecting him, at least not in Arkham. He was looking for Bolton Worsted Mills. I think he's an engineer or something of that sort, peddling machine parts, judging by the stuff in that case. Now, let's get on with it."

We picked up the fellow with some difficulty, because he was quite heavy, and carried him down to the laboratory, where we laid him on the table. Quickly, West began to unfasten buttons, removing the jacket, vest, necktie, shirt and undershirt, directing me to deal with Leavitt's shoes and trousers.

I did as I was told, but without enthusiasm. The suddenness of Leavitt's appearance and the coincidence of his having a fatal heart attack in West's front hall made me dizzy. What was I doing, helping to undress this stranger in West's cellar? I experienced a kind of doubling, in which I seemed to be observing myself. I did not much like the picture. The corpse was not yet cold and emitted a sweaty smell. His mouth had fallen open, showing a couple of gold teeth. His brown eyes stared into emptiness.

"Not exactly a fashion plate, was he?" West said, as he dropped the man's clothing in a corner. "No matter, though. He's exactly what we need – a perfectly fresh specimen, in reasonably good shape. And more or less educated too, if he's an engineer. He ought to be fairly articulate." He was as excited as I had ever seen him, face faintly flushed, eyes shining, like an angler who has finally landed a big one.

I set up the apparatus while West checked over the corpse, making sure it was ready for the procedure. His hands danced lightly over the still form, palpating and taking measurements. Finally, he took up a scalpel and began the business of finding the blood vessels and inserting the needles. I connected the flask of fluid I had just prepared as West made a final check of the electrical apparatus.

At a nod from West I activated the pump. The process worked flawlessly – the violet-coloured fluid flowed in as Leavitt's blood was drawn out. Despite my familiarity with the business, I felt sick at heart. Less than an hour ago, this had been an ordinary man, looking for Bolton Worsted Mills so he could go there to sell his machine parts. Now his blood was being drained away and soon his body would be subject to the chemical orchestrations perpetrated upon him by West and myself.

Like a musician with his instrument, West hovered over the apparatus, turning a knob here, checking a connection somewhere else. His face wore the look of utter concentration I had come to know well. If someone had broken down the door of the house at the moment, I did not think he would have heard. I was distinctly nervous. I could not believe that Leavitt was entirely unlooked-for and expected a knock on the door at any moment.

Once the fluid had been pumped into the body, we prepared to apply the electric current which West hoped would enhance the revivification process. I held the electrodes in place and he activated the machine.

A faint humming sound filled the room. A few seconds later, the corpse began to vibrate gently. I knew this to be a purely mechanical effect, but it startled me nonetheless. After a few minutes West, who had been bending over the body, his stethoscope applied to the region of the heart, looked up at me with excitement.

"We have a pulse. Stop the electricity!"

I did as instructed. Already a faint colour had appeared on Leavitt's pale face. His features remained still, the eyes sunken, but he was certainly alive. We had only to wait for signs of sentience to determine whether the brain was functioning.

I left West attending to Leavitt and went upstairs. I had remembered the case Leavitt had been carrying and intended to bring it down to the cellar. Its contents might tell me something about its owner and whoever might be concerned about his disappearance.

The case stood where I had seen it before, on the carpet near the hall table. But the table was bare except for the fern in its pot. Earlier, West had said that Leavitt had collapsed while he was getting a glass of water for him. Where was that glass? I would have expected it to be somewhere in the hall, most likely on the table. But there was no glass, full or empty, whole or broken, anywhere in the hall. I made a careful search of the floor, thinking that West might have dropped it in his haste to help Leavitt. I found no glass, but under the table, close to the baseboard, there was a hypodermic syringe. It was empty, the plunger fully depressed.

I reviewed again my conversation with West when he called me upstairs. Had he said anything about administering a drug to the man? I thought not. He had said only that Leavitt had collapsed and died while he was fetching the water. But there was no glass, hence no water. It was impossible that he would have disposed of the glass before summoning me. He had been too excited. And as far as I could remember, he had not been upstairs since we had carried Leavitt down to the cellar.

Deeply troubled, I returned to the laboratory, carrying Leavitt's case. West looked up, clearly satisfied at the state of things. "He's coming along nicely. I would estimate that he'll regain consciousness in an hour or so. The damnable thing is that I can't stay. I have to operate on a patient in half an hour. Mr. Leavitt wasn't considerate enough to let us know he was coming. I suppose I should have waited. Two or three hours more or less probably wouldn't have made much difference. But I couldn't pass up the opportunity of a really fresh corpse. Dump that case here, Charles. We'll deal with it later. What I want you to do now is stay here and watch him until I get back. Just monitor the heart rate and respiration every few minutes. If he starts to fail, give him a shot of this – right here, in the arm. And Charles – " he paused at the door of the laboratory, "if he says anything, anything at all, write it down. I wish like hell I didn't have to leave!" He ran lightly up the stairs. Moments later, I heard the outer door of the house slam.

Reluctantly, I turned to our victim, for so I could not help thinking of him. His colour appeared nearly normal, and although his breathing was so slow as to be almost imperceptible, he was certainly breathing. There was no sign of fading. It appeared that West had achieved his goal at last.

The next hour passed quietly. I checked Leavitt even more frequently than West had ordered, making notes of the times and other particulars. It seemed to me that Leavitt was beginning to emerge from his unconscious state. His eyes rolled and a few times his eyelids fluttered. I was glad that we had put the restraints on him, remembering our terrible experience with the prizefighter.

When next I approached the table, Robert Leavitt was looking up at me. Despite my anticipation of this, I felt a stab of fear. This was the first time I had been alone with a subject. I knew how tenuous must be his hold on life; I knew also how much West hoped to learn from him. If I lost him through ignorance or error, West would be terribly disappointed.

I peered into Leavitt's eyes, trying to determine whether there was a functioning brain behind that fixed gaze. Could he really see me? Hesitantly, I spoke his name.

"Mr. Leavitt, can you hear me?"

"I hear you. Who are you?"

"My name is Charles Milburn. Mr. Leavitt, please tell me – what do you remember?

His lips moved soundlessly for a moment. "Nothing. I remember nothing... except music. I was floating through music. The angels were singing." He smiled and closed his eyes. "I thought I was going to heaven, but they didn't want me."

"What do you mean?" I whispered.

"They sent me back. Pushed me out. I felt myself falling, falling through darkness. So fast – then I saw you." He frowned and moved his head from side to side. "That other one – where is he?" He was beginning to get agitated.

"There's no one here but me, Mr. Leavitt. Please calm yourself. You've had an attack and you must stay calm if you want to get better."

"Am I in a hospital? Why is this bed so hard? And why are my arms tied down?"

"It's to keep you from injuring yourself." I felt desperate. "I just have to check your pulse now. Excuse me, please."

"You're a doctor, then?" He grew a little calmer. I performed my simple procedures, murmuring something I hoped was reassuring.

"Wait!" said Leavitt, just as I was finishing my notes. "I know there was someone else, not you. I remember now. I knocked at a door to ask for directions. The name plate said 'Herbert West, M.D.' He opened the door – not you, a little blond fellow... He asked me inside and told me to wait a minute while he got a map. But he came back with a needle in his hand, came at me with it! Where is he? Help! Help!"

He had grown agitated once more, his face a mottled red colour I did not like. His pulse had been somewhat rapid the last time I checked it, and that was before this outburst. I leaned closely over him and pleaded, "Mr. Leavitt, please calm yourself. You're not in danger. The danger has passed, but you must not get agitated."

I felt the situation slipping beyond my control. This was no passive experimental subject, but an ordinary man undergoing a terrible experience. To make matters worse, he now appeared to be having some sort of fit. His face twitched, his eyes rolled wildly and his body grew rigid, straining against the straps that held him down. I could not think what to do. The syringe containing the booster fluid lay nearby but I hesitated to administer it, since Leavitt's symptoms were surely not those of the fading that had characterized so many of our other subjects. For all I knew, it might make him worse.

Suddenly, I heard quick, light steps behind me. West pushed me aside and bent over Leavitt. Grim-faced, he seized a different syringe, filled it from a bottle, inserted the needle into Leavitt's chest and depressed the plunger. Leavitt's face turned scarlet and he let out a roar that went on and on. Then he collapsed, limp and once more lifeless.

"Damn it, damn it, damn it! Too late!" West stood over the body for a long moment, his head hanging. When he straightened up he looked more discouraged than I had ever seen him. But my mind was still reeling with the enormity of recent events and I could not speak. "Well, he's dead," West said. "I suppose we had better start up the incinerator and burn everything. Come on, Charles, snap out of it. You look as though you're going to faint."

I made an effort to pull myself together but I could not bring myself to confront West with the last words of the dead man. His terrified reference to a needle and the fact that I had found such an implement at the scene of his collapse, along with the fact of the nonexistent water glass, suggested that my friend was a murderer. He was a physician who had taken the Hippocratic oath, but he had killed a man simply so that he might use him as an experimental subject. I could not ignore this, as I had previous indications of West's unscrupulousness, but I remembered my uncertainty about the revivifying fluid I had compounded, which we had used on Leavitt. I thought I might have added too much of the activating agent, but in the excitement I had forgotten to mention this to West.

"I think it was my fault," I heard myself saying, as though from a distance. "I made a mistake with the fluid, didn't stop it in time. It was just when you came in to tell me about him. I meant to tell you, but I forgot."

He looked at me for a long moment. I could not tell what he was thinking. Then he said, "This entire episode is a perfect example of why haste and experiments are not compatible. I should have waited. Right from the first I should have waited." After another silence he shook his head slightly and said,

"Let's take another look through Leavitt's pockets and case. There might be something that will give us an idea of how popular he is. We must destroy him and his possessions as soon as we can. Someone might have seen him come here, but no one will ever be able to prove that he was in this house."

"Aren't you going to notify someone – the police, maybe – about his death? I asked. "After all, he died of natural causes. He wasn't a corpse when he arrived here."

West gave me an impatient look. "It would be madness to notify anyone. The next thing you know there will be hordes of policemen all over the house. And how would you explain that hole in his chest, and the incisions? Once the police develop an interest in you it's nearly impossible to divert them from it. You have to develop a relationship with them instead, which is the last thing I want. No, we must consign Mr. Leavitt to the flames. It's unfortunate, but the lost must stay lost this time."

We searched through Leavitt's belongings. There was little enough of interest in his wallet and pocket-book. The case he had carried contained mainly technical literature and samples of machinery we assumed to be used in the cloth manufacturing trade. A letter from someone at Bolton Worsted Mills indicated that he was expected to arrive at some unspecified time during the week. I was grateful for one thing – Leavitt was apparently a bachelor. His address in St. Louis was given as Dempsey's Boarding House, hardly the abode of a married man. I was still unhappy, though. Did Leavitt perhaps have an old mother, or brothers and sisters who would never know and always wonder what had happened to him on his ill-fated trip to New England?

On two matters I insisted, to West's intense annoyance. Before we put the body into the incinerator we replaced his clothing, so that the unfortunate man would not go on his final journey naked. With some difficulty we forced the fellow's limbs back into his shirt, trousers and jacket. I myself re-tied Leavitt's necktie and replaced his shoes.

"Well, are you happy now?" asked West.

"One more thing," I said. "Do you happen to own a prayer book?"

He looked at me incredulously. "No I do not, and even if I did, this nonsense has gone far enough. Let's get on with it."

"No, Herbert. We're not going to burn this man like so much trash. He had the misfortune to meet his end here and we owe him something better than disposal. So I'm going to give him a funeral service. Or would you rather I had a word with the police?"

It was the first time I had defied him. For a moment I thought he was going to strike me, but then that coldness I knew so well descended over him. "Oh, all right. Wait a minute." He ran upstairs. I remembered, too late, the syringe I had found in the hall. Would he realize I had seen it? But when he returned a few minutes later, I could see nothing in his face but amused contempt. He tossed me a copy of the *Book of Common Prayer.*

"All right, Reverend Milburn, do your stuff. But don't take all day."

Feeling foolish, I fumbled with the thick little book. The cataloguer in me noted that it had been published in New York City in 1848, by D. Appleton & Co. A faded book plate bore the name Joseph Ezekiel Derby. Unfamiliar as I was with the Episcopalian liturgy, it took me a little while to find the burial service. The thinness of the onionskin paper didn't help; nor did West's ill-concealed impatience. I read the prayers for the graveside. "In the midst of life we are in death..." The age-old words sounded strangely in Herbert West's underground laboratory, but I hoped that they would serve to appease Leavitt's spirit if it still lingered at the scene of his second death.

West watched me with a strange look on his face, amused scorn combined with a kind of remoteness, as though he regarded the inexplicable busyness of an alien creature. At that moment, for the first time in our association, I felt a disconcerting shift in my perspective – I was no longer part of 'we,' but only 'I.'

I closed the book and laid it down. Then we carried the body down the passage to the incinerator. West opened the door and we slid into it the mortal remains of Robert Leavitt, of St. Louis.

After this I could not wait to get away. West seemed equally glad to see me go. We parted with some vague words about meeting in a few days to discuss future plans, but I did not see him again for upwards of two weeks.

Early in October, a man came to my door. He was from the Boston Police, he said, showing me an identification card. He was investigating the disappearance of Robert Leavitt of St. Louis, who was last seen on College Street near the hospital.

I had been expecting a visit of this sort and successfully maintained a calm exterior. I knew nothing of Robert Leavitt, I said. I had visited my friend Dr. West on the afternoon of

September 15, but I had seen no strangers in the neighbourhood, neither at my arrival nor when I left. With this the fellow had to be content. I knew there was no evidence linking Leavitt to West. I was certain that even Leavitt's gold teeth had been raked out of the ashes in the incinerator and deposited, together with the samples he had been carrying, into the Miskatonic River.

Why did I protect West? Many times I have asked myself this question. The answers formed a kind of circular dance in my mind which ran something like this: Once the body and other evidence was gone there was no point in telling anyone. But why didn't I confront West immediately, or go directly to the police? Because my own position was equivocal; because, despite the doubts about West that had accumulated over the years, I was still his friend. I could not make the transition from friend to accuser as swiftly as the situation demanded, and once the body was gone... But why hadn't I persuaded him to wait before burning everything? All right, but how could I have made sure he wouldn't do it after I had gone? And there was my own responsibility for Leavitt's second death, because I had forgotten to tell West that the fluid was probably defective. If we had administered a correctly prepared substance, Leavitt might have fully recovered. So it was possible that the ultimate responsibility for his death was mine...

There was not a night in those weeks when I didn't lie awake and run all these arguments through my mind. I never reached a conclusion; my ruminations usually ended in a strange waking dream, in which I saw Leavitt approaching West's house and ringing the bell. West admitted him and they talked. My friend's expression was solicitous but I imagined a lurking glee in his eyes. He excused himself and returned a minute later – with death in his hand.

Did he look into Leavitt's eyes as he depressed the plunger? I remembered them – dark grey with amber flecks, full of anxiety. Had he seen the man's terror and carried on regardless? I could not imagine the thought process that led to the deed.

After the visit from the policeman I thought I had better talk with West. Sufficient time had passed that I could approach him without the loathing that had come over me as I looked at the syringe I had found in the hall. At the very least I wanted him to know that I no longer wished to participate in his experiments, now that he had crossed the border between iconoclasm and outright crime. But first I needed to know what had been in his mind when he jabbed that needle into Leavitt.

The following evening I knocked once more on West's door. Almost I hoped he was not home, but forced myself to knock a second time when no answer was forthcoming after half a minute. The door opened. West wore a distracted look.

"Oh it's you, Charles. Come in. I have a visitor, but it's all right. Come in." He showed me up to his private quarters. In the sitting room was a middle-aged man with dark hair and a moustache, wearing a military uniform unfamiliar to me. West introduced him as Lt.-Col. Sir Eric Moreland Clapham-Lee, of the Canadian Army's Medical Corps.

"Sir Eric has been most helpful in securing me a commission in his service," said West. "I'll be leaving for Ottawa in a few days, then on to England and eventually to Flanders or France."

This was a tremendous shock to me. So far, the war in Europe had been a distant newspaper phenomenon. Everyone fully expected it to end soon. It was thought to be no concern of America's. West had never shown the slightest military or patriotic zeal, but he had obviously sought out this Clapham-Lee for the purpose of enlisting in a foreign army.

I said little but thought much. As the others finished their business and West showed his visitor to the door, I perceived a reason for his sudden interest in foreign service. Two reasons, actually.

Feeling once more the estrangement that had descended upon me as I read the burial service over Leavitt, I was careful to have a firm hold on my composure when West returned to the room. "Well, Herbert, may I offer my congratulations. I didn't realize you had suddenly grown militaristic."

"Don't be an idiot, Charles. I haven't a militaristic bone in my body. But surely you realize that this is the only way I'll ever have anything like legitimate access to material for my experiments. Wars produce corpses, lots of them. And before they're killed, they're young men in good health. Governments see to that. Only the healthy need apply for the job of cannon fodder. Well, maybe a few of them will be less than dead as a result of my efforts. And in any case, I'm good at cutting and splicing. So I can be of some use to the not yet dead, too."

And you can get away from Arkham and out of the country before the investigation into Leavitt's disappearance picks up steam, I thought. Aloud I said, "I had a visit from a member of the Boston Police yesterday. I thought you should know."

West seemed unconcerned. "Oh yes, he came here too. I told him I had never seen Leavitt. Case closed. What did you tell him?"

"Only that I had visited here on the day in question, but I never saw Leavitt or anyone who might have been Leavitt. That's all."

"Good, Charles, I knew I could count on you." He produced one of his beautiful smiles, but for the first time it failed to charm me. A part of me was already in mourning but I could not simply give up and go away, turning my back on more than three years of friendship and close collaboration in risky enterprises. I administered my final test.

"But I could have said a good deal more, Herbert. I could have told him about what Leavitt said to me before you came back. And about the syringe I found in the hall."

"Oh, so you and Leavitt had a little conversation, did you? I wish you had told me before. It would have been something to set against the failure. And you didn't write it down as I asked, obviously. Well, what did he say?"

"He said you attacked him with a needle. And before that, when I went up to get his case, I found an empty syringe under the hall table."

"Now Charles, what do you suppose our visitor from the Boston Police would have made of your story that Leavitt himself told you I murdered him? Either he was conversing with you or he was dead. You can't usually have it both ways in this vale of tears. As for the syringe, it's one of the tools of my trade, along with sharp knives and deadly drugs. Its presence in my house is hardly surprising, is it? If something like that turned up in *your* hall, now, it might be a different matter..."

He was actually laughing! There wasn't a trace of defensiveness in his manner, never mind guilt. And what angered me more than anything was the fact that he treated me, his friend and associate, very nearly his partner in crime, the same as an ignorant, intrusive policeman. If he had at least admitted the deed, said "Yes, Charles, I killed him, but in a good cause; let it be a secret between us." If he had said this, the old magic would have done its work. Nothing would now restore Leavitt to life, but this might have saved my friendship.

"I suppose it doesn't matter now that you're leaving, but I came here to say... to tell you that I won't be assisting you with your... experiments any more. Not after this. I admit that I probably contributed to Leavitt's death – the second one, I mean. That's why I lied to that policeman. But I can't condone murder,

Herbert. So this is the end for me. I don't imagine I'll see much of you after this. Oh, and good luck with the war."

He listened with no expression on his face, his eyes focused on something behind me. I turned to go and was halfway down the stairs before he spoke again.

"Will you come to the station to see me off, Charles? Eight o'clock on Wednesday morning. Please come."

I almost kept going without replying. But then I thought, Well, one last time, what harm can it do? "All right, Herbert. I'll be there."

♦ 11 ♦

Wednesday morning was misty, the scarlet blaze of the maples muted to a dull red. I thought I was early, but West was already at the station, talking to a porter who took away his two large suitcases and a trunk. He wore a tweed travelling coat and already looked remote and foreign. Conversation was difficult. What I wanted to say was, "Do you know what you have done to me? You have broken my illusions, and now you are going away, leaving only the fragments behind." But instead I chatted with false heartiness about the weather and the prospects for a pleasant trip through interesting country.

When the train was in the station and passengers were going aboard, he cut me short. "One thing, Charles. It's just as well I'm going away, don't you think? Since I'm my father's son, after all – murder in the blood, you could say. Thank you for your help all these years, and your friendship too. It wasn't unappreciated."

I felt once more his cool, firm handclasp, then he was gone. All around me echoed endingness, endingness.

I walked slowly to the Library. All day I was distracted and irritable. I sent several colleagues away dissatisfied, even hurt, by my manner. At the afternoon break Alma asked outright what was bothering me. Breaking our rule, which now seemed silly, of never discussing personal matters at work, I said,

"West has gone to Flanders, to the war. He's going to be a medical officer in the Canadian Army." Already I could feel an obscure relief stealing over me, just by voicing the fact to Alma.

But her reaction was unexpected. "Really? How did he manage that? I wish I'd thought of asking him about it. You see, I've been thinking it's irresponsible of me to stay here, following my daily round of silly activities while people are killing each other over there. I've heard there are things non-combatants can do, apart from nursing, I mean. I'll have to find out more."

I was shocked, and showed it. "Alma! Not you too! No, I can't let you go!"

"I hardly think it's for you to say, Charles. But don't be silly, it's not as though I'm going tomorrow, or even at all. It's just something that might be worth pursuing. You already know I've been thinking about leaving Arkham. What could be better than this? It's a worthy cause, and a way of postponing a final decision about what to do with my life. I shouldn't have sprung it on you so suddenly, that's all, especially when your friend just left."

She listened to my edited description of West's decision to go, and after a while I felt a little better, but only for a while, because I knew there was another ending in sight. When Alma signed up with the Red Cross as an ambulance driver, it was set at mid-March.

On a morning as clear and frosty as that one in October had been mild and misty, I saw her off at Arkham Station.

"Cheer up, Charles," she said. "I'll write you, of course – more often than West, I'll bet. How many letters have you had from him?"

"A couple of short notes," I admitted. "But I imagine he's fairly busy." My words conjured up a sudden mental image of West in a bloodstained white coat, bending over something unspeakable. "I've been reading that things are heating up again on the Western Front."

We made no promises to one another, Alma and I. It would not have been in keeping with what we had been to one another. I was left with hopes, but not expectations. We walked up and down the platform, talking of trivia. I wanted this pointless interlude to continue forever, and I couldn't wait for it to end. When it did end and the train was pulling away, Alma waving to me through her window, I wished that I could reverse time, just a little. Was it something like this agonized desire that drove West in his efforts to reverse death? If so, I could almost begin to understand his ruthless single-mindedness.

It is always more difficult to be left than to leave. The one leaving has new situations to occupy him or her, new people and places to take in and cope with. The one left behind, on the other hand, has only that which occupied his attention before, but without the presence of those who are no longer there. And in my case there was besides an envy of the new adventures that West and Alma had embarked upon, and which I was unable to.

Shortly after Alma's departure I was seized by such an intense longing for the past, for her and West, that I resolved somehow to follow them. But this was not so easily done. America did not enter the War until 1917 of course, and I knew anyway that I would never make the grade in the Army because of my poor eyesight and bad leg. I had neither the connections nor the resolve to enlist in a foreign army, as West had done. And anyway, I expected the Canadians would have physical standards which I probably did not meet. Besides, West had a valuable skill to offer; I did not think there was much demand for cataloguers. That left services such as the Red Cross and other support organizations. But I knew my motives for joining any of them were suspect. It was not altruism, humanitarianism or patriotism that drove me, but nostalgia, which would not serve me well in any kind of challenging situation.

Finally, I knew that if West had wanted me to accompany him, he would have made sure I did. It was as simple as that. No, Herbert West and Alma Halsey had left the circle of the world I inhabited, as surely as if they had gone to Mars. To put myself in mere physical proximity with either of them now would achieve nothing. The idyll was over and I had my own road to follow.

After a few weeks during which the motions of daily life felt like slogging through ankle-deep mud, I found myself coming to terms with my new situation. In their own way, my war years were as odd and disjointed as the previous three had been. The differences were that the oddness was public, not private, and I was not as happy.

Because of the involvement of my two friends, I had more interest in the War than most Americans. I read every newspaper article I could get my hands on and attended lectures by persons who professed an expert knowledge of the situation, an expertise which often existed only in their own minds. After the sinking of the *Lusitania* in May 1915, anti-German sentiment and patriotism began to develop. A number of strange little societies sprang up in and around Arkham, such as the Arkham Patriots' League, the Miskatonic Musketeers (a group of self-styled 'practical militarists' who went out and practiced marching and shooting rifles in preparation for the ultimate struggle with the Hun), the Arkhamites Against War and the Bolton Catholics for Peace. I attended meetings and demonstrations of several of these groups, not from any conviction, but merely because to hear about the War and related issues made me feel, in some tenuous way, closer to my friends overseas.

It was at one of these events that I met Sarah Enright. She was from Bolton, working as a nurse at St. Mary's Hospital. I found myself next to her at a lecture and soon realized that she was rolling her eyes heavenward at exactly the same times as I was inwardly doing so myself. Chatting together at the refreshment session which followed, we found we had a good deal more in common. For one thing, Sarah was professionally acquainted with West; she had, in fact, worked with him.

"Yes, I know Dr. West quite well," she said. "He's a good doctor, though not everyone thinks so. At least when it comes to surgery, anyway. I've never seen anyone so fast and neat at the job. Very few of his patients develop post-surgical infections. Those Canadians are lucky to have him sewing up their soldiers, but it's Arkham's loss."

"But you say some people don't think much of him."

"Well, of course. When someone's really good at what they do, there are always a few who are happy to find fault. Now I admit, he isn't much for reassuring the patients and cheering them up. But I figure some of the other doctors are just jealous, and as for the nurses, some resented his insistence that everything be sterilized within an inch of its life. And then, of course, he was totally resistant to their charms, which really got their collective goat!"

"Yes, that's Herbert all right," I said with a smile. "He's the most unromantic person I've ever met."

"Unromantic! That's an understatement. 'Dr. Iceberg West,' that's what they call him. But I liked working with him. You always knew where you were, as long as you were on your toes, that is. And he might have been cold, but he was certainly ornamental."

Sarah could not be called ornamental, exactly, but she was attractive enough, with her neat dark hair and trim figure. We became friends. I was glad to have someone I could talk with almost as freely as I had with Alma. But friends was all we were. At this point anyway, it seemed that my desire for anything more had gone away too.

One evening we had arranged to meet outside the Freemasons' Hall, where we were to attend a lecture with the provocative title 'Are There German Spies Among Us?' I waited until the last possible minute, but Sarah did not appear. I went inside and found a pair of seats near the back of the hall. Minutes later she arrived, a little out of breath.

"I couldn't get away in time," she explained later. "You see, my lady was having one of her spells, and I thought I had better stay with her until she settled down."

"Your lady?"

"A lady I look after. It's sort of an extra job I have, three afternoons a week. She's... disturbed, I guess you could say. Some days are better than others, but it's not bad, usually. And it means a little extra money for my mother in Bolton. She still has three children at home, you see. My Dad died a few years ago, so it's not easy for her."

I looked at her with admiration. Here was someone who was dealing successfully with the difficulties of her life, a life not nearly as privileged as Alma's or mine. "Isn't it difficult, this extra job? I would have thought working at the hospital would be enough."

"No, it's not hard, most of the time. You see, she trusts me, and I've come to know what kinds of things upset her, so I can usually tell when she's going to have a bad spell. It doesn't happen that often, maybe a couple of times a month. Usually I'm just company for her. I guess her family prefer to pay someone to be with her, so they don't have to do it themselves. She can be quite interesting to talk to, even though I'm never sure what's the truth and what isn't. She must have been a real lady once. I think she was married, though I've never seen or heard anything of her husband. But sometimes she speaks of a little son she lost."

About this time I had a strange dream. I was in the back of an ambulance, although there was nothing wrong with me, as far as I could tell. Alma was driving. The ground we were riding over was very bumpy, but it was dark and I could see nothing outside except occasional flashes of bright light. "Flares," said Alma. "They set them off to show me the way."

Finally we arrived at a barn, rather like the one where the prizefight had been held. Alma drove inside. I tried to get out but she wouldn't let me. "You can't walk, Charles. Someone will come and get you." Someone did, but I couldn't see who it was. Strangely, they didn't need to lift me because I was floating in mid air, lying on my back. Whoever it was had only to steer me. We went along miles of corridors, some dimly lit and brick-walled, others bright and lined with white tiles that reflected the light blindingly.

Then West was there, dressed in white. I could not see him very well because I was unable to rise from my horizontal position or turn myself. "I'm making you a new leg, Charles," he said. "Then you won't have an excuse not to come out here." I tried to protest that having an excuse wasn't the issue and I didn't need a new leg, but suddenly he was holding a leg out to me and smiling. There must have been many other people in the room, because applause and cheering broke out. West held up the leg as if to show it to this audience. I felt intensely embarrassed and woke up.

All this time, of course, I continued to work as a cataloguer at Miskatonic University Library. Cataloguing was far more difficult and interesting in those days, before widespread acceptance of the Library of Congress's printed cards imposed standardization of methods.

From 1915 onward I was engaged in cataloguing a large collection of books, manuscripts and other materials donated to the Library by Augustus Quarrington. Nominally, he had been a member of the Philosophy Department, but over the years his interests had branched out (some would say slopped over) into areas as diverse as mathematics, Egyptology, quantum physics, phrenology and especially numerology. He was a twentieth century manifestation of the long tradition of interdisciplinary studies begun by such Renaissance scholars as Pico della Mirandola, Johannes Tritthemius and Heinrich Cornelius Agrippa. Quarrington believed, among other things, that there was a secret system of numbers that united all things in the universe. Once discovered, it would yield the key to eternal life and answers to the ultimate questions. Unfortunately he died before he attained this goal, at the age of one hundred and one.

I was first made aware of his demise by a notice in the *Arkham Advertiser* over my breakfast coffee – "Venerable Prof Dead at 101." He had written to me only a few weeks earlier, a rather puzzling letter. My attention fully engaged, I read the article, learning more about the professor's wide-ranging interests and his long career as a teacher, researcher and daring theorist.

Several weeks later, I was summoned to a meeting with Dr. Armitage, the University Librarian and Peter Runcible, my Department Head. Dr. Quarrington had left his entire collection of books, manuscripts and objects to the Miskatonic University Library, with the stipulation that they be kept together and housed separately as the Augustus Quarrington Collection.

Dr. Armitage looked grim rather than delighted at the news.

"We're up against it this time," he said. "I've managed to talk most of our prospective donors out of these notions before it was too late, but Quarrington sprang this one on us. Good God, can you imagine if we had to set up a special collection for every professor's cast-off books and papers – the Joseph Brown Collection on Tropical Liverworts, the Nathaniel Dixon Collection on Medieval Siege Engines, the Professor Bertha Marshall Collection on Transylvanian Doily-Knitting! You know what I mean – they all want a room with their name on it and a separate catalogue too, as though their books are too good to mingle with the common herd."

"Little do our prospective donors know how many of their books prove to be redundant," remarked Runcible. "You remember, Milburn, last year when that fellow from the Classics Department left us five thousand books? How many of them did we keep?"

"Fewer than a quarter," I said. "I spent the better part of a month going through them and deciding which ones to keep. And another week at Gifts and Exchanges to dispose of the rejects."

"Ah, that would have been Professor Hollingsworth," said Dr. Armitage. "It was lucky that I managed to convince him to trust us when it came to dealing with his collection. He'd been hinting that he expected a special room, because he was being so generous – five thousand books, after all! I persuaded him that they would be more useful if they were kept with others on the same subjects. But then, Hollingsworth was a generalist. I find it's the ones who specialize in some esoteric and rarified subject that are the hardest to deal with."

"But sir," I ventured, "that doesn't really describe Prof. Quarrington, does it? I gather that he was interested in a large number of fields. He believed in the interdisciplinary approach, didn't he?"

Runcible let out a barking laugh. "You could call it that, I suppose. Some would say he got lost on the road between philosophy and magic. There is one thing, though." He turned to Armitage. "It's pretty unlikely that many of his books will be duplicates of ones we already have. The question is, are they worth keeping? I mean, really – numerology? It's hardly a science."

"Perhaps not, but it's a subject of interest to some scholars," said Dr. Armitage, "if only as an example of a dubious field of inquiry. But you have a point, Runcible. Prof. Quarrington's materials include a great deal that will be difficult to deal with. No fewer than a dozen languages are represented. Latin and Greek, but also Icelandic and Old Lithuanian."

"That's where you come in, Milburn," said Runcible. "You seem to have a knack for figuring out what to do with the unfamiliar. Foreign languages and so on. And then there are the items that by rights belong in an archive or a museum. Quarrington's manuscripts and... objects he studied for various reasons – rocks and bits of string, and even shoes, I understand. We're relying on your experience as a cataloguer to deal with them."

I thought, 'unfamiliar' to Runcible means 'stuff I'd rather not be bothered with,' but I was flattered that my superior had such good things to say about me in the presence of Dr. Armitage. Aloud, I said,

"Shoes! Surely we aren't going to catalogue them."

"Oh yes, we are," said Runcible, grinning. "Or rather, you are. Why do you suppose we asked you to be here today?"

"Yes," said Armitage. "The bequest states quite clearly that everything must be kept in the Miskatonic University Library, and everything must be catalogued."

"But sir," I objected, "why shouldn't we exercise our right to select appropriate materials for the Library's collections? No one has ever given us things like shoes before. They aren't appropriate."

"True, but in this case there's a complication," said Armitage, looking at me sternly. "I suppose I should have mentioned it earlier. You see, Prof. Quarrington has left the Library a... considerable sum of money along with his books and other materials. A very generous endowment for the Augustus Quarrington Collection. Exceedingly generous. But the will stipulates quite clearly that the materials *must* be kept together, *must* be catalogued and *must* be made available to researchers. Do you understand now, Milburn?"

"Oh yes, sir, I quite understand." I kept quiet after that, wondering just how I was going to catalogue books in languages I had never heard of before, never mind rocks and shoes.

As I began to work with the materials, in a small room formerly used to store castoffs such as broken furniture, old catalogue cards and superseded reference works, I felt like a lone missionary sent to a small savage country, the customs of whose inhabitants were utterly mystifying and a little frightening.

I unpacked the cartons, starting with the books and progressing to the manuscripts, maps, drawings, photographs, natural objects, knotted strings and other bizarre and unlikely items. One box did indeed contain a dozen or so pairs of well-worn shoes, accompanied by a file of notes helpfully entitled 'Shoe Study.'

The most interesting photographs were dozens of close-up views of different people's eyes. I laid the images out on the table, for no better reason than to experience the odd effect of many disembodied pairs of eyes looking up at me. As I regarded them, I became certain that one of them was West's. There was something about the crystalline quality of the irises, the directness of the gaze and the trace of irony I thought I could see in the expression, that was very like him.

Eventually I found it necessary to co-opt another librarian to work with me. Alma, with her scientific background, would have been the ideal choice, but her replacement, Linton Adams, was intelligent enough to be able to work beyond rigid disciplinary boundaries.

It was fairly easy to classify the books – philosophy, mathematics, natural history, chemistry, physics and so on. There was another broad grouping of 'esoteric knowledge,' which included everything from alchemy to astrology, mesmerism, phrenology and divination. There were so many works on numerology that they constituted a category of their own.

The manuscripts were more problematic. In the end I decided to arrange them in strict chronological order, as far as their dates could be determined. With time, it was surprising how readily I was able to date a document from its subject matter and tone. Quarrington's early writings were fairly standard philosophical treatises. As the decades went by they became more varied as to subject and wilder as to substance. Those written in the last years of his life approached the limits of reasonable discourse.

Quarrington believed that he had found a way to test his theories by subjecting individuals to analysis using principles he had worked out over the years, then making specific predictions about the life courses of the subjects. The predictions would be kept secret from them, of course, so as to avoid influencing their choices. Eventually the actual life events could be checked against Quarrington's documented predictions. If these proved to be true, Quarrington believed, it would be possible to project from the lesser to the greater and unlock some of the world's ultimate secrets.

A thick portfolio titled 'Profiles and Predictions' contained dozens of these case histories, probably of students. They were not named but identified by codes, to which the key was either missing or not yet recognized for what it was by myself and my assistants. The data included information such as exact time and place of birth, family history, number of siblings, economic status, education, likes and dislikes. Some were rather peculiar, such as detailed measurements of body proportions and reactions to varying kinds of sounds, intensities of light, temperatures and pin-pricks on a number of sites on the body.

The predictions ranged from fantastically detailed and specific to ominous hints. I found myself reading them compulsively.

Will be thrown from a horse while passing Hooper's Pond, June 12, 1910. Right leg broken, but will recover completely.

Early marriage, five children, early death from tuberculosis. Bad business – should I intervene? But how? Keep her from marrying? – impossible!

Will start out as lawyer, be persuaded to enter politics. Successful. Then possibility of corruption. May do great harm.

This woman will become a nexus. Because of her, many great things will be done, but much pain endured as well. Details unclear.

Many contradictions here – light and darkness in equal measure. Reconciliation necessary or self-destructive impulses may follow.

I kept reminding myself that these predictions were based on rather dubious data. Without knowing the individuals to whom the prognostications referred, it was impossible to begin to investigate their validity. But even without the identifying key, I thought this was a potentially volatile file. I recommended that it be securely stored and consulted only by those who had a sincere and serious reason to do so.

In 1917, with the United States finally in the War, a great change took place in Arkham. Suddenly, many of the younger men were gone, their jobs taken by women. My assistant Linton Adams left for France, along with a few other men from the Library. Fortunately, the cataloguing of the Quarrington Collection was by then nearly complete.

I saw less of Sarah Enright, as she was kept very busy at the hospital with so many nurses overseas. But I found myself in demand socially, much to my surprise. With the general shortage of younger men, anything in trousers that was even semi-articulate was a desirable property. As the War progressed and American soldiers began to return with various disabilities, I was more than once taken for a returnee and my limp the result of a war injury. Admiring women asked me to tell them how it happened. I am sorry to admit that on one or two occasions I did just that, fabricating a lurid tale from bits of information gleaned from newspapers and letters from Alma and West. The latter, I thought, would have been much amused.

♦ 12 ♦

War Letters

Letters... They became disproportionately important to me during the war years, especially those from West and Alma. I have them here before me, so often read that sections of them speak to me from memory. Once, I fancied that I could feel in the paper the touch of her hands, hear from the ink the sound of his voice. But my own fingers and eyes in their seeking have obliterated these fragile ghosts.

Other considerations apart, the letters contain a chronology of those years, which is why I read them now once again.

****

Salisbury Plain
England
Dec. 14, 1914
C.D. Milburn
23 ½ College Street East
Arkham, Mass., U.S.A.

My Dear Charles,

I write to you from an ocean of mud, otherwise known as a camp of the Canadian Expeditionary Force, although it rather resembles chaos. Perhaps the sorting-out process which is our purpose here is as yet invisible to my unmilitary eye.

Not much to say about the ocean voyage, except that I was fortunate enough not to get sea-sick, unlike many of my fellow passengers, including Clapham-Lee. He was laid up for most of it, and only struggled out of his bunk when we were nearly at Plymouth.

Two weeks in London were useful in that I was able to finish outfitting myself. At least there are decent tailors there. Then to this muddy plain, where we medical types have been kept busy with an epidemic of cerebrospinal meningitis.

In my spare moments, I have amused myself with sociological observations. Canadians seemed quite English to me until I was able to compare them with real Englishmen, after which they seemed more like us. I speak here of Canadians born in Canada; there is also a large number of British-born Canadians, fully encumbered with the traditions and prejudices of their native land. They are unfortunately over-represented in the Canadian Contingent. The nuances of social class are further complicated by those of military rank; I think I have managed to get them straight by now. Most of the others regard me quite amicably, I suppose because I have crafted the right sort of facade for myself, tempered with the disarming ingenuousness of the Yankee.

The lamp is guttering and my tent-mate (not for long, thank God!) is muttering about 'lights out,' so I shall dutifully douse and retire.

Herbert.

Boulogne, France
Feb. 10, 1915
My Dear Charles,

Well, we finally got to France. Now we are waiting (I have learned that in the Army one spends a great deal of time doing that) to discover where we are to be sent. There is a rumour that our contingent is to join the 2nd British Army on the Belgian border.

I am not sure which is harder to bear – lack of luxuries or of privacy. I have a different tent-mate here, not chosen by me, you may be sure – a fellow from some outlandish place called Saskatchewan (I had to ask him the spelling), but very English for all that. At least he seems to have had decent training (in eastern Canada), so we can talk shop, although I don't know what we'll do after we have exhausted the topics of suturing techniques, diagnostic methods and so on – reminisce about our dear old home towns, no doubt.

Sometimes I think of my laboratory lying unused in Arkham (although I tell myself I should not) and wonder what the devil I'm doing here.

Herbert.

****

Red Cross Stn. No. 3
Boulogne, France
May 3, 1915

Mr. Charles Milburn
23 ½ College Street E.
Arkham, Massachusetts,
United States of America

Dear Charles,

My first letter from France is to you. I have been here only two weeks, but it seems like forever. I spent the entire first week trying not to faint or vomit, and I was afraid to sleep because of the nightmares. By the second week I was all right, and now I'm completely hardened, on the surface at least.

My job is ferrying casualties from the trains that bring them from the front to the hospitals here. They don't send women drivers to the front. That bothered me at first, but now I'm just as happy it is so. It may sound heartless, but by the time they arrive here, the worst cases have died; the ones that are left are bad enough.

On the days I'm not on duty, I explore the town with some of the others – the original French town nearby, I mean, not the new one of hastily-constructed huts, sheds and tents where we live and work. Boulogne itself is kind of a dull little place, but the countryside beyond is pretty, with its villages and fields. Sometimes we go on picnics, and there are lots of opportunities for me to practice my limited French. But it's not exactly a holiday.

I share a hut with five other women – an English bohemian, a Canadian from Toronto disconsolate over a broken engagement, a would-be Communist from Minnesota and a pair of earnest Australians. They have taken some getting used to, but I certainly wouldn't have met people like them in Arkham! Each has her own reasons for being here – to find adventure, to escape a dull existence, an oppressive family, an unwanted suitor. Oh, Romance! That seems to be behind so many of the reasons – too much, too little, the wrong kind.

Enough. I can feel a Complaint coming on, and I don't want to burden you with it. I'm sure this will be a Good Experience for me.

But I do miss you.
Alma.

I missed her too, more than I ever admitted in my letters to her. And I was a faithful correspondent. I wrote to her about my adventures with the Quarrington collection and about the changeless changes of Arkham. She wrote to me about the people and situations she encountered in her difficult and demanding work. I think perhaps it was in those letters that she began to find her future career. But here I excerpt only those that bear on Herbert West.

****

55 Church Street
Arkham
May 10, 1915

Mr. Charles Milburn
23 ½ College Street
Arkham

Dear Mr. Milburn,

I regret that we have had so few opportunities to become acquainted, for I suspect that we have much in common. But it is not for everyone to walk the road that I have chosen. It has been a long road and an interesting one, and I sense that it is approaching its end. I had my 101st birthday in January, and that is certainly long enough for anyone.

That is why I presume to write to you now, because you are the friend of one whom I regard as my son. I have had grave concerns for Herbert West, ever since I compiled and analyzed data about him as part of my Study of Predictions. As a rule, I refrain from revealing my predictions to subjects or those close to them, for fear of influencing their decisions, but in his case I am breaking this rule.

I speak of his decision to participate in this European war. I think it may be extremely harmful for him to place himself in a situation where violent death is a daily commonplace. I realize that as a surgeon, he is, presumably, on the side of life. Even so, I feel – no, I <u>know</u> – that a situation where many violent deaths occur may create intolerable strains on him, with unfortunate, even disastrous results. Before he can safely enter that borderland, he must undergo experiences that will be painful, even agonizing, but are necessary. I can explain no more now but I ask you to join me in persuading him to return to Arkham as soon as he can. Your presence is necessary for his ultimate well-being, but he does not know this. I do not think you have plans to join him overseas, thus it is especially dangerous for him to remain there.

<u>Do not abandon your friend. Your fates were linked when you read the Necronomicon together. Three and five, and three times five again, but your returnings will be true. Do you be true also.</u>

Quarrington

I did not know what to make of this urgent but irrational plea. West had certainly not consulted me when he decided to go overseas, and I knew him well enough to recognize that any suggestions of mine for him to return would be ignored. And, when all was said and done, had I abandoned him? I thought not; he had not, after all, given me the chance but had abandoned me instead.

****

No. 1 C.C.S.
C.A.M.C.
St. Eloi, Belgium
May 12, 1915
My Dear Charles,

My experience with rain and mud in England was good preparation for my current situation. I have never seen so much mud, and hot water is a luxury I never fully appreciated until now. Indeed, I am inclined to think that hot water, not art, is the hallmark of civilization.

Things began to get exciting here a few weeks ago, which is why I haven't had time to write. I managed to convince those in charge that surgery is my thing, not handing out reprimands to men who have let their feet get rotten or examining their genitals for signs of venereal disease, or seeing that Rules are Enforced. So, just as the Germans began attacking Ypres again I was assigned to the C.C.S. here at St. Eloi.

A C.C.S. (for you civilians unused to the rampant initialisms so dear to the military mind) is a Casualty Clearing Station, the first stop between the field of battle and the military hospital (or the morgue, depending on how things turn out). It is a field hospital of the most basic sort.

Charles, you cannot imagine the intensity after a raid or a battle, with wounded men coming in by the dozens. My efforts back home to keep myself in good physical condition have paid off, because all of us here have been tested to our limits and beyond. I think my record now is three solid days of operating with only the shortest breaks between cases. It's amazing what one can do when one has to.

The casualties are sorted by type of injury and likelihood to withstand transport and surgery. Those whom the stretcher-bearers have assessed as unlikely to survive are left behind in the field – a callous but necessary practice called triage. Even so, when one is finished with a case, there is another ready for one's attention. And another after him, and another. After a cigarette break, one carries on. No, do not imagine I have taken up smoking; that is a kind of joke here – "Everyone fall out for a cigarette. Those who do not smoke will go through the motions." It's about what we need to catch our breaths, so to speak, although we have one fellow here – a Frenchman, naturally – who smokes while operating. When one of the nurses objected to his dropping ash into the wounds, he muttered, "Ah, mais c'est sterile, Mademoiselle," and carried on.

I am sure you think you know the reason I decided to come here – my research. But you must realize that a C.C.S. is not the sort of situation in which one can carry out experiments of the sort we did in Arkham. It is a lovely irony that I should be surrounded by fresh corpses which I cannot utilize. I have heard of men severely reprimanded for leaving their dead comrades' equipment on the field and bringing back their bodies instead. So a dead man is worth less than a rifle, except to his friends; thus the dead must be treated with respect. It's a nuisance, altogether.

I've been hearing artillery at work for some time now, so suspect it will be a busy night. I had better get some sleep while I can.

Herbert.

He remained at St. Eloi for a full year, growing increasingly impatient with what he considered an unproductive situation and with his superiors. In his letters I began to see an attitude like the one that preceded the Commencement Day incident, and wondered whether this was what Quarrington had warned me about. But my hints as to the desirability of a return to Arkham were uniformly ignored. In 1916 he found an opportunity for change and seized it. Or perhaps it would be more accurate to say that he manufactured it.

St. Eloi
Jan. 16, 1916
My Dear Charles,

The ebb and flow of 'personnel' washed a rather interesting individual to our blood-soaked little outpost recently, an Englishman named Morton who was supposedly inspecting something or other. He had a civilian look under the thinnest of military veneers, but he is well acquainted with Sir Eric Clapham-Lee, and for some reason was extraordinarily loquacious.

I already knew, of course, that Sir Eric is a surgeon of considerable repute in England. That was one of the reasons I approached him in the first place. He has great ambitions to revolutionize surgery and open a new field for enterprising individuals. He told me a little of this on the ship from America, before he was felled by sea-sickness.

Morton was elusive as to details, but I gather that a precipitous descent in the Clapham-Lee fortunes may be imminent, due to some financial disaster in the Far East. This, added to Sir Eric's scientific zeal, may furnish an avenue for a quid pro quo.

(War, I have found, induces in me a peculiar combination of ennui and anomie, which time reduces to a low cunning).

<u>Now I will tell you something</u>: Before I left Arkham, I worked out a way to create artificial tissue that is non-specific until it has been applied to a particular place in the body. Once assimilated, it promotes exceedingly rapid healing and reconstruction of severely injured areas. You can imagine how useful it has been here, and how many opportunities I have had to test it. I am quite overjoyed with it. I can put a man back together who has been very nearly destroyed. It may be that his own mother would not recognize him, but he will be alive and unmistakably human. I hope you understand now what I have to offer Sir Edward Clapham-Lee. If I decide to; I shall reserve judgment for the present.

Fondest regards,
Herbert.

Clapham-Lee was only one element in the formula; West himself was the other.

May 10, 1916
My Dear Charles,

Since I wrote you last I decided that I should experience something of life in the trenches. During the fighting near St. Eloi in April I managed to leave my relatively bomb-proof haven at the C.C.S. for an Advanced Dressing Station (an A.D.S. of course – what else?) just behind the lines, as the unofficial guest of the officer in charge there. As it turned out, that worthy fellow met with a bad end when the station was shelled, and it fell to me to direct the removal of the wounded to a place of safety. I found it an oddly exhilarating experience, Charles, dashing about dodging bullets and encouraging the stretcher-bearers, even taking a hand in stretcher-bearing myself. My brain has never been clearer than it was during this episode – an effect of undiluted adrenaline, I suppose. I was tempted to repeat the experience by getting myself transferred officially to one of these front-line stations but resisted, knowing that my talents are put to their best use in the operating theater and my experimental work cannot be done in the field.

Of course my superiors were not happy about this little adventure, although a little thought should have shown them that my presence was a piece of good luck. After all, Briggs would have been killed even if I had not been there, in which case the outcome would have been less satisfactory. But no, Rules were violated, resulting in disciplinary procedures and a blot on my record. Fortunately, I had already written to Clapham-Lee, hinting that transfer to another venue may be of mutual benefit for scientific collaboration. So we shall see what transpires.

Herbert

What transpired was a transfer the following month.

No. 1 Canadian General Hospital
Etaples, France
August 17, 1916

My Dear Charles,
Success! Since my last letter things have changed considerably. The powers that be decided that cooperation is the thing, with surgical expertise best concentrated in places where it can be mobilized to greatest efficiency. And Sir Eric now believes that a certain obscure Yankee may help him achieve his dearest ambitions.

So here I am, near this little French town where the war has sprouted a veritable city of hospitals and supporting institutions. The countryside is quite interesting – sand dunes and pine groves, a little like Cape Cod back home. There is a good view from the No. 1 to the seaside village of Paris Plage. Opportunities abound for exercise and amusement, which somewhat compensates for our close quarters and the everlasting regulations.

Despite which, I am working again – real work, besides what I do in my official capacity. For the first time I have been able seriously to pursue my revivification work. In the warren of buildings here I was able to commandeer a hut that is just adequate for my purposes. Clapham-Lee was helpful in this matter (although I am beginning to develop reservations about his motives). With the abundance of corpses available here, I have already carried out a number of revivifications. Some were like O'Brien and Hocks; I think the violence of their deaths carried over. They came to life filled with the intent to kill, and since the only thing available to be killed was myself, I had to dispatch them. (Finally a use for the pistol I am permitted, as an officer, to carry. Besides target-shooting, that is). Disposal of the bodies is absurdly easy. But I have registered several successes, some of them stellar compared with our Arkham results. With my tissue-regenerating substance, I was able to restore some of these men to the extent that they were able to return to active duty, slightly diminished in mental capacity, perhaps, but certainly functional. The most fortunate were considered unfit for further service and sent home.

Rejoice with me, Charles, because I must perforce keep this secret from my colleagues, even Clapham-Lee – no, him especially.

There are moments when I envy your peaceful haven in Arkham, closeted with your books.

Herbert.

P.S. But most of the time I do not.

My peaceful haven... Yes, I suppose it was that. Most of the time, my work was a refuge from memories and regrets. But every now and then, I would stop whatever I was doing – counting the leaves of plates in a book or holding up a page to the light to discern the watermark of the paper – because of an unbidden image that had invaded my mind – Alma, her hair loose and haloed with light; West's half-smile when he had caught me out in a lapse of logic during one of our arguments. Sometimes an entire minute would pass before I returned to my work.

Audrey Driscoll

Etaples
Oct. 22, 1916
My Dear Charles,

We have just come through several extremely bloody weeks, for me a maelstrom of life and death, to the point that sometimes I do not know whether I am trying to save a living man from death or restore a dead one to life. It has occurred to me more than once that it may not matter. I have plumbed their tissues in pursuit of their lives, swum in their blood, been splattered with fluids from their uttermost depths, seen things that no man (not even I?) should see – hearts laboring futilely in broken bodies, brains pulsating within shattered skulls. I have heard agonized screams and pleas for the mercy of death. Nothing can shock me now. And yes, I have possessed their lives, held them in the palm of my hand, snuffed them out like candles when it suited me. Perhaps some day I will tell you.

And no, Charles, I have not heard or seen any ghosts, rudely evicted spirits wandering about seeking their lost bodies. But then, I do not look for such things. One or two of them were lively conversationalists, quite argumentative. At least one could have been called <u>impertinent</u>. Apropos of impertinence, Clapham-Lee and I continue to dance – a pavane still, not a tarantella.

Yours "in haste," as we used to say in more civilized times.
Herbert.

****

After this, he did not write for several months. But Alma did.

Boulogne, France
January 15, 1917

Dear Charles,

Happy New Year to you too, except I'm not sure we can really call it 'happy' any more. It goes on and on, war without end. I have been here so long that it seems like home. My work has become routine, even though it is horrible. Am I callous, or is it human nature to adapt – even to this?

I've started doing some writing – besides letters, I mean. Nothing much, just opinion pieces and anecdotes about things that strike my fancy. There are so many people here trying to do their best, so many incidents that are strange, funny, poignant. I've been sending some of my pieces to magazines and newspapers in London and back home too (New York and Boston). If I could do this for a living, I would be happy. Especially if you were here too. No, I don't mean that, of course – not while the war drags on. What I wish is that it was over and you were here. We could run away to Paris and live in sin. I would write and you could be a cataloguer at the Bibliotheque Nationale. Wouldn't that be fun?

You asked about Herbert West. I haven't seen him myself, but I've heard things about him. It seems he is getting to be famous – or maybe notorious is a better word – for insubordination, irregularities, automobile racing, target-shooting and so on. And he spends a lot of time going for long walks alone. Some people probably think that's worse than the other stuff. But he's also a brilliant surgeon, gets through the cases faster than anyone and has an astonishing success rate, even with the hopeless ones. He must be a headache for his superiors, which means he hasn't changed much since he left Arkham, or only in degree, not in kind.

The Quarrington stuff sounds fiendishly interesting. But better you than I.

Toujours,
Alma.

****

Etaples
Mar. 28, 1917
My Dear Charles,

Profound apologies for being such a poor correspondent, but I have been, as you must know if you have been reading your newspapers, somewhat preoccupied. In addition to witnessing the decimation of a generation of young men and trying to reduce it, I have managed to make something of some of them. I leave the details to your imagination.

I've also had my hands full with Sir Eric. He is growing tedious. He has plans for a career after the war (in which case he must know something I do not, for it shows every sign of lasting forever – or at least until every man capable of soldiering, English, French, German and Canadian, is dead. But of course, America now trembles on the brink of entering the fray, a reluctant bride who nevertheless must bloody the sheet eventually. So who can tell?)

But Sir Eric – he asks me constantly for Results, for Facts, for Details. And I dispense a few crumbs and try to divert him. In our conversations – many of which take place on the wards at dawn, surrounded by men asleep or dying and the silent, watchful nurses – I have learned that what he desires is to offer to the well-heeled public a means to alter their facial features. Not merely to reconstruct the maimed (which we have both done, I better than he), but to improve or merely change, for reasons of vanity or expedience. He thinks there will be a great demand for this among the wealthy, and if there is only one surgeon who can accomplish it, that person will exercise the power of the monopolist and command large fees. So much for science and the good of all mankind! (There is only one person, as yet, who can do this, and it is not Clapham-Lee!)

I have ended our collaboration, although he does not know that. Unfortunately, I revealed enough to him at the beginning of our association that he is inflamed by the potential. I am running out of diversions. Ironically, the best means to put him off are furnished not by me but by the fortunes of war. When we are more than fully occupied with our legitimate business, he is perforce less tiresome.

Disengage? Counter-attack? Negotiate? Steal a march? Surrender? You see, Charles, how I strategize. And all around me, death in life and life in death, so that I grow weary of it all – even, sometimes, of myself.

Cheerfully,
Herbert.

P.S. I nearly forgot – I've been promoted. It's Major West now. Grand, eh?

****

Boulogne, France
June 25, 1917
Dearest Charles,

Last week I was in Paris on leave. You will never guess who I met there – your friend Herbert West. He was drinking absinthe and was quite convivial, perhaps as a result. He asked me to say hello to you for him and to apologize for not writing more often. So here are greetings and apologies from Herbert.

My duty accomplished, I must say something more: He seemed a little disconnected, as though he was looking for someone to tell him who he was. You know him better than I, in most ways, so maybe you've seen him like that before. Or maybe not. In any case, I think I may have helped him a little. It was, in some ways, an informative encounter. I think he misses you more than he knows or is willing to admit. I miss you too, and know it <u>and</u> admit it, but somehow Arkham seems very small and far away. Remembering it, and even our good times together, is like looking through the wrong end of a telescope.

I'd better stop; I'm not sure what it is I'm saying.

Fondly,

Alma.

This letter seemed to imply more than it said, and I read it repeatedly, trying to extract a hidden meaning, but it eluded me. I expected a mention of this meeting in West's next letter. But he did not write until several weeks later – a strangely uninformative letter, as though he had written it only to fulfill an obligation. Or perhaps it only seemed so to me. He rambled on about surgical procedures, using technical terminology that meant nothing to me (which was probably just as well), and referred to surgeons and nurses with whom he worked, not always in flattering terms. He seemed to have more respect for the nurses, explaining that in the Canadian Army they held actual military ranks, unlike the British Army's nursing sisters. He mentioned, apropos of nothing, that he sometimes found it necessary to shoot rats among the hospital outbuildings, and closed with a token inquiry about my health.

But there was a postscript.

P.S. I met Alma Halsey in Paris nearly two months ago. It has become a leave center recently, and I suppose both of us knew an opportunity when we saw it. She spent much of the time on the dance floor with a rather handsome fellow. When we managed to speak of you, Charles, I was discreet and said nothing to her of the Miss Enright you have mentioned more than once in your letters. H.

Nothing more for nearly three months, then this:

Etaples
Nov. 7, 1917
My Dear Charles,
Greetings from the No. 1, where business continues as usual, both official and otherwise. Birthday greetings, actually, to myself. I am thirty-one today. Three years in the belly of the beast or, more accurately, in its lower intestine. I wonder what

that does to a man? If I ever get back to Arkham, you may be able to answer that question, Charles. I'm not sure I ever will.

Another piece of good news – I have finally come to terms with Clapham-Lee. If you recall, he was being tedious about my research, which he persisted in regarding as a collaborative effort long after anyone should have seen that it was not. A few weeks ago he issued an ultimatum, which proved wonderfully effective. I invited him to my laboratory hut, promising to show him the results of my latest efforts. He has now internalized them absolutely and has no more room for doubts of any sort – a remarkable transformation. I anticipate no more difficulty from him.

Wondrous are the ways of reason, and happy is he who pursues her unencumbered with irrational notions.

Unreliably (but sincerely) yours,
Herbert.

****

17 Norbury Square
London, England
December 20, 1917
Dear Charles,

I hope this finds you well. My own health has finally succumbed to two and a half years of wartime conditions. I am staying with some friends of my mother's here in London. I don't know when (if ever) I'll be able to return to duty, but in the meantime it's lovely to be pampered.

I left Boulogne in November, when it became obvious that I was more of a burden than a help. I suspect my difficulties are at least in part psychological – a form of 'shell-shock,' maybe? But there is a physical component as well; I'll not weary you with the details.

People keep sending me letters from the war, so I am constantly reminded of it. Sometimes I wish I was still there. Not only because of the friends I left behind, but because everything matters there in a way it cannot elsewhere – in Arkham, or even here in London.

Some of the letters are from people who have found out that I've been collecting stories about people's war experiences and getting them published. Recently I had an interesting one from a nurse at one of the Canadian hospitals in Etaples – a curious little tale about an amnesia case that turned up in the middle of November. The man had no identification, though was evidently a soldier. He did not know his name, nationality, place of origin, military unit or rank. He spoke English, was probably British or Canadian, but it was hard to tell, because he had difficulty articulating. No one could remember having seen him before. He must have been in combat, because he had recently healed head and facial wounds which appeared to have been expertly treated, but no one could figure out where. His mental disorder and confusion were such that he was transferred to one of the facilities in England for the care of mental cases.

As if that wasn't enough, a General disappeared from that same hospital several weeks ago. That's right – disappeared. Maybe that's the word they use when a high rank goes a.w.o.l. He's been declared missing, but not missing in action, of course, since he was with the Medical Corps, not a combat officer.

Another tidbit is that the nurse who sent me the story, Alexa MacInnis, is acquainted with Herbert West, has even worked with him. She says he's a good surgeon, but that's not all. "A third of the nurses are in love with him, another third can't stand him, and the rest are scared of him." Interesting, no?

I must close this now. The people I'm staying with are quite convivial types, and tonight we're going to a play, then to supper. They say I need "a real rest," but feel compelled to entertain me. Just to have my own room, good sheets and hot baths is a wonderful rest, without anything else.

I'll write again soon.

All my best,

Alma.

But she did not write. Weeks went by and I heard nothing from her. I tried not to let myself imagine too much, but every now and then my mind conjured up a scenario of Alma dancing with a handsome officer, laughing and flirting with him. Away from the grim business of war, why wouldn't she allow herself to be diverted? And what business did I have to begrudge her that?

Then, just after Midsummer's Day, this arrived:

No. 3, 175 Pembroke Road
London
June 15, 1918
Charles,

A short note to let you know I'll be living here for some time. I'm writing a book about the war and feel I can do a better job on it here. And I'm not sure I'm ready to go back to Arkham, or to America for that matter.

Don't worry about me, but don't forget me.
Always,
Alma.

****

Alma and West weren't my only wartime correspondents. My colleague Linton Adams wrote me several letters, one of which was of particular interest.

Somewhere in Paris
September 7, 1918

Charles Milburn
23 and One Half (what kind of an address is that anyway?)
College St., Arkham, Mass.

Dear Milburn,
Well, I finally made it to Paris. After a pretty ugly time of it in the Marne I got leave, and a bunch of us decided to come here instead of London. So far it's been a blast. You don't know what you're missing, back there in Arkham.

I won't torture you by describing all the fun things I've done (and the girls – ooh la la, they're really something!), but I have a message for you, believe it or not, from someone who says he was a good friend of yours back home. It's a pretty good story, actually, so I'll tell it from the beginning.

A bunch of us boys from the 85th were exploring Montmartre one evening. We went into this little tavern called the Jardin de la Lune. It seemed to be run by some gypsy-type folks. There were fellows playing guitars and girls dancing. We boys were feeling pretty happy by then, but in a while it all changed. I don't know if you've ever noticed this, but if you drink enough, there comes a point where things shift from happy and safe to sort of dangerous, all at once. The music and dancing stopped, and this knife-thrower showed up. That's when I thought: Something else is about to happen. And that's when I first noticed this fellow who said he was a friend of yours.

He was with some other guys, Brits I thought, but it turned out they were Canadians. This guy was American, though, from Boston, as I found out later. He seemed a little crazy, not drunk, but crazy. He didn't do anything out of line, not at first, but there was this look in his eyes and something about the way he talked that made me think he was on the edge.

Anyway, the knife-thrower. He was another one of those gypsy-looking guys, but looked dangerous, had a couple of scars on his face. He worked with a woman – his wife, maybe, but who knows? She was pretty but quiet – intense, you could say – thin with long hair. She stood against the wall and he threw knives all around her, as close as he could get them without hurting her.

We were all yelling and clapping, when suddenly that crazy-looking fellow, West, his name was, stood up and challenged the guy. He spoke French. The knife-thrower didn't much like what he said, you could see that. He was getting pretty worked up, yelling and waving one of his knives under West's nose. I would have backed off, but West just grabbed the guy's wrist and said something to him, very quietly. The gypsy started to laugh but West said it again, whatever it was, and the gypsy caved in. He gave all his throwing knives to West and told his wife to get lost. She seemed kind of puzzled but went and sat down. West went over to her and said something. I think he got someone to bring her a drink. Then the knife-thrower went over to the wall and West started throwing the knives, at him.

Now he got them close, way closer than the gypsy himself had done. He pinned the guy's sleeves to the wall, looked like he gave him a little hair trim too, right on top. He was really good. And you could see that for him it was just great fun. He made quite a show of it. Everyone was impressed, everyone but the knife-thrower, that is. He was getting madder and madder. Finally, West was out of knives. He turned to us and bowed a couple of times. Just then the gypsy pulled one of the knives out of the wall and made as if to throw it at West. Someone shouted and West turned back toward the gypsy. For a few seconds no one did anything. They stood there staring at each other. Then the gypsy threw and West jumped aside, just in time. The knife stuck in a window frame behind him. It seems so slow, writing it all out like this, but it all happened in just a couple of seconds. West got that knife so fast it was unbelievable. He said something like "You don't need two ears, do you?" and threw. It clipped off part of the guy's ear, really.

I don't know where things would have ended up then, but some of the other gypsies hustled up and grabbed their guy and calmed him down. His ear was bleeding pretty badly. The guys West had been with were getting ready to leave, and I would have expected him to go too, but he went over to the gypsies and actually offered to patch up the gypsy's ear. I don't know what they told him, but they seemed pretty easy about it; maybe this knife-throwing pal of theirs made a habit of getting into trouble. And I think they were pretty impressed with West.

Anyway, the upshot was, since West's friends had left (maybe they weren't really his friends, I don't know), we asked him to join us. We were getting ready to move on to a place where things were more civilized and there were more women. But West wasn't interested. He thanked us and said he had other plans. Just then he didn't seem crazy at all. He came over to me and said he'd thought he'd heard me mention Arkham. That's when he introduced himself. I said I was from Arkham, all right, and he asked if I knew you. When I said I did, he asked me to give you his regards. Then he took off into the night. So here I am passing on to you regards from Major Herbert West of the Canadian Army. Strange but true.

Hope all is well in the Dept. and that your brain hasn't been ruined yet by the Quarrington stuff.

Linton Adams

****

Etaples, France
Nov. 15, 1918
My Dear Charles,

It looks as though the show is really over now and it's time to make plans for going home.

I am going to give my medical practice to John Billington, because I'm going to get into something entirely new that I perfected here. It's going to be a bit of a risk but I think I can make a go of it. I'll need my house and laboratory back, so I've told Billington he has to find new premises.

I hope to be back in Arkham in the next month or two.

Herbert.

****

En route to Paris
Nov. 30, 1918
Dear Charles,

I've finished my book and shipped it off to publishers. My mad English friend Nina says I need a change of scene and I want to see what Europe is like now that the war is over, so we're off to Paris. We hope to reach Italy before the weather gets bad, then back to England next year some time.

I'll try to write you. Look out for my stories!

And don't forget me.
Alma

I felt I had lost her all over again.

****

Savoy Hotel
London
Dec. 3, 1918
Charles,
I will be arriving at Portland, Maine on a hospital ship due to depart tomorrow. Expect to be back in Arkham shortly after landing; will notify you by telegram.
Ask Mrs. Fisk to get my house ready.
Herbert.

♦ 13 ♦

A few days after receiving this note I went to West's house. I had been there only a few times since his departure, to make cursory inspections of the premises or to find things West asked me to send him. Before he returned, I had to decide whether to resume some association with him, or to make it clear that I no longer wanted his company. In his house I hoped to find some trace of him that would help me decide.

I wandered through the neat but lifeless rooms, ending up in his bedroom, where I had never been before. It was very simply, almost starkly furnished – a bed, a small table, a chest of drawers and a chair. The furniture was of excellent quality, although old and well-used. Feeling guilty, I slid open a few of the drawers, but found only clean, neatly folded linen, smelling of lavender. The bottom drawer contained a hinged leather case. Intensely curious, I opened it and saw a miniature painting of a woman, delicate-faced and very fair, and a young child, probably West and his mother. On the reverse was the date 1891. In that year he would have been five years old; three years later she would leave her little son and flee – to Arkham? Troubled, and feeling guiltier than ever, I replaced the thing in its case and closed the drawer.

I could not ignore the fact that West had committed at least one murder, but surely his dedicated service in Flanders and France had paid for the death of Robert Leavitt many times over. Why was it acceptable for soldiers to kill each other by the thousands in the most brutal ways imaginable, but not for West swiftly to dispatch a peripatetic engineer so that this individual could (unwittingly, it was true) donate his body to science?

I considered the letters he had written me. Some of them had been disturbing, but I had no way of knowing how much of what he had written was sheer exaggeration. What were the facts? He had pursued the same research as that with which I had gladly assisted him for several years. Some might maintain that it was macabre or disrespectful to use human corpses as experimental material, but was it evil? I thought of the miracles of reconstruction he claimed to be able to accomplish. Surely this had been worth the years of secret labour? On his return to America West would publish his spectacular results and go on to well-earned glory.

But what about the disappearance of Clapham-Lee? Had West had anything to do with it, or was this merely an erroneous intuitive leap on my part, suggested by obscure hints in his letters which meshed so disturbingly with Alma's? He had spoken of reservations as to Clapham-Lee's motives and of animosity between them, but he had said also that these matters had been resolved.

And yet – I remembered his absolute coolness when I had accused him of killing Leavitt. And that disquieting look of calculation he had given me as I emerged from unconsciousness after my fall.

I had run out of facts. Letting my thoughts drift, I could see him, Herbert West, walking alone along a windswept shore, sand dunes on one side, the sea on the other. I watched him in my mind's eye, until I lost sight of him in the distance.

I finished my contemplation with two threads I had not previously woven into my tapestry. One was the letter from Augustus Quarrington. *Do not abandon your friend.* And finally – I could not deny the sudden leap of gladness my heart had taken when I had read that he was coming home.

Herbert West returned to Arkham on the shortest day of the year 1918. It was a raw, foggy night. The street lights were shrouded in fuzzy haloes as I drove to Arkham Station.

He was nearly the last person to leave the train. I had nearly given up, thinking that he had been delayed for some reason, when I saw yet another soldierly figure approaching. He was silhouetted against some bright lights in the distance, so I had only an impression of someone wearing a cap, long coat and tall boots. Only when he got quite close to me did I recognize him. I was surprised that he was still in uniform.

"Charles, I thought it was you," he said.

"Welcome home, Herbert," I said, extending my hand. I felt suddenly constrained and awkward, more so even than on our first meeting, years ago. He seemed utterly exotic, a soldier home from the wars, not someone on whom I had ever had a claim of friendship.

He took my hand, and – could it have been my imagination? – I felt once more that rush of magnetic energy. "It's good to be back, Charles. Good to know Arkham is still here."

"I brought a car," I said. "I thought you would have baggage."

"You – a car? Things have changed more than I thought." As we passed a street light, I saw his face a little more clearly. The same smile, the same edge of sarcasm in his voice. He still wore spectacles but had grown a moustache. The strangeness diminished, but only a little.

"As for baggage," he said, "most of it is coming later. Andre has the rest. Over here, Andre."

For the first time I noticed that he was not alone. A few yards behind us was a man, short and stocky, also in uniform. He approached, carrying a couple of suitcases. "Charles," West said, "this is Andre Boudreau, my servant. Andre, this is my good friend Charles Milburn."

Andre set down the bags and bowed slightly in my direction. "I'm pleased to meet you, Mr. Milburn," he said. He had an accent, French, I thought, but I could not be certain.

"The car is Alma's," I said as we climbed in. "She thought it would be better if it was used while she was away, so she lent it to me."

"And you dutifully learned to drive, I suppose. Well, it's a good thing. Amazing how tired I am."

I said little on the way to Boundary Street, wishing to concentrate on the business of driving. When I had successfully stopped the car in front of West's house, he said,

"Surely you'll come up? I may need you to show me around, remind me of where things are. You have no idea how peculiar this feels."

"Actually, Herbert, I do. To me you seem so..."

"Foreign? I suppose I am, in a way. For four years I have been an honourary Canadian and spent a lot of time with Englishmen. It's bound to have an effect." His accent wasn't quite an English one, but he had certainly acquired an intonation that was not Yankee.

In the apartment, West turned to Andre and gave some directions, speaking quietly in French. The man disappeared down the hall, still carrying the bags. In the sitting room, West took off his coat and draped it over the back of a chair. "Take a good look at Major Herbert F. West of the Canadian Army Medical Corps," he said. "Because after tonight he will disappear forever."

He looked taller than I remembered. I supposed it was the cap, with its unfamiliar badge, and the boots. The uniform of khaki-coloured cloth was, of course, beautifully tailored. I noticed, without comprehension of their significance, the various insignia on sleeves and lapels and the polished leather Sam Browne belt. I was not surprised that West had enjoyed the sartorial aspects of his military role.

"I'm impressed, Major West," I said, not altogether untruthfully. "I'm certain you set a good example to all. Showed 'em that not all Americans were reluctant to join the fray."

"Ah, for me the fray was altogether different from the common soldiers'. Andre would be the one to tell you something about that, but he won't because he's a man of few words now." He tossed the cap on top of his discarded coat and went over to the liquor cabinet. "It's a good thing this stuff keeps indefinitely," he said, taking out a whiskey bottle and finding some glasses.

"To your homecoming," I said, raising my glass.

"And to the future," said West.

"Have you made any plans?" I asked.

"I have indeed. I gave Billington notice weeks ago. He can keep the practice but has to find new premises for it. I need my office and laboratory for my new venture."

"And what will that be?"

"I'm going to specialize – my own specialty entirely. It all comes out of my old research and the work I did in the War – restoration and reconstruction of the human body."

"But is there much demand for that sort of thing outside of wartime? And why here in Arkham? Surely Boston or New York would be better?"

"Arkham suits me. As for demand, you'll be surprised. Quite apart from the usual accidents there are what you might call accidents of birth – people born with deformities of various sorts, external and internal. And people who simply want to look differently from the way they do. Wait and see."

"You mean what that... associate of yours wanted to do? I've forgotten his name."

"Clapham-Lee. I've gone beyond his wildest dreams. Far beyond. I don't waste my time thinking about him now."

After a moment of silence which for some reason was uncomfortable, he said, "You know, of course, that my father is dead."

I had heard of Hiram West's death, which had been caused by a stroke several months earlier. "It was rather unexpected, I gather. Was it a shock to you?"

"Not altogether unexpected. He was over seventy, you know, and had never exercised any restraint when it came to cigars and drink. He never exercised anything except his mouth. Of course it was a shock. But it didn't seem real, over there."

Another brief silence, then, "The West business empire, nicely fattened by war profits, has been divided between my brothers, but Father did set aside a rather generous portion for me. Despite our differences, I must admit that he was decent enough that way. Now I don't have to worry about money while I get my new venture going."

"But what about revivification?" I asked.

"What about it? I've finished with revivification. I've learned everything I can from it."

"But I thought you had some success with it in France. You mentioned several cases."

"I certainly did have success," he said, with a not altogether pleasant smile. "What I mean is that I have now discovered the criteria for successful revivification. They are rather narrow, as I suspected. The corpse must be very recently dead – less than six hours, certainly – and with its major structures intact. That limits the types of deaths from which one can return, obviously. Return in a more or less functional state, that is, and for longer than a few hours. Believe me, during the War I had opportunities to create some novel... composites that fortunately were short-lived. In the interests of experimentation, you understand." Again that less than pleasant smile.

"Returning to the successes, of the dozen or so men I revivified who are, as far as I know, still alive, fewer than half were in full possession of their faculties. The majority had some cognitive impairment, ranging from slight to serious. So the question is – is it better to be dead, or alive but diminished and often dependent on others for the most basic things? I think most people would prefer death."

"But I'll bet their families, the people that love them, would want them alive, however diminished," I said.

"You romantic, Charles. Consider a woman whose husband returns to her in a quasi-vegetable state. Not only has she lost a breadwinner, she has gained, in effect, another child. A permanent child. And no widow's pension or opportunity to remarry."

"Well, maybe you're right. But were they all like that?"

"No, not all. The thing is – I could not predict with any certainty the degree of cognitive impairment. Even in corpses well within the six hour limit, results varied greatly. Now, of course I knew nothing of these fellows' level of intelligence before they died. It may be that some of them did not have far to go to attain the vegetable state. But the fact is that it would take a great deal of experimentation, involving prodigious numbers of corpses, and information as to intelligence before death, to be able accurately to predict results. Your idea of finding volunteers for the cause might be one approach, but I suspect they would be few and far between. To volunteer for such a thing would, to many people, seem to be courting death. I'm rather keen on my new area of practice, and don't want to ruin my prospects by becoming identified as the 'death doctor,' or something like that."

"Yes, I can understand that."

"So, no more revivifications for you, Charles, with all their attendant hazards," he said, smiling. "We can be friends rather than associates from now on."

"Speaking of associates, who is this Andre? Your servant, you said."

"Exactly. And a very good one. I confess that's one thing about the life of an officer I would miss. It was a piece of luck that he was able to accompany me here."

"But where did he come from originally? Is he French?"

"In a way. He's from New Brunswick, Canada, but for various reasons prefers not to go back there. He was my batman and now he'll be my servant – valet, chauffeur, butler, whatever. With the assistance of the excellent Mrs. Fisk, I'll have everything I need. I'm quite looking forward to civilian life."

Part 3

THE NECROMANCER

♦ 14 ♦

Within a surprisingly short time, Dr. Herbert West, reconstructive surgeon, was established in the Arkham medical community. He had privileges at St. Mary's Hospital and the Boston General. He was on several important committees. He taught at Miskatonic University's Medical School. His days as a persecuted student and Allan Halsey's enemy seemed infinitely distant, the misdemeanours of his student years quite forgotten. A number of factors had converged to ensure his success – his war record, the regard of Dr. Welburn Bright, recently retired but still influential, and liberal applications of cash in the right places. Not least of all were West's capacity for sustained effort and his ability to be charming when he wanted to.

As he had predicted, cases requiring his particular talents came from everywhere. He had referrals from all over the United States and Canada, even a few from Europe. He worked out of the same offices on Boundary Street in which his original practice had been, except that the plate on the door now said Herbert West, M.D. Consultant Surgeon.

I did not see him as often as I had before the War. He was very busy. So, for that matter, was I. Peter Runcible had finally found his way into a coveted place in Miskatonic's administration, and I had been appointed Principal Cataloguer and Department Head. My new responsibilities took considerably more of my time and energy. Unlike the old days, when my work had demanded no more of myself than I could spare from my doings with West, I now found myself focussed on my profession nearly to the exclusion of other things.

West and I usually met for a meal or a drink every few weeks. I think I was the only person with whom he could talk freely about certain things. Because of our past collaboration, he had reason to trust my discretion, and since I was in no way in his professional life, he could use me as a confidant and sounding-board, up to a point at least.

Shortly after his return, in a burst of extravagance, West acquired a new car. No product of the American automobile industry, it seemed, was good enough for Dr. West. Instead, he imported from France, at great expense, a Hispano-Suiza H6B.

"It has a top speed of eighty-five miles per hour," he explained. "Excessive, perhaps, but now that I have to go to Boston so often it makes sense to have an efficient vehicle. I hate to be a slave to the railroad timetable. Besides, speed is exhilarating. Some of the officers I knew in France held races on occasion – purely for amusement, you understand. Those country lanes north of Etaples were perfect for it – narrow, lots of corners, peasants and flocks of sheep on the move, Army vehicles, cyclists – it was a veritable obstacle course and a real test of skill. I resolved to get a fast machine as soon as I could."

Soon after he took delivery of the Hispano, West invited me to come for a 'spin' to Kingsport. At first I was impressed by the luxury of the vehicle compared to my Ford, and indeed was exhilarated by the speed with which we left Arkham behind. Then West said, "All right, now we can open her up," and accelerated sharply. We roared down the Arkham-Kingsport road at a truly alarming speed. West, oblivious of my terror, talked with enthusiasm of cylinders and crankshafts and power-to-weight ratios, all the while shifting gears and steering with an ease that made me envious. I was glad we met no other traffic as we accelerated out of curves and crested hills in a way that made me think we were about to become airborne. I found myself wondering how many unfortunate sheep, peasants and cyclists he had run over in France.

Very soon after we left Arkham, we swept down the last hill and into Kingsport, slowing and stopping with a flourish in front of the Town Hall. West looked at his watch and turned to me, eyes shining. "Not bad," he said. "She runs beautifully, don't you think? How would you like to drive us back?" When I didn't reply, he looked at me more closely. "You're quite pale, Charles!" he exclaimed. "I didn't realize you're susceptible to car sickness. You should have told me. Look, the best cure for it is to drive. It's quite simple, and much more fun than that Ford of yours, I guarantee it."

Once I stopped shaking, I acquiesced to his suggestion, recognizing it as a solution to my unadmitted terror. The car was indeed a pleasure to drive, but we returned to Arkham at a much slower speed, rather to its owner's disappointment.

West's Hispano may not have been the only one in Massachusetts at that time, but it was certainly the only one in Arkham. I suspected it cost him a small fortune each year to keep it in good running condition, but he obviously thought it a worthwhile expenditure, perhaps because he knew that citizens of the town never failed to be impressed at the sight of Dr. West in his fancy French car, racing down the Aylesbury Pike or the highway to Boston.

"So, how are you liking Arkham?" I asked, after we had garaged the car and were settled in West's sitting room. "After the War and everything I guess you find it rather dull."

"Arkham is never dull," he said with a smile. "Not to me." Under the professional polish and the trace of the exotic he retained from his overseas experiences, I thought I could see the old Herbert West undimmed. If there was a suggestion of hardness about the grey eyes, a little less sweetness in his smile, who could wonder, considering the things he must have seen? He rarely spoke of the War, never reminisced in the way that seems inevitable among those who have been 'over there.' Almost all traces of Major Herbert F. West had indeed vanished. He had even shaved off his moustache.

The silent Andre was now firmly ensconced as West's manservant. As he served us coffee I observed him curiously. He spoke so rarely I still knew very little about him. He always seemed entirely concentrated on the task at hand. The expression in his dark eyes was one of quietness rather than servility but his devotion to West was obvious. Almost I envied my friend this gem of a servant, even as I continued to wonder about him. There was an oddness about Andre that I could not fathom.

"By the way, Herbert," I said when Andre had returned to the kitchen, "I didn't realize you number knife-throwing among your talents. A friend of mine wrote me quite a lively account about meeting you in Paris."

He looked a little embarrassed. "One's foolish moments always come back to haunt one, it seems. Knife-throwing... When I was at the Med. School there was quite a fashion for it. I suppose it was a sort of bravado associated with all those edged instruments we handled. I became rather good at it. For some reason, there in Paris... Well, the reason was probably absinthe. I admit I could develop quite a taste for that stuff. Just as well it's illegal to import it. But who was that fellow I gave my message to?"

I did not resist the diversion. Absinthe. So that was the reason for the craziness Linton had seen, I thought. Alma had mentioned it as well in one of her letters. Aloud I explained that Linton was a colleague who had worked closely with me on the Quarrington Collection. This reminded me of something. "How well did you know Professor Quarrington?" I asked.

"You are very curious tonight, Charles," he observed, frowning a little. "I took some classes from him. He used his students pretty indiscriminately to test those outlandish theories of his. I have to grant that he at least tried to use the scientific method. I was one of his subjects for a while. He had a notion about a person's eyes being indicative of the presence of some force or other – had a bee in his bonnet about forces, old Q. did. Anyway, he took photographs of everyone in the class, close-ups, and cut them down, keeping only the parts that showed the eyes. I suppose mine are in there somewhere."

"I thought so," I said. "Those eye pictures were one of the things that made cataloguing his collection such an interesting experience. You should come and see it someday. We're going to have a dedication ceremony for the Quarrington Room next week. After that it will be open to all."

"I think I'll postpone the pleasure, Charles. To be quite frank, I have uneasy memories about Quarrington. You'll laugh, but it was exceedingly uncomfortable, being an experimental subject. I was part of his prediction study. The idea was that he would develop a profile of each of us, according to his peculiar criteria. Our part was to tell him what happened to us as we went through our lives, by writing to him at least once a year.

"I have to admit I found the whole thing bothered me more than I would have expected. He asked very detailed questions about rather private things, and for once I neither embellished nor omitted. Afterward I regretted that. I should have told him some real thumpers and observed what he made of them. But I suppose I was rather impressed with the scope of the enterprise and flattered to be one of the chosen. Don't forget, I was only about twenty at the time. In the end I felt I had literally given away a part of myself, and I didn't like that. So I stopped communicating with him."

"Well," I said, "the Professor seems to have retained his interest in you." I told him about the letter I had received.

"He wrote to you, did he?" asked West. "So you knew him?"

"I met him at that University Open House, the same week I met your father. Just before O'Brien. Quarrington insisted on seeing the *Necronomicon*. When I showed it to him he said some strange things, but I put them down to eccentricity. I didn't expect that he would remember me. But he seemed to realize that I knew you."

"He took a special interest in me, for some reason. At one time I thought he meant to make me his acolyte and successor, which was flattering, but hardly the sort of thing I wanted to do. But he told me about the *Necronomicon*. And about you, too."

"*Me*? But that's impossible. That was early in 1911, less than a year after I came to Arkham. He didn't know me then."

"Maybe you didn't know him then, but he knew about you. When he told me about the book, he said I would have to deal with you in order to see it. 'There's more to that young librarian than meets the eye,' he said. 'You could do worse than ask him if you ever need someone to help you with one of your projects.' I had told him a little of my ideas, you see, and how I would go about testing them."

"So you did seek me out. I thought you just turned up at that concert, and asked me to have supper with you as an afterthought."

"It was more of a before-thought," he said. "I had already considered approaching you. It just happened a little sooner than I had planned."

"So Quarrington had a hand in all this, it seems," I mused. "Our collaboration, that is. And everything that followed..."

"Now you sound just like him," West said, sounding a little irritated. "It may be that he was trying to set up a – now what did he call it? Oh, I remember – a 'resonant link.' Quarrington thought that bringing certain individuals together could have great consequences, greater than one might expect from their separate characteristics. Don't ask me to explain it. But maybe that's what he was trying to do."

"And do you think it worked?" I asked. His seriousness was uncharacteristic and I wanted to tease him a little. "Do you think we caused something to resonate by our association?"

"Well yes, I think we did," he said, smiling. "Don't you?"

Alma Halsey stayed in Europe for nearly two years after the War ended. In addition to writing a book about her war experiences (eventually published as *An American Girl at War*), she had undertaken to deliver a series of articles to the *Boston Post* about the situation in Europe from the American woman's perspective. She found this to be such a rewarding occupation that she had extended her stay as long as possible.

I was content for things to remain in a state of limbo as far as Alma and I were concerned. Within myself I did not feel that our affair was entirely over, but neither did I cherish any hopes, or, for that matter, intentions. And emancipated Alma, I knew, travelling all over Europe, interviewing everyone from peasant women to heads of state, would not feel herself under any obligation to me.

I had to admit that my continued state of bachelorhood did not seem to be in any way a failure or hardship. I had interesting work, a few congenial friends, and female companionship of various sorts when I wanted it. There did not seem to be any reason to pursue matrimony. And I, unlike West, was not myself the object of pursuit.

With his recent professional success, the glamour of his war record and the good looks that only improved with time, West was once more eagerly sought after by the ladies of Arkham society. But he was no more susceptible to them now than before.

I was within hearing on one occasion when an articulate, educated and attractive young woman tried to hold a conversation with the elusive Dr. West. It was at some University function involving tea and cakes and sherry. West hated occasions of this sort at the best of times, and attended only if he had to.

Young Lady: Oh, Dr. West, what do you think of this new idea of eugenics? Mr. Leonard Darwin in England says that marriage should be regulated so only the fittest have children. And Mr. Charles Davenport here in the United States agrees with him.

West: Really? I'm not aware of these gentlemen's opinions.

Young Lady: Yes indeed. I think it's a fine idea. People who are healthy and intelligent have a duty to get married and produce more healthy and intelligent Americans. Or some other country will beat us, especially with all those immigrants they're letting in now.

West: Well, I'm sure you'll do your bit to keep America sound, Miss ___.

Young Lady: Thank you, Dr. West. But I was thinking of you. As one of our most respected citizens, you have a duty –

West: Oh, I realize that. I can certainly introduce you to a number of my promising younger colleagues. Now you must excuse me. There's someone I must speak to, and it appears he is about to leave.

A little later, West came over to me, saying, "I am definitely going to stop attending these nonsensical receptions. Next thing you know I'll be hauled away bodily by a tribe of marriage-starved females and torn to shreds as they fight over me. What is it, do you know?"

"It's a natural impulse, Herbert. We bachelors are out of step, especially you. The ladies must think it's altogether unfair of you to turn yourself out so well, to be so... ornamental is one word I've heard, and then brush them off. You're like a bird in courting plumage who doesn't want to court. You should assume some deformity when you go out in society – crossed eyes, or a limp like mine. Or at least wear something wrinkled and ill-fitting."

"Lord, no. That would just bring them rushing over to help me, poor old fuddled thing that I'd be. And up the aisle too, no doubt."

"Well, but – why not? Why this antipathy to marriage?"

"I could ask you the same thing, Charles."

"I'm younger than you. And poor. And there's Alma."

"By two years. And you're not that poor. And if you're waiting for Alma Halsey to come back and propose to you, forget it. That woman has too much spirit. Which she's exercising all over Europe, if I can believe what I read in the *Post*."

"Well, you may be right. But just now I'm happy enough with my life. Marriage would be more of a change than I want."

"I could say the same thing, exactly. I am rather an odd fish, you know – Dr. Iceberg West and all that. It's not so far from the truth. I'm not much bothered by thwarted desire. Not while I have my work."

This was the most self-revealing statement I had ever heard him make on this matter. I remembered it some weeks later at a dinner party he gave at his home. Such gatherings had replaced the drinking parties he had indulged in before the war. He would invite half a dozen or more congenial companions and provide an excellent meal (ostensibly cooked by Mrs. Fisk, although remembering his fondness for cooking I suspected he collaborated with her). Afterward, we would all gather in the sitting room for drinks and the vigorous debates so well loved by our host. Given the interests of those present, the subjects were often of a scientific or medical nature, but philosophy, art and politics were by no means neglected.

Like the old drinking parties, these were all-male affairs. Some of the fellows were bachelors like West and myself, but those who were not knew better than to bring their wives. I thought of my reaction to the not so dissimilar situation when I had been a guest of Hiram West's. That had struck me as graceless and crude. What was the difference, then? Of course the level of education and culture was higher here, but it was more that the informing spirit was in some way entirely different.

On this occasion, two or three debates were going on simultaneously. West and John Billington were having a spirited discussion about something, waving their arms and interrupting each other, but in an obviously good-natured way. It occurred to me that I had never seen West in better form. He was articulate, enthusiastic, full of energy. He's happy, I thought, with a small shock. For the first time since I've known him he's unreservedly happy. So this is the life that suits him. He is doing work that he loves and has made a place for himself in this community. He has made himself. Yes, that was it – West had made himself into what he wanted to be, despite what some would have considered intractable raw material. And if I had in some way contributed to the result, I was content.

Every year a committee of Miskatonic librarians met to decide how to spend that year's allotment of funds for the development of the Quarrington Collection. Several years of association with the eccentric professor's collection had made me think of it as my collection as well. I welcomed every opportunity to add to it and make it a living body of knowledge, however bizarre and unorthodox it might be.

I was also glad of any chance to rummage about in the bookstores of Boston, antiquarian and merely 'used' alike. Especially fascinating was the shop of Humphrey Villard. He had a talent for tracking down the obscure and the rare that was quite astonishing. In 1919, I went to view several works on alchemy that he had assembled for my consideration.

Villard greeted me with the enthusiasm reserved for a customer who came prepared to buy, with an institutional purse at his disposal. He was a short, rotund man, balding but with a halo of curly grey hair remaining, and a beard. His eyes twinkled at me from behind his spectacles. The books in question were displayed in his office, which occupied a kind of eyrie on a mezzanine floor at the rear of the shop. The main floor was given over to antiquarian or collectors' books. Beneath, in the cellar, was a welter of used books, a Mecca for students and parsimonious bibliophiles. The place smelled of books, of old leather bindings and of paper gently decaying into its primal elements.

The works Villard had selected were representative of alchemy from its earliest documented beginnings to the present day. Here were writings of Paracelsus, the *Sylva sylvarum* of Francis Bacon, the *Alchemical Mass* of Nicholas Melchior, the *De occulta philosophia* of Agrippa, George Ripley's *Compound of Alchemy,* as well as more recent writings such as the *Doctrine and Ritual of Magic* by Eliphas Levi. I made my selections quite readily. Villard's integrity as a dealer made my task easy, for I found he had not over-represented the quality of his offerings. We negotiated a little over prices, but only for form's sake. Our business concluded, Villard poured each of us what he termed a libation, and proceeded to extract news from my circumscribed niche at Miskatonic. For him no detail was too trivial. He collected bits of information as eagerly as he did books, and used them as a kind of currency with his customers.

Villard had followed my adventures with the Quarrington material with interest. From time to time he would try half-seriously to persuade me to part with some particularly desirable item he knew to have been in the old eccentric's possession. Now he turned to me with a mischievous look on his face. "I hope you haven't spent all your money," he said. "Because I have something you won't be able to pass up. A genuine piece of Quarringtoniana."

"Now what could that be?" I asked.

"Well, I don't know exactly what it is. But it was certainly written by the man himself. I'm familiar with his handwriting. It looks as though it refers to some other body of documents. Here, have a look."

He handed me a sheaf of papers. One look told me what it was, and my heart leaped strangely.

There were several sheets. Written in Augustus Quarrington's unmistakable circular hand and violet ink was a long list of names in alphabetical order, each with a date and an alphanumeric code. Surely this was the key to the file called 'Profiles and Predictions!' It would permit the matching of those documents to actual individuals. Anyone wanting to verify Quarrington's predictions would find this information invaluable. By itself, however, it was nearly worthless.

Villard was watching me, a little smile on his face. I said, "Well, it certainly is by Quarrington, as you say. But without whatever it refers to, it's of limited use."

"Exactly. That's why I saved it for you. I thought it was a safe assumption that 'whatever it refers to,' as you so coyly put it, is in your collection."

"It's not my collection, as you know quite well. It belongs to Miskatonic."

He waved off the distinction. "You organized it, you catalogued it, you know what's in it. It's your collection. Now, are you interested in this item?"

"How did you happen to acquire it, anyway?"

"Well, you know I name no names. Let's just say that it turned up when the Professor's personal items from his home were dispersed. I gather his heirs were distant relatives. I suppose an ancient bachelor like him wouldn't have any close family. Anyway, this turned up in an envelope carefully affixed to the bottom of a drawer from Quarrington's desk. The underside of the drawer, if you follow me. Whoever found it assumed it must be valuable because of the pains taken to hide it, and so brought it to me. What do you think?"

"I think I would be interested in this item, if only because it's a document in Quarrington's own hand. If I can match it up to something already in the collection it may gain in value. How much are you asking?"

"I could ask how much you're willing to pay. I suspect it would be quite a lot. I saw how you nearly choked on your drink when you looked at it. Those are names, now, and dates – quite recent dates, too. I'll bet this is a list of people, students probably, about whom Quarrington gathered data to test one of his wild theories. It's probably a missing link for you. But I'm a reasonable man. I know this list is useless without the data to which it refers, and that the data is most likely in your Quarrington Room, under lock and key, I hope. And I want you to buy more books from me, Mr. Milburn, so there's no point in being greedy over this." He named an entirely reasonable figure, which I paid gladly.

While one of Villard's assistants packed my purchases into cartons, Villard turned to me and said, "Alchemy is a fascinating subject. Have you read much about it?"

"Not systematically," I replied. "Why do you ask?"

"Because I was quite interested in it once. Oh, don't imagine me with crucibles and alembics. I'm too lazy for that, and too clumsy, if you must know. But there's a mystical side to it. So many things can be viewed in an alchemical sense. It fairly cries out for analogies. And far from being a dead thing of medieval times, it was practiced, both in the practical and spiritual sense, until quite recently. Maybe still is, by some. And it unites pre-Christian thinking with some of the central mysteries of Christianity."

I thought about this on the way home. Whether because of my delving into the Quarrington material or for some other reason, I had lately begun to suspect that there were subtle connections between seemingly disparate parts of the world. Sometimes I thought I could hold up two thoughts, as it were, one from the part of my mind that reasoned and analyzed, one from the part that felt and guessed, and see a kind of kinship between them, as though a door had opened between two sealed chambers.

♦ 15 ♦

Early in 1920, Arkham experienced an exceedingly cold and snowy period that lasted for several weeks. One night there was a loud knock at my door. Before I could respond, it opened and West came in. He was pale and agitated.

"Herbert, what is it?" I asked. "Are you sick?"

"Yes. No. No, I'm not," he said. "It's just that..." He took off his hat and ran a hand through his hair. He threw the hat onto a chair and began pacing nervously. Suddenly he stopped and looked at me. "I've been to Sefton Asylum," he said.

"What were you doing there?" I asked. "Checking on John Hocks? Don't tell me he's started to talk!"

"Stop babbling, Charles. You don't know what you're talking about. Hocks is still there and unchanged, as far as I know. I've kept a watch on him for years, without setting foot in the place. I hate going there. It's like a prison whose inmates are doubly confined, first in their madness, then physically. But... With luck, she didn't know me. That wouldn't be surprising after all... Damn it, now what should I do?"

I had never seen him so bothered. "Herbert, I don't know what you're talking about. You have to explain it to me from the beginning if you want my advice. And for God's sake stop that pacing. It's making me nervous. Take off your coat and sit down, and tell me what happened."

He did as I suggested but seemed about to jump to his feet again. "So if you weren't at Sefton to see Hocks, what were you doing there?" I asked.

"Even lunatics need surgery on occasion, Charles. The asylum has an arrangement with St. Mary's, to the effect that any of us doctors contribute our services as needed. They had an accident there this morning. One of the inmates was burned while working in the kitchen. It was nothing much; I expect the fellow will be perfectly well inside of a week. But when I was leaving, I saw... someone. And it's possible she knew me. Recognized me."

"Who was this person?" God help me, I was intrigued. "Every man has a few secrets," West had said to me once, and I knew he was no exception. "A... resident?" Given the possibilities, I could not bring myself to say 'inmate.'

"I don't know," he said, standing up and raking his fingers through his hair again. "That's the damnable thing – I don't *know*! But if I can guess, so can others. Your friend Nurse Enright, for example. She was there. No doubt it'll be all over Arkham by tomorrow."

"I don't think so," I said. "Miss Enright is discreet and sensible. She wouldn't talk irresponsibly."

"That doesn't make any difference. Things like this always get out. There's only one thing to do – see Holberg and find out more about her." He picked up his coat and began to put it on.

"You're going?" I asked stupidly. It appeared that he had found an answer to his dilemma, whatever it was, but not from me. "Who's Holberg?"

"The director of the asylum. I'll see him when I go back tomorrow to check on my patient. Perhaps he'll tell me something about... her."

Suddenly he stopped in front of me, one arm in a coat sleeve. "This is the sort of thing that cracks a man's foundations."

"I don't know what you mean. You haven't really told me anything."

He ignored this. "I have to go now. Thank you for your... attention."

When he was gone I sat for a long while, thinking and staring at the dying embers in the fireplace.

The following day Sarah Enright and I met for lunch at a cafeteria patronized by students and others who perforce valued cheapness over culinary excellence. From the first I could see that Sarah had something to tell me. Her face was animated and her eyes sparkled. "I have a piece of news I think you'll find interesting. First hand too, not gossip."

"Wait a minute," I said. "Is it about Dr. West?"

"Yes. How did you know?"

"He told me about it himself. I think it was something of a shock for him."

"I could see that. It was quite amazing. One second he was his usual self, you know, cool as anything, walking along next to mousy little Dr. Spencer. Then he saw her and changed completely, just like that. He got white as a sheet. And those eyes of his – for a second or two he looked... well, crazy."

"Sarah, I hope you haven't, that you won't say anything about this to anyone else. But can you tell me a little more about this person? Is she a young woman?"

"No! At least sixty, maybe even seventy. She's the lady I look after sometimes. Miss Anna Derby. I told you about her, remember? Yesterday I was taking her back to her room when we met Dr. West. You know, I never realized it before, but they look sort of alike. Are they related?"

This detail was new to me, and possibly crucial, but I tried not to show it. "I don't know. Why is she there, at Sefton?"

"Well, I suppose because she isn't fit to live alone. She's not sane."

"But does she have a family here in Arkham?"

"Not here. Boston. At any rate, Mr. Robert Derby hired me to visit with her three times a week. They have the same name, so they must be related, but I'm not sure just how."

"Who's Mr. Derby?"

"He's a judge. He lives in Boston now, but the family used to have a house on High Street. I don't know whether it's been sold or only rented."

"I see. Sarah, do you think this lady recognized Dr. West?"

"I don't know. She was sort of... upset the rest of the day. I asked her what was troubling her, but she wouldn't say. I was afraid she'd get one of her bad spells again."

Sarah had been looking after Anna Derby for six or seven years. During that time her condition had remained much the same. Sarah was not certain what her trouble was, but the symptoms included long periods of silence and short ones of intense agitation, during which she had to be confined or restrained because of an urge to wander. Once or twice she had slipped away but was found before she left the asylum grounds. In between, she had periods of near normalcy, although there was always a certain vagueness in her manner. "There's something sad about her, Charles," Sarah said. "It's as though she lost herself somewhere."

"Perhaps she did," I said without thinking. "And now, it seems, she's been found."

A few evenings after this, history seemed to repeat itself in the form of another loud knock at my door just as I was beginning to think about going to bed. This time it wasn't West but his servant, Andre Boudreau.

Without waiting for a greeting, he burst into excited speech. "Monsieur Milburn, you must come now! The Doctor, he needs your help." As if he thought I would follow him into the winter night just as I was, without a coat and in my slippers, he began to turn away, but I laid a hand on his sleeve.

"Wait, Andre, please – Has something happened to Dr. West? An accident?" I thought of John Hocks. Could he have escaped from Sefton?

"No, not an accident. He needs for you to help him, in the laboratory."

We stood and looked at each other, Andre Boudreau and I, in my doorway, with cold air invading my sitting room through the open door. The laboratory! I was surprised that West would have admitted anyone else into this secret. I thought I was the only other person in Arkham who knew about the place.

"Come in, please, Andre," I said. "Of course I'll help Dr. West, but I can't go out like this. Sit down and wait while I get ready."

He complied, but lapsed into silence while I got into coat, boots and hat. Further details were not forthcoming. Considering the urgency of the summons and not keen on running the several blocks to West's house, I asked Andre to crank up the Ford. As I expected, his cranking was far more efficient than mine, and we were on Boundary Street in a few minutes.

Andre hustled me down to the laboratory without ceremony. I was surprised to see both doors to it standing open, the concealing one that doubled as shelves of wine bottles and the iron door itself. Inside, the place looked both familiar and unfamiliar. I had a fleeting impression that it was more crowded than before, with pieces of equipment unknown to me. But the sight of West bending over a table took me instantly to the past.

"Here he is, Doctor," said Andre. "*Voici* Monsieur Milburn."

"Thank you, Andre," said West, turning toward us. "Please leave us now."

"Are you sure, Doctor?" said Andre. "I thought we would be – "

"Not tonight," West said shortly. "I'll call you if I need you. Charles, come here."

Andre left, but slowly and with a long look back at us as he closed the door. I turned to West.

His face was pale and somehow ravaged, with a kind of flickering nervousness about the eyes. As I approached him, I saw a sheet-covered body on the table and the familiar revivifying apparatus standing ready nearby, complete with a flask of the violet-coloured liquid.

"What is it you want me to do, Herbert?" I asked. "And are you sure you're all right?"

"No, I'm not," he said, impatiently. "As for what I want you to do, the answer is 'Everything.' I only hope you remember how." He turned away from me, clutching at his head with both hands. "My God, this is horrible!" he muttered, as though to some third person, but Andre, obeying his orders, was no longer in the room.

"What do you mean, everything? How can you – ? It's been years since I've had anything to do with this, you know that, and why can't you do it?"

He swung around. "Too many questions!" His voice was harsh but the distress on his face frightened me more than his anger. After a brief struggle with himself, he assumed a semblance of calm but I could see that it was a forced calm.

"Charles." He came close to me and made as if to put his hands on my shoulders, then dropped them to his sides. "Listen carefully. I cannot do this revivification, but... it must be done. I have to do it, or rather, you have to do it, for my sake. Please, Charles."

He was pleading with me, something I had never imagined. "All right, Herbert, I'll try, but I don't know if I can."

"You can. You will. I'll be right there to tell you exactly what to do. Everything's ready. Go wash your hands. Go on, quickly!"

I could not argue with his desperate urgency. I washed as directed and struggled into one of West's lab coats. Mustering all my determination, I approached the body on the table.

Even through the sheet, I discerned several things about the corpse: it was small and thin, surely no more than five feet tall. At first I thought it was a child, but certain anatomical details told me otherwise. The body was that of a woman.

This wasn't the first time that we had worked with a female corpse. Several of our subjects in years past had been women, but that could not be the reason for West's apparent distress. The sex of a corpse had never deterred him; I had been the one to be intimidated. West had laughed at my modesty and insisted that the female subjects be stripped naked and treated like all the rest. "She's dead, Charles. She's not going to blush because you see her hidden assets."

I took a deep breath and prepared to remove the sheet, but before I could do so, West was plucking at my hands, nearly dancing in his agitation. "No, no, no! Leave that one alone!" he cried, and I saw then that the head of the corpse was shrouded with a separate cloth from that which covered the body.

"Why, Herbert?" I asked. "Is there a reason you don't want me to see her face?"

"Because I say so," he replied. "She's my – my subject, and it has to be done this way. Here, I'll show you. Like this."

Carefully, he folded down the sheet, exposing the neck and shoulders but stopping short of revealing the breasts. "There, now get on with it, for God's sake!" He thrust a scalpel toward me, and it was all I could do to make myself take it.

"Who is she?" I made no move to begin, thinking he was more likely to be informative now than after the job was done.

He drew in a breath sharply for an angry reply, but clamped down on it with a twist of his lips. "That's irrelevant. She's a subject. I can't tell you any more. Physician-patient confidentiality, you know." Another grimace, intended to be taken for a smile. "Now come here and... do it. Please, Charles."

Begging didn't become him, and I was short on cruelty. I bent over the corpse. The dead woman had not been young, judging by the loose and wrinkled skin of her neck, which made West's fit of apparent prudishness even more peculiar.

He positioned the head and showed me exactly where to make the incision to expose the jugular vein. "Right there, that's right," he said. "Come on, you need to exert more pressure. Steady and even." But when the blade began to part the flaccid flesh, he abruptly turned his face away, clutching at the edge of the table. For a second I thought he was going to faint, but I had to concentrate on the job in hand. When I had finally inserted the first needle, I felt a rush of relief, but this was only the first of many steps. West looked, if possible, even paler but there was a steely determination in his eyes.

He insisted on being the one to uncover the corpse's lower extremities, and again he exposed only enough of the body for me to locate the femoral artery, folding and tucking the sheet carefully to ensure that the pubic area remained covered. This time he looked away before I began cutting the skin. It was bluish-white and the texture of crepe, with small broken veins like purple hieroglyphs on parchment among sparse grey hairs.

West had told me long ago that there was no point in revivifying old people because they were too weak to sustain the forced return to life. Invariably, they retreated swiftly into death. Why, then, was he so insistent on performing the procedure on this elderly woman?

I nearly asked him this question, but one look at his eyes, which darted from me to the corpse and back in a feverish way, made me keep silent.

Once the needles were in place, West grew calmer and regained something of his old manner. All at once, he was in charge of the proceedings and I only an onlooker. He activated the apparatus to administer the revivifying fluid, adjusting the taps and watching the meters.

Once the flask was empty, West covered the body again, adding a light coverlet over the sheets and adjusting the cloth that covered the face as though to make sure that it would not impede respiration, once it began. I was about to ask him the reason for these departures from his normal practice, when he forestalled me.

"Thank you, Charles, for coming so promptly and being so helpful," he said, with a facsimile of his charming smile. "I cannot tell you how crucial your assistance was tonight."

You could tell me if you chose to, I thought, but knew that it would be useless to say so.

"I'm sure you're tired now, and want to go home," he continued, steering me toward the laboratory door. "I'll have to ask you to show yourself out, since I can't leave my... patient alone."

At the door of the laboratory I stopped and looked at him closely. His outward manner was calm, but underneath the surface I sensed nervousness and confusion. He didn't seem to know what to do with his hands, and there was a distinct tremor in his fingers. No wonder he had felt unequal to the surgical parts of the procedure. I had a dozen questions I could not ask, but took a chance on a suggestion. "Herbert, I can stay if you want me to. You don't look well."

He hesitated and I thought I saw a flicker of relief in his eyes, quickly suppressed. He glanced back at the silent form on the table behind us and sighed. "Thank you, no, Charles. I must... I can do the rest myself. Good night."

He swung the heavy door to close it, but before it could clang shut we heard a faint, whispery voice, rising to a thin wail.

The ensuing look of sick distress on West's face convinced me. I pushed the door open.

"I'm staying," I said. "You need help here. Both of you."

West's face was almost as white as his lab coat. "All right, Charles," he whispered.

Together, we returned to the table, where by now our patient was jerking feebly and uttering incoherent sounds. Before either of us could do anything, she started to scream and thrash.

"Not there, not now, never, don't do it, I won't go, leave me alone, I have to go back, I hate him, hate him, hate..."

I stepped forward, realizing that West had not used restraints on this subject. Here was another difference, but this was no time to comment on it. The woman's movements had dislodged the cloth that covered her face. It slipped to the floor as I bent over her. Her eyes were unfocussed and her breath came in gasps. I smelled antiseptic and something foul beneath it.

Suddenly she seemed to see me and went limp. "Who are you?" she asked, sounding almost calm, but then she quickly turned her head toward West. His face wore a look of uncertainty and questioning I had never seen before. His lips moved as though he was about to speak.

To say that the woman's face changed would be a gross understatement. It was transfigured. Years seemed to fall away as delight dawned in her eyes and a smile like sunrise rearranged the pallid flesh. West's smile. For the moment it lasted, the resemblance between them was unmistakable. "*Lawrence,*" she whispered, then cried the name aloud while struggling to lift her arms from under the blanket that covered her.

West backed away. "Charles, she's raving! You talk to her. I can't." He turned around, raising his hands to his face. "Oh God, why did I start this?" he muttered.

The woman had almost succeeded in sitting up. "Lawrence, come back!" she screamed. "I saw you... yesterday? You were there! They tried to fool me; someone told me you were Hiram, but I knew you. I'd know you anywhere! I tried to find you, but... something happened and I couldn't. Come back, come back!"

Exhausted, she collapsed into the mess of blankets. Her eyes were closed, her mouth open, showing yellowed teeth and shrunken gums.

I had to reassure her. "He'll come back soon, I promise you. My name is Charles Milburn, I'm a friend of his, but I don't believe we've met. "

"Friend of Hiram's?" Her face became grotesquely contorted, full of hate. "Get away from me! Where's Lawrence?"

She whipped her head around toward West, but he backed away as though from a viper about to strike and stood several yards away, apparently paralyzed.

"I don't know anyone called Hiram," I said, bending closer. "What is your name, can you tell me?"

"Annie, Anna, Annalinda, anatomic, annihilated Anna. You'll be a dead woman Anna, unless – Unless. It was less than that, ha-ha!" She laughed, a loud, ringing laugh that sounded completely wrong in that underground laboratory.

Her laughter stopped as suddenly as it had started. "Who are you?" she asked again.

"Charles Milburn. May I call you Anna?"

"If you like." Her eyes, swimming like bluish agates in wet, red-rimmed sockets, grew vague. "Who did you say you are? Another doctor? Enemies, doctors, nice ones... You look like a doctor."

"Not really a doctor." I was floundering. What was I supposed to say to this woman, and what the Hell was the matter with West? He had revivified her with some intention in mind, but he had not bothered to tell me what that intention was and now he was apparently terrified to go near her. I wished Sarah was there.

Trying to forget that she had been a corpse not so long before, I made myself take Anna's hand in mine. It was cold and bony, a bag of loose sticks and marbles. Her nails were long enough to be slightly curved and pressed into my skin. "I'm not a doctor," I repeated, "but I want to help you. Suppose you tell me about Lawrence. Maybe we can find him together."

"Yess," she breathed. "Find him." She pressed her lips together, emphasizing deep, vertical lines that showed her determination. The rekindled life within her was focused entirely on one idea. Behind the grotesque and pathetic mask of age, with its wrinkles and sparse grey eyelashes, was a hot desire that frightened me.

I reached out and pulled a nearby stool toward me. It wasn't comfortable, but it would have to do; I was afraid that if I let go of Anna's hand, the tenuous rapport I had established with her would vanish. I spared a glance for West. He stood with his back against a laboratory bench, his hands clenched at his sides, watching us. I wondered what he would do if Anna survived this ordeal – take her back to the asylum or give her a room in his house? In any case, he would have to face her. An uncharitable part of me was maliciously amused.

Anna looked at me, her eyes narrow with suspicion. "Why should I believe you?" she asked.

"Lawrence," I prompted gently. "Who is he?"

"Oh, wouldn't you want to know?" A smile, ghastly and inappropriate in its teasing roguishness, disfigured her patrician features, and the question came out in a teasing sing-song, as did what followed. "Lawrence Dexter... Lorenzo, *amato*." The smile lingered on her lips, transformed somehow to sweetness.

I thought hard, staring at a row of glass vessels gleaming on a distant shelf. (*Alembics*, I thought, but of course they weren't). I had to question her carefully, because this was something precious to her. "How did you meet him?"

"At the Convivium. He knew the secrets. About the enemies. But they got him, then they got me."

She was wandering. I tried to steer her back to reality. "When did he tell you these things?"

"How? When? Where? Why? You sound like the doctors that tied me up and asked me things again and again and again. How do I know you aren't one of them?" Her voice had grown shrill. I glanced toward West again. He was sitting on a wooden box, elbows on knees with his forehead in his hands.

"I promise you, I'm not an enemy," I said. Gently, I let go of her hand and held both of mine out, palms turned toward her. "See, I have no weapons. And I won't take you anywhere unless you want me to. You were telling me about when you met Lawrence."

"Jeremy was four years old and little Hiram was seven. And big Hiram, my husband – " She laughed, a cracked, crazy laugh, and when she spoke again it was in the sing-song voice. "He had other fish to fry. Little fish, little fish. Lots of little fish in Hiram's net." She sang the sentence again, her voice quavering in a way that stirred the hairs on the back of my neck and made West press his knuckles to his lips.

"I was lonely." Anna's voice was calm again, and now plaintive as well. "All those women with their sorry-faces – I could tell they whispered about me behind my back. But they didn't know about Lawrence Dexter and the Convivium of the Secret Wisdom. I had my own secret." She smiled, a little cat smile.

I took a chance with another question. "What was he like, Miss Derby? Lawrence Dexter."

"Like me," she said, still smiling. "Like he was my brother. Except his eyes were grey."

She closed her eyes and I saw a glitter of tears on her wrinkled cheeks. "He loved me, but Hiram would never let me go. But I had my son."

"So you had three sons?" I held my breath.

"Two and one, that's three. Only I had to pretend to... make up to Hiram. To fool him."

"I'm not sure I understand," I said.

Another flirtatious smile. "Come now, I don't have to spell it out for you, do I Doctor? You should know about these things."

"And when was he born, your son?"

"He was my November boy, my little Francesco... "

A violent movement from West caught my eye. He had jumped up and was staring at the woman on the table.

"Did you say – *Francesco*?" It came out in a whisper.

"My son?" she murmured. "That was his name. Not Herbert. Not West. That was Hiram's name but my son wasn't Hiram's."

"Herbert! What's wrong with you?" I ran around the table and grabbed his arm, resisting his attempt to shake my hand off. "I don't know why you made me revivify this woman – your mother, don't try to tell me otherwise – but now that she's alive you have to talk to her. You *have* to!"

He looked at me, on his face an expression I had never seen before, as though something had broken in him. And – could it be? – I thought there were tears in his eyes. "Come on," I said, gently shaking his sleeve, "there's nothing to be afraid of. I'll be right here."

"No, I can't. She's too... it's horrible. But Charles, ask her... ask her for me – why did she leave?"

I was about to argue with him, but I could see that a change was coming over our patient. Her breath came in gasps again and she was staring fixedly at the ceiling. I hurried over to her

"Anna, can you hear me?"

A long interval of silence while her mouth moved as though she was chewing the words. "Yes..." She swallowed, the movement of her throat pulling at the fresh sutures in the loose skin of her neck.

"Anna, tell me – why did you leave your children?"

This time her voice seemed to reach me from a distance, as though she had retreated down a long hallway." "Lawrence... dying... in New York City."

She took a long, shuddering breath. "I wanted to... come back, but Hiram – "

I waited, but she did not speak again. "Hiram. What did Hiram do?" I prompted.

This time there was no recognition, no conversation. She stared at the ceiling and raved. The words she intoned were beyond comprehension, as though she spoke in an unknown tongue.

"Gyazgin komgolz bagha dord, kagha weerpa dagha merdolon saava." There was more, and it all sounded like this.

West recoiled violently, clapped his hands over his ears and almost ran to the far side of the room. For a moment I thought he was going to leave altogether, but he stopped near the door.

Anna's eyes rolled back in her head, and she gasped "*Francesco...*" The name struck more forcibly for being suddenly understandable, like a familiar face emerging from darkness. Then she slumped back onto the blankets, apparently lifeless once more.

"Herbert! Come here, I think she's fainted!"

"No! I can't listen to that gibberish she's spouting. You don't know – "

I went over to him and grabbed his arm. "She's not saying anything now, she's unconscious. Maybe dead. Come on, you're the doctor – do your job!" I frog-marched him back to the table.

Perhaps the lifeless appearance of our victim reassured him. It was, after all, the normal outcome of these experiments. After a moment he went through the motions of checking for vital signs. There were none.

He drew up the coverlet over her face and stood in silence for a long moment. Then he bent over the still form, murmuring something I could not hear, nor did I want to. I went over to the door and waited for him there.

I did not intend to visit West the following day, thinking it best to leave him to his own devices. The more I thought about what we had done in the cellar laboratory, the more it seemed like a grotesque dream. I remembered the steel blade laying open the bloodless flesh, West's uncharacteristic agitation and the irrationality of the entire proceeding. I wondered how he had managed to acquire the corpse and move it into his laboratory.

After a night of restless sleep I cancelled all my obligations for the day and drove to Boston. I visited a number of libraries, paging through bound copies of newspapers a quarter century old and making notes. As I drove back to Arkham, I was certain that West would be interested in the information I had compiled, but was at the same time reluctant to deliver it.

The next day a discreet notice appeared in the obituary section of the *Advertiser*, of a funeral service to be held that evening for Anna Derby West "of Arkham, suddenly deceased at the age of 70 years."

Anna Derby West. So he had publicly acknowledged their relationship.

I remembered that Sarah was working an early shift at the hospital and made my way there instead of to my office at the Library. With luck I managed to catch her on a break. The ordinary human noise of the hospital's cafeteria insulated us like the tumult of a storm and we were able to talk in its privacy.

"Sarah," I began, "that woman you told me about, Miss Derby – "

"Oh, Charles, she's dead! She got sort of upset last week. I told you about that. Well, next time I was there – that would have been two days after – she was having one of her bad spells. I couldn't get her to settle down. A couple of days after that she ran away. She was gone by the time I got there for my shift with her, but she didn't get very far, poor lady. One of the orderlies found her just a few hundred yards from the gates."

"Are you sure she was dead?"

"She wasn't, then. They took her to St. Mary's, here in Arkham. They can't really cope with medical emergencies at the asylum. But she died about half an hour later. Hypothermia."

"I'm sorry, Sarah." Then I thought of something. "When did that happen, exactly? Her death, I mean."

"Let me see..." She thought for a moment. "Late Saturday afternoon, about five or six o'clock."

Saturday afternoon. Andre had summoned me to West's on Saturday night.

"I don't suppose anyone has told Herbert about this – Dr. West, I mean. Perhaps I should – "

"Oh, but he was there!" Sarah looked up at me, the tears on her cheeks incongruous with her sudden vehemence. "He was just leaving when they brought her in, but he stayed with her until... until the end." She found a handkerchief, wiped her eyes and blew her nose.

"Sarah," I said, "did you go into the emergency ward with her, or did you wait outside?"

"I went in. If I'd been just anybody, they wouldn't have let me in, but since I work here, no one stopped me. And I felt it was my fault, somehow. The last time I saw her she told me she had to find an old friend whom she'd seen a few days ago. The way she said 'friend' I figured it must have been an old flame. I tried to humor her, thinking she would forget the notion when she calmed down, but I guess it didn't work."

"And Dr. West – what was he doing there? He doesn't work in Emergency, surely?"

"No, of course not! I don't know why he was there. But after Miss Derby died, he signed her body into the morgue and did the paperwork, listing her possessions and so on. She didn't have much, of course, poor thing. Just her nightgown and robe and a handkerchief. She'd lost her slippers, I guess." Sarah let out a choked laugh. "But she still had that blessed walnut."

"Walnut?" I asked. The word seemed absurd. And I had seen no such object in West's laboratory.

"Ever since I've known her, Miss Derby had this big walnut she kept in her pocket. If she liked you, she'd show it to you but she'd get quite fierce if anyone tried to take it from her, so I made sure no one did. It must have been a souvenir from her home, or maybe she just thought it was. Maybe it wasn't even always the same walnut. There are walnut trees on the grounds at Sefton, you know. Sad, isn't it?"

I agreed. I was beginning to think the situation was much sadder than either of us had realized.

There were few mourners at the modest funeral – West, of course, and Sarah, one or two of the staff from Sefton Asylum, and a tall, pale man who was introduced to me as Robert Derby, the dead woman's cousin. I observed him curiously during the brief service, but could see no trace of a family resemblance between him and West. Speaking with the man later, I had an impression of a melancholy nature, and of one serious to the point of lugubriousness. What sort of family background, I wondered, had produced this morose individual? Perhaps it was not surprising that Anna Derby had wanted to distance herself from her family, even at the cost of marriage to Hiram West. At least the atmosphere around him had been one of optimism and energy, however crude.

Afterward, I invited West to join me for an early supper at a restaurant I found congenial to both palate and wallet. He had previously professed scorn for the place, but this time accepted my suggestion of venue without comment. He seemed resigned and dispirited, a state in which I had not seen him before. This, and the formal black garb of mourning had the odd effect of making him look both older and younger. Toward the end of the meal I figured it out – his face looked worn, but the grey eyes that looked out from it were the eyes of an orphan.

I noticed something else. On the third finger of his right hand, West wore a ring, an emerald in a curious setting of a style I had never seen before. I was surprised because he never wore rings, as a rule. He had declared at least once that rings were a bad idea for surgeons because they retained impurities, got in the way and could potentially damage the hand on which they were worn.

I did not like the idea of his being alone and at loose ends that evening, so after the meal I asked him back to my quarters. Again, he accepted my invitation in a way that implied that he did not really care what he did just then.

"Would you like coffee or something stronger?" I asked as I hung up our coats.

"Coffee would be splendid," he said, following me into the kitchen.

I expected that he would speak of his mother's revivification, now that we were away from the public ear, but he talked of trifles while I busied myself with the coffee pot. A book lying on my table caught his attention. "You're reading Paracelsus? His writings on alchemy, I see. Are you hoping to augment your fortune by making gold from lead, Charles?" He smiled at me with something of his old manner.

"If I were, I would surely have had to ask for your help before now," I replied. "No, it's for the Quarrington Collection. I'm adding to the books on alchemy, so I thought I had better learn something about the subject. It's really quite interesting."

He opened the book at random and read, "*Nihil enim aliud mors est, nisi dissolutio quaedam, quae ubi accidit, tum demum moritur corpus... Huic corpori Deus adiunxit aliud quoddam, puta coeleste, id quod in corpore vitae exisitit.* Hmm. Something about death, and the body, and... God. That's as close as I can get, but I'm sure *you* can translate it perfectly."

He handed me the book, and to humour him, I translated.

"'For death is nothing but a kind of dissolution which takes place when the body dies. To this body God has added a certain other thing of a heavenly nature, that of the life which exists in the body.'"

"Well," said West, "I agree with him about the dissolution. But the rest is nonsense. There we part company, Doctor Paracelsus and I."

"But why, Herbert?" I asked. "I'm not sure that Paracelsus is referring to any kind of supernatural phenomenon here. In fact, I think a perfectly reasonable interpretation of that statement would be that he is speaking of the thing you have been looking for all these years – the key to the mechanism of life."

"Well, for one thing, he says that this 'certain other thing' is of a heavenly nature. To me that is a meaningless statement. The mechanism of life is an earthly phenomenon."

"Ah, but the alchemists were intensely earthy men," I countered. "They sought the sublime in the terrestrial. At least, they began with the earthly and sought by their art to achieve the heavenly."

"Exactly – *art*, not science. Now I suppose there's no harm in artistically inclined individuals dabbling in these pre-scientific ideas, using them as vehicles for their creative impulses, but that's not science and never will be. So don't expect me to have much sympathy for these notions. But you seem quite taken with them."

"Yes, I am. They contain so much – the beginnings of science and the medieval way of thinking about natural phenomena, but also a kind of spiritual discipline which is still valid today."

"Really? How can that be? But then, I know nothing about spiritual disciplines." He was only politely interested, but at least the topic had diverted him from his earlier dejected state.

"The practice of alchemy, in its purest form, was accomplished both in the laboratory, using matter, and spiritually within the alchemist himself. One of its tenets is that the process cannot possibly succeed if the motives of the alchemist are less than noble, a quest for material gain rather than enlightenment. The work is necessarily complex and lengthy, requiring many repetitions, failures and new beginnings. You know, Herbert, reading about it I've been reminded of all those revivification experiments we did together. You must remember telling me that even the smallest increment of knowledge was worth the effort, and that all the repetitions were absolutely necessary."

"Knowledge, yes, but... Well, I can see the parallel, even though I disagree with your implication. But I fail to see the connection between what the alchemist did to the matter in his vessel and his inner state."

"It's a mystical connection," I replied, knowing quite well that I was entering territory he unequivocally rejected. "The idea was that by struggling through all the writings, however contradictory, and following the tortuous operations in the laboratory, the alchemist brings about both an outer and an inner transformation, that at one and the same time he finds the Philosopher's Stone in his vessel and in himself.

"The symbols are exceedingly powerful. I suppose that's the appeal of it for me. It's a self-renewal through reconciliation of the opposites in one's own nature. You destroy your old self, as it were, by subjecting it to intense scrutiny in order to find the good qualities, and seeking balance in reconciliation. Then, speaking in alchemical terms, this First Matter is allowed to rot to blackness, in a death which precedes the rebirth and transformation. It's a sacrifice, a symbolic return to the womb. To me, that's the point of the whole thing, the giving of oneself into the mystery to achieve rebirth, and finally the exaltation of the new self in a red dawn." I stopped, out of breath and feeling a bit silly.

"I can see you're quite taken with all this," West said again, with an ironic smile. "In fact, I've never known you to get so worked up about an idea. Are you going to ask me for a little corner of my laboratory now, in which you can pursue these transformations?" His words were light, even gently mocking, but he frowned a little as he spoke.

"I don't think that will be necessary," I said. "But I do find it fascinating."

I had quite forgotten about the coffee while I was speaking, and West, in his neat-handed way, had dealt with the brew and assembled cups and other necessary items. He picked up the laden tray and looked at me.

"I suppose you're thinking of the supposed worthlessness of the unexamined life. But what would prompt one to begin such an examination in the first place?"

"I'm not sure, but I think it would be quite compelling, if it was necessary. You would drive yourself to it, whatever your will or thoughts about the matter."

He looked skeptical. "Really? And have you experienced such a compulsion yourself?"

"No. Not yet, anyway. But I'm certain that is how it would be."

"Well, I hope you tell me about it when it happens. It should be an interesting phenomenon to observe."

We went into my sitting room, where West took his usual place in the armchair and leaned back with a sigh. "Thank you for this, Charles. These past few days have been very... difficult." There was a small silence, broken only by the crackling of the fire in the fireplace.

"I can imagine," I said, "but I have to ask you – why didn't you tell me everything right at the start?"

He looked away, as though he had a pressing need to study the prints on the wall. When he turned back to me it was with an expression of mingled embarrassment and defiance.

"I didn't actually intend to involve you at all," he said. "But when it came to the point – you know, the incisions, all that – I couldn't do it, and you were the only person I could ask for help."

"She was your mother," I said.

It wasn't a question, and he did not answer it. "I think it must have been seeing me again that set her off," he said. "You see, I went back to Sefton the following day, both to see my burn patient there and to find out more about... her. Dr. Holberg tried to be informative, for one of his tribe. He spoke eloquently of hysteria, neurosis, mania, and a dozen other conditions, none of which he bothered to define in any understandable way. For all I know, she suffered from all of them, or none. I came away knowing little more than when I went in, except that the woman's name was Anna Derby West and she had been a... a resident for more than twenty years. So I asked him if I could see her myself. That was perhaps a mistake."

"What did you say to her?"

"Nothing. I didn't get a chance. The fool of an attendant who took me to her introduced me. Well, to be fair, I didn't think to ask him not to do that. So when the fellow said to her, 'Here's Dr. Herbert West to see you, Miss Derby,' she nearly fainted. Then she started to scream, which was most uncomfortable, for me at least. I suppose that's one thing about an asylum – you don't expect anything normal. There was no possibility of a conversation, never mind a happy reunion." He shook his head and fell silent.

"Why did you revivify her?" I asked. "Did you really think it would be a happy reunion?"

"No, of course not!" He sounded angry. "But just imagine – after twenty-five years your missing mother turns up in a lunatic asylum! Wouldn't you want to find out how she got there? And since no one at the asylum could tell me, there was only one thing to do."

He got up from his chair and turned away from me, to the dark mirror of a nearby window. "I happened to be there when she was brought into the emergency department and stayed with her until she died. The next step was obvious. Moving her body from the morgue to my laboratory was easy; Andre and I managed that quite well. But I couldn't bring myself to... touch her, to do the things that had to be done. It wouldn't have been... decent." He turned around, his face pale. "But I had to know!"

"To know what?" I asked, gently.

"About her madness – what it really was. Whether she remembered me, and... why she left." He shook his head. He came back to his chair and sat down, leaning toward me. "I tried to tell myself it was only another experiment, but it wasn't, of course. I couldn't maintain scientific detachment."

"I don't think she recognized you," I contributed. "Not as her son, anyway. She thought you were someone else and being told your name was West confused her."

He stared at me. "Who did she think I was?"

"Lawrence Dexter."

"Who?"

"Don't you remember? She called you by that name when she saw you, before you... ran away."

"I 'ran away,' as you put it, because it was obvious that she was insane. Especially that gibberish she spouted at the end. I'd heard something like it before – " He broke off, biting his lip. "Right there, one of my questions was answered and I knew there was no point in asking her any others."

"On the contrary, talking with her brought up questions I thought I could find answers to, and I did. There actually was a Lawrence Dexter – "

"That's absurd!" West interrupted. "She was... wandering in her wits. All that stuff she said, it was meaningless. You of all people should have known that, after all those subjects you tried to interview years ago. The whole thing was a waste of time."

"You won't think that after you hear what I found out."

"I don't know if I want to." But he made no move to leave.

I consulted the notes I had taken. "Lawrence Dexter was an Englishman. I don't know anything else about him before he came to America, but in the Eighties he was the head of a society of occultists called the Convivium of the Secret Wisdom. He lived in New York City and gave lectures all over the continent. Spiritualism and magic were quite fashionable at the time."

"So he was either a fraudster or a lunatic. What of it?"

"I found notices of his lectures in Boston newspapers in 1885. 'Evil Entities Lurk Beyond the Curtain of Everyday Life. Mr. Lawrence Dexter of the Convivium of Secret Wisdom reveals the truth. Discover the secrets of the Ancient Gods.'"

"What did I tell you? A lunatic," said West. "And probably a fraudster too. I don't imagine these revealing lectures were delivered for free."

"My point," I said, "is that your mother must have attended one of these lectures and become acquainted with Dexter. Eventually they became lovers."

West fixed me with a steely look. "What are you suggesting, Charles?"

"I'm not *suggesting* anything, only reminding you of what your mother said. They met in 1885. When she was talking about him she called him 'Lorenzo, *amato*.' That means 'beloved.'"

"I know damned well what it means!" West growled, looking at the carpet and clawing at his hair.

"She said she had to 'make up' to Hiram, her husband, so he wouldn't guess, and that her son Francesco was born in November. November 1886, I'm guessing."

"Coincidence." His face was pale, his pupils dilated. He looked dangerous but self-controlled.

"You told me years ago that your mother was half Italian, and that you thought she had a love affair after your second brother was born. She said she and Dexter looked alike. That must mean that he was blond with grey eyes, like you. When she saw you in Sefton she thought you were him, and the other night too. Your middle name is Francis. I'll bet she called you Francesco. That's too many coincidences."

He jumped up and took another turn around the room. I was half-afraid that he was going to take a swipe at me, but he did not.

"So now I have a long-lost twin brother called Francesco. I suppose he's the one I lied about to you all those years ago, and now he's come back to haunt me."

"What do you mean?"

"Just lately I've found myself hypothesizing about this outcome or that outcome in a way I never have before, exactly as though there's a little pest plucking at my sleeve, saying, 'But have you thought about this? What if this happens? Or that?' It's maddening."

"How do you explain it?"

"I don't. Charles, you have to understand this – I was a child of eight when my mother disappeared. After she left, it was as though I tied off all the blood vessels that connected me to her, as one does when amputating a limb. A part of me atrophied and died after that, and yet I managed to live – quite successfully, by some measures. You know that. But now – it's as though someone has grafted onto me that stranger that was my young self, and I can't do anything without him popping up and saying, 'Here I am, what are you going to do about me?'

He laughed bitterly. "Now you tell me that I'm the offspring of a madwoman and a man who believed in some sort of lunatic theory, and so was probably himself unbalanced. And I grew up in the house of a criminal. On the whole, though, I would rather that Hiram West was my father. He may have been a murderer, but at least he was sane."

"As sane as any murderer, I suppose."

He ignored this. "For years I thought he'd killed her. I don't know where I got the idea – bits of things I overheard and saw, I suppose. They must have formed themselves into a shape of horror in my mind."

He stopped pacing and looked at me. "So what else did you find out about this Dexter?"

"He died in August of 1895, in New York. Someone shot him, but it seems that no one was charged with his murder. Maybe it wasn't murder, only an accident. He lived for several days but was never able to give a statement."

"August of '95," West said, slowly. "That's when my mother left. I was eight."

"Another... coincidence?" I asked, carefully.

"All right, Charles," West said, "the dates are damnably suggestive, I agree. I suppose she might have gone to Dexter when she heard he was dying. Perhaps she intended to leave Hiram and send for me later. I don't know. But something went wrong and she ended up in Sefton."

"She said things that suggested Hiram had something to do with that, and with Dexter's death as well."

West swiped a hand over his face. "I wouldn't put it past him. By the way, did you say you had something stronger than coffee?"

I fetched some whiskey and poured two glasses. "Sarah Enright said she was paid by Judge Derby to visit with your mother at Sefton, and when he died that responsibility went to Robert Derby. He was at the funeral service, wasn't he?"

"Yes, he's a cousin. His father was my mother's uncle. There has never been any warmth and friendliness between the Wests and the Derbys. I can understand why, now. Well Charles," he continued, with a forced smile, "didn't I say this would crack my foundations?"

"Why? After all, you are what you are, regardless of who your parents were. And you know you can trust me to keep all this to myself." Especially, I thought, given my role in the revivification of Anna Derby West. Now I was as culpable as her son, when it came to 'offering an indignity to a dead body.'

"Well, and what am I, then?" asked West. "Do you know? A man is the product of two things – the physical inheritance from his parents, and his upbringing. My upbringing was delivered by Hiram West and the tutors and others hired by him. But the other? There's a theory, propounded by Dr. Henry Maudsley, a British psychiatrist, that mental as well as physical disease can be transmitted from parent to child. So while I may not be mad now, it's very likely that I am infected with abnormality."

"But you have no reason to think so, do you?" I persisted. "Apart from these ideas about inheritance, I mean?"

"There have been times when I have found myself considering the possibility," he said, slowly. "In France during the War, for example. No, I can't rule it out."

I remembered some of his letters and a chill settled over my heart. It was as though he had laid aside his brilliant veneer and revealed darkness beneath. "But that wasn't exactly a normal situation, surely? For anyone that was there I mean, not only you. And don't forget that I'm the son of a suicide, but I don't expect that I'll be driven to do what he did."

"That's not the same. Suicide can actually be a rational choice, in some situations. And your father, from what you've told me, was a perfectly ordinary, competent individual until his bank failed. This is... insidious. And probably inescapable."

"But nothing about you has changed since you found out about all this," I said. "You're exactly the same person you were before." The person who murdered Robert Leavitt, my mind supplied helpfully.

"The person I was before was living in a state of blessed ignorance. Then I saw a clear road before me. Now it's full of hidden pits. You'll think me ungenerous and selfish, but it's probably just as well she expired before she was able to say more. Other considerations aside, explaining her recovery would have been an awkward business, since several people were there when I declared her dead."

He was groping for his usual ironic manner, like a man trying to find a weapon in the dark, but it eluded him. It was time to change the subject.

I saw that he was fretting with the ring I had noticed earlier, turning it around and around on his finger, as though it bothered him. "That's a very distinctive ring," I said. "I've never noticed it before."

"That's because I've never worn it before. But it seems appropriate now. You see, it came from *her*. My mother." He took it off and passed it to me.

I looked at the ring closely, turning it around under the light. The emerald was quite large and very fine, with a spark of fire in its clear green depths. But it was the setting that I found most puzzling. I could not guess of what metal it was made – some curious alloy, very pale gold in colour, heavy and hard, yet with a sheen that was almost pearly. Even more peculiar were the designs carved into the metal. They had been executed with great skill and precision. The motifs appeared to be geometrical in nature, but I could not begin to guess from what cultural or artistic tradition they emanated. The intricacy and grace of the interweaving lines and curves spoke of a highly evolved technique, but to me, at least, they were utterly unfamiliar.

"Do you know where this came from?" I asked, at length. "Where did your mother get it?"

"I really don't know," he said. "I doubt that it's an heirloom of the Derby family. There's nothing of the solid Yankee about it, is there? But then, I seem to remember some of the old Derbys were seafarers of one sort or another. It may be that one of them brought it back from some distant place."

He did not seem particularly interested in the ring and I did not persist in questioning him about it. He stared at the floor for a moment, then looked up at me and said, "Quarrington predicted that I would go mad, you know. That's another reason I wasn't keen on him toward the end."

"What do you mean?"

"It was that big prediction study of his. You know the one, I mentioned it a while ago. Mostly he didn't tell us subjects what he had predicted, so it wouldn't influence us and skew the results, but with me he let one detail slip. It surprised him so much that he forgot himself. I remember him poring over the notes he had made about me. He closed his eyes and looked like he was in pain or something. Then he looked at me and said 'You will die twice, Herbert West.' After that he clammed up. At the time I didn't worry about it much. At twenty or nineteen, or whatever age I was then, death seemed so remote that it didn't matter whether it would be once or twice. But I've thought about it since and decided he was telling me I would go insane – the death of the mind, you see, before the death of the body. He liked to speak in metaphors, Q. did."

I leaned closer to him. "You haven't asked for my advice, but I'm going to give it anyway. Your mother's life was sad, even tragic, but it was her life and now it's over. Your father is dead too, whoever he was. Forget them. Well, not entirely, but there's no reason to brood about them like this. As for all this stuff about madness, there's no point in thinking about that, either. You have work to do, work that you love, so do it. These other things will look after themselves. If you're infected with madness, as you say, worrying about it won't make any difference. And if you're not, then it's madness to worry. And if you do go mad, I'll make sure you're treated well."

"In that case, Charles, the kindest thing you could do would be to shoot me. The very thought of becoming one of those dribbling idiots at Sefton fills me with horror. But thank you, Dr. Milburn, for your opinion. I shall surely consider it. There's a practicality about it that appeals to me."

He got up to leave and I saw him to the door. "Quarrington wrote me a letter shortly before his death, when I was in Flanders, full of dire warnings. He warned me not to lose sight of you, Charles, that bad things would happen if I did. I've taken that much of his advice anyway. You're the only one I could talk with about all this."

I recognized in myself a desire to comfort him, but didn't know how, so I put my arms around him in a brief, awkward embrace, which he neither resisted nor reciprocated. He felt frailer than he looked. "It'll be all right, Herbert," I muttered, and let him go.

I listened to his footsteps receding down the stairs and something I had read recently came back to me, unbidden and complete. A cryptic sentence from Paracelsus: *He who would enter the Kingdom of God must first enter with his body into his mother and there die.*

Later, I realized that I had forgotten to ask West when his mother had given him the emerald ring. Had it been when he was a child, before her departure from the household? Or during the brief encounter before her death? It didn't really matter, but it bothered me, like a loose thread in a garment or a chip in the rim of a cup.

That night, I dreamt the question and an answer. West told me that she had not given him the ring as such, but only a large walnut. "She handed it to me and said, 'This is for you. He would have wanted you to have it.' And I put it in my pocket and forgot it. But later, after she was gone, I cracked it open and found the ring. Like this."

He opened his hand, disclosing a walnut. Then he clenched his fist on it, producing a cracking sound, and opened his hand again, like a conjuror. On his palm lay the emerald ring. West laughed. "It was only a walnut," he said.

I knew, of course, that this was a dream. But it lodged in my memory like the truth, and I never asked him for another.

Despite my sympathy for him, West's revivification of his mother struck me as grotesque and pathetic. I have read a good deal since then about the theories regarding heredity that were being propounded at the time. West had probably been aware of them when they were newly in vogue, and for some reason they had resonated strongly in his rather arid materialistic philosophy, which allowed no room for the unexplained. When he discovered that his mother was an asylum inmate, his fear of hereditary insanity must have prompted the desperate urge to interrogate her unfortunate corpse after her sudden death.

Moreover, by this time I had begun to suspect something else about him. There was only one explanation for certain of his idiosyncrasies. I had read my Plato. I knew what sort of love was discussed in *Phaedrus*. I knew also that in our time such individuals were considered by many to be hereditary degenerates. The knowledge that he himself harboured this abnormality must have been a heavy burden for him.

The thing that made me almost certain was an incident which took place at one of West's dinner parties. Things were at the stage where most of the guests were in a state of animated eloquence. John Billington was playing the piano and West was singing a duet of some sort with one of the others, rather badly. I had been talking with a new member of West's circle, one who was unusual in being older than most of us, and without a medical connection. He was a professor of physics, James Williams by name. As West and his companion concluded their performance to cheers and applause, I became aware that Williams was no longer attending to what I was saying. Neither was he cheering or applauding. He was gazing with a fixed and hungry stare at West, who was laughing and clapping his singing partner on the shoulder, entirely given over to the enjoyment of the moment, eyes shining, fair hair falling over his forehead. Suddenly, West became aware of Williams's stare and gave him such a look that I expected the man to fall over dead from the sheer icy intensity of it. He excused himself and left the room.

An hour or two later, the party had degenerated into something of a brawl and I was feeling unwell. West was nowhere to be found, so I went to get my coat. In the relative quiet of the entrance hall, I heard voices nearby. I looked around the corner and saw West and James Williams a little distance away. West leaned a shoulder against the panelling, one arm folded against his chest, a drink in his other hand. Williams had his back to me, but I could see his hand tentatively touching the lapel of West's jacket, plucking the cloth nervously between thumb and fingers as he spoke.

I could not hear what they said, for it was a conversation carried on in murmurs, mainly by Williams. His voice rose a little at times, taking on an imploring note. West's replies were brief, but I was struck by his manner – teasing, almost coquettish, with an ironic half-smile. I must have made some involuntary sound or movement, for suddenly he glanced in my direction. Unperturbed, he flicked Williams's hand from his lapel as though it were a bit of fluff. "Not now, James," he said, then, in a louder voice, "Charles, surely you're not leaving already?" I turned away from Williams's stricken face, embarrassed.

Williams left without a word while I was making my good-byes and (I heard later) quitted Miskatonic and Arkham some months subsequently. The day following the dinner, I mentioned the incident to West. "James Williams seemed upset about something when he left the other night."

"He's an importunate fellow," said West. "Just because I invited him to dinner and a small debauch, he thought... Well, never mind what he thought, but he seriously misjudged his potential. Not very good in a physicist. Oh, you don't understand? Well, never mind."

I didn't ask him any more, but I wondered. Had there been a miscommunication between the two of them? Had Williams recognized a kindred spirit and leapt to conclusions? Or had West given him reason for hope, then changed his mind?

None of this troubled me, particularly. What did, in fact, was this very lack of trouble, and the realization that the scene I had witnessed had intrigued me, rather than repelled.

Now that the usage of the years had dimmed West's glamour a little, it seemed to me that I was fated to be his confidant and, in an odd sense, his guardian. His peculiar upbringing and idiosyncratic values predisposed him to dangerous excesses, but he used me as a kind of Everyman on whom to test some of his ideas and plans. I had a twofold responsibility – to protect the world from him, and him from the world. I wondered which would prove more compelling.

With the arrival of spring, Anna Derby's remains were laid to rest in the Derby family plot in Christ Church Cemetery, rather than by the side of her husband in Boston. West insisted on this. "She was quite clearly dissociated from Hiram, no longer his wife in any sense that mattered."

"What do your brothers think?" They had attended neither the funeral service nor the burial.

"They have no feelings about her, one way or the other. As for me, I don't see much of them now. They had to make other arrangements when I was in Europe, and I decided not to be available to them when I returned."

"What do you mean, 'other arrangements'?"

"I used to do the odd bit of work for them. Strictly off the record, of course. But no more. They'll have to deal with their own dirty linen. And don't ask me to explain that, because I won't."

♦ **16** ♦

In the summer of 1920, Alma Halsey returned to Arkham. She knocked on my door one Saturday afternoon. I was unprepared for her arrival and was surprised by the upspringing of joy I felt when I saw her. I lifted her off her feet and whirled her around several times before setting her down laughing.

"Such exuberance, Charles!" she said, kissing me on both cheeks. "Oh, I'm so glad to see you again! I hardly know what to ask you first."

We spent the afternoon and evening talking. Alma was in Arkham for a short time only, staying with her parents. She intended to settle in Boston, where she would be writing a series of articles for the *Post* on various aspects of modern life as they pertained to women.

"It's exactly what I wanted to do even before I knew it," she said. "Those months of wandering around Europe showed me that."

"So journalism's gain is librarianship's loss. And mine, too, it seems."

"Now Charles, you have to own something – or someone – to lose it. And I'm going to be in Boston, for God's sake. That's a lot closer than I've been in five years. If you want me you'll know where to find me. So what have you been doing all this time, besides cataloguing?"

"Reading about alchemy."

"Why?"

"For the sake of the Quarrington collection, mainly. But I admit I find it fascinating. If I had lived hundreds of years ago, I might have tried to become a practical alchemist."

"Is there any other kind? But somehow I can't see you cooking and distilling all sorts of things, trying to turn them into gold. You'd probably set yourself on fire." She laughed and drained her glass.

"Well, it is the spiritual side that appeals to me." Her laughter had fallen harshly on my ears and I was happy to change the subject as I poured her another drink.

Eventually, our conversation turned to West.

"He's doing quite well these days," I said, "specializing in what he calls 'reconstruction.' You know, repairing serious wounds so as to minimize scarring. But there's also... renovation, I guess you could call it. Some people – film stars, mainly – want to have their faces improved. Better noses and chins and so on."

"You mean people come to Arkham to have Herbert West slice up their faces?" She was aghast.

"Boston. There aren't enough good hotels in Arkham for the recovery period. West seems quite amused by the whole thing. He says he doesn't care who he operates on as long as it's technically interesting."

"Hmm. I always thought he had more than a little of the ghoul about him. Well, he's not getting anywhere near my face with that scalpel of his."

"Your face doesn't need improving, Alma."

"Thank you. Speaking of West, I heard something rather odd. Mother told me that his mother died just a few months ago. But it seems that he hadn't even known she was still alive. Is that true?"

I gave her an edited version of the story but could not conceal the fact that Anna Derby had been an inmate of Sefton Asylum for many years before her death.

"Hiram West for a father and a madwoman for a mother," said Alma. "What a legacy. I suppose it explains a few things."

She was getting uncomfortably close to a sore point. "I'm not certain what you're suggesting, Alma. Well, perhaps I am, but I'll choose to ignore it for now. I think he has come to terms with his mother's... situation by now. And it's been a few years since Hiram died."

"But his older brothers are carrying on in their father's footsteps, by all accounts, and with youthful gusto. I've heard that they're getting into the liquor business, now that the Eighteenth Amendment has passed. Young Herbert would do well to stick to his last, or rather his blade."

I was glad when we went on to other topics, glad also to find that Alma and I still had much to say to one another. I had feared that our past connection would create unease between us, or that after her travels I would seem dull and provincial. Quite late in the evening I walked her back to her parents' house.

"Let's not lose track of each other again, Charles," she said in parting.

"Well, it wasn't I who went away."

"But I came back."

After Alma's amused reaction to the topic of alchemy, I had not told her how my interest in and knowledge of it had grown since my involvement with the Quarrington collection – that I sought out books about it at every opportunity, entering a world full of fantastic beasts and elaborate symbols, whose complicated literature hid more than it revealed, but was nevertheless nearly addictive. As I read the texts (which seemed often to contradict one another) and studied the illustrations (of winged dragons, self-devouring serpents, hermaphrodites, green lions and unicorns expiring in the laps of maidens), I had glimpses of a great secret – the reconciliation of good and evil in a mysterious duality. Light and darkness were contained in a single nature redeemed by the Great Work, by sacrifice and resurrection. The writings rarely mentioned gold. The Golden Flower, yes, but also the Blue Flower, the Emerald Tablet, a progression of colours from black to white to yellow to red. I was fascinated beyond reason and opened each book as though it was a door to a magical realm.

But there was no one with whom I could discuss this interest, neither my librarian colleagues nor my friends. Alma dismissed it as a medieval curiosity and West thought it frivolous and irrational. I perforce kept this secret to myself, even as it permeated my thoughts.

I never admitted the possibility of magic.

In the years after his mother's death, Herbert West reached the pinnacle of his career. The specialty he had created nearly single-handed was now taught in several medical schools, which meant that he was in demand as a lecturer as well as a practitioner. His patients ran the gamut from factory workers to the luminaries of stage and screen. I found out about the latter mainly from Sarah, since West was uncompromisingly professional when it came to revealing confidential details about his patients. On the few occasions that he related some of the particulars of a case it was the technical aspects that interested him, not the notoriety of the patient.

He had not emerged entirely unscathed from the events surrounding his mother's death. Those who knew him knew better than to refer flippantly to asylums or madness in his presence or, for that matter, to mothers. Anyone who transgressed, whether through malice, clumsiness or ignorance, was treated to a glacial stare and instantly rebuffed. I detected an increase in his reserve, a lessening of that devil-may-care insouciance that formed a good part of his charm. He was quicker to take offence and to express anger.

One day in the early fall of 1922, I was reading the newspapers over my morning coffee, when a small item in the *Arkham Advertiser* caught my eye.

A Strange Wanderer on the Aylesbury Pike

Travellers on the Aylesbury Pike early Tuesday morning were surprised to see a strange, apparently human being shambling along. It seemed to be disoriented, since it changed direction several times, once crossing directly into the path of an oncoming automobile. Arkham Police were notified and picked up the individual, who was in a poor state of health.

Doctors at St. Mary's Hospital said that the main problems were exposure and mental confusion, but evidence of recent surgical procedures was noted as well. Staff at St. Mary's said that no patients had been reported missing.

The individual expired later that day, without giving a statement. Investigations continue.

This snippet induced in me an intense disquiet. The reference to recent surgery and the fact that the individual could not be accounted for by the hospital pointed to West, with his secret laboratory, his surgical adventurousness, flexible ethics and love of experimentation. What had been the nature of the surgery, I wondered, and why was no gender used in reference to the unfortunate creature?

West had stated categorically on his return from the War that he had finished with revivification, due to the limited success of the procedure and the expansion of his interests into other areas. With his practice, his teaching and other commitments, as well as the research he carried out openly at the Medical School, he would have little time for clandestine pursuits. But this shambling figure – I could visualize it now, lurching from one side to the other of the busy Aylesbury Pike, a vacant stare on its face, a face that had been altered from its original lineaments, perhaps? I reread the story, but it gave no details as to which parts of the body had been operated upon. I wondered if Sarah had heard anything.

This local story was overshadowed by a spectacular incident from New York City. The previous night a celebrated diva of the Metropolitan Opera, a silvery-voiced French soprano named Eleonora Desanges, had been nearly killed in a savage attack by her former lover, an artist called Alexander DeGrassi. A knife had been involved, with the result that both the singer's throat and face had been slashed. 'She Will Never Sing Again,' mourned one headline; and 'Diva's Beauty Ruined,' proclaimed another. The major city papers wallowed in the story, dredging up every detail they could find about Desanges' career and stormy private life. Cheated of the spectacle of a celebrity's death and funeral, they made the most of her disfigurement and the ruin of her career.

Both of these events, the local and the international one, were on my mind when I joined West for lunch at the Miskatonic University Faculty Club later that day. He preferred this venue for dining to the even more exclusive Doctors' Lounge at the hospital. "Too insular," he said of the latter. "I get tired of shop talk, and for some reason physicians in a group tend to be rather coarse. I prefer the company of mixed academics. The cooking is better here too."

He was in an ebullient mood. "It's lucky we decided on lunch rather than dinner today, Charles. Andre and I are leaving for New York City this afternoon."

"What, on the 2:30? That's a late start. Why not tomorrow morning, on the 8 a.m.?"

"It's too urgent for the train. I'm driving to Boston, meeting a pilot there and being flown the rest of the way. We should arrive before dark."

"Flown to New York? Why?"

"The Desanges case. I'm going to reconstruct the beautiful Eleonora and her voice. Naturally, there's a certain urgency to get on with it."

"But the papers say it can't be done. She'll never sing again, they say."

"Oh, she'll sing again. Maybe not exactly the same way. The silvery voice may become a velvety voice, or a honeyed one, but she'll grace the Met's stage again, I guarantee it."

I was a little taken aback by his aggressively optimistic attitude and wondered whether his record of successes had caused him to abandon scientific caution.

"How can you be so sure? Have you ever done an operation like this before? The papers said her throat's been slashed. Wouldn't that have destroyed the vocal cords?"

"I think I have more accurate information on the state of Mlle. Desanges' vocal cords than the fellows who wrote those newspaper stories. And as for doing such operations, in France I patched up slashed throats, faces and body parts of all kinds, most of them successfully."

"Oh, I believe that. But how many of those fellows were opera singers? Scars are one thing on a soldier, quite another on someone who makes her living on the stage."

"This is my specialty, Charles. I assure you I have repaired injuries much worse than these. And not in any crude, scarred way either, as you seem to think. It's true that there were no divas in combat in the Great War, although I did work on a couple of nurses who were cut by flying glass when the Germans bombed the hospital at Etaples. The exact techniques will depend on the precise nature of the injuries, of course. But based on what her doctors have told me, it's entirely reasonable to expect a full vocal recovery.

"And the face should be routine. Mlle. Desanges may emerge from this ordeal more beautiful than ever, in fact. There has been no loss of tissue, merely injury. Loss would have made it a rather more interesting procedure. Now specifically..."

He launched into a description I soon lost track of, which was just as well, because it involved references to skinning, flaps, retraction, excision, swelling and other grisly matters which were not a happy accompaniment to a meal.

Over dessert, I ventured to mention the Aylesbury Pike incident.

"Yes, I did notice something in the *Advertiser*," West said, addressing himself to a piece of apple pie. "The story reminds you of John Hocks, doesn't it? You needn't worry. According to my informant at Sefton, Hocks is the same as ever." He looked at me, smiling, with such a guileless expression in his grey eyes that I felt ashamed of my suspicions.

"You don't know anything more about it, then? I thought you might, being... connected with the hospital and all."

"Not a thing. I wasn't there yesterday, for one thing. Better ask your pal Sarah. This is excellent pie, by the way. You should have some."

"I wonder where that person could have come from," I persisted, "if not from the hospital. And did you notice the article didn't say whether it was a man or a woman? Why would that be?"

"Well, the *Advertiser* doesn't exactly hire the best reporters, you know. Most of those go to the big cities, like your friend

Alma. As to where the thing might have come from, my guess would be Sefton Asylum. They're not terribly vigilant when it comes to escapees, as we have reason to know. It's a wonder they've managed to hold onto Hocks all these years. And it's a sad thing, but the inmates of such institutions eventually begin to look like one another, men and women alike."

"But the evidence of surgery?"

"Even lunatics need surgery on occasion. You know that as well as I do. Again, the details were mostly absent. That little story has certainly taken your fancy."

"Well, but it just sounded so – "

"So much like something I'd be mixed up in, is that it? You're getting suspicious in your old age, Charles. I have enough surgery to do without making a hobby of it. And now I must be off."

That night I went to West's house. Brooding over our conversation for the remainder of the afternoon had convinced me that I had to investigate further. This would be my only chance.

To enter the house uninvited in his absence was not only illegal but possibly dangerous. Had I not already seen that Hiram West's son or not, he had a ruthlessness equal to Hiram's when it came to protecting his interests? And with his peculiar ethical make-up, the borders of friendship were closer to home than one might imagine. But I had accepted my undeclared role as guardian and conscience, and could not elude it.

It was with a good deal of unease that I approached the house on Boundary Street late that night, armed with a couple of flashlights. For the first time I noticed how peculiarly well situated the place was for one who valued, indeed required, secrecy. The grounds were extensive, the rear consisting of shrubberies, while the part close to the house and street was conventionally landscaped. West cared nothing for gardening, but employed a man to keep the grass cut and the shrubs pruned. Beyond this buffer zone the neighbouring houses were comfortably distant.

West had never asked me to return the keys he had given me when he left for the War. I tried one of them in the outer door, almost hoping that he had changed the locks since his return. But it turned easily and soon I was standing in the hall where Robert Leavitt had died.

The house felt occupied. I told myself that this was only because I remembered my previous solitary visit, just before

West's return from Europe. On that occasion, empty for four years, the place had been lifeless and sterile; now it was inhabited, a home. But already nervous, I could not ignore the feeling that someone was there. Perhaps Andre had stayed behind after all? To dispel my unease, I called out, "Hello! Is anyone here?" There was no answer, only a thick silence followed by the non-sound of my own blood circulating.

Whatever I was looking for would be in the laboratory. Lighting my way with a flashlight, I descended to the cellar and moved the hinged section of shelves that concealed the door. My second key fitted its lock and I entered the room, closed the door and turned on the electric lights.

The last time I had been in this room was more than two years before, when I had helped West with the revivification of his mother. On that occasion I had an impression that West had re-equipped the place, but now there was no doubt of it. New apparatus had been added, most of it for purposes unknown to me. The most striking objects were a fully-equipped operating table under powerful lights, and a kind of vat with a constellation of glass vessels connected to it by tubes and rubber hoses.

On shelves at one end of the room stood a dozen large vessels full of an iridescent, violet-coloured liquid. Looking more closely, I saw that several of the jars contained cloudy shapes, as if the stuff were coalescing to form distinct entities. There was something disturbing about these shapes, to the extent that I was happy to look away from them, but not before I was reminded of the *homunculi* that Paracelsus and other alchemists had claimed to have coaxed from the *prima materia* by their arts.

Sitting down on a stool, I tried to think. During the War, West had written to me about the beginnings of his work in what he called reconstruction and renovation, saying that it involved the revivifying fluid in some way. He would need large amounts of the stuff for his normal practice, even if he no longer did revivifications.

I could explain what I saw, but was this innocent explanation the correct one? I had known West long enough that logic produced another explanation, one which I could no longer ignore. Why did he revivify corpses? Because he wanted to. Because he was able to. It was a way of exercising his will to a degree impossible for others. He had never published anything about revivification, whatever his original intentions, and never would. Why would he give away to the world the secret of his unique power? For him, it was no longer research.

But what about the operating table? Even I recognized that this was no longer the simple slab that we had used for Leavitt and his predecessors. Its presence seemed to negate West's recent declaration that he did not engage in surgery as a hobby. But no doubt he would not regard it so; he would call it research. All right, but why was he doing research here in the cellar, when he had a fully-equipped facility at the Medical School at his disposal? Inevitably, I was led back to something hidden and secret.

I poked about, opening cupboards and drawers. For the most part, their contents told me nothing, but in one drawer I found a pistol, surely a non-standard piece of lab equipment if ever there was one. Target practice? On what? Florence flasks that had somehow offended him? I looked at it for a long time before I closed the drawer.

I was about to leave when I remembered the annexe, the other room to which I had never been admitted, even when I was West's collaborator and accomplice. It was still locked, and I had no key. Frustrated, I thumped my fist against the door.

I nearly screamed when a deep groan sounded from beyond the solid wood. My heart seemed to stop beating, then started again with a heavy thudding that filled my ears with a rushing sound. My nerves twitched with a futile impulse to run. When it lessened I pressed my ear to the door. Nothing. I struck the door again. This time I heard a cracked voice raving, "O God, o God, o God," repeated many times, then fading away. I stood frozen, ear to door, for long moments during which my brain contained only one phrase, echoing the words of the unknown occupant of the locked room: *No, not this. No, not this. No, not this.*

A sentence from the *Rosarium philosophorum* swam into my mind: *"For our stone, namely the living western quicksilver which has placed itself above the gold and vanquished it, is that which kills and quickens."*

Finally, thought returned. What could I do? Obviously, I could not break down the door alone. Should I summon the police? I crept back into the main laboratory and tried to analyze the situation.

Clearly, it was alive, and human, and suffering. But who was it, and why was it here? Did West have an actual patient here in this cellar? Could there be a legitimate reason for someone to be alone in that room, in pain or suffering? I thought of the little West had told me of his 'renovation' work – surgery performed solely to alter someone's facial appearance. I supposed it was possible that an individual who wished to have such a procedure done in secret was being accommodated in this hidden room. But West expected to be away for a week. Surely he would not leave someone unattended for that long a time? Whatever else he might be, West was conscientious when it came to his living patients. His perfectionism would allow no less.

Despite my confusion, one thing seemed clear. I had to try to communicate with whoever was behind that door. I went back to it and rapped on the wood. "Who is there?" I called. "Are you all right?"

Silence. And silence. And silence. There was no response to my rappings and calls.

At length I gave up and went upstairs. I went to West's study, hoping to find something there to explain the presence of someone in the locked annexe. His desk was, as usual, awash in books and papers, but they seemed to be exclusively of a professional nature and told me nothing. The filing cabinets were locked, as were the desk drawers.

The other rooms were orderly, as always. Except for his study, West managed to occupy a place without leaving much evidence of his presence. I wandered aimlessly around, trying to extract from the familiar surroundings indications as to the thoughts and motivations of their absent owner. I looked in the sitting room mirror, but all I could see in its tarnished and wavy glass was my own anxious face. And over my shoulder the opposite wall, on which hung the three paintings by Walter Dixon Taylor.

I went over and studied the pictures once more. I had grown no fonder of them with the years and now found them more disturbing than ever. West had been evasive when I had invited him to speculate as to what might have inspired the artist to paint these images, and why it was West to whom he had given them. Now, with the evidence of his secret doings fresh in my mind I could not help but wonder again. Had Taylor known of West's private research? Or had he been inspired by something less tangible? I could find no answers to these questions, not in this room, nor in any of the others I had visited.

That left only West's bedroom and the small adjoining room where he kept his wardrobe. Only here did I have a sense of his presence. A bathrobe was draped over the foot of the bed and a shirt and tie hung on the back of the single chair. A couple of books lay on the bedside table. I went over to see what he had been reading. Hugo's *Les Miserables*, in French, I noticed, and an English translation of the *Meditations* of Marcus Aurelius.

Suddenly I felt exceedingly uncomfortable. Why was I prying into my friend's personal things? Whatever he might be doing in his laboratory, surely he was entitled to privacy in the place where he slept. I left immediately.

By the time I reached my own home I had come to a decision. I would return to the laboratory each night and try to speak to the occupant of the locked room. The nature of any response I would elicit might tell me what to do next.

And I would meet with Sarah Enright and carefully question her about anything she might know about West's recent professional activities. She might not have much direct knowledge, but she would certainly have heard gossip. Finally, I would have to have a serious talk with West at the earliest opportunity.

Sarah and I met at our usual cafeteria the next day. I had given much thought as to how I should pose my questions to her. She knew, of course, that West and I were friends of long standing, and therefore would think it peculiar if I started asking about things that she would expect me to know already. Thus I began by chatting about the strange incident on the Aylesbury Pike. Had she actually seen the afflicted individual?

"No, but I talked with someone who did. She said it was very peculiar. No hair, for one thing. And there were these partially-healed incisions all around the face. Nicely done, too, she said."

"Was it a man or a woman? The paper didn't say."

"It was a woman. But you couldn't tell right away."

"Because the face had been altered?"

"That, yes. But the breasts had been removed."

I felt sick. This was much worse than I had expected. I forced myself to maintain a light tone of voice.

"I heard a rumour that it might have been someone who had run away from Sefton."

"Who knows? I imagine the police checked there. But you want to know an odd thing? There's a body missing from the morgue."

I looked up quickly. Too quickly, perhaps. "Oh really? There couldn't be a connection, surely. Unless it's possible for someone to be put in the morgue before they're really dead."

"I doubt it. Anyway, I wasn't suggesting there is a connection, only that it's another strange thing that's happened this week."

"Yes, it surely is that. Sarah, don't you think it's wonderful that Dr. West has been called to New York to operate on that opera singer?"

"It certainly is. This should really put Arkham on the map."

"Tell me, what's it like to work with him?"

"Well, he's very quick, very demanding, but fair. He expects us nurses to know our stuff and do it without being told. And he's polite. He doesn't yell at us or call us names when we make mistakes. But he isn't what you'd call friendly. He's pleasant enough, but that's just on the surface. Underneath there's ice. I've only noticed that in the last year or two. He wasn't like that before."

"What's he like with patients?"

"Chilly. He's a great technician. If I had to have an operation, I'd want Dr. West to do it. His patients get fewer infections and recover faster than anybody's. But if I had a disease that couldn't be fixed with surgery, he's the last doctor I'd choose. He has no interest in explaining things to patients. You see, it's not enough to tell someone they have a tumor and they have three months to live; no I can't do anything; good afternoon. Next patient. People who are getting that kind of bad news need time to talk and ask a lot of questions, and hear the same answers in different ways. Dr. West – it's more than just not taking the time. It doesn't even occur to him that it needs to be done at all. So it's a good thing he's a surgeon. But I'd hate to be the person he tells that he can't do something for them. 'Well, Mrs. Smith, I can't eliminate that squint of yours without cutting an important nerve to your brain. So resign yourself to it.'"

She sounded so much like West that I laughed in spite of myself. Sarah started to laugh too, and it was at least a minute before we could stop.

"What about the other doctors? How does he get along with them?"

"Well enough, on the surface. Most of them recognize his competence but don't feel close to him. Others hate him, but I think that's mostly jealousy. One thing I've heard is that he uses too many new techniques on patients before they've been fully tested. So far he's been able to get away with it, but one day he'll slip up. That's what some of them say, and I think they can hardly wait for it to happen."

"That sounds pretty drastic."

"Oh, it's only one or two. Mostly Dr. James Hobson. He's a friend of Dr. Halsey's."

I remembered my encounter with Hobson at the Halseys' reception ten years ago, and diverted our conversation into other channels. Although I was almost sure that the wanderer on the Aylesbury Pike was West's handiwork, no one else had as yet made the connection. He must have once more taken a corpse from the morgue, with the objective this time not revivification, but surgery. A kind of vivisection on the recently dead? Or would that be revivisection?

I returned to West's cellar three more times during his absence and forced myself to hammer on the locked door. Each time I heard only silence. Was the person I had heard still alive? Had I even heard anyone in the first place? Without any evidence to support this I hesitated to call the police. I began to wish I had not bothered to pry into West's doings. All I had accomplished was to acquire some disturbing and inconclusive information about which I did not know what to do.

Eleonora Desanges made a spectacular recovery. Fewer than six months after surgery she was on the stage again. Critics filled their reviews with words such as 'rich,' 'warm' and 'velvety.' Her tone was likened to amber, honey and a fine old wine. As for her face, there certainly were no scars apparent. Some said that she was more beautiful than before, her face more distinguished and finely sculpted. West was referred to frequently as a magician. Newspaper reporters and magazine writers appeared on his doorstep, demanding interviews.

"It's ridiculous, Charles," he said. "There was some fairly complex surgery here, but nothing out of the ordinary. Why, if those people wanted to hear about something truly amazing, I could tell them about a fellow I worked on in France in 1918. His name was West, like mine, that's why I remember it. Peter West, that was it. Part of his face had been blown away. It was not merely slashed, Charles, it was *gone*. Luckily the bones were more or less intact. I managed to make a new face for him. It took three months and a large amount of a certain substance I believe I've told you about. But when he finally left for home, he had a face. A decent-looking one too. Now that was surgery worth making a fuss about. But no one wants to hear about Peter West from some place called Manitoba, and everyone wants me to tell them for the fiftieth time about Eleonora Desanges."

I made the right sounds in response to this, but I was thinking about a shambling form on the Aylesbury Pike. And about sounds from behind a locked door.

The storm of celebrity reached its zenith when West received word that the President of France had awarded him the *Legion d'Honneur* for, as the letter put it, 'saving a national treasure of France.' Reporters from several French publications, and some British ones as well, descended on Arkham. It was months before West was left in peace.

I still have the clippings and articles. Looking at them a few days ago, I was impressed by the sheer volume of material. An article from a British magazine included a photograph of West. I had forgotten how young he was then, only thirty-five. His pictured face seemed to gaze out beyond me, the clear eyes looking into some unguessable distance.

Here was a man, I thought, who had made the dead come to life, who had snatched the dying from the brink of death, who had made a new face for a man, who had restored the voice of Eleonora Desanges. Was it right to judge him by the rules that applied to me, to Sarah, to the rest of us ordinary plodders? Was it so surprising that he would rewrite some of them to suit himself?

♦ 17 ♦

Thou wilt never make from others the One that thou seekest, except there first be made one thing of thyself.
Gerard Dorn: "Philosophia meditativa"

In 1923, Herbert West's star fell from the sky. The first intimations of disaster were harmless enough. In January, I was in Boston on Library business and went to see Alma, who was living in an apartment in the South End. As always, we had a good deal of catching up to do. Alma asked me about various Arkham colleagues and friends, and I was eager to hear about her burgeoning career as a journalist.

At length, a silence fell between us. Alma broke it by saying, "Something interesting, Charles – recently I happened to meet a journalist I'd known in England. She's writing a series of stories called 'Mysteries of the Great War.' One of them is about the disappearance of General Clapham-Lee – remember him, that associate of Herbert West's I mentioned in one of my letters?

"I remember." I felt a trickle of unease.

"Well, this journalist, Kate Winter, says that she has spoken to the man's son, Edward Clapham-Lee. He's a doctor in London. He said something about following up a lead in America, in Arkham, to be precise. What do you think of that? I was sure

West had something to do with Clapham-Lee senior's disappearance."

"Wait a minute, Alma. Just because Arkham was mentioned, it doesn't necessarily implicate West. There are twenty thousand people in Arkham."

"Ah, but only one of them was recently written up everywhere for performing miracles of surgery on a famous singer. This Edward Clapham-Lee specifically mentioned that." She sat back in her chair, looking pleased with herself.

"Well, what did you say?"

"What did I say to Kate? Merely that I was acquainted with Herbert West and that he'd been a Medical Officer with the Canadian Army in France. But I don't think that was news to her."

When I returned to Arkham, I lost no time in telephoning West to tell him that I had a matter of some urgency to discuss with him. He seemed irritated, but said he could see me that evening.

In his study I recounted what Alma had told me. "Now I don't know anything about Clapham-Lee except that he was an associate of yours. But I thought you should know about this."

"Well I do, as a matter of fact. Edward Clapham-Lee has already been in communication with Professor Hobson."

"Hobson!" He was one of West's undoubted enemies.

"Yes. I can imagine what Hobson told Clapham-Lee about me," West said. He did not look particularly distressed, however.

"But Herbert, is there anything for Edward Clapham-Lee to find? That you'd rather he didn't, I mean."

"There is, but in effect there isn't. Have you ever read Poe's *Purloined Letter*? It's like that. Hidden in plain view. Is that all of your urgent business?"

"No, actually." Now that I had come to the point I was more nervous than I had anticipated. "Herbert, I need to talk with you."

He gave me a look in which exasperation was mingled with amusement. "Here I am, Charles. So talk. What are you getting at, exactly?"

He was not helping me at all. I felt as though I had been digging a hole and had managed to fall into it. But I kept digging.

"I think you've been revivifying corpses and operating on them. That strange person – woman – found on the Aylesbury Road last fall, I'm sure you had something to do with that, even though you told me you didn't." Having found it exceedingly difficult to get this far, I didn't have the courage to admit I had searched his house too.

"Before I respond, let me ask you something. It seems you've been doing some investigating. What, precisely, is your purpose? Do you consider yourself a minion of justice? Or are you going to join Alma Halsey in the journalistic profession, if it can be called that? Or do you fancy that our friendship gives you the privilege to pry into my business and play the role of my conscience?"

The coldness and sarcasm of his tone dismayed, then angered me. I was glad of the anger because it gave me courage. "None of those, Herbert," I said. "I thought you would recognize friendship when you saw it. I don't propose to exercise moral judgment on you, but there are others who'll do just that, Professor Hobson for one. I'm sure they're ready to pry into your affairs, as you put it. If you're engaged in activities that break their rules, you're vulnerable to attack. Like Allan Halsey was. Remember him?"

West began to laugh. He laughed loudly and long, with what sounded like a trace of hysteria. When he stopped, he said, "Well spoken, Charles. All right, you've convinced me you have my interests at heart and I must admit that you of all people have never shown any signs of betraying me. Unfortunately, I must disappoint you. I will say only that you were right about that wretched creature on the Aylesbury Road. It was indeed my... creation. But don't exercise that vivid imagination of yours by speculating about its sufferings. There were none. I took good care to ensure that, but it was criminally careless of me to let it escape. That's all I'm going to say on the subject, and in the interests of friendship I think it's time you left."

He showed me out of his house without another word.

I did not see much of West after that. Whenever I met him on the street or on the campus, he was cordial enough but he no longer invited me to his home.

One evening early in March I stayed late at my work and it was after seven o'clock when I locked the door of the Cataloguing Department. The great hall on the main floor of the Library was warmly lit and full of students consulting the card catalogue and making notes. There were only a few weeks before papers were due and examinations impending.

Outside, I was surprised at how dark it was. At my usual quitting time, it would not even be dusk, but the additional two hours had made a greater difference than I had expected, especially since the day had been an overcast one. The lights around the campus quadrangle seemed dim, as though they fought an unequal battle with the night. A cold blue mist had gathered, obscuring the Administration Building opposite.

I felt a weight settle on my spirit, as though inhaling the dark air had poisoned me. I had intended to go to Alfred's Restaurant on Main Street, a frequent haunt of mine as an alternative to the uninspired meals produced by my landlady's cook. But the prospect of the familiar routine of ordering soup and a cutlet from the motherly Mrs. Alfred ("A very good choice, Mr. Milburn; you won't be disappointed") and chatting with other lone diners about the weather or whatever we were reading in our newspapers, seemed futile and drab. But no more so than an even more solitary meal in my apartment. It was too late to find a colleague for company and I was getting cold, standing irresolute in front of the Library, an obstacle to hurrying students. For lack of any better idea, I started toward Main Street.

Halfway down a narrow passageway between the Library and the Arts Building, I saw someone cross its far end at right angles to my own path, a hurrying figure clad in a long coat and a hat. It could have been anyone, but I thought it was West. I quickened my steps. If I could get within hailing distance, I would greet him. Maybe we could share a meal and find our friendship still intact.

The light at the near end of Howard's Alley was burned out and in my hurry I had forgotten the irregularities in the brick pavement, where water always collected in wet weather. My shoes were in need of repair and to avoid puddles, I slowed down and picked my way, trying to remember where the depressions were. Even so, I plunged one foot ankle-deep before I was clear of the treacherous section. By then, West was only a dim silhouette against the lights on distant River Street.

I broke into a run, cursing the puddles and the limp that slowed me down. I was further delayed on Main Street by a glut of cars crawling past a broken-down truck. I managed to negotiate a zig-zag course among them, but by the time I reached River Street, I had no idea where West had gone. Shops were shutting for the night and only a few people were on the sidewalks, going home from work or to some evening entertainment.

Not surprisingly, the promenade along the Miskatonic was deserted on this damp, raw evening. A row of yellow lights marched eastward and westward. As I passed each lamppost, my shadow raced along before me or lagged behind, as though growing tired of the chase. The dark river water gurgled along the wall but no one lingered in the riverside park, with its wet benches and leafless trees. With a pang of sadness, I remembered my walks here with Alma on summer evenings long ago. My leg was starting to hurt and I was hungry. Whether or not it had been West I had seen, he was gone. I had lost him.

Because of this useless detour, it was too late to go to Alfred's. They closed promptly at eight, and it was now ten minutes to. There was nothing left but to go home.

I took a final look up and down the river. Far to the east, where the promenade ended and the lights blurred together into a dim yellow glow, I saw someone moving. Someone. A man wearing a long coat and a hat, who might have been Herbert West.

I decided to follow, despite my sore leg and my hunger, and a suspicion that it was a futile effort. But now, even if I did catch up to him, he would be no longer a friend met by chance. Now he was my quarry. I would have to think of a reason for following him. Perhaps the simple truth would do? "Hello, Herbert, I saw you from Howard's Alley, and wondered if you'd want to join me for supper. I really hated the thought of dining alone, so I followed you all this way." It sounded absurd and pathetic. He would either laugh at me or be annoyed. And where was he going, anyway? Was this why he was too busy to spend time with his old friend – because he had to walk the streets of Arkham by night?

He continued along River Street, past a row of ancient houses that leaned together in the mist as though to reassure one another that they would stand for another century, having already survived more than two. I nearly lost him again in the greater dimness here, where buildings hid the river vista and more street lamps were burned out. But I could hear his footsteps, faintly – each one a small, precise tap on the pavement. Surely this had to be West! His steps always sounded like this, quick, deliberate, purposeful. I would have to keep just far enough behind him that he wouldn't notice me if he happened to turn around. I no longer intended to get his attention, but wanted to see where he was going and what he was up to.

We were now in East Arkham, the nucleus of the old town, which had degenerated into a slum. The gambrel-roofed houses, no longer occupied by solid Puritan burghers, were a teeming warren of foreigners – Poles, French-Canadians, Italians, even a few Syrians, not to mention native-born Americans who had fallen into poverty. Cheap rooming-houses tottered against one another, with vacant lots here and there, like missing teeth. The few shops were dimly lit and patronized by furtive figures who rummaged among unthinkable merchandise in the dingy aisles. From taverns occasional sounds erupted, of drunken conviviality.

West ignored all this. He kept moving at a steady pace, past crooked doorways, decrepit automobiles, slinking cats. He did not speak to anyone we passed, not the tired-looking workmen in their patched jackets and flat caps, nor the women of indeterminate age huddled in coats and headscarves, nor the rabbles of skinny kids, one of which nearly knocked me down as they raced by, sniggering.

But I would not lose my way... Ironically, this disreputable part of Arkham was not unknown to me, and my familiarity with it was a result of my friendship with West and my failed love affair with Alma.

I no longer cherished any illusions about my situation. My father's bankruptcy and suicide had been the first of my misfortunes. If not for that, I would by now be a professor of classics at some prosperous college. I would probably have a wife and two or three little children. On a night like this one, I would be warm and dry before my own hearth after a good meal, not walking the cold streets with holes in my shoes and a chill on my heart.

True, I had a profession which, while peculiar, satisfied me. Once I had a woman who (I thought) loved me, and a friend who was remarkable, a law unto himself. But I had lost them both. (I saw again that chimerical hearth and home, except this time it was Alma by my side. I saw West, rapt and exalted, waiting for life to emerge from death). They were so different from one another that I could not explain their removals from me as mere quirks of individual fancy. No, I thought, realizing that it had begun to rain, a cold rain that could turn into sleet at any moment – it was largely because of my loyalty to West that I had lost Alma. And where had that loyalty brought me? To this drab street, alone in the rain, following someone who was most likely a stranger.

I stuck my cold hands into my coat pockets and wished that I had brought gloves. Both of my feet were wet, my bad leg hurt and my hunger had evolved into a feeling of faintness. Moreover, I could no longer see West. He must have made a couple of quick turns I had missed. It was time to abandon the chase.

Was it only by coincidence that I found myself on Powder Mill Street? There was a house where lonely fellows like me were welcome, provided we had a few dollars in our pockets. I had come to know it during the war years. The furniture was elegant, in a way, and the atmosphere both welcoming and secretive. That was part of its dubious charm. The ornaments in the parlour were familiar to me by now – artificial flowers under a glass dome and a plentitude of embroidered cushions. A plaster copy of a statue from India that reminded me of Mr. Burton's book in the Library's vault. Some naughty Japanese prints. Lamps with fringed and bobbled shades, intended to cast a discreetly dim light.

Well. So much for the parlour. One of the women looked like Alma. Or at least, that was what I told myself. She was blonde, her body strong and supple, not full-breasted. With her hair cut short or hidden under a cap, she could have passed for a boy. She called herself Sadie; I never knew her real name. Our transactions were just that – transactions, but conducted with a certain grace. When I told her I was a librarian, she said she read books sometimes. I did not ask her about them; there were others with whom I could discuss books. From her I wanted something else.

I was cold, wet and hungry. The sensible thing would be to go home and warm up the greasy chop and mashed potatoes awaiting me on the covered plate on my table. I would follow them with a small glass of whiskey (the remains of a supply procured for me by West) and the illusion of company offered by the characters of the novel I was reading. Then I would go to bed.

But my rooms were a long way off and the rain had turned to sleet. I could telephone for a taxi, afterward. I had done that before. I went up the steps and rang the bell. Someone always answered the bell, and tonight was no exception. "Oh sir, my but you're wet! We haven't seen you in a while. Come on in. Sadie'll be glad to see you. Just wait in the parlour for a few minutes and I'll tell her you're here."

An hour of warmth, companionship, intimacy. Cheap at the price.

Later, after the taxi had deposited me in front of my house, I got my car and drove westward along College. Near the hospital, I parked on a side street and walked slowly along Boundary Street, past West's house. A light burned in the porch and another somewhere on the second floor. But it was a dim light and even though it shone through the parlour windows, it was not in the parlour. In the hall, perhaps. His study was dark. As I stood and watched, someone passed the parlour windows, a dim silhouette, dimmed even more by the panes of coloured glass. Only once. Then all was as before.

So he was home now, at any rate. But perhaps it was only Andre I had seen. Or someone else. A guest? There was no point in speculating. I knew nothing, not even whether there was something I should know.

I went home again, and to bed. As I waited for sleep, I wondered if West might have been seeking in East Arkham something like that which I had found in the end. Probably not; Arkham may have been haunted by evils of its past, but I did not think that its Puritan roots would have indulged aberrations such as his. I thought I knew now at least one purpose of his trips to larger cities. I envisioned him in a parlour rather like the one I knew so well – dim, velvety, suggestive. A curtain was drawn aside, and from behind it emerged a young man, dark, faun-like, his face grave and beautiful, with high cheekbones and a mouth of self-possessed irony. He held out his hands, whispering...

I could go no further with these imaginings. As I slipped toward sleep, I thought again of sweet, seductive Sadie, the alluring way in which her eyes feigned innocence while her hands and mouth betrayed experience. I saw her head on the pillow in a halo of bright hair, her lips slightly parted, her eyes like opals...

Sleep is like death, some say, except that the dead do not dream.

♦ 18 ♦

He [the artifex] must have a most subtle mind and an adequate knowledge of metals and minerals. But he must not have a coarse or rigid mind, nor should he be greedy and avaricious, nor irresolute and vacillating. Further, he must not be hasty or vain. On the contrary, he must be firm in purpose, persevering, patient, mild, long-suffering, and good-tempered
Geber: Liber perfecti magisterii

One day in late spring I looked up from my desk to see Sarah Enright in the doorway, looking a little uncomfortable.

"Principal Cataloguer and Head of the Cataloguing Department," she read the name plate on my door. "What a title! It beats most of the ones we have in the hospital."

"True power is never measured by the length of one's title. Come in, Sarah. I never thought I'd have a chance to welcome you to my domain."

"I wouldn't have come, except I'm going to be away on a week's leave soon, and there's something I have to talk to you about."

For some reason, I suspected that the thing Sarah wanted to talk to me about concerned West. Gossip is an irresistible commodity to most people and, as far as I knew, that handy listening post by the shelflist still worked. So I suggested an early lunch break.

There was a pleasant corner off the main campus quadrangle, with a couple of benches, a scrap of lawn and a large rose bush which was just starting to open its fragrant flowers.

Sarah didn't waste time with preliminaries. "I think your friend Dr. West is going crazy."

I nearly dropped my sandwich, but managed to ask, "What makes you think that?"

"Well, maybe crazy is too strong but he's sure acting strange. For one thing, he's working much too hard. He's taken on two other doctors' surgeries, Dr. Peterson's and Dr. Little's. Peterson's sick and Little's going on a trip somewhere. And he's losing his temper. Now Dr. West never loses his temper, even when he's mad at someone. But yesterday he yelled at Nurse Dempster for forgetting to put out an instrument, and today I heard him yelling at Dr. Shortt. Shortt was yelling too, but... And he just doesn't look right."

"What do you mean?"

"Well, you know how neat and tidy he always is? Not today. That suit he has on, he's been wearing it for days. Sleeping in it too, by the looks of things."

This sounded bad. "Is he at the hospital?"

"No, I think he's in his office at the Med. School. But he's due to operate again this afternoon."

"When did all this start?"

"I first noticed it last week. But I think he's been doing extra operations for a couple weeks. It's just catching up with him, I guess."

Talking to West certainly had not helped before. He had told me to mind my own business months ago. But Sarah had taken the trouble to come to me, and she was not even West's friend. I was. "Sarah, I hope you don't mind, but I have to cut our lunch short."

"Be careful, Charles. I'll bet you haven't seen him like this."

West looked up with a glare as I peered into the doorway of his office. His face was pale and unshaven, his hair wildly disordered, necktie loose and vest unbuttoned.

"What are you doing here?" he asked.

"Herbert, I shouldn't have come, perhaps, but – " My second mistake, I realized, was to have come unprepared.

"So why did you?"

"I heard you were in some sort of trouble. Maybe I can help."

"Yes, of course! How would you like to do a splenectomy in half an hour? Or maybe you could give a lecture on skin grafting techniques later this afternoon. Look, Charles, this is neither the time nor the place for a visit. If I have troubles, they're mine and I neither want nor need your help. Now please leave."

His voice grew quieter as he spoke, so that the last sentence was delivered in a near-whisper. There was something disturbing about this decrescendo. His eyes were huge in a face that had surely grown thinner since I had seen him last. Murmuring an apology, I left.

But before I gave up I went to the hospital and sought out the office of the Chief of Surgery, Dr. Harold Shortt. I had never met Dr. Shortt, but I could not think what else to do. I waited for twenty minutes in his antechamber until a starched but ornamental female (was she a nurse or a secretary?) conducted me into the presence. Dr. Shortt bore a striking resemblance to the Bolshevik leader, Vladimir Lenin, with which his Yankee accent seemed at odds.

I introduced myself and said, "Dr. Shortt, I'm a friend of Dr. Herbert West. I was in Dr. West's office just now, and I must say that he doesn't appear to be himself. I thought I should bring this to your attention, since I understand he's carrying a heavy workload these days. I'm concerned that he may not be fit to do all the surgery he has taken on."

"You're a librarian, Mr. Milburn?"

"That's right."

"What makes you think you can tell whether a physician is fit to do his job? Do they teach that in Library School?"

"No, but I've known Dr. West for many years. His appearance and behaviour today are most uncharacteristic. Believe me, I wouldn't have troubled you if I didn't think there was a good reason."

"Mr. Milburn." Shortt stroked his beard and began speaking in what I assumed to be his lecturing style. "Physicians are trained to endure long hours. It's part of our calling. True, at times we become a little testy when we're under pressure. But knowing our limits is part of the job. I'm sure Dr. West is perfectly capable of operating or he would not do it. Now you must excuse me. I have another appointment."

I could do no more. I went back to my office, deeply troubled.

Late that afternoon, finally immersed once more in my own work, I became conscious of a small commotion in the outer office. I looked up when someone threw my door open without knocking. It was West. He looked, if anything, more dishevelled than before. He leaned over my desk and without preliminaries said,

"You presumptuous bastard! What did you think you were doing when you went to Shortt? By taking it upon yourself to judge my competence you played right into his hands. You would have done better to plunge a knife into my heart. So listen well, because I'll say this once only – I'm finished with you. I don't want to see you or hear from you again."

Before I could find my voice he was gone.

As if this wasn't enough, there was a disturbing story in the *Arkham Advertiser* a day or two later: a dangerous lunatic had escaped from Sefton Asylum after nearly twelve years of confinement. He had been known as the 'Wild Man of Arkham' at the time of his incarceration early in 1912, when he had committed a heinous deed. Officials at Sefton were not prepared to speculate as to how this individual had managed to break out of the facility and elude capture, but the police warned residents of the district to be vigilant, since the escapee was considered extremely dangerous.

Nothing more happened until a night in July. I sat near an open window, listening to the small unknown sounds outside. It had rained earlier and the air had a blessed coolness. I could smell the freshness of wet grass and leaves, and the perfume of night-scented stocks. It had been dark for nearly an hour and I was thinking that it was time I went to bed, but inertia kept me where I was.

Just then I heard light steps coming up the front walk and the verandah stairs, followed by a sharp knock on my door. It was West. Without a word, I held open the door and stepped back. He came in, murmuring a greeting, and fell into an armchair. When I had switched on a lamp I was shocked at his appearance, even after the terrible scene a few weeks earlier. He was no longer unkempt, but looked exhausted, the customary elegance of his clothing a harsh contrast to the weariness in his face. He sat for a moment with closed eyes, then looked up at me and said,

"Well, Charles, it's all up. The career of Dr. Herbert West has been rather like a meteor – fiery, fast, and now finished."

"What do you mean?"

"Well, for one thing, Hobson and Edward Clapham-Lee are plotting against me. And for another, I'm being sued."

"Sued? By whom?"

"The family of a patient, of course."

"What patient?"

"A Boston banker, George Hurley."

"He's dead?"

At this he began to laugh. "No, he's not dead. That's the problem, actually. Things might be better if he was."

"I don't understand. You'd better start at the beginning."

"Yes, except I'm not sure where the beginning is, really." He thought for a moment. "I suppose it was about six weeks ago. Hobson and Vladimir began hinting that a certain member of the staff was not bearing as much of the load as the rest of the stalwarts. This individual was getting undue attention from the press and the public by performing frivolous surgical pyrotechnics while the rest of them were putting their weary shoulders to the wheel."

"Excuse me, Herbert, but who is Vladimir?"

"Shortt, of course. He looks just like Lenin, wouldn't you say? You must have noticed, when you went to warn him about the unstable Dr. West. You played right into his hands, unfortunately, but now I know I can't blame you for everything."

"You mean this is a plot of some sort?"

"I think so. You wouldn't believe it possible, would you, that a couple of elder professor-doctors would use patients as pawns in a game of this sort, but it certainly seems that way. The long and the short of it (and yes, I meant that) was that I foolishly accepted what I saw as a challenge. Peterson had just done a bunk, supposedly because of his nerves, and Little simply had to go off to visit his old mother in darkest Ohio. So I took on their work. After all, I told myself, it wouldn't be anything like my workload during the big pushes in the War. But of course I was the only one at war here. Everyone else was just following their regular routines.

"I should have known better. That day you came to see me I had just about reached the end of my rope. I eased up after that, but the damage was done. Word leaked out that West was finally slipping. Then along came George Hurley, fat and fifty, with his hernia. Not the sort of thing I usually do any more, but Hurley wanted *his* hernia fixed by the same hands that had repaired Eleonora Desanges' face. So I thought, what harm could there be in it? After all, I can do hernias in my sleep.

"The trouble was, first, that the gentlemen of the Boston press had been alerted of Hurley's insistence. One or two lively little stories appeared in the papers. The other thing was that at the last minute I found that my assistant was to be Pokey Campbell – Dr. Patrick Campbell to you, Charles. Now his job was to look after the anaesthesia, which is trickier than you might think. It requires constant monitoring of the patient's state, so that he is maintained at a steady level of unconsciousness but not pushed into a state of excessively deep unconsciousness, otherwise known as death. Well, Pokey isn't the most reliable individual in the world. He's too shaky to hold a scalpel, so has been relegated to minding the gas canister. Generally, I avoid him like the plague, but that day (just three days ago, how much longer it seems) everything went wrong. When I got to the operating theatre, there was Pokey goggling at me over his mask. I knew I was in for it then. I would have to do the surgery and monitor the anaesthesia too. Never mind that I hadn't slept in a week. Yes, I know I should have refused to go ahead, but... Vladimir and Hobson had me figured out, all right.

"Well, you can imagine what happened. The hernia was a little trickier than I had expected. Part of the problem was that Hurley is a fat man, and everything took a little longer than usual. The outcome was good, though, very good, or would have been except for one detail. I had been too busy to check Hurley's state. Pokey was off in dreamland somewhere, and by the time I'd sewn Hurley up he was just slipping over the edge. I alerted Campbell to the fact that he had let the patient die, thanked the nurses for their help and left.

"That's when I made my real mistake. Damn it, I didn't want to give in! I got my revivification stuff and when I came back Hurley was still on the table. I guess no one knew what to do with him after I left so abruptly. Well, I set up the gear and pumped old George full of fluid before anyone showed up. He'd been dead less than an hour; maybe that's why it didn't take very long for him to come back. But of course he was still under the anaesthesia. Actually, it was interesting. I'd never revivified someone who was in that state, but I suspect it contributed to the less than happy result. The nurses came in with Dr. Shortt (who else?) to get Hurley declared dead, and there I was, hovering over him and telling everyone, 'He's alive!' And he was, too, and still is, but in an apparently infantile state.

"His family is determined to sue the negligent surgeon who reduced this pillar of the community to such a pitiful condition. And Drs. Hobson and Shortt are encouraging them, I might add. Ironic, isn't it?" He closed his eyes again.

"So what might happen if they sue? I suppose you'd have to pay damages of some sort." I knew he was independently wealthy but had no idea of the amount that might be involved in a case of this sort.

West waved that aside. "That would be the least of my troubles. If it were only the family and a neat little lawsuit, I could weather it. But you can't imagine what a Godsend this is for Hobson and Shortt. They've been busy for weeks, keeping notes on my mistakes, real and imagined. They'll start up committees of inquiry and investigation and hound me out of Arkham, and out of my mind too."

"Have you considered leaving Arkham? You should be able to do well anywhere."

"You'd think so, but there's also the Clapham-Lee business. A war on two fronts, I'll have, just like the bloody Kaiser. And I think my brothers are working on a little project of their own."

"What Clapham-Lee business? You'll have to tell me more about that. I really don't understand it."

"Neither does Edward Clapham-Lee, although he thinks he does." West laughed again.

"I have to ask you, Herbert. Did you kill Clapham-Lee?"

"Not if you know where to look. But what I did or didn't isn't really the issue. The issue is one of perception. Edward Clapham-Lee, along with a cadre of lawyers, police and journalists, is likely to be hanging around my neck for the foreseeable future, sending out allegations of dark deeds committed in the shadow of the Great War. And Hobson and Shortt will be sniffing around too – well, I'd rather be stood up against a wall and shot. That at least would finish the business quickly."

"I think they do that in France. Here in America it's hanging, usually." This was my sorry attempt to deflect his increasing hysteria.

"Well, even that would be preferable. Oh, and – " He laughed yet again, a little too heartily. "This is priceless. The Wild Man of Arkham is free once more and possibly still wild. Of course, you and I know him as John Hocks."

"I read about it in the newspaper. I thought about telling you, but decided you probably knew."

"I did indeed. Mr. Hocks paid me a visit one evening. Unfortunately for him, I was not 'at home,' as they say."

"What do you mean, he paid you a visit?"

"Just what I say. He came to the door. When Andre opened it, he ran away, but I'm sure I've seen him slinking about in the shrubbery since then. No doubt he too has a score to settle with me, and is just waiting for his chance. I don't dare go about unarmed these days." He pulled a pistol from inside his jacket, a gesture I found more disturbing than reassuring.

He stood up, returning the weapon to its place of concealment. "Look, Charles, I won't keep you much longer. I'm thinking up a plan of sorts to deal with all this, and I'll need your help. Have you taken your summer holiday yet?"

I couldn't have been more surprised if he'd asked me to dance. "No, I'm scheduled to take it in a couple of weeks. Why?"

"Could you advance it by a week or so – say to next week? This plan of mine – it should take you four or five days at most. Well, maybe a week. That's if I decide to go through with it. It's... drastic. But it cannot possibly succeed without you. Will you help me?"

When had I ever refused him my help? I didn't like the signs of paranoia I saw in him, or the tinge of hysteria in his manner, but I thought the fact that he had a plan in mind was a good sign. "Of course I'll help. And I should have no difficulty changing my vacation to next week."

"Good. Now Charles, I may ask you to drop everything and come in the next several days. If I go through with this thing it'll take all our time and attention. And nerve too."

"Like our old experiments," I said.

"Just like that."

He did not seem ready to leave. Twice he started for the door and both times came back. There was a moment of awkward silence, then he said, "At a time like this, I wish I... It would be good to have someone who..." He came closer to me.

"Charles," he said, "it's not... lack of desire, but desires that are abnormal."

I had no idea what he was talking about but that word, 'abnormal,' reminded me of his obsession with what he thought of as his flawed heredity. These troubles must have reawakened it.

He stood silent before me. The dim light from the lamp in the corner cast shadows beneath his cheekbones and in the caves of his eyes. He had disarranged his hair by running his hand through it and it fell over his forehead. In that moment I felt pity for him, something I once would not have thought possible.

He was now so near to me that I caught a faint scent of narcissus, probably from the stuff he used on his hair. His eyes were rapt, enormous, his lips slightly parted. Slowly, he raised his hand. His fingers brushed my cheek, the line of my jaw, flitted lightly over my lips. He made as if to snatch his hand back, but I caught it in both of mine. In my ears I heard a high, sweet, constant note, as though a harp-string had been plucked and reverberated in the silent room.

I held his hand, thinking, Of course he's troubled, and for the first time in his life he needs simple comfort from another human being, but he doesn't know how to ask for it, with all his nonsense about abnormality. Gently, I drew him toward me and embraced him. His slight body was full of tension. "Herbert, it'll be all right," I said. "You'll find a way out of it. And I'll help you, you can be sure of that."

He relaxed a little and laid his head on my shoulder like a tired child. The moment lengthened as if to eternity, then passed. He drew away from me with a sigh.

I wanted to reassure him further, but didn't know how. "Herbert, if you're thinking... I know about you... And it's all right – "

"It's all right with you, is it? Are you sure?" he asked, mockingly. He kissed me on the lips, hard. It felt like an attack, and I stepped back involuntarily, wiping the back of my hand over my mouth.

West laughed. "Is it still all right? I admit, there have been times when I've wondered about you. Do you ever wonder? I can tell you now, you probably don't know what you have inside of you. Maybe you never will." He moved toward the door, then turned back. "Charles, you've been a good friend to me. Better than I deserve." And then he was gone, into the darkness. I stood for long moments with my hand pressed to my lips, until the perfume of night-scented stocks had obliterated the scent of narcissus and the turmoil inside me had subsided.

The next day I went to Dr. Armitage and told him that urgent business required me to take my vacation the following week instead of the one after. He readily agreed. "And what are you going to be doing with your two weeks?" he asked.

"Well, I have business here in town first. Then Cape Cod for a week or so."

"Ah, you young fellows have all the fun! Footloose on the Cape, and I'll bet you won't be lonely, either."

I nearly started to laugh. Under the circumstances, I thought, that was quite ironic. "I don't intend to be alone, Dr. Armitage," I replied.

"Good luck to you." He waved me out of his office.

I had decided that I needed an objective opinion on the matters that West had told me about. Sarah Enright was pretty well my only source of information in the Arkham medical community, apart from West himself. While I valued her insights, I needed to talk to one of the doctors, who would be better able to judge how plausible were West's ideas about a conspiracy. After some thought, I remembered John Billington. He had taken over West's practice in 1914. Since then, he had moved it to Bolton, as that was where most of his patients lived. But I was fairly certain he retained ties with the Arkham medical community and with Miskatonic. I telephoned him and made an appointment.

Billington's office was about half way up the hill from the river, with a view over its sinuous curves. Behind the building, the walls of the Cathedral soared skyward.

Billington greeted me cheerfully. He was a stocky, brown-haired fellow. With his shirt sleeves rolled up, his vest half-unbuttoned and jacket discarded on a nearby chair, he was a complete contrast to West. I had to admit that were I in need of medical help just now I would feel better in Billington's hands.

"And what can I do for you today, Charles Milburn? I don't believe I've seen you as a patient before."

"I haven't come to see you in a professional capacity today, Dr. Billington," I said. "Not for my own sake, anyway. I would like your opinion on a matter concerning our mutual friend, Dr. Herbert West."

"West! What's he gotten himself into now?" He smiled, but a small frown creased his forehead as he spoke.

"Well, I'm not certain. Suppose I describe the situation as Dr. West has explained it to me." I laid out the main points of the Hurley business, delicately hinting at West's suggestion that Drs. Hobson and Shortt had inveigled him into making unwise choices. Of course I omitted any mention of the revivification, merely suggesting that West had managed somehow to resuscitate the patient, but with unfortunate results. I said nothing about the Clapham-Lee matter, either. West had refused to give me any particulars, and it was unlikely that Billington would know anything about it anyway.

When I had finished, Billington sat for a while without speaking. He lit an evil-smelling pipe and puffed on it. Then he got up and looked out of the window. Finally, he said, "West is a peculiar fellow. I can't say I know him well, even though we had some classes together. And there were all those discussions at his dinner parties, of course. But he wasn't exactly forthcoming about himself.

"At first I had an idea he was a pure materialistic optimist. But about the time he went off to the War I had begun to think otherwise, that it was just a veneer over something else. I guess I started to wonder when he pulled that graduation stunt. Remember that?" He laughed a little.

"Well, anyway, eventually I began to think he was a lot more finely balanced than he seemed. As long as things were going in a way that he could cope with, increased intensity didn't seem to matter – he'd just spin faster, you might say, and leave the rest of us in the dust. But if something came along that he couldn't fit into that peculiar world-view of his, it would throw him off completely for a while. Then – well, it was such a contrast – near-hysteria, wild accusations, a kind of self-destructive mania. Luckily, these episodes never lasted very long. He'd think up some sort of plan and be in control again."

"But would it be a good plan? I mean, a reasonable one?"

"Well, they usually worked out. There might have been better ways to deal with the situations, whatever they were. But West always came out on top in the end."

"Dr. Billington, would you say that Dr. West is... well, crazy?"

"No, only that he doesn't always cope well with uncertainty. I always wondered how he managed over in France during the War."

"Do you think he has any reason to suspect a conspiracy against him?"

"Not a conspiracy, no. But I know for a fact that he has enemies. Serious ones, going right back to his Med. School days. That Halsey business, for one thing. Sure, a lot of those old guys are out of the picture now, but a few are still there, and they have some big grudges against West. You see, he has an unfortunate tendency to go a little too far. It's totally uncalled-for too, like throwing rocks at a wasp nest. I heard him thank old Shortt once for the amount of business he generated for West's father – the undertaker, you know. Shortt was going through a phase where he lost a lot of patients. West said it so politely, too, and in such a complimentary tone, that Shortt just about fell for it. When the real meaning seeped through, he almost burst. By then West was down the hall, laughing his head off.

"That kind of thing doesn't win many friends. Or the deep-freeze treatment he gives people sometimes. But then West, you see, takes on this air of martyrdom, claims people hate him, et cetera. And he's never managed to grow out of this habit.

"All those innovations of his, too – he'd rush ahead and use them on patients, then complain of persecution when something went wrong and he was reprimanded. In fact, that's one place where I was pretty sure he'd come to grief in the end. He's good, really good, but a doctor can't use patients as experimental subjects willy-nilly. Something is sure to go wrong, and now probably something has. But he does have enemies, yes. Does this help, or have I just confused you with my ramblings?"

I assured him that he had been most helpful. As I was leaving, something else occurred to me. "Dr. Billington, have you heard... can you tell me anything about that fellow that escaped from Sefton, the Wild Man?"

Billington eyed me curiously for a moment, as if wondering what my question had to do with West. "I'm not up on his case, naturally," he said, "but I gather his physical state is not good. He's subject to convulsions, apparently, but given his history cannot be regarded as anything but dangerous. Surely you haven't seen him?"

"No, I haven't," I said, "and I hope I won't. Goodbye, Dr. Billington."

"West is lucky to have a friend on his side. I hope he realizes that. Good luck." But I noticed that he didn't offer his own help.

That Saturday, after I had finished work, I left my office with the good wishes of my staff ringing in my ears. I had two weeks of leisure time ahead of me, except for the days I had committed to West's plan, whatever it might be. By Tuesday, having heard nothing from him, I was beginning to hope that his troubles had resolved themselves. After a late lunch, I fired up Alma's old Ford, which I had bought from her after her return from Europe, and headed toward Kingsport. I needed to get away from Arkham and its troubles. I turned off on the same dirt road that Alma had taken on that long-ago day before the Great War, when she, West and I had spent a lazy afternoon on the high cliffs.

The place was just the same. Here I still am, it seemed to say. You come and go, but I remain. The wind blew over the cliff top, stirring the grass tussocks that clung to the thin soil on the rock. On the far horizon was a bank of high-piled cumulus clouds, their battlements and crenellations like the gates of heaven. I had intended to walk north, into a valley and up the slope beyond to the higher cliff top on the other side. But when I descended, I found a steep, brush-grown gully that discouraged further exploration. Out of the wind it was hot and airless. A dense green smell of growing things filled the place. No birds sang, but a humming of insects told of multitudinous beings pursuing their lives in this remote place. Underfoot, leaves of past summers had accumulated in a thick brown mat of humus through which the green grass had pushed. I stood for long minutes, relishing the atmosphere, so alien to me after my desk-bound existence. Eventually, the heat and insects became oppressive and my imagination began to turn every moving shadow into the shambling figure of John Hocks. I turned and toiled back up the way I had come.

Lying down on the cliff's edge, I looked over the rim. Immediately below me, rocky shelves and ridges thrust out, obscuring the narrow strip of gravelly beach and making me forget that there was a drop of several hundred feet beneath my elbows. It was rather exhilarating to lie there, as though suspended in the blue air of high summer, with the constant wind raking through my hair. For some time, I lay and watched the clouds. They slowly reshaped themselves, new forms ever arising, a constant succession of shapes superimposing themselves one on the other in an almost orderly way that reminded me of polyphonic choral music, where the overlapping voices make shapes of sound. I heard again the *Miserere* of Gregorio Allegri, as it had been sung at the Cathedral recently. The achingly beautiful, ethereal melody floated to my mind's ear like the finest wisps of cirrus cloud high above.

> *Tibi soli peccavi, et malum coram te feci;*
> *Ut iustificeris in sermonibus tuis,*
> *Et vincas cum iudicaris.*
> *Ecce enim in iniquitatibus conceptus sum*
> *Et in peccatis concepit me mater mea.*

> Against you alone have I sinned and done evil
> In your sight: it is right that you pass sentence
> And just that you give judgment.

For behold, I was born to transgression,
And my mother conceived me in sin.

Ecce enim veritatem dilexisti;
Incerta et occulta sapientiae tuae
Manifestasti mihi.
Asperges me hyssopo, et mundabor:
Lavabis me, et super nivem dealbabor.

Yet since you delight in truth,
You have shown me the
Secrets of your wisdom.
Sprinkle me with hyssop, and I will be clean.
Wash me, and I will be whiter than snow.

For some reason these words from the Fifty-First Psalm reminded me of West. I should have asked him to come along today, I thought. It would have done him good. Perhaps next week, after the business, whatever it is, is finished. I fell to thinking then, about West and his troubles, real or imagined. After my talk with John Billington I had sought out Sarah Enright and asked her if she had heard anything about the Hurley incident.

"Yes I did. The nurses that assisted at that operation are friends of mine. They said it was very strange. Just as Dr. West was finishing, he checked Hurley's vital signs and pronounced him dead. 'Thanks to you,' he said to Dr. Campbell, and left the room. The nurses didn't know what to do and Campbell had made himself scarce. They talked about it for a while and decided to go to Dr. Shortt. Shortt wanted to see Hurley for himself, so they all went back to the operating room. And there was Dr. West, only this time he said Hurley was alive. And he was, too. Shortt checked for himself. The trouble was, when he came out of the anaesthesia, he was like a child."

"Sarah, were your friends convinced that Hurley was dead?"

"Well, I imagine they took Dr. West's word for it. Neither of them would have gotten a stethoscope and listened to his heart, I don't think, but they would have felt for a pulse in his wrist. If they said there wasn't one, I believe it. And he wasn't breathing, either."

"And how is he now?"

"Stronger, but still can't talk or do anything for himself. Maybe he'll come out of it, maybe not."

It occurred to me that Hurley's diminished capacities could have been caused solely by the oxygen deprivation resulting from over-anaesthesia. That is, even if he had not died and been revivified, he might have ended up in the same state. In which case the fault was entirely Dr. Campbell's. From what West had told me, it was nearly impossible to predict someone's post-revivification mental capabilities. But of course he could not very well present this argument to colleagues and a public who were ignorant of, and not receptive to, the entire concept of revivification.

Under the sun and wind my anxieties diminished somewhat. Perhaps Hurley would recover. And West, with his resourcefulness, would surely come up with some way of confounding his enemies, even as I had tried to reassure him the other night.

The other night... Only then did I permit myself to think about what had passed between him and myself at the end of his visit to me. A need for simple human comfort, I had explained it to myself then. But I could no longer deny the internal cataclysm I had experienced when I had held him in my arms. Even his harsh and mocking kiss had excited me as much as it had repelled.

While I had thought of West as a fortunate being in the centre of things, I had admired him like a distant, brilliant star. But when I learned something of his history I found that we had things in common. Could it be that the most important difference between us was that as a child I had known that my father was a good man, and that my mother loved me?

Thinking of these things, I drifted into sleep, and had a dream.

West and I were walking up a steep, grass-grown slope toward a belt of storm-twisted oaks. Above us, the sky was luminous with dawn. Beyond the oaks, the ground fell away sharply into a gully. I hesitated at climbing down, but West did not.

"Come along, Charles," he said, with a characteristic trace of impatience. "Look, it's quite easy. Here, take my hand and I'll make sure you don't slip." Despite the impatience, he smiled up at me. The slanting light touched his hair with fire, but left his face in shadow. Somehow, we found ourselves on the far side of the gully. Before us now was a house built on the very rim of the cliff. West went to the door without hesitation. "Here it is at last," he said. "This is the place where I will be married." He opened it and went in. I followed, full of fear and sorrow which clutched at my heart. By the time my eyes had adjusted to the green dimness inside, West had opened another door in the far wall of the house, one that swung out into sun-shot space.

"Herbert, wait!" I cried in a panic. I ran forward, but my progress was slow, as though I ran through thigh-deep water. Just as I reached him, he said, "You've been a good friend to me, Charles. I'll see you on the other side." He stepped over the threshold into a blaze of light. I tried to follow but could see only swirling mists before me. Far below, a white wave crest spent itself on rocks and sand. Terrified, I jerked myself backwards, and woke up.

A paralyzing sense of loss and loneliness filled me. The bright day had faded and an enormous copper-coloured moon was rising out of the pale mists that hid the place where the sky and sea joined. I got up, feeling cold and stiff. It took a long time for the mood of the dream to disperse. Even when I arrived at home I was haunted by it still.

That night I did something unusual for me. I went to Water Street, to a tavern I knew, and drank until I no longer cared much about anything. It was like a crude version of one of West's brain-clearings, and without his diverting company. But it worked.

♦ 19 ♦

One is the stone, one the medicine, one the vessel, one the method and one the disposition.
Reitzenstein: "Alchemistische Lehrschriften"

When I awoke the next morning, I knew what I had to do. Despite an aching head and queasy stomach, I went to the Library, letting myself into the silent building with the key that was one of the few privileges of my rank. I went to the wing where the Quarrington Collection was housed. Off the main room was a small office for the use of researchers or librarians working with the material. Here, in a locked cabinet, was the thick file called Profiles and Predictions and the key to the codes by which the documents within it were identified, which I had bought from Humphrey Villard.

After discussing the matter with Dr. Armitage, I had restricted access to these documents, because of the nature of the information they contained about persons still living. Like the *Necronomicon*, they could be consulted only after approval by a librarian, but the criteria were different: for the present, only a person represented in the file or a member of his immediate family could see the material, and then only the file that pertained to that individual.

The names in the index were listed in alphabetical order. I turned to the last page and found West, Herbert F. It took me a few minutes to determine how the documents were arranged by their code numbers, but finally I found the one designated DX.37-31-59.

It was a fairly thick document, and I hesitated before looking at it. Why was I doing this? Because I wanted to know whether everything that had happened to me since I came to Arkham was governed by chance or something else. Because I wanted to find out the nature of the 'resonant link' that Quarrington had supposedly created between West and myself. Because I wanted to know what fate Quarrington had predicted for Herbert West.

The first page contained biographical and statistical information on subject DX.37-31-59. Date and place of birth and physical characteristics: Boston, November 7, 1886. Height: 5'6". Weight: 137 lb. Hair colour: Blond. Eye colour: Grey. Yes, this was West, all right.

Much of the data, although interesting in a way, meant nothing to me. I learned that the subject had showed marked reactions to blue and green light, to the F# dominant chord, to pin-pricks on certain spots on the palms of his hands. If I had been a tailor I could have made a suit of clothes for him using the detailed measurements Quarrington had taken. But a lot of it struck me as meaningless mumbo-jumbo. Impatiently, I turned the pages. Here was a transcript of an interview. The writing was rapid but legible. The questions were marked, logically enough, Q., the replies by the subject, S. It was dated October 15, 1906. West would have been not quite twenty years old.

Q.: How would you characterize your relationship with your father?

S.: Until I was 15 I wanted to kill him. I made plans several times. Then it occurred to me that it would be a better revenge to follow my own road at his expense.

Q.: Why did you want to kill him?

S.: Because he mistreated my mother. For years after she left I thought he had murdered her.

Q.: Was this a reasonable belief?

S.: I think it was, yes. He is his own master. No one else sets his course for him. If he wanted her dead, he would kill her.

Q.: How did you feel about this moral code of your father's?

S.: I hated it, but understood it too.

Q.: Explain, please.

S.: Laws are created by men. Those who are able to, by cleverness or strength, may set them aside.

Q.: What about your mother? What are your feelings for her?

S.: I don't have any now. After I finished mourning her disappearance, I put her image away and tried to forget her. I nearly convinced myself that I was motherless, that I had created myself from things I found in my father's house.

Q.: And your brothers?

S.: They are much older than I, and care for different things entirely. I deal with them only when I must. We have a working arrangement. But I think the younger of them hates me.

Q.: Why is that?

S.: He seems to blame me for our mother's disappearance. I don't know why that is.

Q.: Have you had any relations with women?

S.: Not really. I kissed a girl once, but thought better of it.

Q.: How do you deal with your sexual feelings?

S.: I try not to have any.

Q.: Why?

S.: Because I find them disturbing.

Q.: Have you had any sexual experiences at all?

S.: Yes.

Q.: Explain, please.

S.: I'd rather not.

Q.: Why not?

S.: I find this subject disturbing.

Q.: It is necessary. Tell me, when did the first of these experiences occur? How old were you?

S.: I was nine years old. And it was not by choice.

Q.: *Nine?* Who was the other person?

S.: Persons. There were two. One of them was my brother, the younger one. He was 14.

Q.: I see. And was this experience repeated?

S.: No. The next time I had a knife.

Q.: Did you tell your father?

S.: No. I knew he preferred not to know about my little troubles.

Q.: What are your feelings toward your brother now?

S.: Indifference. I cannot afford to hate him.

Q: And afterward? Were there any other experiences?

S.: Yes. Not many. I try to avoid such entanglements.

Q.: Why?

S.: I feel as though I am drowning. Or complete revulsion. There is no middle ground. I can't explain. Please don't ask me any more about this.

Q.: What is your greatest fear?

S.: Being locked up. Losing the power to act.

Q.: What is your greatest desire?

S.: To be a spy in the house of death.

Q.: Explain, please.

S.: I want to know exactly what happens when someone dies. So that someday, perhaps, I can reverse it.

There was more, much more. West's interests and ideas on various topics, the places he had visited, his means of travel to these places, the significance of different numbers in his life. Eventually I stopped reading. I felt for him a great compassion. Behind the clinical questions and answers of the text, I could visualize the two of them, Quarrington, his blue eyes gleaming from under bushy eyebrows, scribbling down the answers given by the pale young man before him. I guessed how much it cost West to give some of these answers, how hard he drove himself to do it. 'For once I neither embellished nor omitted,' he had said to me, surely in reference to this very interview.

I turned to the last part of the document then, to Quarrington's assessment and predictions. I reminded myself that West did not know what was written here. Quarrington described him as

...an unstable element with great potential for good or evil. To avoid the pain of his invisible wounds, he has created for himself a cold veneer that separates him from others. To discover his excellence it may be necessary to do him harm, perhaps destroy him.

The things revealed by his body are at variance with those shown by his mind. This is very bad. He will work at cross-purposes with himself and do great harm unless he is transformed and unified. He will die two deaths. I do not know yet whether actual or symbolic. Before this he will fumble in ignorance with the ultimate things.

The salvation of this man is in the hands of one who loves him despite the above. Without this he may go down into his darkness and become a creature of pure evil. But if he passes through the ordeals that await him with the help of his friend he will be transformed into that rare being – one with power in his hands who subjects himself to the greater Power. A resonant link is absolutely necessary to ensure his salvation.

I had read enough. My headache was worse, and I was beginning to feel resentful – toward Quarrington for speaking in hints and metaphors, toward West for dragging me into his troubles and complexities. All I wanted to do was go home, drink a quart of water, and sleep for the rest of the day.

At home, I opened the windows, closed the curtains and threw off my clothes. I filled a large glass with water, drank it, refilled and drank again. Just as I was about to fall into bed, there was a knock at my door. Cursing, I wrapped myself in a bathrobe and went to see who it was.

Andre Boudreau stood on my doorstep with his usual calm demeanour. He appeared to be dressed for a journey and carried a duffel bag.

"Hello Andre," I said. "What brings you here?"

"Good morning, Mr. Milburn. Dr. West would like you to join him for supper this evening. Eight o'clock. And the business afterwards, he says."

'The business.' This was the summons, then. He expected me to drop everything and come prepared for something requiring time, attention and nerve. Just now, I did not feel equal to such an enterprise and almost asked Andre to tell Dr. West to choose another day. But then I remembered his distress and my promise to help him.

"Thank you, Andre. I'll be there. But it looks like you're going away."

"Yes, I go to Boston. An overnight trip. I return tomorrow afternoon. The Doctor, he asked me to take some papers there." He indicated the bag he carried. "He has some troubles now, yes? And you will help him? You are his friend, I know."

"Yes, he has troubles," I said. "And I'll help him, if I can." This was one of the longer conversations I had had with Andre. My exchanges with him before this had consisted of greetings and expressions of appreciation for the services he rendered to me as his master's guest. I studied him, wondering again about the strangeness I had always seen in him, but never understood. I decided now that part of it was his singularity of purpose. He never seemed to be in a hurry, nor to have any personal concerns. And yet, he never seemed dissatisfied either. "Are you happy working for Dr. West, Andre?" I asked.

"Yes. I work for him always. He gave me back my life."

"Gave you back – ? Oh, I see. You were wounded in the War and he healed you."

"Not just wounded. I was dead. He gave me back my life. Now I serve him always." He smiled then, a smile that showed very white teeth and made his face come alive in a way I had not seen before.

"I see. Well, good luck on your journey, Andre. And thank you."

When he had gone I sank down on my bed. How had I not guessed the truth before? Andre was one of West's successful revivification subjects! The man I had just spoken with had been dead and had been restored to life by Herbert West. The fact that I had not realized this in five years was eloquent testimony to the effectiveness of the procedure in this case.

I slept for several hours. When I awoke it was early evening and time to prepare for the business at hand. Something about the formality with which Andre had spoken the invitation made me take more than usual care with my preparations. I washed thoroughly and put on clean linen and one of my better suits.

It was a soft golden evening. A haziness around the descending sun spoke of possible rain later on. West himself admitted me into the house on Boundary Street, since Andre was still away. He looked like a bridegroom, in a beautiful summer suit of some light-coloured fabric, with a vest and necktie in pale contrasting colours. His face was thinner, but his remarkable grey eyes were full of light.

"Welcome, Charles," he said, formally shaking my hand. "Come into the parlour. It's good of you to be so prompt, particularly since you are in a fragile state, I see."

I mumbled something about overdoing it the night before, but I was encouraged by the ebullience of his greeting. Surely it meant that he had found a way out of his troubles. Perhaps Hurley was better or West had come up with a really devious plan.

The room looked emptier than I remembered it. The paintings by Dixon Taylor, the ebony clock and the silver candlesticks were no longer in their accustomed places. Some articles of furniture were also absent. The phrase 'cleared for action' came to mind. So he is leaving Arkham, I thought. That's why he's happy.

"Dinner first, then business," said West, conducting me to the dining room. "Mrs. Fisk has quite outdone herself on our behalf. Unfortunately, she has had to go home early, so we must be content to dine *a deux*."

The meal was indeed dainty and varied. My host served me himself, making sure that I tried a little of everything, and that my wine glass was replenished when necessary. The grace with which he did these tasks spoke of the pleasure he found in them. He himself ate little, but with evident enjoyment. Our conversation was leisurely, of matters without urgency. I was reminded of the first supper we had shared, long ago.

On West's hand was the emerald ring his mother had given him. This was the first time I had seen it since her death, and it made me a little uneasy.

"I learned something from Andre this morning, when he came by with your invitation. He was one of your revivification subjects, out there in France, wasn't he? One of the successful ones."

"Yes, and it has certainly taken you long enough to figure it out," he said, laughing a little. "I thought you realized it from the first, so didn't bother explaining. What was it that finally tipped you off?"

I admitted that Andre himself had told me. "But how did it happen? Can you tell me more about that?"

"Of course. What harm can there be in it now? It was in August of 1917. There were some terrible battles that month – Lens and Hill 70. And that was before the real carnage of Passchendaele. When I first saw Andre he was still alive. He was waiting with some others for one of us to attend to him, but he died before anyone managed to do so. There was something about him... a great desire to live, unlike the resignation that so often appeared in men as near to death as he was. I hoped to return him to the life he had been so reluctant to leave, so I took the risk and revivified him. The trickiest part was dealing with his injuries before the new life ran out of him. I had more tools at my disposal by then, so I managed it. Then it came down to the old question of mental capacity. It was soon evident that he was a complete amnesiac. Not a scrap of memory remained to him of anything before his death.

"His Army records said his name was Andre Boudreau, from somewhere in New Brunswick. An *acadien*, he is. So I began by speaking to him in French. Eventually he regained the power of speech, and I found he retained the ability to learn. I pulled some strings then, and had him returned to a semblance of active service as my batman. The fellow I had before was keen to see action, so everyone was happy. I thought that the simple tasks I would require of Andre would be an excellent test of his abilities. And as you have seen, he has performed brilliantly these past five years. Between them, he and Mrs. Fisk have quite spoiled me." He looked a little sad, as though a cloud passed before his sun.

"Do you pay him?" I asked.

"Of course I pay him! Do you imagine that I would take advantage of the fellow because of his situation? My transgressions are of a different sort. When the war ended, I made it clear to him that he was free to go home if he wished, but the concept had no meaning for him. So he chose to stay with me. He must have quite a good bank account by now. He should do well enough, even if I – More dessert, Charles? No? Well, in that case we may as well go to the study and get on with the business."

In the study I had another surprise. The place had been tidied up. Gone were the heaps of papers, and the books were for once arranged neatly on the shelves. Looking more closely, I noticed that an attempt had been made to group them by subject matter.

West smiled. "It's not up to your standards, I'm sure, but you have to give me credit for trying."

"Very commendable," I said. "But surely you won't be able to find anything now?"

"Oh, believe me, that won't be a problem. And now – "

"Herbert," I interrupted, "are you leaving Arkham? Is that why – ?"

"I suppose you could say that. Or perhaps Arkham is leaving me. I will explain everything in good time. But first let me fill up your glass."

I was already feeling the effects of the wine I had drunk during the meal, but made no objection. West's hand as he poured was quite steady and I noticed that he drank nothing himself.

"So this is the same plan you mentioned the other night? Hurley is no better, then?"

He shrugged. "It's hard to say. He's no worse, at any rate, and may improve in time. But that's not really the issue any more. The plan is this: I'm going to disappear. With your help, Dr. Herbert West of Arkham will cease to exist. And under cover of his funeral I shall, with luck, leave to make myself anew elsewhere. I'll be a clean slate. A *tabula rasa*."

"*Funeral?* Oh, you mean you're going to fake your own death. But surely that's too – " I was feeling somewhat muzzy-headed, and thought I might have misunderstood him.

"No. I'll fake nothing. To put it simply, Charles, I am going to die. Tomorrow at dawn, or to be more precise, at seven a.m.

You will deal with the authorities. Once they're satisfied with the situation and I'm officially pronounced dead, you will revivify me. And you'll arrange my funeral, whether I need it or not."

I could only stare at him in horror. I looked at his face for an indication that he was making some sort of elaborate joke at my expense. There was none. Under the blitheness of his manner he was quite serious. "Herbert, that is utter madness. You can't possibly mean to do it."

"Yes, it's mad, and yes, I intend to do it. The very madness of the thing is what will make it work. You see, once the machinery of death takes over – the death certificate, the obituaries, the funeral, all that – everyone will think they know exactly where I am, so no one will look for me anywhere else. Except you, but you'll have your hands full for a few days." He grinned like a child who has just pulled off a trick on an incredulous adult.

I had so many objections I didn't know which one to voice first. "But Herbert, you could end up like... like George Hurley. Or worse." Visions assailed me of his mercurial personality lost behind dull, clouded eyes and slack-jawed idiocy. "Remember, I was there when we did all those revivifications. All those poor wretches, struggling up from death only to lapse back into it, or looking at us with glassy eyes, or raving insanely. And what about Hocks and O'Brien? Do you really want to end up like that? What in your life could possibly be worse?"

"There's always a risk. But most of those cases you remember were morgue denizens. If the procedure is carried out well within six hours after death the chances of success are much better. I am confident of that. Look at Andre. Oh yes, I don't deny it, the whole thing is an enormous risk. But consider – if it succeeds I'll be free of all that nonsense." He waved a hand in the general direction of the campus. "I can begin anew, make myself all over again."

"But surely you can do that without killing yourself first, by God! Why not just resign, sell up, say goodbye to Arkham and begin anew somewhere else? It doesn't even have to be in this country – London, Toronto, Paris, anywhere."

"It would follow me. Make no mistake, Charles. Once this kind of mud sticks to you it's impossible to wash it off. No matter where I go as Herbert West, someone will always turn up with a shovel and do some digging. My life will never be my own, and I can't tolerate that."

"So change your name. You'd have to, anyway, if this crazy scheme of yours succeeded. So just do that, and skip the dying."

"Too simple. As long as I'm known to be at large there's always the chance someone will find it worthwhile to come after me. You don't seem to realize how serious my situation is."

"On the contrary, I've been thinking a lot about your situation, and I can't see that anyone has anything to charge you with. There's no evidence. Whatever you've done, I'm sure you haven't left anything around that could be used against you."

He smiled, a tight, hard smile. "You give me too much credit. I've been careful, but it's impossible to hide everything. Over ten years or more, it's inevitable that people will have seen or heard things. And on a few occasions, I've slipped up. That Aylesbury Pike business, for one. It's only a matter of various individuals pooling their knowledge. Then the police will turn up on my doorstep, warrants in hand and *carte blanche* to search my house from attic to cellar. The very existence of my private laboratory and the incinerator would be enough to incriminate me, in some minds, anyway. Then there are other things... I have destroyed a good deal, these past weeks, but it's impossible to do it all."

"You give me the horrors, Herbert. Is there so much, then? More like Leavitt, I mean?"

For a second, weariness flitted over his face. "I promise you, I'll tell you everything. Tonight. But first I must ask you to give me your word that you will carry out this plan as I have described it to you."

"Describe it again. In detail. First of all, how are you going to die? Surely you don't expect me to kill you?"

"No, Charles. I'll take care of that part myself. Once I'm dead, you'll leave here, making sure that no one sees you go. When Mrs. Fisk finds my body, she'll notify you and the police. After they've done their bit and you have the certificate of death in hand, you will revivify me, and we'll see what happens next."

"So you've informed Mrs. Fisk of her role in all this," I said. "When she finds you she'll be putting on a performance, is that it?"

"Don't be an idiot. Mrs. F. is an excellent housekeeper, but I had no intention of making her an accomplice. Or Andre. That's why I sent him away. No, Mrs. Fisk will be entirely unprepared, which is why her performance will be quite natural and unforced. You're the only one who will be called upon to do any acting."

His lack of discernment amazed me. "Have you considered the effect on Mrs. Fisk, to come in to work and find her employer dead on the floor, when he was alive and well the night before?"

"No," he said, looking surprised. "What effect?"

I threw up my hands. "Herbert, you really are the limit. Look, I think it had better be me that finds you. I told Armitage and one or two others that I have some business here in town before I leave for my holiday. The business will be with you. We'll have had a pleasant evening here and will arrange to meet tomorrow morning, to discuss... investments. That's it, you'll be giving me advice on investments. When you don't answer the door, I'll call the police, because I'll have no reason to expect you not to be here – " I broke off in horror, realizing how readily I had fallen in with his crazy plan.

"Very good, Charles! You see, you're a conspirator after all. Certainly, go ahead and spare the good Mrs. Fisk's feelings, if that's what you want. She usually arrives about half past nine, by the way. But I think you're making too much of it. After all, I'm only her employer."

"For the last five years," I said. "And before the War, too. And what about Andre? He'll come home only to be told that you're dead. He's devoted to you. It was written all over him when he talked to me this morning. And he knows you're having troubles. He asked me if I was going to help you. And I will too, though I don't know why. I've never known anyone so oblivious to the feelings of those who love him."

Realizing what I had let slip, I got up from my chair and went over to the window to hide the fact that I was blushing. Outside, the evening was melting into night. The world beyond the window seemed infinitely remote, as though it was withdrawing from me. I thought: I will see and hear and think and do unimaginable things before I walk freely in those streets again.

I glanced at West. He was staring into space, looking as though someone had hit him. In a way, I supposed I had. "Love," he said, "is an irrational emotion. But surely you're misinterpreting the situation. Mrs. Fisk is a practical woman. I don't think you would find her fainting over my corpse. As for Andre, he's devoted, yes, but it's only because of his dependence on me since his return to life. It's the devotion of a good dog, nothing more."

"I could argue with you on both those points," I said. "But I won't. Because you're missing something obvious here, aren't you? Someone, rather. Me."

"*You?* But I'm telling you everything. You're a privileged creature."

"Exactly. I've been privileged to be your friend, all these years. Over that time it was inevitable that I would develop some feeling for you. Friendship, yes, but more than that. And now you ask me to help you kill yourself. Think about that before we continue."

He was silent for a moment. Then, "That's why I'm asking this of you," he said. "You are the only person in the world of whom I can ask this. Without you it would be only suicide. But you can restore my life to me – no, even better, you can give me an entirely new life."

I remembered then, reluctantly, the words I had read just that morning. Quarrington's words: *The salvation of this man is in the hands of one who loves him.* Now I knew. Now I understood. If he was a bridegroom, his chosen bride was death. And I, it appeared, had no choice at all.

"All right," I said, leaving the window and returning to my chair. "I think I understand why it has to be me. But what I don't understand is why you have to do it at all. Tell me that part again."

He poured into my glass the last of the wine, his hand trembling ever so slightly. I picked up the glass and watched the light glow ruby red inside it.

"Everything has its price," West said, "and sometimes it's necessary to pay before the bill falls due, because by then it will be too late. That time, for me, is now. Don't imagine that I haven't been tempted to wait, on the unlikely chance that things might work out by themselves, but I know that once in the clutches of the law, one's choices become very limited.

"When I was sixteen or so, in Boston, I attended several trials – associates of my father's. Their names and the crimes they were charged with aren't important. After that, I resolved never to become enmeshed in the machinery of justice. It wasn't that I objected to justice in the abstract, but to her servants. She may be blind and impartial, but they certainly are not. It wasn't even the corruption that disillusioned me, but the way in which a man charged with a crime becomes the property of the state. Even if he is found innocent in the end, the mark of the shackle remains on him forever. That's something I will risk the shadow of death to escape."

"But don't you believe that a man should be accountable for his deeds?" I fell easily into my old role of devil's advocate.

"Yes, but not to smug officials who visibly enjoy their petty power over the accused. Not to corrupt judges who hand out punishments with hands that are unclean. Think of it this way, if you like – I'll just skip a few steps and put my self – my entire self

– at the disposal of what you call God. Cut out the middleman, you could say."

"So you see it as a kind of trial by ordeal?" I was intrigued by this, not only the idea itself, but the fact that West had suggested it. "I think you're becoming a Romantic, Herbert."

"Perhaps I am. But there are other reasons. I couldn't tolerate imprisonment. The firing squad, yes, even the noose. Hanged, drawn and quartered, I don't care. But not incarceration. I'd rather take my chances with your friend Thanatos."

"I hardly think it will come to that, do you? Investigations, maybe a trial, but in the end – "

"Wait until you've heard everything I'm going to tell you, then ask yourself that question again. A few days ago, I went to see Hocks again, actually see him, there at Sefton, in his cell. They kept him in solitary confinement all these years, you know. Twelve years in a room eight feet by ten, without a window. That was my doing, I admit it now. If I hadn't meddled with him, he would have been peacefully dead all this time, dead and rotten. Instead, he was... a horror. He looks... bleached, like something that's been living in a cave. His hair is white and his skin... dead white. But his eyes were the same." He shook his head, then rested his elbows on his knees and studied the floor.

"Why did you do that? Go to see him? I thought you hated going there."

"I did, and do. It's a prison. I suppose I thought it was time I followed up on that particular experiment. Better late than never." He smiled, or rather moved his lips in a spasm that vaguely resembled a smile. "After viewing the results, I took the only logical course of action. I bribed one of the warders to let him escape."

"*What? You* are responsible for Hocks's escape? Why, Herbert? He's dangerous! You know what he did that other time – those terrible murders." I jumped to my feet. "We can't, we have to – "

"Relax, Charles," West said, with something of his old manner. "Hocks isn't the man he was then, any more than I am. He'll do no more murders, except mine, if I let him. I'm certain he's lurking nearby, probably waiting his chance in the shrubbery. Have you heard of any other sightings? I assure you, there will be none. The good people of Arkham may rest easily."

I decided not to argue the point and let West resume his explanation.

"Then there are my brothers. I suspect they're planning a surprise for me as well, a fatal surprise. Over the years, I found it necessary to work out a number of *quid pro quos* with them, but a few months ago I told them things had changed and I couldn't guarantee my end of the deal any more. This made them anxious, because all they have on me is misuse of dead bodies and 'unprofessional conduct,' while I have information about their doings that could lead to serious entanglements with the police.

"Once they find out I'm under investigation myself, they'll have even more reason to hasten my demise. Why? Because it's likely that some prosecutor will think he can capture two Wests for the price of one, by negotiating something with me. That's how Lady Justice really works. Whatever plans Hiram and Jeremy have in mind for me, revivification will not be an option afterward. Their enemies tend to make their exits in ways involving dynamite, fire or corrosive substances."

"Well, but if a prosecutor wants to negotiate with you, why not? Surely that would be better than – ?"

"And here I thought you were a man of principle! Well, I suppose I can have no pretensions to honour now, but they are my brothers, after all. Their mother was my mother. And besides, to enter into those negotiations would make me as much a property of the state as being charged and tried myself. It's not whom you dance with that counts, but the fact that you're at the ball.

"The other thing is one you know about already. Ever since my mother turned up, I've wondered about my heredity. This fear was confirmed in retrospect by things that happened in France, before I ever knew that she was a madwoman. It's completely illogical (perhaps I am becoming a Romantic, for which I must surely blame you, Charles), but I see this… experiment as a way to escape the legacy of my parents – madness and murder, or simply madness. It'll be a kind of reverse birth, and a test, like you said. If I can come through it reasonably intact, mentally and physically, I'll be a different person.

"It's the ultimate experiment, isn't it? All these years I have presumed to drag others back from death. I think it's only right that I take that journey myself now. There's only the one chance, of course, but think of the possibilities!"

His face lit up with genuine enthusiasm. Almost I found myself swept along with him. It was true that none of our subjects had known what was being done to them. West would be going willingly and with his eyes open. But no, it was still absurd.

"Aren't you afraid of death?" I realized with amazement that I had never asked him this question before.

"No. Truly, I'm not. It's dying one fears, not death. The method I'll use is completely painless. I'll pass from life to the unknowingness of death in a matter of minutes."

"But if it's forever? If the revivification doesn't work, for whatever reason?"

"Then I'll never know, will I? No, I'm not afraid."

He didn't look at me as he said this. His glance slid over me and fell to the carpet.

"But your work! It's been so important to you. Now it'll remain unfinished, unless you – "

"My work here is finished, in any case. My future as Herbert West contains only lawsuits, inquiries, investigations, lawyers, trials, sudden violent death or a long imprisonment. I've already heard that the Massachusetts Medical Association is preparing to suspend me until investigations have been completed. No, that life is finished, and I reject the other options open to me. That leaves only one road, a dark one, but it's the one I choose."

Jumping to his feet, he began to pace around the room in his old manner. "That's it, you see! This is what I *choose*. This is my *choice*. The other way I become only flotsam on someone else's river."

He stopped before me, and asked, "Well, what's your answer? Will you help me once more, for the last time?" His tone was light but I thought it was a forced lightness, and his face was set in anxious lines I had never seen before.

I was beginning to see that his state of mind was far more complex than I had imagined. This was more than simple despair at recent reversals. What I saw before me had taken his whole lifetime to develop. No longer did I believe that I could bully or argue him out of his desperate scheme. But still without understanding, I tried.

"What if I say no? What will you do then?"

"The same, probably. I have no desire to live under the terms I am being offered. So I think I would do anyway what I have resolved to do. Except that without you there will be no returning."

I did not reply immediately. Were his words mere histrionics? I did not think so. Deluded he might be, but he was sincere. If I turned my back on him now, he would surely die.

And I, who had made such an issue of my friendship for him, would be proved a liar. Whether by heredity, temperament or inclination, or perhaps only by mischance, he was alone as I could not even begin to imagine. He was Outside, nearly completely so. He had only one tenuous link to the ordinary world. That link was me. He had only me.

"Yes, Herbert," I said, "I'll help you. And maybe not for the last time."

He looked at me without speaking. Then, "Thank you, Charles. I am enormously in your debt."

He sat down again, facing me, and said, "That's why I'm telling you all this. Because I need to settle my account. I'm willing to pay the price for what I've done, but someone has to know what it is I'm paying for. You're that someone." He smiled once more, the smile that had captivated me from the first. "Are you ready to hear the confession of Herbert West?"

"Yes, I'm ready." But I was afraid.

He took a deep breath. "All right. Well, you already know about Leavitt."

"Yes, Leavitt," I said. "What were you thinking when you stuck that needle into him?"

"All I could see was the opportunity he represented. I desperately needed good experimental subjects and there were none available. Then he came along, a stranger, far from home and pretty much unlooked-for here. I asked him in and made some pretext to leave the hall for a minute while I got the drug. I didn't let myself think. I came back and hit him with it."

"Was he the only one you murdered?"

"No. Clapham-Lee..." He paused. "Charles, Brigadier-General Sir Eric Moreland Clapham-Lee, D.S.O. was a greedy opportunist."

"And that justified killing him?"

"No, of course not, but I didn't know him at all when I told him about my research."

"You told him about revivification?"

"No, only about the tissue-regenerating substance. You see, when I met him in 1914 he was one of the foremost surgeons in England, and he seemed to welcome progressive ideas. I needed a congenial colleague with whom to discuss my new work. Someone who understood the technical points. So in a moment of enthusiasm, I told him about it and invited him to collaborate with me. This was shortly before the War began. When it did, we were both keen to go because of the possibilities for furthering our research, as much as anything else. And we did. Or I did.

"Clapham-Lee played me like a fish, handing out privileges in exchange for data. That's how I got my laboratory, there at Etaples, and some equipment and other things. But in 1917 he revealed his true motives. He saw the whole thing as an opportunity for profit – clinics that would cater to wealthy people who wanted their faces altered, for whatever reason. He wanted to establish them immediately after the War ended. To him it was only a business opportunity, not scientific research at all! He thought he was flattering me by asking me to be a partner in this venture, although I suspect he was planning to get me out of the picture as soon as he could. He and my father would have gotten along beautifully.

"Finally he had everything but the details, the actual formula for the stuff. I was pretty sure he'd been trying to work it out in secret, but without success. So he gave me an ultimatum: either I reveal everything to him or he would suspend my special privileges and bring the whole weight of Army rules and regulations down on my head. This came at a bad moment for me, and so for him too. I decided to excise his arrogance. One night I agreed to meet with him in my laboratory, on the pretext of negotiating terms. I killed him there and revivified him later. Much later. He was alive, but only in the physical sense. The body functioned but the mind was gone. He was a complete amnesiac, like Andre but worse, because he had lost the ability to learn. I made a new face for him and when the incisions had healed sufficiently, I let him loose. He was quite the little mystery until they shipped him off to England."

"Wait a minute, Herbert," I said. "You took this man's life, then gave it back, but stripped him of his mind, his memories, his links to his family, friends, even himself, and let him go into the world with nothing? Surely that was excessive?"

He sighed. "Yes, it was excessive. And it's coming home to me. Hobson told me just last week that Edward Clapham-Lee expects to be here soon, bringing with him an 'associate,' a casualty of the War who is instrumental in his search for his lost father. Now I have no doubt that this individual is Sir Eric himself. Whether his son has figured that out, I don't know. Perhaps Clapham-Lee left some written documents naming me. Perhaps he has even managed to remember something and regained the power of speech, unlikely though it seems. I imagine his son hopes that the sight of me will prompt a return of memory in this 'associate' of his, who will then make significant revelations. Little does he imagine how significant. I have no idea whether this would work and don't intend to find out.

"After Leavitt, I thought I would be doing the world a favour, taking myself and my murderous tendencies to a place where killing was permitted, even encouraged. But I was wrong.

"The War... Time passed so quickly then. The great battles, Ypres, the Somme, Vimy Ridge, Passchendaele – that's when I really lived. The times in between for me were full of meaningless routine and vices without pleasure. I lived for the bloody times, when men were lined up twelve deep in the triage area, with trainloads arriving every hour. I worked like a butcher at my trade, in reverse you might say, except for the amputations, of course. When I'd done what I could for the living, there remained the dead. Some I restored to true life, as I have told you. But the others... Sometimes I created unique monstrosities for my own amusement – all short-lived, fortunately. I shot any that showed signs of persistence."

He looked at me, and the contrast between his clear grey eyes and the horror of his words made me shudder. I remembered how at the prizefight, he had been the only man unmoved by the brutal spectacle. He had recalled me to myself when I had allowed the frenzy to overwhelm me. Had it been the War that had changed him, or something in himself?

He thought for a moment, looking down at his hands. "I was almost relieved when Clapham-Lee delivered his ultimatum and gave me a reason to stop. Even so, I couldn't resist taking my revenge on him.

"That was the worst of it. What do you think of your old friend now, Charles?"

"That was the worst? But what about that strange wandering creature on the Aylesbury Road?" I had not forgotten the mutilations Sarah had described.

"That was like the corpses from the morgue you and I worked on before the War. A mindless thing. I was surprised that it managed to escape."

"How did that happen?"

"There was a major misfortune. You'll laugh – the incinerator broke down. I discovered that just as I was preparing to dispatch the creature when it had served its purpose. I didn't want to keep it on the premises, alive or dead. So I decided to take it out to Hangman's Hill, finish it off and bury it. But it got away."

"But the... the mutilations that you did on it. What were they for? Torture?"

"No. That's something I've never done. They weren't mutilations, either; it was practice for surgery. If people weren't so squeamish about these things, some human bodies could have quite useful careers after death. And the anti-vivisectionists might be appeased too, but I doubt it. No, they'd probably form a Society for the Protection of Revivified Entities or something of the sort.

"But that's nothing new, of course. The public can display an astonishing degree of irrationality, especially under the influence of the popular press. Take Robert Knox, for example."

"Who was he?"

"A physician in Edinburgh, Scotland. About a hundred years ago. You may recognize him if I said that he was the best customer of Messrs. Burke and Hare. No? They were murderers, Charles. Every medical student is told their story, why I'm not sure. A cautionary tale, perhaps. Some think it exemplifies the adventurous beginnings of the profession. To me it says only that there are always men willing to sell and others who are prepared to buy. But Dr. Knox, now, he's a little more interesting.

"He was an anatomist at a time when dissection of corpses was considered by the ignorant public to be an extreme violation. Some thought that it would interfere with the process by which body and soul would be reunited at the Last Judgment, so there were severe restrictions placed on the kinds of bodies that could be used for scientific purposes – those of criminals, mostly. I suppose it was thought that their souls were doomed anyway, so it didn't matter if they couldn't find their bodies again. Demand far exceeded supply, of course, so the vacuum was filled in ways other than legal ones.

"Burke and Hare murdered sixteen people, mostly by suffocation, and delivered the corpses to Knox, who paid well and asked no questions. Eventually they were caught and Hare was persuaded to testify against Burke in return for his freedom. Burke was convicted and hanged. Ironically, his corpse was turned over to the anatomists for dissection. A Professor Alexander Monroe was the lucky recipient. Hare went free. Knox, on the other hand, was neither charged nor tried, except by the press. They hounded him relentlessly, despite his claim that he didn't know that the corpses he bought were the products of murder.

"He was an old Army surgeon and showed considerable resilience in the face of the mob. He formed a committee to make an impartial inquiry into his conduct, and it cleared him of legal responsibility, but even that didn't turn public opinion. Knox was shunned. His colleagues didn't come to his aid because he hadn't gone out of his way to curry favour with them and was considered arrogant. Now who does that remind you of?" he asked, with a smile. "And he didn't do any murders himself, only bought the products of murder. He died a poor man and possibly a broken one, in London.

"I don't imagine that there's much difference in the public mind between Edinburgh a century ago and Arkham today, when it comes to these things. No matter that many are now enjoying health and freedom from pain as a direct result of my work with revivified corpses. That wanderer on the Aylesbury Pike, about whom you've been so concerned, contributed directly to the prolonging of the life of a worthy woman, a wife and mother who was stricken with cancer of the breast. Removal of those organs was the only possible solution, and I accomplished the procedure with minimal disfigurement by working out my techniques on that unfortunate creature." He stopped speaking, his face a little flushed.

"And you're absolutely convinced that these creatures were mindless?"

"Absolutely. It would have been impossible to use them as I did otherwise."

"Could they talk?"

"No, of course not. No more than a stone can talk."

"There was at least one who could. I know, because I heard it."

"Oh? When was that?" He looked startled.

"I came here and looked around while you were in New York, operating on Eleonora Desanges. Those keys you gave me back in 1914, remember? I didn't have one for the laboratory annexe, of course, but I heard someone in there, groaning and calling out to God. Only once, though."

He sighed. "Why didn't you tell me?"

"I was afraid to. You were angry enough at my investigations as it was."

"You're right, I was – then. I know better now."

"One final question – how many were there in all, of these creatures?"

"Eleven."

"So. You killed Leavitt on impulse and Clapham-Lee for revenge. In France you created and killed things you call monstrosities for your own pleasure. You left that wretched groaning thing alone in your cellar. And you revivified ten other corpses to make creatures you believed to be mindless so you could carve them up for practice."

"Yes, that sums it up very neatly. What price love now, Charles?" His face was still and empty. I felt sick.

"Didn't you... Don't you feel any... regret, remorse? Is that why – ?"

"You forget, Charles, that I was present when these deeds were done. I saw no pain or suffering as a result of my actions. It has never been my desire to cause suffering."

"But Clapham-Lee... He was your friend, wasn't he? Or a colleague at least. And whoever that was in your cellar – I heard despair in his voice."

He stared at me, eyes burning coldly in his white face, which suddenly looked ten years older. "Despair. I know what that is now. Isn't that enough for you, Judge Milburn? What's your verdict?"

I stood up and placed myself before him.

"You realize, Herbert West, that you're in my power now. I could choose to denounce you to the law. I could watch you kill yourself and go away, leaving you dead. Or I could go away right now, leaving you alone to deal with your troubles. You've made me your judge, jury and executioner. And I can play that last role by doing nothing at all."

"Exactly. But whatever you decide, for me there are only two possibilities. Death, or death and revivification. The second choice is yours alone."

I remembered once more the March day I had first met him – the springing vitality, the excitement he radiated, the suggestion that he moved about wrapped in his own special atmosphere. He had captured me that day, and if I had made attempts during the following twelve years to free myself from this enthrallment, my efforts had never been very serious. For me, a world without Herbert West was a diminished world. Even now.

But how could that be? He was a self-confessed murderer, a cold-hearted exploiter of helpless creatures, a liar and a deceiver. Surely the world would be better without him? For all I knew, his present desire for death was to be welcomed and encouraged by all right-thinking people. If I revivified him I would be responsible for inflicting him on the world again. Indeed, I already bore that responsibility, ever since the death of Robert Leavitt. But there were factors at work that had nothing to do with me.

Feeling restless and cramped, I went to the window. Outside, instead of the darkness of a summer night, was a strange blue twilight. The familiar trees and nearby houses were gone, as though shrouded in mist. Directly under the window stood a man, a thin grey-clad figure. His hollow eyes stared up at me out of a white face. Suddenly, I knew him. John Hocks. He was not alone. Behind him was an inchoate mass of heads, shifting and bobbing, appearing and disappearing. There were dozens of them.

"Herbert, come here! Look!"

West came over. "Yes, it's Hocks. I've seen him standing there like that the past three nights. He just stands and stares, but he's usually gone by morning. Well, his wait will soon be over."

"But... those others, who are they?" Having watched them, I realized that they shifted as a single mass, a miasma of ghosts. The mist around them made it difficult to discern details, but I thought I recognized some of them. There was Kid O'Brien, his broken nose and bloody face making him stand out from the rest for a moment. Another might have been Robert Leavitt, and still others reminded me of faces I had seen lying still in death or grimacing in renewed agonies. More than a few were monstrosities – beings with feet where hands should have been, with multiple arms or a plague of extra ears. One figure wearing a military uniform was headless, and another, similarly clad, bore a too-large head on a small, wiry body.

"What others?" West said. "There's no one else out there, only Hocks. Come on, it's getting late and we have a lot to do." He drew the curtains and steered me away from the window.

So he could not see them. Their message, it seemed, was for me alone. I thought it would be more than my life was worth to try to leave the house on Boundary Street before I had engaged with my appointed task.

"All right," I said. "You'd better tell me exactly what you want me to do."

As the night turned toward dawn, West showed me how to carry out his desperate plan. "Timing is crucial," he said. "All the official business must be finished before you can revivify me, and that has to be done as soon as practicable after my death. That's why I'll administer the drug at precisely seven in the morning. Worthies such as the medical examiner do not begin to stir until after eight, so you'll have enough time to go home, change your clothes and put on a performance of strolling out to call on your friend Dr. West, to get his opinion on investment opportunities."

These details reminded me again of the absurdity of his scheme. "Herbert, think about what could go wrong! What if the medical examiner doesn't come until it's too late?"

"Then you'll telephone Billington or one of the others I've told you about and get him to sign the death certificate. Don't forget, you'll be distressed at the death of a friend. You'll have a good excuse to be irrational and persistent. Make the most of it. Now let's go down to the lab."

As we descended the stairs to the main floor, rain-washed air wafted through an open window on the landing, cool and refreshing on my hot face. It provoked in me an intense nostalgia for ordinary things – rain and sun, sleeping and waking, work and conversation, friendship and love. I almost said to him, "Herbert, that's enough of this nonsense. Let's go back upstairs and have another drink. You can tell me what you're really going to do and then I can go home." But then I remembered John Hocks and the mob of phantoms, and reluctantly put away this naïve idea.

In the laboratory, everything was ready. The apparatus was set up and on a bench nearby stood a flask of the familiar violet-coloured liquid. West picked it up and held it to the light, making the iridescence sparkle and shift.

"Here, you might say, is the essence of Herbert West," he said, smiling. "It's possible to create a formula unique to an individual by adding substances extracted from the living organism. Obviously, this was impossible in cases where the subjects were dead before they ever came into my hands. One day it may be possible to reconstruct an individual from such a substance alone. A wonderful thought, isn't it?"

He reviewed the procedures. They were still familiar to me, despite the years that had passed. Just as I was beginning to think I knew what I was doing, a thought struck me. "Herbert! The funeral – who'll be buried, if not you? If you're alive again, I mean?"

He laughed. "I thought you'd never ask. I'll introduce him to you now."

He unlocked the door of the annexe and motioned me inside. On a table lay the body of a man, dressed formally in a navy blue suit, with a red necktie and polished shoes. He looked like West, startlingly so – blond hair, clear-cut features, high cheekbones. But these eyes were closed forever. These lips would never smile.

"Who is he?" I whispered.

"His real name doesn't matter. Call him Francis West, or Francesco – my troublesome twin brother. He'll stand in for me – or lie in, rather – if all goes well."

"But where did he come from?"

"Really, Charles, I should think by this time you could work it out for yourself. He was a member of a gang, shot in some brawl. It wasn't the bullet that killed him, but loss of blood. I saw the body at one of Hiram's establishments some time ago. He looked rather like me, and I thought it might be an interesting exercise to perfect the resemblance. It might be handy to have a double, even a dead one. He is, of course, embalmed. It will be your task to haul him upstairs so Hiram's men can pick him up. Of course, if I stay dead it will be burial for me and the incinerator for this one. Or *vice versa*, I don't really care."

"Let me understand this, Herbert. This fellow was dead. You brought him here and revivified him. Then you surgically altered his face to make him look like you."

"Exactly. Look, I had to give him new hair too. His own, alas, was brown, and I thought a wig would be a rather cheap device. It turned out rather well, didn't it?" He looked immensely pleased with himself, a craftsman admiring his own good work.

"So he was alive for some time?" There were only the faintest of scars to be seen, and only when I looked closely.

"A couple of weeks. And don't worry yourself about his sufferings. There were none. When the time came I dispatched him very kindly. Just as I will dispatch myself."

West removed his spectacles and placed them on the face of his double, making the resemblance between them nearly perfect. "You see, he'll do admirably," he said. He picked up the glasses and handed them to me. "I don't need these any more, but they must be found near my body, or it will look suspicious."

He looked at his watch. "It's time. Oh, before I forget – I want you to have this." He held out the emerald ring. Before I could say anything, he grasped my right hand and slid the thing onto my finger. "I think you'd better wear it when you do the revivification," he said. "Don't ask me why. Don't ask me anything now. It's too late."

He went to a cupboard and took out a small bottle containing a clear fluid, then to a drawer, from which he removed a hypodermic syringe. Then he left the room, moving quickly and purposefully. Panic rose in me as I followed him up the stairs. I found it difficult to breathe.

"Herbert, wait! Surely you don't have to do this. Surely there's some other way."

He half-turned toward me. "Surely I do. After all you've heard you must know that I cannot do otherwise." The bridegroom was ready; the bride awaited him impatiently.

We went into his bedroom, full of morning light, filtered through the thin white curtains. It was the beginning of a beautiful summer day and Herbert West was preparing to kill himself.

He set the bottle and syringe on the chest of drawers and removed his jacket, hanging it carefully on the back of the chair. He rolled up the left sleeve of his shirt. Then he picked up the syringe and drew it full of the drug from the bottle, carefully adjusting the amount.

"This will do the job in about a minute," he said. He put the deadly thing on the bedside table, next to the spectacles I had placed there already. He came over to me and held out his hands. "Charles, you've been a good friend to me, and for that I thank you, regardless of the outcome of this, our last adventure." He smiled at me with such kindness that something broke within me, some jagged thing that had pressed on my heart since I had heard his terrible confession.

Standing near him as I was I could see that he was afraid. His left eyelid twitched and there was a faint dew of sweat on his upper lip, on which a light stubble of moustache was visible. I pressed his hands. "Herbert, please don't do this."

"I have to." Abruptly, he pulled his hands from mine and lay down on the bed. He picked up the syringe with his right hand and turned his left arm so that the inner part, where the veins showed blue through the fair skin, was toward him. He placed the needle against the skin and pushed it into the vein. His lips moved without sound, then set in a thin line as he clenched his jaw. He pressed the plunger and shot the poison into his body.

For a little time, nothing happened. Then he said, faintly, "Charles, your hand..." I took his hand, and he gripped it hard. His eyes were fixed on mine. "Charles, if I'm... impaired when I come back, if it's too late and I'm a hopeless... kill me. Promise me that!"

"I promise," I murmured, hardly thinking of the implications.

His eyes widened, the pupils enlarging, and grew unfocussed. His hand became limp in mine. I placed my palm over his heart and felt it beating, yet ever more faintly, then not at all. He was dead.

Despair washed over me in a black wave. I felt myself falling and falling, was forced to my knees. I laid my head on his chest and wept.

♦ 20 ♦

The son is become a warrior fire and surpasses the tincture, for he himself is the treasure and he himself is attired in the philosophic matter. Come hither, ye sons of wisdom, and rejoice, for the dominion of death is over, and the son reigns; he wears the red garment, and the purple is put on.
Tractatus Aureus.

Some unknown time later I raised my head. My watch said seven-thirty, a concept which was, for a while, meaningless. I could not imagine why I had fallen asleep kneeling by my bed. Too much to drink again, Charles, I said to myself. No wonder I had nightmares. Finally, the thinking part of my brain began to function once more. It was a beautiful July morning in Arkham and Herbert West was dead.

His eyes were still open, and their empty stare horrified me so much that I pressed my fingers on the eyelids to close them. Then he seemed only asleep, the long lashes lying on his cheeks. He was so recently dead that the characteristic pallor, indicative of the pooling of the stilled blood, had not yet begun. The horror I had felt at his revelations of the night before was gone, dissolved in the fact of his death. Now I felt only pity. I pulled down his left shirt sleeve and fastened the silver cufflink. It was time to do what I had promised.

But I hesitated, standing there next to his bed. I thought with weary revulsion of the long chain of links that had to be forged for his salvation. I could not do it. I wanted only to stay with him. I wanted to be dead myself. It would be so easy. The drug bottle stood on the chest of drawers. The empty syringe lay on the counterpane where it had fallen from his fingers. I had only to refill it, lie down beside him, and do as he had done.

What stopped me, strangely enough, was the thought of my father. He had given in to his despair, without any thought for me or my mother. I did not want to die a suicide, and the son of a suicide. Surely I could prove myself stronger, for the sake of my friend? And I had given him my word. "All right, Herbert." I brushed the fair hair from his forehead and touched his cheek. Then I left the room, taking the syringe and the drug bottle with me.

I descended to the cellar once more and closed the hidden door to the laboratory. Following West's instructions, I left the house by way of the rear door, which opened from the back hallway into the shrubbery behind the house. But before I could find my way to the street, a figure glided from behind some bushes and confronted me.

I say 'confronted,' but in truth he did no more than stand in front of me. In the light of the new day, I saw him clearly. He was nearly skeletal, the bones of his face covered only by dead-white skin, except for his lips, which were the colour of liver. What was left of his hair was white too, giving him the appearance of an albino. But his eyes were not the white-lashed, rabbit-like sort commonly seen in such individuals. They were dark and muddy, peering from deep sockets like wary animals.

Perhaps I was beyond shock, or perhaps I had known all along that this encounter was necessary.

"John Hocks," I said, "what do you want here?"

"Hocks." His voice was deep but faint, as though it came from a hole in the ground. "They called me that once. But not any more. Now they call me Will." He smiled, showing blackened teeth. "It's a joke. Because I won't."

"You won't... what?"

"Do what they want. And I won't die. Until he does." He twitched his hand toward West's house. "The one who raped me."

"What do you mean, raped?"

Another twitch of those liver-lips. "Well, what would you call it? Every day, every night, I feel it inside me, can't forget, ever."

"What is it that you remember?"

"I was in the water. I sank down, down, fighting all the way and kept fighting down there in the darkness, gasping for air. Air! Air! How I wanted it! But all I got was water, cold and heavy inside me. It went on and on. In the box under the ground, I kept drowning. Then finally, peace – until *he* made me live again, forced life into me like a shaft of heated iron. It was a violation. Because I had given it up and it wasn't his to give back to me. I ran and ran, tried to spew it up so I could fall into the sweet peace again. But I couldn't do it. He put something in me that wanted... blood, it wanted life, any life. I killed, I ate, ripped, drank. But all I ever wanted was the dark, and sleep." His words came more slowly and farther apart, as though he was a clock running down.

"He thought you might have been able to return fully to life. That was his intention."

"It wasn't his to give back. He stole my death, and I'm here to get it back from him." He grinned again, showing the waste of his blackened teeth.

"You're too late, then, John Hocks. Herbert West is dead. He lies dead in this house."

For the first time, he showed surprise. "Dead? How do you know?"

"I was with him when he died. Now I'm going to find people to help me bury him. And John Hocks, I tell you that before he died, he said to me that he was wrong to bring you back to life. He was sorry."

"Aah." He drew a long breath, and I heard a kind of sticky creaking, as though the fabric of his body shifted and strained. "All right, I'll... wait. When I see them take his body away, I'll know. I might even leave you a present. But if you're lying..."

He lurched toward me, and it was as though all the ghosts of West's victims looked out from his eyes, avid for my blood. I pushed past him and plunged blindly into the shrubbery. Once on the street, I ran. After a couple of hundred yards, I slowed down and looked back. He hadn't followed me, and I almost wondered whether my encounter with him had been a hallucination born of weariness and anxiety.

At home, the first thing I did was to pour away the drug remaining in the bottle, if only to stop myself from using it. I smashed the bottle and the syringe, and wrapped the fragments and the needle in a handkerchief.

I washed myself and changed my clothes, hoping to dispel the effects of a sleepless night, too much wine and emotional strain. I was afraid to lie down, lest I fall asleep and waste precious time. At eight-thirty I set out again, taking with me the handkerchief containing the glass fragments. I strolled through the Miskatonic campus toward River Street, trying to look casual and unhurried, even though all I could think about was the ordeal before me, and the fact that every passing minute diminished my chances of success.

Once I reached the riverside promenade, I deliberately slowed my steps and paused as though to admire the view. The flowing water swirled against the wall beneath me and the fragments of glass sparkled briefly before they disappeared forever. Then I went to Alfred's Restaurant and tried to put on a convincing performance with eggs, toast and coffee. But I had to force myself to swallow, and finally abandoned half the meal uneaten.

The closer I got to West's house, the more aware I became of the pain in my heart, of fear and apprehension at what lay before me. I was afraid that in my absence Hocks would have broken in and violated West's corpse in such a way that revivification would be impossible.

As I approached the house, three black crows peered down from the roof. I had never seen crows there before. It was as though they were inspecting me. Was I ready for the task? I had served only the briefest of apprenticeships before the summons came. Fear surged up again but I told myself that I was a necessary part of the events being played out here.

I went up the walk, up the steps and across the porch. The crows flew away, croaking harshly. There was no sign of Hocks, but maybe he was still lurking in the shrubbery. I rang the bell. I rang and knocked many times, as West had told me to do. Finally, I looked in one or two windows and went around the corner of the house and looked in the garage. Then I made my way to the house next door. Its occupant, a lawyer, was an acquaintance of mine. I explained that there appeared to be some trouble at Dr. West's house and asked to use his telephone. It was already quarter after nine. West had been dead for more than two hours.

I told the police officer who answered that I had had no response at the home of Dr. West and suspected that all was not well there. I had arranged to meet him at nine o'clock, I said. A little persuasion was necessary to convince the policeman that action was needed. Might Dr. West be at the hospital? I assured the man that this was not the case, but he should certainly check if he wished. Had I looked to see whether Dr. West's car was in its garage? Yes, I had done so, and yes, it was there. These details seemed to satisfy him and he said he would dispatch a couple of officers.

It was a long ten minutes before they arrived and forced open the door. I had left the second floor apartment unlocked, since West had told me this was his usual custom.

The policemen climbed up the stairs, but I lagged behind. They had to be first on the scene. I could hear their voices and footsteps above me. When I detected an increase in the volume and urgency of their tones, I knew they had found him.

The elder of the two, Officer Hatch, came out of West's bedroom to meet me. "I have some bad news, Mr. Milburn," he said. "Dr. West is dead."

Even with my knowledge, his words fell like a blow. I stumbled a little, and Hatch grasped my arm. "May I see him?" I asked.

"All right, but don't touch anything. We have to look over the premises."

I did not have to play at grief as I entered the room. It took me hard when I saw my friend lying as I had left him. Hatch gave me a few moments, then asked, "Who was his next of kin, do you know? And did he have a doctor? We have to find someone to issue a death certificate."

Time reversed itself to the previous night, when I had asked West this same question. I saw his wide-eyed look of mock surprise. "What would I want with one of those fellows? I'm never ill and even if I was, I could deal with it as well as any of them, or better. What you must do, Charles, is make sure they summon good old Dr. Tillotson."

He went on to tell me that there were two physicians in Arkham who were called upon to examine dead persons not known to have any doctor attending them. One was Dr. Stanley, an eager young fellow, very keen on the latest methods. "He wouldn't hesitate to recommend a post-mortem in the case of an apparently healthy thirty-six year old man who has died suddenly," West had said. "And that would surely be fatal to our enterprise. Now I happen to know that Stanley is away right now. He goes to Maine for two weeks every summer. Fishing, I believe. In his absence, Dr. Tillotson is called. His methods aren't nearly so rigorous. And he's open to... negotiation."

Now I said, "Dr. West's next of kin are his two brothers in Boston. And I don't believe he had a doctor. He was rarely ill."

"Is that so?" said Hatch. "I suggest you go into the parlour and wait, Mr. Milburn. We have to ask you some questions, but first I'll telephone Dr. Stanley." He went into the study.

An alarm bell went off in my head. Could it be that West had been mistaken about Stanley and his fishing trip? Or perhaps he had already returned? Holding my breath, I hovered in the doorway to the study. What would I do if it were Stanley who was to come after all? Surely he wouldn't remove the body immediately? I would have to be prepared to do the revivification in whatever interval of time was allowed me between the departure of the officials and the removal of the body. But would they leave me alone with it? And what would they do when they realized there was no longer a body to remove? Well, but there was one. But it was already embalmed. The progressive-minded Dr. Stanley would surely realize this. I grew dizzy, contemplating these possibilities. After a few minutes I heard Hatch say, "I see, Miss. So he won't be back until next week? No, I need someone right now. I guess I'll try Dr. Tillotson."

Relief made my legs weak as I went back to the sitting room, but panic returned when I checked my watch. It was almost ten o'clock. West had told me that if I was not able to begin the revivification by noon, I may as well not bother. "Unless you're curious to see what sort of curiosity I'll be by then. But that's your business entirely."

Hatch came back, followed by Foskett, his associate. While they waited for Tillotson, they questioned me about my relationship to the deceased and my doings of the past two days. I told them that I had dined with Dr. West the previous evening. Afterward we had talked until quite late. I made a point of mentioning that West had complained of a headache several times in the course of the evening. He and I had arranged to meet again at nine the next day to discuss some investments about which I wanted his advice. I showed them the papers which I had fortunately remembered to bring with me – prospectuses of mining ventures in Colorado. On receiving no response to my ringing of the doorbell, I had summoned them. The rest they knew.

After this they asked me the same questions all over again, only in a different order, using different words. I knew this was intended to disconcert me and cause me to vary my answers if I was lying. "Did Dr. West have much to drink last night?" asked Foskett suddenly. No, I assured him, which was the truth, he had had only a little wine with the meal. They left me and went to investigate the dining room and the remains of the supper.

Some unknown time later, the doorbell rang and Foskett went to answer it, returning with Tillotson in tow. The latter was a short, beefy man, red-faced from the climb up the stairs. He carried a medical bag in one hand and a fat cigar in the other. He greeted Hatch with a grunt, and indicated me with his cigar-holding hand. "Who's this?"

"I'm a friend of Dr. West's," I said, going over to him and holding out my hand. "Charles Milburn. I'm looking after things here until Dr. West's brothers in Boston have been notified."

Tillotson transferred the cigar from hand to mouth so he could shake my hand, then took it out again so he could talk. "Is that so? That seems irregular to me. He has no family here, eh? Is there a Mrs. West?" He looked around as though he expected such a person to materialize from the air.

"Dr. West was a bachelor," I said.

"Hmm. Well, it takes all kinds, I guess." He vanished into the bedroom. I followed, not caring if he thought that was irregular too.

After his initial reaction, Tillotson did not object to my company. In fact, he seemed pleased to have an audience for his comments and heavy-handed witticisms. He asked me the same questions I had answered twice already for Hatch and Foskett. I was careful to mention West's fictitious headache and otherwise to say exactly what I had told the policemen. It pained me a little to see the fumble-fingered way he dealt with West's clothing, including the fact that he had neglected to put down his cigar and scattered ashes over the body. "Gee, look at these clothes," he muttered. "Was this guy a pansy or something? Is this what he was wearing last night?"

I hoped he did not expect an answer to the first question since I wasn't about to give him one, but in response to the second I said that yes, Dr. West was dressed as he had been the previous evening, except that he had removed his jacket. I noticed that Tillotson was careful to unfasten West's cufflinks and push his sleeves up in order to look at his arms. When he picked up the left arm, I grew tense.

"Was he a dope fiend, do you know?"

"Dr. West was extremely moderate in his habits," I replied. "He certainly did not have a drug habit, if that's what you're suggesting."

"So how do you explain this?" He pointed to the mark on West's arm made by the needle.

"I don't explain it, but I know he wasn't a dope fiend, as you put it."

"Well, maybe not, but it looks like he had a reason to prescribe something for himself." He looked at me closely with bright blue eyes that seemed rather too intelligent. "Dr. West was having some kind of trouble, wasn't he? A lawsuit, I think I heard."

"Yes, there was something like that," I admitted. "But surely you're not suggesting..."

"Oh, I'm not suggesting anything," Tillotson said. "But it's kind of funny for such a young man to drop dead suddenly like this."

"Indeed, and I assume you have been called in to determine a probable cause of death, not to make irresponsible allegations."

"No need to get testy, now, Mr. Milburn. All right, here's how it looks to me. An aneurysm, probably cerebral. He comes in here last night, pretty late from what you say. He's feeling not so good, takes off his glasses, hangs up his jacket over here and lies down until he feels better. Only he never does. He hasn't been dead very long, maybe five or six hours."

Less than four hours, you old fool, I thought. But not much less.

"But the thing is," Tillotson continued, "it's pretty hard to tell for sure with these things. An autopsy would be needed for a definitive answer. Which would also settle the question of suicide."

"Dr. Tillotson," I said, "as far as I am concerned, the question of suicide exists only in so far as you yourself have raised it. Do you see any evidence here to indicate suicide? Perhaps you should speak to the police officers about it, since they were first to arrive on the scene."

He looked annoyed. "Well, of course I'll have to see what Hatch and Foskett turned up. But what I'm getting at is, since you're representing the family, what there is of them, do you feel there's any percentage in further investigation?"

"I, and Dr. West's brothers too, I'm sure, are concerned only that this sad event be handled properly and promptly. If Officers Hatch and Foskett have found no evidence that Dr. West's death was anything but natural, and you yourself support this view, I do not think any further investigation is needed, no."

"In that case, I'm sure we can come to a mutually satisfactory arrangement," said Tillotson, grinning.

With a mixture of relief and disgust, I realized he was finally getting to the point. "Indeed, Dr. Tillotson. Perhaps I could offer you fifty dollars for your expenses." I held out the money, hearing West's voice in my mind. "Fifty ought to be about right. More than that would only make him curious."

"I'm much obliged, Mr. Milburn. Now, if we could go into Dr. West's study, I'll make out the death certificate. 'Apparent brain aneurysm,' I'll put for cause of death. Will that do?"

"If that's your professional judgment, certainly," I replied, unable to keep a chill out of my voice.

Tillotson chuckled as we left the bedroom. "'Professional judgment.' Oh, that's a good one," he said.

Finally they were gone and Herbert West was officially dead. I looked at my watch and was startled to see that it was eleven o'clock. West had been dead for four hours. I went back to the bedroom. Tillotson had left his clothing disordered. Clumsily, I rearranged the rumpled shirt, buttoned up his vest and straightened his arms so that his hands lay at his sides. His hands, which had done unimaginable deeds, both wonderful and vile, but would do no more unless I found in myself the resolve to carry out the rest of the work. "Get on with it, Charles," I whispered, but in truth I felt like weeping.

The first thing I did was telephone Hiram West at his office in Boston. I did not know him well, having met him only once or twice when he was in Arkham. He was a silent man, very different from his bombastic father, but with an alertness that suggested the silence was by no means empty.

"Mr. West, this is Charles Milburn, from Arkham. I'm afraid I have some bad news for you, concerning your brother Herbert."

"Oh yes?"

"He died last night. It appears to have been a brain aneurysm."

"Were you there? Did you witness his death?"

"No. No, I didn't. I dined with him last night, but when I returned this morning, he was dead."

"Why did you go back?"

His manner reminded me of my questioning by the police, but I explained about my fictitious prearranged meeting with West. "I would like to express my condolences," I added, "and to offer my assistance in making some of the arrangements here, if you wish."

"That would be helpful, Mr. Milburn. I will telephone our Arkham establishment immediately, to advise them of the situation. Where is the body now?"

We agreed that he would notify Jeremy, the third brother, and arrange for obituary notices in the Boston newspapers. I would do the same in Arkham. The funeral was to be three days hence. I could expect the undertaker's men to come and collect the body that afternoon.

This business concluded, I turned my attention to the main purpose of this insane enterprise. I had decided that I would begin by carrying West's body down to the laboratory, and that of his double to the bedroom. That way, no matter when the undertaker's men arrived, the correct corpse would be available. If I was unable to revivify West, or in the event I decided not to, I would cremate him in his own incinerator.

As I was going down the stairs to the ground floor, I was startled to hear a key being inserted into the front door. It opened to reveal Mrs. Fisk, West's housekeeper. "Oh, good morning, Mr. Milburn," she said. "I didn't expect to see you. I had an idea that Dr. West would be having a late morning today, so I thought I would come a little later than usual."

She was a middle-aged woman, tall and strongly built, with abundant hair that may have at one time been some shade of blonde, but was now a curious mixture of silver and bronze. Her only other noteworthy feature was a pair of blue-green eyes, as remarkable in their way as West's grey ones.

"I'm afraid I have some bad news, Mrs. Fisk," I began, and told my tale once more.

She was silent for some time after I finished speaking. "I'm very sorry to hear this, Mr. Milburn. He was so young. Would you like me to lay out the body? I know what to do. I suppose West's Funeral Home will be handling the funeral, but it's not decent to leave the poor man lying there, is it?"

I had not anticipated this suggestion and felt panicked. This would mean more delays. Already I had barely an hour in which to begin the revivification. Then I remembered how awkward I had always found the business of undressing the corpses West and I had worked on. I had already been dreading that part of the operation, especially in view of my emotional entanglements with him. Mrs. Fisk, with her steadiness and experience, was a Godsend.

"Yes, that would be extremely helpful. Dr. West had no family close by." Forget his brothers, I thought, remembering West's suggestion that they were planning to kill him. This woman, Andre and I – we were his family.

West's bedroom was filled with cool, bright light from the north-facing window, tinged a faint green from the leaves of a large chestnut tree outside. He still looked only asleep. I brought in a basin of water and Mrs. Fisk followed with towels and washcloths. Unlike Tillotson's coarse joviality, which had grated on my nerves, her comments, delivered in a calm, low voice, provided a welcome distraction from the inner turmoil which threatened to overwhelm me as we removed West's clothing.

"He always wore such beautiful clothes," Mrs. Fisk said. Look at this vest, now. Pure silk, that is. And the best linen for his shirts. That's right, just hold him up like that while I take it off."

I had been correct in thinking that dealing with the body would be easier with her assistance. She sponged poor West down while I held his limbs steady, or turned him this way and that.

"How was he to work for, Mrs. Fisk?" I asked. Having heard so much of horror from West himself the previous night, I was curious as to how she saw him.

"He was wonderful. Well, for one thing he was a very tidy man, so that made it much easier for me. And he was always polite. He wasn't always friendly, but that was all right. I don't expect to be friends with the people I work for, but I want them to treat me like a human being.

"He was sort of lonely, wasn't he? I'd be preparing one of those dinners he gave for his friends, and he'd come into the kitchen to see how things were going. Then he'd offer to stir something or cut something up. 'I feel at home in kitchens,' he'd say, and he was a good cook too. And more often than not, he'd get me arguing about something.

"He liked to argue, you know, for fun. At first I thought he was trying to make me mad so I'd quit, for some reason. But that wasn't it. He just wanted me to take the opposite side and start firing back at him. God was one of his favourite subjects. He had a whole list of reasons why God doesn't exist, and I'd come back with my reasons why he does. Or whether it's all right to own slaves, or to execute criminals. He'd argue both sides of those, different days. It sure made some jobs go faster. Peeling potatoes, or apples, or shelling peas, for instance. 'Let's chop some logic along with these vegetables,' he'd say. I'll miss that."

Her words conjured up a vivid image of the two of them in the kitchen, a pan of potatoes between them, West gesturing eloquently with a paring knife while he argued God out of existence. Despite my sorrow, I smiled. "Yes, he loved a good argument," I said. "I had a few with him myself."

"And he wasn't cheap," Mrs. Fisk continued, "either with his time or his money. He'd be out day and night, as long as there were sick people that needed doctoring. He worked too hard, I thought. I wouldn't be surprised if that's what killed him. And he didn't sleep well. That's always a sign of trouble."

"How do you know that, Mrs. Fisk?"

"I can't count the times I'd come in on a morning and find his bed hadn't been slept in. Now maybe he made it up himself, but I don't think so. When he was a regular doctor, before the war, I figured it was because he'd been called out all night. But later, after he began doing his special work, that couldn't have been it, could it?"

"Maybe he had emergencies at the hospital," I said. And thought, Maybe he was busy in the cellar.

"I don't think he was a really happy man, Mr. Milburn. Sometimes I thought he was missing something. Oh, I know people said he should have gotten married, but that's not what I mean. He was missing something inside and didn't know where to look for it."

"That's an interesting thought, Mrs. Fisk."

"And he didn't eat right. I don't think he ever had three meals a day. I'd leave him something for dinner every day before I went home but most times I think Andre had more of it than Dr. West. Look, you can see how skinny he was getting."

It was true. He was lightly built but had always looked fit and well-muscled. Now his ribs stood out too starkly, and the cords of muscle on his arms and legs.

"He was a good man," said Mrs. Fisk. "I've heard people say he thought he was too good for Arkham, and that he was cold-hearted. But if that was so, I wouldn't have expected him to bother with my John."

"What do you mean?"

"My son John. He works at Bolton Worsted. A couple of years ago he caught his hand in one of the machines. I thought he'd lose it for sure. Dr. Billington said it would have to come off because there was too much damage and it would get infected and cause blood poisoning. But I said 'Wait until I ask Dr. West.' So Dr. Billington called him and said we would get John out to Arkham to see him. But Dr. West, he said 'No need for that, I'll come over in my car right now.' And he brought John back here and fixed his hand. How? I don't know how. But John was back at work in a month and you can barely see the scars. And when I asked Dr. West how much I owed him, he said, 'Nothing at all.' How about that?"

By now we were finished. West's body lay on the bed, straight and clean, covered with a sheet.

"Now what do you think he'd want to be buried in?" asked Mrs. Fisk. "He had so many suits of clothes it's a wonder he could keep track of them."

"I'll pick something out before the undertakers come," I said. West's double was already wearing a suit. "Definitely a second-best one for him," West had said, laughing.

Mrs. Fisk finally left, after I had told her the anticipated time of the funeral and asked if she would help with the preparations for the reception which would follow the service. Finally I was alone, and now there was every reason for haste. West had been dead for nearly five hours.

And yet I hesitated still, thinking once more of the things he had done. Two murders, certainly. Even if Clapham-Lee had been insincere and an opportunist, even though he was alive now, after a fashion, West had killed him. And to bring him back to life deliberately in a diminished state, without any of the sustaining ties to others, without the power of reason, surely this was cruelty elevated to a Rococo pitch. But he had given Andre Boudreau's life back to him too, and Andre seemed to be a happy man, and devoted to West.

Then there were the mindless creatures. Eleven of them, if I could believe what West had told me, including one who had ended as a public spectacle before expiring, and others who must have endured periods of half-existence in the cellar. And what about the 'composites' he had mentioned? I had not been able to make myself ask him for details about them, but I had seen some of them in the vision from the window. One who could contrive such abnormalities was himself an abnormality.

"He will fumble in ignorance with the ultimate things," Quarrington had said in his final assessment of West. He might become a creature of evil, but would be transformed with the help of his friend. I was that friend, the only one who could attempt that transformation, if I chose to do so.

And whatever West had done, his servants loved him. Mrs. Fisk, that good, sensible woman, had said unequivocally, "He was a good man." But would she have so described him had she known what I knew? Or if West had not paid her as generously as he had? She had seen him heal her son without expectation of payment. But did that deed negate the others?

What balance could I use to weigh his heart?

Thoroughly confused and troubled, I went once more into the bedroom and looked at his face. The remoteness of death had begun to take over his features. Soon, I thought, he will be as marble. *It's now or never.*

Where *is* he now? I saw him inject the drug. I watched the mechanism that was his living body slow and stop working. Here lie his flesh and bones, but the thing that made him Herbert West, the doctor, the necromancer, my friend, where is that? *What* is that?

Despite my urgency, this conundrum did not yield. It resisted me, as it had resisted better men, philosophers, mystics and poets, throughout the ages. *"Behold, I show you a mystery."* There was no point in hammering against that door. Either I had faith or I did not.

"It can't be just mechanism, Herbert!" I spoke aloud in the silent room. "If you were standing here you'd know it too, God damn it!" I was angry – at West for putting me in this predicament, at the world for its imperfections, its cruelty, the flaw at the heart of things that manifested itself in the corruption of Tillotson, the falseness of Clapham-Lee, the perfidy of West's brothers, in West himself and his transgressions; finally, in the corpse of this young man, dead before his time and by his own hand.

I'll do it! I decided. If West was less than perfect, so also was the world he had inhabited. If I could, I would restore him to it as I had promised. The world deserved to have West in it. "He must be transformed and unified," Quarrington had said. Well, I knew of only one way to achieve that.

Once he was alive again, his fate would be out of my hands. Perhaps he would only die again. Or maybe he would be free to find that missing piece of himself, to seek his own completion and face the consequences of his choices, including John Hocks. I was only an instrument, not the maker. I laid my hand on his chest. "I'll bring you back, Herbert, if I can. I swear it."

First we had to descend into the cellar, the abyss from which he would be reborn or in which he would be utterly destroyed. I ran downstairs, unlocked and opened the secret door, fumbled in the blackness for the electrical switch. Then I climbed back up the many steps, no longer hurrying, telling myself to conserve my strength. I wrapped the sheet around West's body and picked him up. Strangely, the corpse had not yet begun to stiffen. As I shifted it to get a better grip, his head lolled against my shoulder and I smelled the perfume of narcissus from his hair, and from the sheet he was wrapped in, the scent of lavender.

West was not a large man, but despite his recent loss of weight he was a heavy burden for a fellow with a game leg who was not particularly athletic. By the time I had negotiated the stairs to the ground floor, I was breathing hard, and as I reached the cellar I was afraid that I would drop him. At last we were in the laboratory. I set him down on the table with relief and rested before I went into the annexe. "I'm going to fetch your fetch, Herbert," I said, with a laugh that surprised me.

The gangster was about the same size as West, but seemed heavier. Of course, now I was climbing up, dragging the dead weight against the pull of gravity. I was also squeamishly aware that this fellow had been dead not for several hours, but for several months. Despite West's assurance that he had done "a first-class job of embalming, guaranteed leak-proof," I felt my nerves recoil as the corpse settled against me. It was as though it radiated deadness, that its state was contagious. There were no lingering perfumes here, only a cold stench of the preservatives with which he had been filled.

I had to rest twice on the way up, propping the corpse on the banister to reduce the weight on my arms. Finally, I deposited it carefully on West's bed. Mindful of Mrs. Fisk's admonitions about decency, I arranged the limbs and straightened the clothing. West's second-best suit was far better than most people's best ones, and the fellow looked quite splendid when I had finished. West's gold-rimmed spectacles gleamed on the dead face, the lenses reflecting blandly the cool light from the windows. From a little distance he looked almost uncannily like Herbert West. Satisfied, I returned to the laboratory.

The apparatus was assembled and ready. The flask of violet-coloured fluid (the essence of Herbert West?) stood nearby. "Here we are again, Herbert," I said, "in the laboratory, about to begin the work."

I unwrapped his body and laid it straight on the table, arms at his sides. Now it was unmistakably a corpse, like so many others I had seen in this place. His skin was cool. Not cold yet, but strangely cool, like kid leather over the bones. His flesh had already begun to shrink and settle, loosening from the bones, revealing the hollow of the abdominal cavity and the narrow valleys between the ribs. His head rolled a little to one side and as I tried to straighten it, I saw that one of his eyes had slipped slightly open, showing a sliver of gummed white and giving his face an idiotic, leering expression. Even his hair felt dead. Repelled, I pulled my hands away. This was no longer my friend. This was only the dross left behind after the vital spirit had departed. Its future was not life but corruption.

I remembered a disgusting story by the mad Edgar Poe, for whose writings West had an inexplicable fondness. He had insisted on reading this tale to me once, complete with theatrical effects. It was titled, if I recall, "The Facts in the Case of M. Valdemar." A man at the point of death was hypnotized (although Poe said 'mesmerized,' using the term current in his day) and so remained sentient even after death had occurred. After several months, during which he was in a state of 'sleep-waking' or trance, the hypnotist for some reason awakened him, at which point, exclaiming repeatedly that he was *dead*, the unfortunate man dissolved, all in a minute (and here I quote, the phrase having stuck in my mind), into "a nearly liquid mass of loathsome – of detestable putrescence." Surely that was the only fate possible for the thing that lay before me.

I wanted to run from the lab and the house, to leave Arkham and never come back. But I could not. If I abandoned him now, he would haunt me forever. I could not escape this obligation. With something like a sob, I unstoppered the flask and poured the fluid into the reservoir of the apparatus.

The few times I had performed the delicate operation of inserting the cannulas into the correct blood vessels, West had been at my side to help and instruct me. Now he was the subject, I the experimenter, and an error on my part would mean permanent death for him.

I checked the apparatus, making sure that all the connections were properly made and secured, the instruments assembled and ready to hand. Minutes were slipping by, and each one was precious. Each one's passage might mean an irreparable loss to him or increase the chances of the arrival of outsiders.

But I could not bring myself to begin. This was a process which, once started, had to continue, to success or failure. Surely it would be a failure, I thought, wearily. How could this collection of glass and rubber, steel and chemicals, bring a dead man back to life, no matter what I did with it? Yes, I had witnessed such transformations in this very place, but never one that had been entirely successful. Never mind that Andre Boudreau was supposedly an example of success; I could not be certain that the fellow wasn't deluded, and I knew that West lied without hesitation when it suited him. What good would it do, I asked myself, to mutilate his corpse, to make it vibrate and flail its limbs and utter garbled sounds? Did I want to see his face (now so still, like a locked casket of wonders) twist into grotesqueness, his eyes grow muddled with agony as he tottered on the brink of the abyss?

The alchemists had spoken of exactly this moment – the beginning of the Great Work, a perilous enterprise which could not be hurried but which, once begun, had to be pursued to its end. The instrument had to be worthy of the power that wielded it. I did not think I was worthy. I had been pressed into service, shaped quickly and roughly, and here I was, my materials ready around me, but my hands trembling, my will vacillating and weak.

Did the alchemist ever succumb to despair, I wondered, as his candles dimmed in the cold dawn light? Did he ever look appalled at his crucibles and alembics, the powders he had ground with his gritty pestle, the liquids he had distilled in his stained flasks? When all was said and done, those things were dead matter. He could move them here and there, heat them, mix them with this or that, but without the intervention of a mystery, in the end the stuff would be as dead as before, no matter how much he had made it fizz and bubble in the fever pitch of excitement, with the bellows labouring and the furnace glowing like the fires of hell. He did not possess the elusive element, only believed that it existed in the world, to be pursued, courted, hunted. He had to give his whole life to that effort. His hopes, fears, sweat, frenzy, tears and despair were necessary ingredients in the search. They had to be incorporated into the work, or it would come to nothing. Unless I was prepared to take the dark road equipped only with my tiny flickering flame of love and faith; unless I was prepared myself to perish in the effort, I had no business here.

Having relished this unhappy irony to its fullest, I began to pray. It was a formless prayer, without an object, without style, almost without words, merely a sincere and anguished intention that my fingers and eyes and tired brain be equal to the appointed task. I bowed my head over the table as I murmured, as if to ask my dead friend for the help he could no longer give, and noticed that in my haste I had spilled some of the revivifying fluid. A small pool of it lay on the surface of the table, near West's left hand. Without thinking, I dipped my fingers in it and brought them to my mouth.

The stuff tasted of salt, of metals, of blood. I felt it too, as a warmth and vibration on my tongue. A wind of energy swept through me, blowing away the weariness of the sleepless night and the long, anxious day. The air in the room rippled and glowed. The emerald on my finger burned with a radiant fire. In my mind I found a knowledge of the veins and arteries, their complexities and those of the tissues and structures in which they were embedded. Suddenly I laughed out loud. I was the chosen instrument, and here before me was my material.

For the first time I could look at his naked body without constraint, as though it were my own. Now he looked like an image of himself, his skin glowing faintly golden under the incandescent lights. I had been brought to this place to do these things for him. At this moment, I was nearer to him than a brother, a lover, a friend, as near as his mother when she began the labour of giving birth to him. I laid my hands on his chest and ran them down the length of his torso. I could feel the link, alive between us.

"Here I am," I said aloud, neither knowing nor caring to whom I spoke. "Use me." I kissed him to seal my promise, and began.

I tilted his head back to expose the throat. Then I picked up a scalpel. I felt as though someone else's hands guided mine as I made the incision, unthinkingly applying the force needed to part the tissues. There was the jugular vein, a dull blue cable embedded in the flesh. I picked up the cannula and inserted it, feeling the slight resistance and give as it slid inside. Once it was secured, I located the femoral artery, made the incision unhesitatingly and slid in the arterial cannula. All was now ready. Nothing could be gained by waiting, and much might be lost.

I opened the main valve and activated the pump. Into his body I introduced his own essence, watching the pressure meters, watching the hitherto empty flask fill with his red blood. It did not take long before the fluid reservoir was nearly empty. I closed the valves, withdrew the invading instruments and sewed up the two small incisions as he had shown me, wincing every time I pushed the needle through the skin. But he showed no sign of feeling it. He was still dead.

Now his immediate fate was out of my hands. I felt dizzy with relief, but could not disengage myself. I remained with him, talking to him, telling him that I was here, I had done what he had wanted me to do, I was waiting for him to come back. I called him by his name, I called him brother and beloved friend. I was caught between hope and sorrow, but it was too early to mourn or to rejoice. So why not hope? He had been dead less than six hours and the means of his death had been such that the body's mechanisms were intact. But another part of me watched with sorrow, thinking: *This is like a dream in which I found my heart's desire, but when I awoke, it was gone.* Remembering my final promise to him, I took the pistol from its drawer and laid it nearby, hoping I would not need to use it; indeed, I did not think I would be able to.

Then a strange thing happened. I had a sensation of wearing clothes that did not fit me, but it was more fundamental than that. My *body* did not fit me. My vision, too was disturbed, as though my familiar spectacles had been turned into powerful magnifying lenses. Then something fell into place, and I was – myself? The air in the room rippled again, and I was looking down at my own face. It was myself lying dead I was looking at. No, I was Herbert West, bending over the body of his dead friend, Charles Milburn.

We were together then, as we had never been before. As I laid my hands on his body I could feel his hands on mine. As I watched his face, I could see my own, lying still in death beneath me. In the time out of time as I waited for life to return to him, a door opened in the fabric of the world and my essence merged with his. I thought his thoughts and my own in the same moment.

There was only one thing to do, there was only one person, only one in the whole world, who could do it. And he lay dead in this place I had created for my work. This was my *métier*, the body on the table was the instrument I played, and the work was approaching its resolution and finale.

Who am I? Lately it feels like I have a raging mob in my mind. I am plagued by that other, *who calls himself my friend, but keeps reminding me of things I do not want to know. I already know everything I need to – I use the things of the world as my mind tells me to use them, to further knowledge. What can I do besides this?*

Why must I keep thinking about what he would say? He is not a scientist. He lives by his nerve impulses and jumbled emotions. "But, Herbert, do they suffer while you do that to them? How can you do that?" Well, I can and I do. They do not suffer or if they do, I know how to deal with it – a snip here, a nick there and their sufferings end. So why do these useless thoughts gather around me like the Furies gathered around Oedipus? If I can't sleep, soon I won't be able to work, and I can't sleep without nightmares. Or drugs, which I know will be the ruin of me in the end.

Which way do I go now? Tell me that, my opinionated friend. My colleagues and my own brothers conspire against me. Those things I made in France haunt my sleep and Hocks waits outside my window. And Clapham-Lee... Oh but what a piece of work he was when I finished with him! How beautifully vacant was his gaze! But the way he tried to cling to me when I was turning him loose... I had to hit him to make him let go. He was like a frightened little child on the first day of school...

No! Why must I remember this stuff? It's all his *influence. Charles Milburn, that overdeveloped conscience on legs. I should have finished him off long ago, in 1914...*

Damn it, why do these thoughts insist on crowding in, unproductive meanderings that waste my time and energy? What will I do, now that he is dead? All right, but with luck maybe he won't be dead for long. And if he is, I will just have to find another assistant, or go on alone. There is no one like him. Now what does that mean? He wasn't all that clever, really. He kept muddling up his thoughts with emotions and getting sidetracked. I shouldn't have listened to Q. I should have found someone with a knowledge of scientific principles and methods. But there's no one like him. No one who knows me as he does. Without him I have no mirror. Yes, and I can run free in the world without his tiresome scruples to weigh me down.

"Run then, until you have run your course. Without him you are a mirror reflecting blackness, a self-consuming fire, a dead stone. Don't you know who he is? When all roads lead you to the abyss, Herbert West, he is your bridge, your only hope. I told you this in 1911, and now I'm telling you again."

Damn you too, Quarrington, and your metaphors and crazy notions! Wait, something's happening here. Yes, he's alive!

I came to myself with a quivering jolt. The air around me sparkled with iridescence. It was July of 1923 and the body of Herbert West lay on the table before me. I was Charles Milburn again, and something was happening. A miracle was happening. Forty-seven minutes exactly had elapsed since I had mingled the revivifying fluid with his blood. Now I thought I felt a slight flutter under my fingers when I held them to his wrist. No, there was nothing. Seconds later, another flutter, then a third. With shaking hands, I groped for West's stethoscope, clamped it to my ears and applied the business end to his chest. Yes! There were heartbeats, faint and far apart, but unmistakable.

Exultation swept through me. I felt my own heartbeats pounding in my ears. Resolutely, I ignored them and concentrated on the matter at hand. I must not fail now, through carelessness induced by excitement.

"Once there is a pulse," West had instructed, "it is crucial that the subject begins to breathe. If respiration does not begin spontaneously, it must be induced."

I watched for signs. There was no movement of his chest and the mirror I held to his lips remained unclouded. There was only one thing to do. I placed my left hand on his forehead and my right under his jaw. I held his nostrils closed and opened his mouth. I placed my mouth hard on his and breathed steadily once, waited a second or two, and breathed once more. Nothing. I repeated this several more times. In between breaths, I felt for his pulse. It was still there, faint but discernable. Finally, as I inhaled in preparation for another breath, I saw his chest begin to rise and fall. He had a pulse. He was breathing. He was alive.

I felt a wildness growing inside me. I wanted to shout and caper. I wanted to run up into the street and yell, "He's alive! He was dead and now he's alive and I don't care what any of you might think!" But of course I did none of these things. I was Charles Milburn again, and a dreadful anxiety warred with my elation. I had, for the moment, done everything I could. Now I could only watch, hoping that my efforts would not be proved vain by a relapse into death, or worse, a state of subnormal life from which I would have to free him. Quarrington's prediction that he would die two deaths would be as good then as if he lived another thirty years.

For an unguessable time I hovered over him. Already the signs of death were receding. Once more he looked only asleep. Despite the struggles of conscience I had experienced, despite my ambivalence about what I was doing, some innocent part of me was full of an unreserved joy as I watched. For the first time, I indulged freely in hope.

I grew dizzy, as though I was being drawn out of myself, becoming lighter than air. A fragrance filled the subterranean room, of the dewy earth on a summer morning, of rain on parched earth. The light glowed intensely golden, as though the sun itself had descended into this underworld. The body before me, Herbert West's body, was transfigured, made more beautiful than he had ever been in life. His skin grew lightly flushed, as though his blood ran with exultant vitality. His hair was pure gold.

"It's the red dawn!" I cried. "He is made anew; he was washed clean by his death, whiter than snow, and now he lives again, filled with the *elixir vitae*. Here is the quintessence, the magistery!"

I was *with* him, as though we shared the same blood and breath. I had given him my life in a great wave of love and hope. "It's enough," I babbled, as the room spun around me. "I've done everything now and it's enough, thank God, it's enough. Herbert, say something! Speak to me, please speak to me! Show me that you're alive!" I bent over him, grasped his shoulders and gazed once more into his living face.

His eyes moved under the closed lids. He lifted his left hand as though to brush aside some obstacle. Then he opened his eyes, those ice-grey eyes I had thought I would never see again after the final slide into the unfocussed stare of death. But I did not know what he saw. I did not think it was me. His lips moved, silently articulating words that I could have sworn were, "Only now..."

Then he spoke aloud, to whom I did not know, except that it was not to me. He stared past me in a way that would have troubled me had I not already been troubled, and said, "Fire and darkness, the sword, the putrescence... Then the twisted road... the place of life in death. Oh no, I will not speak of it. Not to anyone."

He closed his eyes and appeared to fall asleep.

♦ 21 ♦

Never look outside for what you need, until you have made use of the whole of yourself.
Gerard Dorn

There was a sudden clang of the doorbell. I cursed silently the mischance of an interruption at this crucial moment. It was probably the men from the mortuary. Well, there was a body upstairs for them. I had to stay here. Then I heard footsteps in the hall above. How could that be, when I had locked the door after Mrs. Fisk? It sounded as though someone was approaching the door to the cellar stairs. *Hocks, it must be Hocks! I have to keep him out of here!*

I glanced at West. He was breathing normally, to all appearances only asleep. I left the room, carefully closing the door and the hinged section of shelves that concealed it. Then I ran up the stairs.

In the hall I nearly collided with Andre. "Mr. Milburn!" he said. "What are you doing here? Where is the Doctor?" He looked more disturbed than I had ever seen him.

"Andre, I have some bad news for you, I'm afraid. Dr. West died early this morning."

"He is dead?" He set his bag down on the floor. His face grew still and closed. "How did it happen?"

"It was something called a brain aneurysm. A blood vessel bursts in the brain. It can happen unexpectedly and is nearly always fatal."

"May I see him?" he asked.

"Yes, of course," I said. "He is in his bedroom."

I followed him up the stairs even though I was on fire with impatience to get back to the laboratory. Here was another complication! That Andre knew about the laboratory in the cellar I was aware, but I did not know whether I could trust him with the secret of West's revivification. Why was he back so soon, anyway? I was certain West had said he would be away until the late afternoon.

I watched him as he approached the bedside. His face was impassive as he looked at the corpse of West's double, lying serenely on the bed. To my surprise, he stayed only a few moments before rejoining me. "I'm ready now," was all he said.

Ready for what? I wondered. "Are you all right, Andre?" I asked.

"I am all right. There will be a funeral, yes? Let me put these things away. Then I will begin the preparations." He started down the hall towards his quarters.

I didn't know whether to admire his stoicism or to regard it as some strange after-effect of his own death and revivification. Just then, the door bell rang again and Andre came back to admit two men who said they were from West's Funeral Home.

They were youngish fellows, dressed in black suits that seemed at odds with their cheerful everyday faces. I had never seen either of them before, but evidently they had been advised of my existence, for one of them addressed me by name.

"Mr. Milburn? We're here to pick up Dr. West's body now, if that's convenient."

"Yes, I was expecting you." I hoped my appearance was not too wildly dishevelled. I conducted them to West's bedroom. "The body is ready for burial," I said. "His housekeeper, Mrs. Fisk, and I have done all that was necessary. Dr. West told me several times that in the event of his death he did not wish to be embalmed. So all that is needed is to select a suitable casket. I imagine his brothers would prefer to do that."

"But we've been given instructions to embalm the body," said one of the fellows. "By Mr. Hiram West himself," said the other.

"I will speak to Mr. West," I replied, wishing I felt as calm as I sounded. "I was a close friend of Dr. West's, and I am confident that I understood his wishes in this matter."

They did not object further. After all, it was nothing to them, as long as there were no negative consequences from their employer. West had been quite clear on this point. "The fellows from the mortuary won't care. The less they need to do, the better. It's Hiram you'll have to deal with but I think you'll be able to convince him quite easily. He's used to my contrary notions. And if he and Jeremy have been planning my exit, they'll have other things to think about."

The undertaker's men went back to their vehicle and returned carrying a stretcher. With practiced ease, they transferred the body of West's double onto it. I held my breath lest something make them realize that it was already embalmed. That would be a matter for gossip and speculation, all right! I could see the headlines: *Arkham Doc Embalms Self Before Death*, or more likely, *Body Was Already Embalmed, Doc's Friend Arrested*. But they made no comment, and I saw nothing unusual in their expressions as they carried the corpse down the stairs and to the waiting hearse.

Finally, I was able to return to the laboratory. Andre was nowhere in sight. I assumed he had gone to begin his preparations, whatever they were. I opened the doors with hands that shook once more with fear and hope. Would he speak to me? With horror, I remembered my promise to kill him if he was intellectually or physically impaired. Almost I hoped that he was dead, rather than that I should have to make this terrible decision.

The table was empty. There was no body on it, dead or alive. There was no sheet. The apparatus and the two flasks, one empty, the other full of blood, were the only things to show that the revivification of Herbert West had not been a hallucination on my part. For a long minute I could only stand and stare. It took my mind that long to absorb the fact of his absence. Then, frantically, I began searching. What if he was delirious, or demented? Visions of a shambling form on the Aylesbury Road came to mind, and the look of crazy glee on John Hocks's face.

I looked first in the annexe. It was empty. Neither there nor in the main room was there any place where something as large as a body could be concealed. Next, I ran down the passage to the incinerator. I opened the heavy door and looked inside. Nothing. I called his name, many times I called, but heard nothing in reply. I was forced to conclude he was no longer in the cellar. So he must be elsewhere in the house. The main floor offices were locked. So was the rear door, to my relief. But I had left the main door unlocked while I was upstairs with the undertaker's men. It was possible that he had gone out that way. But why? Naked but for a sheet? Disoriented? I was completely perplexed. In all my speculations I had not considered the possibility of his disappearance. I sat down in the hall and tried to think.

Laying aside any thoughts as to his motives, I tried to reconstruct the sequence of events. West must have left the laboratory while I was upstairs with the two men. But where had he gone? The only logical possibility was out the front door. The rear door and the one to his offices were both locked, and I should have seen him if he had gone up to the living quarters. A man wearing nothing but a sheet should be easy to find, I reasoned, and a man who had returned from death only an hour before could not be very fast on his feet. I ran upstairs and shouted to Andre that I had to leave. I thought I heard a reply but did not stay to make sure.

Intending to be methodical, I began by circling the block. I would then proceed in an increasing radius. As I rounded the corner onto narrow Hill Street, a figure emerged from an overgrown lot that adjoined the woods near Hangman's Hill. My heart lurched with hope, but it was dashed when I recognized the emaciated, rag-clad form of John Hocks.

He must have been lying in wait for me. "Ha, it's you, you running man! I watched you run away, like you were scared of me. Stupid you, because I knew what I had to do and I did it. I watched. I saw them take him out. They put him in a... one of those things with wheels, and they went away. He's gone!"

It took me a moment to comprehend what he was saying, because of the hollow, whispery quality of his voice. It was as though the organs that produced it were deteriorating. "Yes, Dr. West is gone. They took him away to bury him. Does that make you feel better?"

A crafty look stole over his features. "I didn't see anyone bury him. Who knows what those men are going to do with him? They could make him alive again, just like he made me. How do I know they won't do that, huh?" He thrust his face toward mine and leered at me, releasing an indescribable stench.

I had never been less inclined to talk with this creature, but had no choice. This was yet another part of the price I had to pay. "You have to believe me. They're going to bury him. If you watch at Christ Church Cemetery, three days from today, you will see. My word on it."

"Your word as a gentleman?" he said, obviously aping something he had heard once. He stuck out a dirty, skeletal hand, and in my eagerness to be done with him, I took it in mine. It felt like a bundle of sticks in a bag, but his grip was surprisingly strong.

"My word as a gentleman," I said, and tried to withdraw my hand. Hocks laughed and squeezed it more tightly.

"Not so fast, you! I know how to do this. You know my name. Will. What's yours?"

"Charles." I hoped he would be satisfied with that.

"All right, Mister Charles," Hocks said, relinquishing my hand after a final squeeze. "But if I don't see a funeral at Christ

Church, I'll come looking for *you*." He turned abruptly and shambled away into the trees toward Hangman's Hill.

I continued my search for West but was soon completely exhausted. A black certainty grew in me as I lurched wearily up and down the streets that I would not see him again, especially if Hocks saw him first and recognized him. I needed to rest before I could do anything more. Once home, I lay down on my bed without bothering to undress, and fell asleep.

I awoke with a start. My watch had run down, but I thought it was early morning. The chiming of the mantel clock had awakened me. Six o'clock. I got up and put myself in order once more, but failed to do the same with my thoughts. I could not stop wrestling with the conundrum of West's disappearance. Where could he have gone, so soon after emerging from death, naked but for the sheet I had wrapped him in? The added complication of Hocks made me groan aloud.

Feverishly, I scanned the morning newspaper as soon as it came, fearing to see a story about a mutilated corpse found in an unlikely place. Except that this time it would not be an itinerant farm labourer or an unknown tramp, but a prominent physician of the town. But there was nothing of the sort. Relieved and anxious at the same time, I went back to my brooding.

The problem was that to the rest of the world Herbert West no longer existed as a living entity. To everyone except me, he was dead. His body was at the mortuary, awaiting burial. This made it impossible for me to tell anyone about his disappearance, to ask for help in my search for him, or even to make any but the most cautious inquiries. If I revealed the secret of his revivification to anyone and was believed, I would negate the entire purpose of this terrible adventure. And if I added that the escaped Wild Man of Arkham was the dead and long-forgotten John Hocks, who was seeking the missing man with evil intent, I would very likely end up in Sefton myself.

I telephoned St. Mary's Hospital and asked the person who answered whether there had been any emergency cases brought in the previous night. No, she said, it had been exceptionally quiet. I thanked her and hung up before she could ask me to identify myself. I considered sounding out Sarah Enright, but had no heart for the circumlocutions that would be necessary. She knew me well enough to see beyond my surface wretchedness and guess that something troubled me besides the sudden death of an old friend.

About mid-morning my telephone rang, causing me to spring up in a near-panic. Perhaps it was West! It was, but not Herbert. Hiram West had arrived in Arkham and was at his late brother's home. Would I please come over immediately, he said. I did not like the tone of the summons, but decided to go, if only to resume my search along the way.

I took a circuitous route to Boundary Street, peering behind fences and hedges, detouring down alleys and paying special attention to vacant lots, but to no avail. Too soon, I was at West's house.

Both Hiram and his younger brother Jeremy were there. They had made themselves at home. Jackets and hats had been deposited on the furniture, suitcases reposed on the floor. Jeremy had obviously investigated the liquor cabinet. As I entered the sitting room he greeted me by raising a glass and asking if I would like a 'snort.'

The two elder West brothers favoured their father in looks, being rather stocky, with dark hair and prominent eyes. Looking at them, I remembered West's uncertainty about his parentage.

West had explained to me some time ago that on their father's death, Hiram Jr. had assumed control of the above-board business enterprises, while Jeremy managed the less savoury ventures. This certainly seemed to be reflected in their appearance; Hiram was dressed as soberly as a banker, while Jeremy wore a suit whose stripes were a little too wide and lapels a little too generously cut for good taste. His manner was jovial, altogether in contrast with his brother's laconic style.

Hiram motioned me toward an armchair. He sat down on the sofa next to Jeremy, facing me. He looked at me hard with eyes that I noticed for the first time were an odd light shade of hazel.

"Who killed him?" he asked.

It took me a moment to understand, so unexpected was this question. "No one killed him, Mr. West. He died of a brain aneurysm."

"That's the official explanation. I want the truth."

"Why do you think that isn't the truth?"

"Because Herbert was only thirty-six. And he had never been sick, as far as I know."

"Except in the head," said Jeremy, lifting his glass to his eye and peering at me through the amber liquid. "But at least he always had good booze on hand. So here's to Herbie." He raised the glass in a mocking toast and drank.

Audrey Driscoll

Hiram ignored him, except for an eloquent chopping motion of the hand in his direction. "Well, Milburn?"

"I know of no one who would have wanted to murder your brother," I said. "Listen, I'll describe exactly what happened. That's all I can do." I told them what I had told the police the previous morning, about the dinner and my late departure on Monday, and our agreement to meet again on Tuesday morning. My arrival at the house only to get no response and my subsequent decision to summon the police. Their investigation and that of Dr. Tillotson. "After they left I telephoned you," I finished.

"Yes, and after that?"

"After that Mrs. Fisk, Herbert's housekeeper arrived, and she and I laid out his body."

"Why did you do that?" asked Hiram, giving me another keen look. "You should have known there was no need for that."

"Forgive me, Mr. West, but I believe I was your brother's closest friend. Several times during our association he mentioned to me that when his time came to die he wanted only the simplest treatment. 'I want to make sure that I dissolve to my fundamental elements and return to the earth,' was how he put it. Of course, he was speaking in a purely theoretical way then, but when he died I saw no reason not to comply with these sentiments."

"Yeah, that sounds like the sort of wacky idea that Herbie would have," said Jeremy, earning himself another chop from Hiram.

"All right, but why not just give those instructions to the undertaker's men? Why on earth would the two of you trouble yourselves that way? It's so... primitive."

"Mr. West, I understand that as one connected with the undertaking business you would naturally think that. But for Mrs. Fisk and myself, it was a way to do one last thing for him. And I think it's what he would have wanted." I stopped, realizing that what I was saying was too sincere for these men.

Hiram continued to look offended. Jeremy smirked at me unpleasantly. I remembered, too late, that I was still wearing West's emerald ring, and that I had been turning it around and around on my finger as I spoke. Had these two ever seen it before? I curled my hand into a less conspicuous position.

"What about that French fellow who worked for Herbert?" asked Hiram. "Where is he?"

"Andre Boudreau. He was in Boston. Herbert sent him on an errand on Monday morning. He was to return yesterday afternoon."

"Well he didn't. At any rate, he wasn't here when we arrived this morning. Only that housekeeper, Mrs. Fish."

"Mrs. Fisk. Andre isn't here now, you say?"

"We haven't seen him."

"Maybe he killed Herbie," said Jeremy. "That would explain why he's taken off."

"Never mind that now," said Hiram. "All right, Milburn, let's see if I have this straight..." For the next half hour we went around and around the events of the previous two days. The brothers fired questions at me in a way that seemed entirely practiced, as though they did this sort of thing frequently. They were far more thorough than the policemen had been. I concentrated hard on my simple narrative and did not deviate from it. Finally, I became annoyed, and decided it was time to show it.

"Look, Mr. West," I said to Hiram, "I can tell you no more than I already have, several times. I suggest you speak to Officers Hatch and Foskett, and Dr. Tillotson. Mrs. Fisk also, if she's still here. I'm sure she can confirm some of what I have told you."

Hiram looked at me as though he suspected some kind of trick. "Stay here," he said to Jeremy, and went off toward the kitchen. I had no fears on Mrs. Fisk's account; from what I had seen of her, I was certain she could handle Hiram West. I was less certain about myself and Jeremy.

He was smirking at me again. "So are you one of them too?" he asked.

"I'm sorry, I don't know what you mean."

"You know, like Herbie." He assumed an exaggerated, limp-wristed pose. "Pansies!"

I remembered what I had read in the Quarrington papers and felt a burst of anger at the brute before me. "I don't think you could have known your brother very well if you can make a suggestion like that," I said. "And you're hardly in a position to accuse others of wrongdoing."

He ignored the second sentence. "I'll bet you knew him really well, didn't you?" he said, still smirking.

The return of Hiram fortunately spared me from making the reply I wanted to make. I knew that it would do no good to show my antipathy to Jeremy. That would change his casual baiting of me into active enmity, which would complicate matters in a way that could only be harmful.

"The housekeeper can't tell us anything more than Milburn has already," said Hiram. He turned to me. "So what was he up to anyway?"

"What do you mean?"

"Herbert. What were all those experiments of his about?"

"He had several areas of research. I suppose the primary one had to do with how wounds heal and how body parts can be reconstructed. He acquired this interest during the War and managed to develop it into a specialty of his own."

"Like that opera singer," interrupted Jeremy. "I didn't think Herbie had it in him to play in that league."

Another chop from Hiram. "Herbert was doing some sort of experiments with corpses. I know that because he used to take unclaimed bodies from our mortuaries sometimes. You know about that too. I remember you from that fight ten or eleven years ago. A man was killed in the ring and you and Herbert took the body away. So what was he doing? Working on a cure for death?"

I laughed weakly. "That would have been a good one! He wanted that fighter's body so he could do tests on physiological changes after death. He was still a student at the time, if you remember. As for other bodies, I don't know. Perhaps he needed them as dissection cadavers for his students. I know they're difficult to obtain."

Hiram gave me a look that suggested he would have liked to dissect me if that would help him get at the truth. "Milburn, did you murder him?"

"No!" The word burst out of me with more force than I had intended. "He was my friend. The last thing I wanted was his death. You insult me by suggesting that."

This time he made the chopping motion at me. "Never mind that. When there's enough at stake, friendship doesn't matter so much. I know that. So do you. What's in it for you, now that he's dead?"

I had little experience with men of this type, whose first consideration in any issue was the weighing of profit and loss. They believed I thought that way too. Taking a deep breath, I said, "Mr. West, you are mistaken. I was your brother's friend, not his business associate. I didn't understand his research and he didn't tell me much about it. I gained nothing by his death. If you believe that I was engaged in some kind of criminal activity, murder or anything else, you should talk to the police. I've told you everything I know and will not take up any more of your time. Now I must have a word with Mrs. Fisk."

As I went down the hall toward the kitchen, I heard Jeremy mutter, "What did you expect? Goddamn pansies."

Mrs. Fisk was preparing lunch for the guests. She looked grim but greeted me cheerfully enough. I commiserated with her on her recent encounter with Hiram. Then I asked, "Mrs. Fisk, where is Andre?"

"Gone. When I came today he wasn't here, and his things are gone."

"But where would he go?"

"I don't know. Andre was a good enough fellow but he didn't talk much. He did love Dr. West, no question about that. Maybe now that he's dead Andre decided to go back to Canada."

"Perhaps, but I would have expected him to stay for the funeral. Unless he knew – " I broke off suddenly, realizing what I had nearly said. But Mrs. Fisk had other concerns.

"Mr. Milburn, these two... gentlemen, are they married, do you know? Will it be just the two of them, or should I expect some ladies to arrive?"

I replied that I thought both of the West brothers had wives and reassured her that I would ask them to tell her of their plans. I also said that if it didn't occur to them to pay her for her time I would make it good to her, at whatever hourly rate she had been used to receiving. "Because you're under no obligation to them."

"Oh, it's all right. I want to do it for Dr. West's sake. But those two are a pair of prize petunias, and no mistake."

When I was halfway down the stairs to the ground floor, Hiram leaned over the banister. "We'll be watching you, Milburn, so don't think you can get away with any funny business."

I turned and looked up at him. "I have no intention of doing that, whatever you might mean by it. I plan to be at Herbert's funeral. I'll see you there."

The funeral of Herbert West was held three days after his death. For some reason, his brothers had decided to make a spectacle of the event. A charitable interpretation was that this was their way of atoning for their unworthy intentions toward him. But it was more likely that they saw it as an opportunity to advertise the services offered by West's Funeral Homes. "This is the deluxe version," they were telling Arkham. "Show the world how much you care. Make a splash!"

The service was held amid the gloomy splendours of Christ Church, the Episcopalian cathedral, which was decked out with massive floral arrangements. A large choir had been recruited and several of the Wests' establishments must have contributed their staffs to serve as ushers and ornamental place-holders. I was surprised not to see a brass band on the premises.

For the citizens of Arkham, the funeral was the occasion for a great outpouring of curiosity. The church was full. Nearly everyone who was anyone in the University, medical, or business communities was there, including many who had known West only by repute or not at all. I saw Mrs. Fisk in the crowd, accompanied by a youngish man I assumed to be her son.

Sitting together was the group of elder professor-doctors who had been West's real or perceived enemies since his student days, among them Drs. Shortt and Hobson, and Allan Halsey. I do not know if I imagined it, but the latter seemed to wear a look of triumphant satisfaction. I turned away, not wishing to see any more of it. For the first time I was glad that Alma was not there.

I was shown to a place immediately behind the seats occupied by Hiram and Jeremy. Everywhere I saw examples of the duplicity and evil of human nature. It was in me too, in the burden of dark knowledge and lies I carried. This very ceremony was one gigantic lie perpetrated by Herbert West and myself.

A magnificent casket of mahogany and brass occupied the focal point at the head of the central aisle. I wondered what West would have thought of it. Perhaps it was a kind of loss-leader, having outstayed its welcome in some showroom due to high price and over-ornamentation.

A clergyman unknown to me before that day, and probably to West as well, delivered, in practiced, unctuous tones, well-worn sentiments on the mystery of death and the bliss of the life to come. The choir delivered the appropriate hymns at the appropriate intervals.

No fewer than three eulogies were given. Dr. Welburn Bright, now over seventy and long retired, spoke sentimentally about young Dr. West and his brilliance, including his war record and innovative surgical techniques. I detected some muttering at this from the professional old guard. Then the current Dean of Medicine, who also happened to be the president of the Massachusetts Medical Association, which West had said was preparing to expel him, intoned a few platitudes whose perfunctory nature made me squirm. Then it was my turn.

I mounted the pulpit and stood for a moment regarding the congregation. The hundreds of faces merged into a blur, from which only four stood out – Sarah Enright, Mrs. Fisk, Hiram and Jeremy West. It was to them that I addressed my words.

In an episode of black humour, West had written a eulogy for himself as a kind of joke. In a way I wish I had been able to deliver it, but I could never have said with a straight face things like, 'Even as a student at Miskatonic University Medical School, Dr. West displayed a laudable concern for public morals, including those of his Dean.' Or, 'Dr. West was anxious to ensure that every citizen does his utmost for the cause of medical research, to the extent that he employed several individuals in this capacity after their demise, thus extending their productive lives.'

Instead, I spoke of his devotion to the prolonging and improving of life and his generosity. To those who could not afford specialized surgery, he had delivered his services at no cost. In conclusion, I said that with his death, a certain energy and optimism had vanished from among us.

To end the service, I had hired three students from the Miskatonic University Music School to perform excerpts from the string trio arrangement of Bach's *Goldberg Variations*. The brothers had objected, arguing that it was secular, irregular and a waste of time, but I insisted, emphasizing that it would take only ten minutes.

They did well, my three young players, considering how short a time they had rehearsed. They played the aria and the first three variations, then the aria once more. As the measured, beautiful melody unfolded, flowered and returned to its initial simplicity, I found myself giving in to the grief that had haunted me since that terrible morning, only three days before. I thought again of the deliberation with which West had gone about planning and executing his suicide. I thought of his final refusal to evade the horror of the things he had told me in his confession and his entire willingness to accept responsibility. Had this been courage or madness? I found that I no longer cared.

Two of the undertaker's men opened the casket so that the mourners could file past the body before they left the church. The crowd surged toward it with an eagerness that offended me. I hung back and scrutinized all individuals that were of a height and build similar to West's. It would be just like him, I thought, to turn up in disguise at his own funeral. There was no one that could have been he, but a pair of men, strangers to me, lingered for several minutes. One appeared to be urging the other to look at the corpse. Eventually they moved on.

The casket was carried out of the church by four minions of West's Funeral Home, large burly men curiously similar in appearance to one another, as though they had been selected for their physiques over other criteria. The pallbearers performed a largely symbolic role. They were men I remembered from West's dinner parties, John Billington among them. I looked at the odd combination of solemnity and excitement on their faces and wondered what they would think if they knew the truth.

Only his brothers and I went to the graveside. They had decided that he should be buried in the Derby family plot, beside his mother. On discovering that I was acquainted with Robert Derby, Hiram had asked me to negotiate this point with him. He had agreed easily, too easily, I thought. Looking at him, I realized that the lugubriousness I had seen several years ago had become a deep melancholy. I wondered how long it would be before he followed in his cousin Anna's footsteps, to Sefton Asylum or some similar place.

As I watched the casket being lowered into the earth, I noticed a movement some distance behind the onlookers standing across from me. A deeper shade had formed beneath the nearby trees, like a localized mist, except that there were faces in it, emerging and receding. In front of this shifting crowd was John Hocks. There was a kind of solemn triumph on his face and when he recognized me he nodded and winked. When I looked again, he was gone, as were his misty companions.

At first I allowed myself to interpret this weird visitation with hope: if Hocks had believed me when I told him to watch for West's funeral, he must not have tracked down and killed the true West. But surely he and his tribe of ghosts would have sensed that the man they sought was still alive. In that case their presence and Hocks's mocking wink may have signified that West was dead.

Later that day I attended a reception at the Boundary Street house. Mrs. Fisk and an army of helpers had been hired to prepare the rooms and provide refreshments. I remained in the background and observed the other guests as they engaged in their social pavanes. Several of them came over to me, eager to talk about West's passing. Most were sincere, but in a few faces I thought I saw an expectant curiosity.

One of these individuals was John Billington. "I have to admit," he said, "that I was shocked to hear of his death, especially after that talk we had. It's occurred to me since then that some of us who were friendly with him should have rallied around and helped him instead of leaving him at the mercy of his own extreme tendencies."

I thought: Too bad you didn't have these noble ideas a few weeks ago, when they might have done some good. After all, he only made you a gift of the practice that's providing you with a living. Aloud I said, "I'm sure Herbert would have appreciated that, but surely it couldn't have made any difference to the aneurysm that killed him?"

"Don't tell me you believe that aneurysm explanation," said Billington. "I'm as certain as I can be without evidence that he killed himself. It's only logical."

"Just because something is logical doesn't mean it's the truth," I replied. "And you're right about there being no evidence to support that notion. In fact, Billington, if I were you I wouldn't go around making allegations like that. You could get into trouble."

He was annoyed and soon went on his way. I decided I was tired of the charade and was about to make my farewells, when I came face to face with Professor Hobson. I intended to elude him after the barest of social amenities, but soon realized that he wanted to introduce me to someone. "Sir Edward," he said, "this is Charles Milburn. He was a friend of Dr. West's. Mr. Milburn, I would like you to meet Sir Edward Clapham-Lee."

I studied the Englishman's face as I shook his hand. Yes, there was a resemblance between him and my memory of the officer I had met in this very room nine years before. He had the same narrow, quintessentially English face, with its high forehead, long nose and receding dark hair. Then I turned my gaze to the older man who stood a little behind him, a man whom Hobson had not troubled to introduce. He seemed old, but could not yet have been sixty, surely? His manner was vague and he did not engage in any conversation, merely gazed about with an amiable but empty look on his face. His face... I studied it as closely as politeness permitted, but saw nothing that suggested a family relationship between him and the younger man. But neither could I see any evidence that his features had been altered surgically. Was this the man who had been found wandering nameless and without memories in a military hospital in France? Was this in fact Sir Eric Moreland Clapham-Lee?

Edward Clapham-Lee regarded me with as much curiosity as I had him and his companion. "I'm delighted to meet you, Mr. Milburn," he said. "My associate here was in France with the Canadian Army at the same time as Dr. West. Unfortunately he's an amnesiac as a result of his war experiences. I'm trying to help him recover his identity. I thought that perhaps Dr. West might have mentioned something in his letters to you that could be of help. It would have been late in 1917 or early 1918."

I looked him straight in the eye and lied. As far as the world was concerned, Herbert West was dead. I had not gone through the anguish of the past week only to turn around and help his enemies, no matter how good their cause. "I'm very sorry," I said. "I have no recollection of his mentioning such an individual in any of his letters to me. And unfortunately, I have not kept the letters, so it's impossible to go back and look."

After this, there was little between us to sustain a conversation, and the pair soon departed. I realized as I watched them go that it must have been they who had paused so long by the open casket. No memories had been triggered, it seemed, by the sight of West's double, but my last sight of the two Englishmen was revelatory. From behind, with their faces invisible to me, the resemblance between them was unmistakable – it was in their stance, the way they held their heads, the way they moved. The younger man held his father's arm to help him down the stairs. I watched them out of sight, but I had no intention of following them with my burden of knowledge.

The day after the funeral, once I was sure that the West brothers had left Arkham, I went to Herbert's house again. Thoughts of the flask containing his blood had been troubling me. I would have to dispose of it somehow, for left as it was, its contents would undergo the loathsome changes of putrescence. I had dreamt more than once that West had stood before me, pale and gaunt, looking at me reproachfully. "In the blood is the life," a voice intoned. But it was not his voice.

The prospect of returning to the scene of his revivification filled me with a mixture of dread and irrational hope. In truth, I still expected to find his corpse.

To my relief, the electricity in West's house was still working. I switched on the lights over the cellar stairs and descended. In the laboratory, my eyes went immediately to the table where West's body had lain.

A body lay there again. I nearly screamed when it sat up and turned toward me. Then I recognized John Hocks. "What are you doing here?" I asked, masking my fear with anger.

He looked better, less cadaverous and decently dressed in a suit, with shirt, vest, necktie and all. My first thought was that he must have taken the clothing from West's wardrobe. His voice was distinct but faint, as though it came from a distance.

"Well, well, it's Mr. Charles, Dr. West's friend! Good evening to you, sir! As for what I am doing here, well, I was resting. In peace. No harm done, I assure you. And what about you? Why are you here? Looking for your friend? Don't you know he's gone? There's no one here but *us*." He grinned at me, sitting tailor-fashion on the table.

"I'm here to make sure everything is in order, the way Dr. West would want it to be," I said. "How did you get in, Hocks?"

"Oh, I have my ways. And that's a good thing, since no one tells me the truth. Not even you, Mr. Charles." He slid off the table and came toward me, shaking a finger.

"I figured it out, even before I came in here, and when I did, well, it was crystal clear, in a manner of speaking."

"What are you talking about?"

"Dr. West, of course. I would have said 'the late Dr. West,' but he isn't, is he? Not late at all, but alive again. That wasn't him they put in that hole in the ground. You can't fool me, not anymore. We're going to hit the road soon, we Friends of Herbert West. We're going to find him and make him remember us. We'll be with him every night, sing him lullabies, tell him stories, give him interesting dreams. Some day he'll know he shouldn't have interfered with us."

"He already knows that, Hocks. He told me so, before he died, and I told you."

"But he didn't tell *me*, or the others. It's not your business any more. You have other concerns now."

His manner had changed; he was stern and dignified, and I realized that I could see shelves and a bunsen burner that were behind him, as though he was transparent. He reached over and picked up the flask containing West's blood. "This is what you came for, isn't it? I said I would give you a present. Well, here it is."

I tried not to look at the flask, but I could tell that its contents were a very dark colour.

"What makes you think I came for that? What is it, anyway?" I wasn't prepared for Hocks to be so perspicacious.

"His blood, of course. The blood of the necromancer. A precious substance. As his assistant, you are the inheritor."

"And who are you? You're not really John Hocks, are you?"

"It took you long enough to figure that out, didn't it, Charles Milburn? Yes, I know your name, but you don't know mine. Not all of them, anyway."

"Where is he?" I asked, trying to keep my voice steady. "Since you know so much, can you tell me that?"

"Where is who?" said the Hocks-thing, mockingly. He grinned. "All right, I'll stop playing games. You want me to tell you where Herbert West is, so you can go rushing after him.

Well, I won't do that. He has to remake himself without you. He's finished with you."

"Will I ever see him again?"

"Maybe. It depends." He held out the flask. "That's enough talk. Take this and listen to me. Come back here in ten days and you will see what there is to be seen. If you choose. It's up to you."

I had to obey. I went over and took the flask from his hand. As my fingers closed around its neck, he vanished. I heard a sound like a gust of wind, and the clang of a distant door closing.

The flask felt warm in my hand. Moments before, it had been full of dark red blood, but now the liquid was black, bubbling and heaving behind the glass. I set it down with a shudder and ran for the door.

A lighthearted jaunt to Cape Cod was out of the question, but I had to get away from Arkham. After a little thought I gathered together a few necessities and went to Kingsport.

There were a few boarding houses in the old town, mainly for summer visitors. It was to one of these that I went, an old house, seemingly ramshackle but solid enough, clinging to the steep hillside like a barnacle. The landlady showed me to a white-painted room at the far end of the house. One of its two windows looked north to the great cliffs, the other east to the ocean.

When I had unpacked my few belongings, I sat down in a chair by the eastern window and looked out to sea. I felt something like peace for the first time in days – since I had lain on the cliff near here, only one week before.

Then, inexplicably, I had a strong sense of West's presence. It was as though he had come into the room. The door was closed but the atmosphere was charged with his peculiar energy and the still air rippled with an invisible current.

"Herbert?" I spoke aloud, without constraint. "Are you here? What happened to you? Please tell me."

As suddenly as it had come, the feeling vanished and I felt foolish, talking to the air. But it had been so strong. I wondered again if he were dead, and this had been the final leave-taking of his spirit.

As I was preparing for bed that first night, I noticed something. The sheets and pillowslips were clean and smelled of sea air and wood smoke but to the counterpane there clung, very faintly, the scent of narcissus.

I slept well that night, and all the subsequent nights of my stay in that place. I had no dreams, or if I did retained no memory of them.

For a week I laid down the burden of speculation and lived only in the present. I spent the days wandering Kingsport's crooked streets, occasionally talking with some of the inhabitants, or sitting on the wharf, my mind rendered blank by sun and salty air. Once I climbed up one of the cliffs to see the town from above and to feel again the strange charm of the high places.

On the last day of my sojourn, as I walked slowly along the strip of beach that divided the cliffs from the tidal zone, I saw something shining silver among the pebbles and picked it up. It was a button, a rather odd one, with an elaborate pattern of twisting and interlocking shapes. I caught my breath. West had had a jacket with buttons just like this one. He had told me that he had them imported from Spain, and that the pattern was thought to be Celtic in origin, with a connection to a pagan god of medicine. I wondered what the chances were of someone else having buttons like these.

That evening, I sought out my landlady. Had someone else from Arkham stayed in the house recently? No, she said, I was the first visitor from Arkham in several weeks. It occurred to me then that West, if he had been here, must have named some other place as his point of origin. I gave a brief description of him and asked if someone like that had been a guest recently. She thought hard but could not be sure. For several days she had been ill and her husband had dealt with the guests. She would ask him.

A while later, when I had nearly given up, she returned. Yes, her husband remembered a fellow who looked like the one I had described. He'd stayed three nights and left the day before I arrived. Her husband thought the fellow was sick. "Looked like death was peering over his shoulder. Good thing he had that French fellow with him," was how he'd put it. He had mostly stayed in his room, which, she said, was the one I had now. The other man seemed to be his servant. Where had they gone? She didn't know. They had settled their bill and left without saying anything about their destination.

Back in my room, I sat by the window, watching darkness gather over the ocean. He had been here, and Andre with him. I realized now that Andre must have been part of West's plan. He must have coached him in his role, just as he had me. I could not find it in myself to resent this deception. He had been preparing for something that would be unthinkable to most people. Who could blame him for hedging his bets? At least I could lay aside my fears that he was dead in a ditch.

I searched the room thoroughly, looking for another sign of his presence, however trivial, but there was nothing. He could not have known, after all, that I would come here.

When I got back to Arkham, I found a story in one of the newspapers that had accumulated in my absence: *Wild Man Dead*, said the headline. *The corpse of the so-called Wild Man of Arkham, recently escaped from Sefton Asylum, was found in a wooded area near Christ Church Cemetery. The state of the body indicated that death occurred several days ago, probably the result of starvation and exposure. In 1911 this individual was confined in Sefton after killing four people. The true name and antecedents of the unfortunate wretch remain unknown. His body was buried in the potter's field at Hangman's Hill.*

The next day I forced myself to return to West's laboratory. It was ten days since the disturbing encounter with the entity that was not Hocks. I hoped it had been a hallucination and for proof went back to look at the flask, fully expecting to find the repulsive results of advanced decomposition.

The flask was where I had left it, but now it contained a substance like wax or resin, pale yellow in colour and faintly aromatic, redolent of spices or exotic herbs. I looked at it for a long time, thinking that someone must have switched flasks, but who?

Wondering if I should have the substance analysed by a chemist, I set the vessel down. As the glass touched the surface of the laboratory bench, there was a faint but distinct crack. The flask broke neatly into three parts, which fell apart with a musical tinkle. Among them gleamed a lump of purest gold.

♦ **22** ♦

Our gold is not the common gold.
Rosarium philosophorum

I was still in a fragile condition when I came home from work one day to find Alma literally on my doorstep, talking with Marcus Desmond, my landlord.

While they finished their conversation, I had a moment to observe her. She looked different. She had had her hair cut and was wearing some fashionably shapeless garment. I could not tell whether these changes were improvements but resented them just the same. They seemed to challenge me in some way, to make demands to which I felt unequal.

I invited her inside and offered her a drink. She took a cigarette and an amber cigarette holder from her bag and spent a few moments fitting them together. In the not so distant past I would have seen this only as an opportunity for some lighthearted teasing. Now I thought how ridiculous it was that she would take such pains to appear sophisticated.

"I'm afraid I've acquired this disgusting habit," she said, but did not seem particularly regretful. "You look funny, Charles." She blew a cloud of smoke toward the ceiling. "Sunburnt and sort of worn. What have you been up to?"

"Lazing around in Kingsport for a week." I shrugged. "It should have been the Cape, but after West's funeral I didn't feel up to that. I would have asked you to come, but you were away."

"Yes, Chicago for the past three weeks. It seemed like three years. Not my favourite town. I would have much preferred the Cape, with you. I was sorry to hear of his death, Charles, for your sake."

"But not for his sake, obviously." I felt suddenly angry. "You never could bring yourself to admit that he had some good qualities, could you? And now you're probably thinking 'Good riddance, but isn't it a pity that poor Charles has lost his best friend.'"

"Don't be so touchy! No, I didn't like him much, but I admit that he had some good qualities. Almost everyone has a few. I meant to say that I was sorry not to be at the funeral, again for your sake."

"That's perfectly all right, Alma. I managed, with a little help from his brothers." Yes, I managed, I thought. I managed to drag him back from death, after watching him kill himself first. Then I managed to lose him forever. Oh, you don't know the half of it, Miss Halsey, so keep your pity to yourself.

I should have made some excuse to cut short this unfortunate visit and see her at some later time when I was feeling less sensitive. But I didn't. And Alma, with her usual zest for facts to string together pressed on, seemingly unaware of my growing anger.

"Those two!" she said, referring to the West brothers. "They regularly make headlines in Boston. Hiram the businessman and Jeremy the crook. And Herbert – you know, I've heard some very strange rumours about his death."

"Oh? And what might those be?" I tried to sound uninterested, but felt a rising apprehension.

"Everything from a drug overdose to suicide to murder. Six months ago, I would have thought any of those to be pretty unlikely. Except murder, maybe."

I choked down a reprehensible comment and remained silent.

"So is there any truth to them?" she asked finally, when she saw that I wasn't about to volunteer a reply.

"I'm surprised you'd even bother to ask. It seems you have some very loquacious friends here in Arkham, with vivid imaginations. I can imagine who some of them are. But listen to me – if I see so much as a hint, a *hint*, mind you, in anything you publish that the death of Herbert West was by causes other than natural, I will sue you for libel so fast you won't know what hit you."

"I see I've hit a nerve," she said, getting up. "I think I'd better go. But before I do, I'd like to say something: if he hadn't had the good fortune to die when he did, your friend West would have eventually been revealed to be just as much a criminal as the rest of his family. I wouldn't be surprised to find he'd done more than one murder himself. So I'm giving you a choice – our friendship or tending a shrine to Herbert West. Think about it and give me a telephone call when you've decided. But I've read the text of that eulogy you gave. If you were the Pope, he'd be canonized already, I guess. So I won't hold my breath."

She picked up her handbag and left. I heard the sound of her heels tapping down the stairs, then silence.

After this, Arkham became hateful to me. I felt there was a widening gulf between myself and the community in which I had lived and worked for more than twelve years. I thought that friends and colleagues were avoiding me or looking at me strangely and discussing me in ways I should not have been happy to hear. My state of mental health was less than robust. I can see that now, but at the time I felt that I was trapped in a glass bubble filled with a poisoned atmosphere.

I became increasingly isolated. Friends turned away after I repeatedly refused their invitations or lashed out at them in unreasoning anger. Sarah Enright had moved to California in pursuit of adventure and opportunities. I was in a worse position than West shortly before his downfall, for at least he had had me.

Thoughts of him brought no comfort. That winter, as I walked in the dim evenings across the campus or in certain narrow streets of the town, I felt I was being followed. I would turn around quickly only to see no one behind me (except perhaps the suggestion of a dark shape disappearing around a corner). Even as I looked for Herbert West in any stranger I met, I feared that one day I would indeed meet him, face to face with only the cold winter air between us. What might he have become since his death? I did not know which would be worse – to see the face I had known so well transformed by evil and violent intent, or empty of reason and cognizance, a blank mirror reflecting nothing.

On bad nights I would think about what might happen if I found him, alive but impaired in mind and body. I imagined us wandering over the land, from town to city to village, weary but fearful of pursuit and capture. *Again and again, I try to teach him his name, but fail. Every night I watch him sleep only to wake in terror, clutching me, whimpering. Until the last awakening in the last of a thousand dirty rooms. His gaze is fixed on me, empty as ever. I scrabble for the pistol that has been years-long ballast in the never-unpacked bag of my possessions; I aim and fire, twice.*

By the spring of 1924, I had had enough. I tendered my resignation to Dr. Armitage and accepted a position at Harvard College. It was of a lower rank than the one I was leaving and Cambridge was a more expensive place than Arkham in which to live, but I did not care. Like West, I wanted a fresh start, a *tabula rasa.*

One of my last acts as a librarian at Miskatonic University was highly reprehensible. Even now I have twinges of professional guilt. I visited the Quarrington Room by night, to look for the last time at the document correlating names to the codes used in Quarrington's Profiles and Predictions. Unfortunately, I had a small accident with a bottle of indelible ink which should never have been brought into the room in the first place. Only a small area was affected, on the last page of the document. And when I departed, the file labelled DX.37-31-59 went with me.

On my last day in Arkham, I visited the Derby plot at Christ Church Cemetery. For a long time I stood regarding a grave on which the headstone had been placed only a few months before. The carving and inscription on it were familiar to me, for I had myself commissioned them. It had been necessary to make a particularly generous contribution to the Cemetery Improvement Fund in order to overcome official objections to the image on the grey granite stone – a serpent devouring its own tail, the alchemical symbol for unity, for eternity. The inscription said

Herbert Francis West
1886-1923
Life from Death.

I had done everything I could. I laid a sheaf of lilies on the grave and went away.

Part 4

PROVIDENCE

My story might well have ended with my departure from Arkham, were it not for recent events that have made necessary this bridge of words, linking that time with this, 1923 with 1938. The waters spanned by that bridge may have seemed placid and shallow but in truth were full of deep whirlpools and sunken debris.

I was never quite able to stop wondering what happened to Herbert West. This was the centre of the spiral, the ultimate source of pain, the wound that refused to heal. In that cataclysmic week of July 1923, I discovered within myself the 'resonant link' created or identified by Quarrington. It was powerful and disturbing – a bond of love, both that which in Greek is called *agape*, the exaltation of friendship, and the fiery and volatile *eros*. Our separate fates had converged and become entangled for some purpose beyond my understanding. When I performed the ceremony of revivification in the secret chamber I felt, no, I *knew* that I was an instrument in the hand of another power. I had yielded myself to it for the sake of friendship and love, but when my work was done, I was allowed to fall back to earth while West flew away like the phoenix from its fiery nest, never looking back at the broken tool left behind.

In the years immediately following his disappearance, I had a recurring dream: I entered a room, sometimes the bedroom in which he died, sometimes a room I had never seen before, very bright, with a view of the distant sea. I went in and he turned toward me and held out his arms. I embraced him with joy,thinking, *At last, at last!* He threw back his head and smiled at me. As though for the first time, I saw his beautiful face transformed by passion. He closed his eyes, murmuring, "Kiss me, Charles." But invariably, as I bent to place my mouth on his, I awoke. At first this dream came several times a year, leaving me, for a day or two, agitated but happy, restless and excited. As the years passed I experienced it less frequently, then not at all.

When the dream left me I thought, Now I have lost completely the secret glory of life. Now all that remains is to grow old. But all these years later, a few fragments of the old magic remain. Sometimes when I listen to music, or at the fall of an evening in spring, when the very air seems green and the mingled fragrances of growth and blooming steal into my window, I experience again a little of that ecstatic certainty.

Long ago, West explained to me that energy is stored in chemical bonds and that the breaking of those bonds releases it into the world. I wonder if something analogous happens with human experiences, with lives, with relationships. In the seething welter of human interactions, as friendships are formed and broken, as passions are felt and expressed, vast amounts of psychic energy must be released. Where does it go? How is it used? I do not know, but find a little comfort in the thought that some unknown force must control these dynamics, just as the known cycle of organic growth and decay drives physical life. Even as the rotting leaves in Michael O'Connor's compost heaps sustained the flowers in my mother's gardens, so perhaps the breaking of the bonds between Alma, Herbert and myself, the hidden turmoils of our lives, the energies released when body and spirit part, in some way served to sustain the eternal mystery. Or so I hope.

****

It began again a few weeks ago, with an engraved invitation in the mail:

Miskatonic University
Anniversary Reunion
1738-1938
All alumni, faculty and staff, present and former, are cordially invited to join in celebrating two hundred years. An opportunity to reunite with old friends and colleagues...

Something made me pause as I was about to put the invitation into the fire. Perhaps it was the familiar MU crest, perhaps the thought of old friends and colleagues striking a warm note in a life that has not been overly blessed with either. After some thought, I replied that I should be delighted to attend.

When I went to the bank to withdraw funds for my journey, on impulse I also obtained access to the small box of valuables I kept in the vault. I removed West's emerald ring and put it on my finger. After I left Arkham, I had intended to show it to an expert in order to find out more about its ultimate origin. But something made me change my mind. The more I looked at it, the more I became convinced that it should be kept secret. I was afraid that its strangeness would be revealed as a cheap sham, or that it was a genuine rarity that would attract unwelcome attention to me. Above all, I felt in some obscure way that its time had not yet come, so I had put it away and forgotten it.

It was a shock to see how little Arkham had changed since 1924. As I entered the city centre I began to see differences – a few buildings gone or radically altered. But the city's profile on the skyline was unchanged. At one and the same time I experienced a sense of homecoming and the strangeness of arrival in a place unknown. If I had come by train, the illusion would have been nearly perfect – almost I might have been my young self, newly arrived to take up my post at Miskatonic University Library in 1910.

The first day there was a speech by the President of the University, followed by a reception and a concert. By then I had already encountered a number of former colleagues. To my surprise, they greeted me with apparent eagerness. This confirmed that my last days at Miskatonic had been distorted by pain and anxiety. I was heartened by these encounters, but they were not the reason I had come to Arkham.

The following day I visited the Library. The old building was still there, but had acquired a few more architectural excrescences. Not only was the marriage of styles not a happy one, the new wings had spoiled the proportions of the college quadrangle, but I had to agree that the additional space gained thereby was welcome.

I was secretly glad to see that the Cataloguing Department still occupied its old quarters. The Department Head, a formidably well-educated young woman conversant with all the latest theories, showed me around my old haunts. I had not been away from my work long enough to lose the ability to talk shop, and did so with considerable enjoyment.

I debated with myself whether to visit the *Necronomicon* in its vault of steel. In the end I decided against it. Whatever role it had played in my life was finished. I had no desire to experience again the unsettling effect it had had on me many years before. The link that had been forged by its power had either dissolved forever long ago or still existed.

Instead, I wandered the streets of Arkham, indulging in memories. It was just after four in the afternoon when I set out. The day had been cool and bright but now fog was gathering on the river and seeping along the streets. I could see the taller buildings of the central area and the spires of several churches floating above the mist. There was a blueness in the air, a colour that spoke of clearness and yet imposed itself between my vision and the things I looked at. I remembered what I had seen from the window of West's study the night before his death, and knew that this would be no ordinary stroll down memory lane. After a while I was no longer sure whether it was 1938 or 1923 or 1911 or some other year altogether.

From my old rooms on Peabody Street, I proceeded to French Hill, where Alma had lived, then along College. I felt that a throng of my old selves followed me – the Charles Milburn who had been West's trusting assistant, the one who had been Alma Halsey's lover, the guilt-ridden being who had wrestled with the dilemma of friendship with a murderer. I watched him kiss Alma with a hungry eagerness, gaze in distress at the death-struggles of Robert Leavitt, and read letters from France that contained more than he wanted to admit to himself.

As I was passing the mass of buildings that was St. Mary's Hospital, I noticed a movement on the opposite side of the street. Three men, coming toward me. The third was rather the worse for drink, it seemed, and was being supported by his companions. Suddenly, one of them began to sing. The tune was that of the national anthem, but the words were different. I kept on my way, and they on theirs. I did not interfere with them, even if that were possible. I had no desire now to see John Hocks revivified, nor to join in the hunt for him afterwards.

Before I knew it, I was standing in front of West's house on Boundary. It was still there, the abyss of his death and the crucible from which he had been reborn. I almost expected it to glow with hidden fires. But it was only a house.

It had been smartened up with new paint and an elaborate brass knocker. There were two name plates on the wall beside the door: Law Office, one said. Donald R. Murray. The other said James Foster, M.D. I was about to turn away when someone emerged, a fellow of about forty, carrying a medical bag.

"Dr. Foster, I presume?" I asked.

"Yes. Is there something I can do for you? I'm just leaving for the day, but..."

"I'm revisiting old haunts here in Arkham, and I wonder if you could tell me anything about this house."

"You used to live here?" There was a gleam of interest in his eye.

"No, but a friend of mine did – Dr. Herbert West. He died many years ago."

"Herbert West," he said. "I believe someone mentioned that name when I bought the place ten years ago. He died here, in the house, is that right?"

"Yes, in 1923. He lived on the second floor. You must like the house, though, since you've stayed here as long as you have."

"It suits me. The offices are just what I need for my practice, and it's handy to the hospital. And the rooms above bring in a little rent every month. Now, if it's ghosts you're looking for, you should talk to Murray, my tenant. I doubt if he would have seen anything, though. He's a hard-headed young fellow." He laughed, showing white teeth that gleamed in the dusk.

"Oh, I'm not thinking about ghosts," I said. "Merely looking for old memories. Do you get much use from the cellar?"

"Hardly at all. There isn't much to it, is there? Just that little storage room behind the furnace. But it suits me as it is. Now you must excuse me."

He hurried off and was soon lost in the shadows. So the hidden rooms had not been discovered, either by Foster or whoever had owned the house before him. Possibly not by West's brothers, either. I wondered again where he had spent the hours between my last sight of him and his departure. And where was he now? To these questions the gathering dusk gave no answer.

Where now, indeed? My hotel was on River Street. The logical route would be to follow Boundary Street northwards, but a small detour would take me to Hangman's Hill. My pilgrimage would be incomplete without a visit to that place. I was growing tired but was determined to see the thing to its end.

In the graveyard I could just see the markers and one or two freshly made mounds. As far as I could tell, the place was much the same as it had been in 1911. I could not tell which grave was that of John Hocks.

I turned toward the wood that lay between me and the road. Among the trees I thought I saw figures moving. They manifested into discernable entities as I drew nearer. At first I could not imagine what they were, but then I knew. They were West's mindless creatures, aimlessly wandering. Why here? I wondered. Had he brought their ashes here, not wanting, despite his disavowal of such fancies, to have them near his house? I tried to count them, but was unable to fix on any one long enough. They walked without purpose, without destination or awareness, of me or of one another. Two or three of them came near enough that I saw their faces. They were recognizably human, but as empty of expression as stones. Neither joy nor hatred, fear nor pain, could trouble them ever again. He had been right about that. So what was it about these beings that froze my heart? Was it that they were capable of movement, unlike other things entirely without mind? Yes, it was their incompleteness that made them travesties of human life. This perversion of the life force for his own purposes must surely have weighed heavily against him. But it was no longer for me to reckon that up. I had made my choice fifteen years before and could not change it now. Hardly knowing what I did, I began to say the Prayer for the Dead. I bent down and picked up a handful of earth, scattering it over the place where I had seen the wandering shapes. This was all I could do. I turned away and bent my steps toward the lights on River Street.

On my last day in Arkham I went to Christ Church Cemetery, even though I was fully aware that it was not my friend who lay in the grave marked with his name. There is something in human nature that demands a tangible monument, and this one was as good as any. If it wasn't Herbert West who lay under that stone, it was certainly a good part of myself. For all I knew, West had no grave as yet, except the one within himself, and, in a strange way, the house on Boundary Street. But that was an empty grave.

I made my way to the Derby plot and found the stone. Grey granite, with his name and dates. The self-devouring serpent. 'Life from Death.' There were flowers on the grave – a few purple asters and some bronze-coloured chrysanthemums. Who had put them there?

I stood for a while, wondering. Then I heard steps behind me, and a voice.

"Still tending the shrine, I see, Charles." I turned around and saw Alma Halsey.

Like me, she was middle-aged, in her early fifties, still slender, with an elegance that I did not remember. Her hair was more silver than blonde but her eyes seemed bluer by contrast, and had lost nothing of their clarity and sharpness.

"Alma," I said, "you're here after all."

"I've been avoiding you, Charles," she replied in her forthright way. "I wasn't sure you'd want to see me again, even though it's been so long. Ironic that we should meet here, isn't it?" She indicated the grave. "Wasn't he a Christian, Herbert West? That looks more like a pagan symbol to me. I'm surprised it was allowed."

"I had to do some serious negotiations to get permission to put the stone here. And no, it's not exactly a Christian symbol, even though it stands for eternity. West wasn't a Christian, not at all."

"An atheist, I suppose?"

"An agnostic, I think. He didn't deny the existence of God, in theory, but without direct experience consigned God to the unknowable. But did you come here to...? Those flowers..."

"I came to see my parents' graves. But yes, I put those there. I thought I owed him an apology. You too, Charles." She laughed, sounding embarrassed. "It was a shock to see you here, big as life. I nearly slunk away, but knew that would pretty well negate my noble intentions."

I went closer to her. "Alma, all that is in the past. It doesn't matter any more."

"But it does. It does. Sometimes it seems to matter more than the present."

I was surprised at her words and the sorrowful way in which she said them. She had always been the optimist, the forward-looking one who had jollied me out of gloomy thoughts.

"Not true. Look, I have my car here. Suppose we go and have dinner somewhere. It's a little early, but the past needs to be diluted with the present. And some good food and wine."

"All right, Charles." She laughed. "Oh, I'm so glad you turned up!. I should have known better than to come here alone." Already she seemed more cheerful.

In a restaurant on River Street (which may have been called Da Vinci's once), I encouraged Alma to talk about herself as we waited for our meals to come. She had had an interesting life, moving from place to place, newspaper to newspaper.

"Finally I got sick of being rootless," she said. "Now I teach in the School of Journalism at Columbia and do some freelancing. I have more time to think and lately I've been thinking a lot about you and our friendship, all those years ago."

"And what have you concluded?" I asked, trying to inject some lightness into my tone. I was afraid she would fall again into the mood of melancholy I had seen at the cemetery.

"That I never did understand you. I thought I knew what was good for you, and when you seemed to think differently, I resented that. And there's something I should have told you right from the start."

"What, Alma?"

"The real reason I resented Herbert West. Years ago, when he was an undergraduate at Miskatonic, I audited some courses – math and biology. About 1906 or '07, this would have been. West was in one of the biology classes. I couldn't help but notice him."

I nodded. I knew what she meant.

"I guess I became infatuated with him," Alma continued. "It was his intelligence, his style, his joy in argument, his beauty. I even wrote him a poem, a sonnet. It was meant to be a kind of intellectual tribute, but... I guess my emotions showed. I gave it to West in class one day.

"He read it and handed it back to me, very politely. 'I must thank you for the compliment this represents, Miss Halsey, but I cannot accept it,' he said. I asked why not, logically enough. He said, 'I don't want you to cherish any illusions about me. To me you are nothing more than an intellect. I'm sorry, but that's the way it is.' Then he walked away. I was mortified. I thought he had insulted me. I quit the class and avoided him afterward, which was easy enough. When I heard he had entered the Med. School, I went out of my way to put him in a bad light to Papa every chance I got. I convinced myself he was a bad sort, and you have to admit he did himself no favours a lot of the time. But when I told you he wasn't my type, I was telling the truth, because by then I had convinced myself of that."

I thought for a moment. "I think you misunderstood him. He was trying to tell you something about himself, not insulting you."

"Oh, and what might that have been?"

"Well, that he wasn't interested in any sort of romantic involvement. But not because of anything specific, you understand. Not only you, any young woman would have gotten that sort of reaction, I think."

"Hmm. I wondered about that, later. I thought he was just cold and stuck up, but you're telling me he wasn't attracted to women at all, is that right?"

"That's it. He didn't want to give you the wrong impression, but there's no easy way to say something like that."

"Hmm," she said again, with a strange little smile. "Well, Charles, I must say I didn't expect these insights from you. You certainly are a deep one."

"Is that better than a Romantic? You and Herbert were always calling me that. You never married, then?"

"No. My life's been too unsettled. I was always racing off somewhere. I have to admit there were times I was happy to have my work as an excuse."

"Well, there you are. You made the choices that seemed best at the time."

"And you? You're still a bachelor? Why do I ask? It's written all over you."

I was not sure what she meant by that. I am rather proud of my ability to keep myself presentable. I decided that it must have been my air of self-sufficiency to which she referred.

"Yes, but unlike you I cannot plead an unsettled life. If anything, mine has been too settled. I suppose I'm just not the marrying type."

She looked at me for a moment. "So while I was gallivanting around Europe after the War, you and West were still bosom buddies? I was jealous of him, you know, even when you and I were lovers. I somehow felt all along that his claim on you was greater than mine."

I tried to give her part of the truth, at least. "At times, I suppose. But there were plenty of times when I hardly saw him for weeks on end. I suppose I became a little muddled about some things after you left."

She shook her head. "What a pair we are. Or aren't, rather. Charles, why didn't we get married?"

"You were too busy trying not to conform. And I – well, I don't know. Perhaps I just didn't relish acquiring a mother-in-law."

She laughed out loud. "Oh Charles! She was rather awful to you, that time I introduced you. Things were so different then, weren't they? Sometimes I look back and wonder what I should have done differently. It's as though I missed a turn somewhere. Do you ever feel that way?"

What could I say? Between us lay the gulf of lies I had created even when we were lovers and friends. I had never told her about my involvement with West's experiments, or the dark roads down which I had followed him. As far as Alma Halsey was concerned, the grave on which she had placed her propitiatory flowers that day was indeed the final resting place of Herbert West.

I knew that if I wanted to reestablish any kind of relationship with her I would have to tell her the truth. But until I knew that West was indeed dead, dead for the second time, finally and forever, I was not at liberty to do that. I knew Alma – her sharp mind and talent for spotting patterns. Retired from journalism or not, she would not be able to resist the allure of the story. It was ironic – if there was anyone who might be able to help me find out what had happened to West, it was she. And I could not tell her. Despite the softening of her attitude toward him, I feared that for her the search would become a crusade to bring a criminal to belated justice. I could not permit this. Not after the agonies of my own choices. Not until I knew what he had done with the life I had helped restore to him. So I looked right into her blue eyes and said,

"Yes, I often feel that I'm an entirely different person from the one I was all those years ago. I remember things I said and did, and it's like watching a stranger. I've felt that pretty strongly these past few days, walking around Arkham. You know, sometimes I think we need two chances to be young. One for practice, then a second one after we've learned a thing or two, so we can finally get it right."

"So you feel that way too. I wonder if it's another effect of growing older. We don't get another chance, though. But it's not too late, surely, to change things, even now?"

She looked so forlorn that I nearly wavered in my resolve. I nearly said, "Alma, I don't know whether it's too late or not. I won't know that until I know what happened to him." Instead, I took her hand and said, "Alma, it's never too late, not while we are alive."

I thought I saw a gleam of tears in her eyes, which she attempted to conceal by looking down at our joined hands on the table. She said, "That ring you're wearing – it's beautiful, but very odd. Where did you get it, if you don't mind my asking?"

I did mind, rather, but decided to tell her the truth. When it came to this ring, the truth at my disposal was limited. "From West, actually," I said. "He left it to me in his will. His piano, his books and this ring. I think his mother gave it to him, but where she got it is anyone's guess."

"I see," she said. "Or rather, I don't, but it certainly is unusual. The funny thing is, I'm sure I've seen something rather like it before. Not a ring, but jewellery with similar patterns. I can't remember where, exactly." She looked closely at my face, and seemed about to ask me something else, but thought better of it.

We went on, then, to speak of other things. That, at least, had not changed. Alma and I had always been able to talk to one another. Except that last time in Arkham, of course.

As we prepared to leave the restaurant, she said, "Oh, before I forget – I have something for you – a letter from someone who must have lost touch with you when you moved from Arkham."

"Oh really, now who could that be?"

"Just a minute. I have it in my bag. Yes, here it is. It's from someone called Francis Dexter, in Providence." She held out the letter to me.

I took it from her, and it was as though an enormous mechanism moved in the heart of the world and a door swung open that had been closed for fifteen years. I did not need to look at the handwriting on the envelope. My primary effort was directed to maintaining a neutral expression as I glanced at the letter and put it in my pocket. But my heart was beating so hard I was sure she could hear it. Francis Dexter, of Providence...

"Hmm, I wonder who that could be. The name isn't familiar. How did you come by this, Alma?" I had to distract her. Would the supposed fact of his death withstand the quickness of her mind? We had met by the grave, with his full name inscribed on the stone before us.

"It was here in Arkham, two or three months ago. I was walking down College, past where you used to live, when who should come out of the house but Marcus Desmond. I hadn't seen him in years, but he asked me in for a visit as though it had been just the week before. We talked for a while, and then he asked if I ever saw you, because he had a letter for you. It had arrived a few weeks before. It was lucky he remembered it before it got buried in some heap of papers. I guess he must have had a forwarding address for you once, but probably lost it. You know Marcus. Anyway, I said I didn't see much of you these days, living in New York and all, but he insisted I take it. 'You get around more than I do, Alma,' he said. 'I'm sure you'll see Charles before long.' Well, it occurred to me if I needed an excuse to look you up, this was as good a one as any, so I took it. And last week when I was getting ready for this trip I remembered it and brought it along. And here you are."

By now we had come to the hotel where she was staying. "It's been wonderful to see you again, Alma," I said. "I hope we don't lose touch again. We may not get a second chance to be young again, but I hope we may have a second chance at friendship. And the next time we see each other, I may have a story to tell you." She looked at me questioningly, and seemed about to say something, but before she could, I kissed her cheek and said good night.

Then I went to my own room to read his letter.

****

Kingsport again. I drove out here before starting on my journey, so I could watch the sunrise and think about the future. I slept fitfully last night. I could not stop thinking, doubting, wondering, hoping. Finally, at four o'clock I gave up, packed my belongings and settled my bill with the sleepy fellow at the desk.

The morning mist is rising from a turquoise sea as smooth as glass, and on the far horizon a bank of purple clouds is edged with flame. The day is full of promise. I should have a pleasant drive south.

All of my night thoughts come down to a single question: who is Francis Dexter? Is he only Herbert West under a different name? I do not think so. Has he become, as Quarrington predicted, one who has power in his hands, yet subjects himself to a greater power? West acknowledged no powers greater than logic and mechanism. But as I read his letter, I thought I could hear echoes of the old prognosticator. Could it be that in the transformation from West to Dexter some other inheritance has been bestowed? Even his handwriting is different. I have read the letter so many times already that I have memorized parts of it, especially the last few paragraphs:

Certain things of which I am not now at liberty to speak have persuaded me that the resonant link between us is as valid a force now as it was in 1923 and before. You know what was achieved by that power years ago. I think that before I die my second death I will need to call upon it again.

In a way, that ultimate experiment we performed in 1923 went on for years, perhaps is still going on. I can say with perfect truth that I have been remade. Is Francis Dexter a better man than Herbert West? I think so, but the ultimate judgment is no longer mine.

Charles, I need your help once more. If you are thinking as you read this, Fifteen years of silence, then he has the audacity to ask for my help again, all I can say is: Yes it is so. Once again, the choice is yours.

Yesterday was warm and today it seems that we have slipped from spring to summer. There is a garden here, which has become Andre's pride and joy. And mine too, in a different way. The early roses are beginning, Andre tells me, and the lilies promise well. Please come.

Yours in hope,

Francis Dexter.

I remind myself that I *know* nothing. Herbert West was not the most truthful of men. How can I tell whether or not this is also true of Francis Dexter? I cannot. There is no one with whom I can verify his statements. For all I know, Dexter may be an even more practiced deceiver than West. His eloquent, nearly hypnotic sentences tantalize and seduce with references to secrets I have been unable to share with anyone for fifteen years. I recognize this, but have let myself be tantalized, just the same.

As he says, the choice is mine. And ultimately, it must be made on the basis of belief rather than knowledge, just as in 1911, when I followed a fascinating stranger into the unknown. There is no need for further debate with myself. I have decided what I am going to do.

When I go home to Cambridge I will write down all my memories of those days. I want to get them straight, so that when I tell Alma this story I will have the truth in black and white. But now I am as free as I have ever been in my life.

First, I will go to Providence. The roses and lilies in his garden may have faded, but the year turns toward the good darkness and will turn to the light again. It is time to begin.

END

A Note from the Author

I discovered the works of H.P. Lovecraft through a handful of little Ballantine paperbacks whose covers were embellished with pictures of grotesque heads. One was splitting open – despite an iron band and padlock around the forehead – to release a horde of little red bats. Another was a mixture of rat and human, complete with a tail sprouting from the cheek. Over the years, I acquired more paperbacks as I tried to find and read all of HPL's stories. Some of the Ballantine books contained lists of the titles, and I can still see the tick marks I made as I succeeded in tracking down the tales. Only "Herbert West, Reanimator" remains unticked. The occasional comments about this story I came across in books about Lovecraft were disparaging, but that only increased my curiosity about it. Why was it so elusive? I didn't read that story until 1998, when I found it by accident in a library.

The commentators were right – it's not one of Lovecraft's best works. But it has something not often found in HPL – a memorable main character who does more than witness the weird. Herbert West was compelled to reanimate corpses, and the nameless narrator of the story was, apparently, compelled to help him. Why? That's the question I began to answer with this book. I didn't realize it would take three more books to finish the task. I devised a life story and family for Herbert West and sent him on a journey that takes him around the world and ends with a return to Arkham.

Readers familiar with "Herbert West, Reanimator" will recall that the unnamed narrator of that story was also a medical student and, later, a physician. When I decided to write a novel based on the story, I deliberately made my narrator, Charles Milburn, a librarian. I knew I could never do a good job of representing the knowledge and attitude of a medical man of the early 20th century, but I am a librarian. Lovecraft mentioned the Miskatonic University Library in several of his stories, so nothing could be more natural than for Charles to be employed there.

Music I listened to while writing this book: J.S. Bach's *Goldberg Variations*, in performances by Glenn Gould and Murray Perahia, as well as an arrangement for string trio performed by a group called Triskelion. This music found its way into the narrative. Loreena McKennitt's album, *The Mask and the Mirror*, specifically "The Dark Night of the Soul" was a huge influence on the atmosphere and the way the story developed.

For more of my views on writing and other topics, read my blog at http://audreydriscoll.com

Other Books in the Herbert West Series

Book 2. Islands of the Gulf Volume 1, The Journey

To Andre Boudreau, Herbert West is The Doctor, who saved his life in the Great War. Andre will follow him into Hell if necessary. Margaret Bellgarde knows him as Dr. Francis Dexter, attractive but mysterious. One day she will be shocked by what she is willing to do for his sake. But who is he really? He doesn't know – and the possibilities are disturbing.

Book 3. Islands of the Gulf Volume 2, The Treasure

Abandoned and abused, young Herbert West resorts to drastic measures to survive. At Miskatonic University he becomes a scientist who commits crimes and creates monstrosities. Decades later, haunted by his past, he finds safety as Dr. Francis Dexter of Bellefleur Island, but his divided nature threatens those he loves and forces him to face the truth about his healing powers.

Book 4. Hunting the Phoenix

Journalist Alma Halsey chases the story of a lifetime to Providence, Rhode Island and finds more than she expected – an old lover, Charles Milburn, and an old adversary, renegade physician Herbert West, living under the name Francis Dexter. Fire throws her into proximity with them both, rekindling romance and completing a great transformation.

All four books are available as ebooks at Amazon, Barnes & Noble, Kobo, Smashwords and the Apple iBooks store. If you have questions, please contact me at Audrey.d@telus.net

Audrey Driscoll is a librarian and cataloguer (but not at Miskatonic University). She lives, writes and gardens in Victoria, British Columbia.

Preview of Book 2 of the Series
Islands of the Gulf Volume 1, The Journey

Part 1, Andre Boudreau

I'm not the kind of guy who sits down and writes his life story. Other people do it, and good luck to them. The Doctor, now, he's got a story to tell, and I am happy to talk with him about old times if it helps him to remember things for his book. But me, Andre Boudreau, why should I do that? I'm the one who polishes his boots and sews on his buttons, and makes sure the coal is delivered on time. Someone has to do all that, and he's lucky it's me, because I am a man who can do what needs to be done.

A couple of weeks ago he comes to me and says, "Andre, I want you to write down all about your life, everything you can remember."

I see a way to wiggle out of that. "But Doctor, you know I can't remember much from before – "

"Yes, but you can remember what happened *after* that. I know, because I hear you yarning with the tradespeople. So just remember it all in order, and write it down."

"Yarning's different," I say. "You don't have to tell things in order. And you don't have to tell the truth."

He laughed at that. Oh, I know for sure *he* doesn't always tell the truth. I had him there, all right. But he wasn't about to give up on the idea.

"Well, at least start remembering. As for the writing down, it will have to be a collaborative effort. I can think of someone who could help you with that part. But you have to do your own remembering."

"All right, Doctor. But don't expect too much."

He was right, there's a hell of a lot stuffed into my brain. It's like a trunk that's been packed in a hurry by someone who doesn't care. You pull on one thing and six others come flopping out.

I guess I've been thinking about trunks and packing because I just did a lot of that. A few weeks ago, the Doctor and I moved into this house, on College Hill, Providence, Rhode Island. There aren't a lot of miles between here and Arkham, but there were for the Doctor and me, since we left there fourteen years ago, in 1923. A whole world of miles.

You could say we've both been to Hell and back. I didn't see the Devil, but I think he did.

I don't have memories of my childhood. My first memories are of blackness. I came out of blackness. I was a very small thing, a little spark in the blackness. That was all, for a long time.

Then I began to see. Only for short moments, like when there's lightning at night. Except it was slow lightning. I'd open my eyes and see things, but I didn't know what they were. Now I think they were the roof of a tent, the inside of a train, the ceiling of some building. A face. Another face. Faces coming and going. Sometimes I heard groans, screams, someone praying in words I couldn't understand. Maybe it was me. I couldn't feel anything, though. There was no pain. I wasn't even cold. Then the darkness again, for I don't know how long. It wasn't really me who saw and heard these things, just a little part of me acting like a scout for the rest, which was back in the blackness, waiting for the scout to report so it could decide what to do next.

There was one picture clearer than the rest – I saw the angel of death standing before me. He was beautiful and terrible – all white and silver, with eyes like ice. He looked at me for a long time and said, "No. Not this one. He's already dead." So I thought, "There's no need to hold on anymore," and let myself slide back into the blackness. As I went I said goodbye to everything – my childhood, family, comrades, my newly hatched young man's ambitions and lusts. I wasn't going to go back to New Brunswick after the war to show them how things worked in the big world. Goodbye, everyone. Goodbye Maman, Papa, Nicholas, Michel, Roger, Paulette, Marguerite, sweet little Louise. Goodbye, Grassadoo, goodbye Andre. Short but sweet, it was. Now it's all gone.

I don't know how long it lasted. I don't think I'll ever know. But it was nothing. There was no "I" any more. It's like trying to think of what there was, before there was anything. Before God made the world there was nothing, they say. But there was – No, nothing. My mind can't think this thing. So I say only: there was nothing.

Then, my first new memory. It was only a feeling. Hot, like fire. Fire was running all through me. I was a man made of fire and heat, my shape burning a hole in the nothing. A red mist swirled through my head and I could feel my heart pumping. No, *being* pumped, by something outside me. It was like a machine had taken over and was running me, running too hard and hot and jerky. It felt dangerous. It felt *wrong*. It was worse than dying. I was terribly afraid. Maybe I was in Hell and this would go on forever.

Then I opened my eyes. No, that wasn't it. My eyes were opened, like somebody pulled a string. Light stabbed into my head, and the pain it made joined the heat in my body. I saw the angel again and thought, "I must be in Heaven. But why does everything hurt, and why am I so afraid?"

He was different now, not like the death angel I saw before. He was white and golden now. There was a brightness behind his head, and his strange bright eyes seemed to look right into my soul. I was still afraid, but I could feel his hands touching me, cooling the heat in my body. Then I was in a river, moving faster and faster. Was I going to drown? I didn't care any more. It was too much trouble to care. I closed my eyes and gave up. If the angel wanted to, he would save me. If not, it didn't matter.

There is a carved wooden angel in the church at Grassadoo, New Brunswick, where I was born. When I went back there in '23, it was still there. I almost remembered it. When I saw it, I felt my breath go in sharp and I thought, "It's Raphael!" That was my name for him. And my second thought was, "Yes, that's why. That's who he reminded me of."

The carving was very old. It was made from a piece of wood from the beach, and its shape was made by the shape of the wood. So he had short hair, this angel, painted yellow, and a halo that the carver had made from a different piece of wood and stuck on with pegs. His wings were kind of small, but that didn't matter, because they were the right shape, and he wasn't going to fly anywhere. He had bright blue eyes, but the look in them wasn't very angelic. Something about the way the carver had painted them made it look like the angel wanted to fight instead of praying and singing hymns.

One of my younger brothers told me that I used to tell him stories about that angel when we were boys. "You called him Raphael," Michel told me. "And you said you used to argue with him in church."

Well, I couldn't argue with Michel about that. Who knows, maybe I did tell him those things. Michel said I told him I could hear the angel's voice in my head. I would complain to him about things that made me mad, and he would help me.

"How did I say he helped me?" I asked.

"He would tell you the reasons for things. Like when Papa had to shoot your dog. Or when Maurice and Peter drowned in the big storm. You said that Raphael would say to you, 'Are you going to lie down and die because of this, Andre? Because if you do I won't be your friend anymore.'"

So what am I saying here? Yes, there is a wooden angel in the church at Grassadoo. Yes, I'm pretty sure I called him Raphael when I was a boy. And when I woke up again, in 1917, when I came out of the blackness, I thought I recognized him. I just kept looking at him, because that was all I could do. I didn't know who I was, where I was, or why I was there. There was only him.

The strange heat was gone. I almost missed it, because now I could feel pain – four or five different kinds, if I thought about it, or I could just let them mix together into one big pain. I was afraid to move, because some of the pains felt dangerous, like they would get much worse if I gave them a reason to. I could feel liquids oozing out of me in places, soaking into the bedding and making cold spots. Was I still in the river? Maybe I was lying in mud on the shore. But no, there was a ceiling over me, so that couldn't be it.

I looked at that ceiling for a long time. I got to know it really well, the colours, stripes, streaks and knots. It was made of corrugated iron laid on wooden beams. A bright shiny streak in the metal drew my eye. Nearby was a patch of rust that looked like a face with a beard, and a bunch of dark spots, like little black stars. One of the beams was light and plain, another had dark and light stripes, and a third one was all dark, with a couple of knots in it. I counted seven spider webs in the angles between the metal and the beams.

I looked at that ceiling until my eyes got tired and closed. I had a dream about sailing a little silver boat in the sky, with a man who had a bushy red beard.

When I woke up, it was dark. I started to get scared. And mad. Why was I all alone? I knew there was something wrong with me, even if I didn't know what. I was thirsty and I had to piss. "Screw the pain," I thought, and turned my head so I could see more of the place. When I tried to get up I found out that my arms and ankles were held down with clamps. I couldn't get loose, no matter how much I struggled. I felt my bladder let go and that's when I started to yell, like a baby in his crib. I don't know how long I yelled, but nobody came.

When I woke up again, someone was with me. There was still pain, but I could feel heat in the places that hurt –not the dangerous heat like before, but a good heat, as though something was working hard to fix my body. I wasn't thirsty and the sheets were dry. "Someone is helping me," I thought. "Maybe it's the angel."

He was still there, tucking the blankets around me, pulling them up to my chin. That was what woke me up.

I could see him better now, and I wondered – was this really the angel? I didn't think angels wore clothes with buttons. And I didn't think they ever got tired. This man was tired. I could see it in his eyes. That was another thing – his eyes weren't blue, like Raphael's, but grey, the colour of river ice before it melts in spring.

He must have seen me looking at him, and he spoke to me for the first time.

"You're going to live, I think. I wasn't sure at first, but it's been twelve hours now. The hemorrhaging has stopped and you're a little stronger. Tomorrow I'll move you to a place where you can be looked after properly. Can you speak? What's your name? Can you tell me that?"

I couldn't say a thing. I had forgotten how to talk. I could understand his words, but I didn't know how to make any myself. And my name? I didn't know that either, and that scared me all over again. He must have seen that, because he touched my shoulder and said,

"Never mind. It's too early for that. Enough that you're alive. Don't worry, I'll look after you. I want you to live. You'll be the tenth – one of a select company. Go to sleep now. I'll be back later."

I didn't want to sleep. I wanted to think about all this. I would be the tenth what? What was wrong with me? Who was he? And who was I? But I felt a little bee sting in my arm, and then I was sliding asleep.

This time I dreamt that I was on a train, going up a mountain. Part of me was trying to enjoy the trip, but another part kept wondering what would happen when I got to the top. Would the train go roaring down the other side? It went slower and slower. Then there was a jolt and a shake, and I was flying. I woke up, and it was morning, and all the birds were singing.

****

Notes from the Case-Book of Herbert West.

August 16, 1917, 2:20 a.m.
Subject #17.8.5R (non-experimental)

Subject was dead approx. 6 hours. Time between administration of fluid and revivification: 95 minutes. Time elapsed since revivification: 12 hours.

Vital signs: respiration normal; heart rate, 70; blood pressure, 120/60.

General appearance: good.

Injuries: trauma of lower left abdomen, right thigh and left arm. No broken bones. No foreign matter left in wounds. Instilled regenerating substance. Installed drains. Subject stabilized. No further loss of fluids.

Prognosis: excellent.

Cognitive abilities: unknown as yet; subject unable to speak.

****

When I opened my eyes again, I knew I was somewhere else. The light was different – daylight, not lamplight like before. I was in a big bright room with windows. And other people. I could see the end of a metal bed, past where my feet were. In the distance, another bed. Grey blankets. I turned my head one way and the other. More metal beds and grey blankets, and in each bed, a man. "Hospital," I thought. Then, "What's a hospital? Why did I think that? Who are all these men? Who am I?"

There were people moving around the room. Women, dressed in blue and white. "Mothers," I thought. But where was he? "I'll be back." That was what he'd said. But now I was somewhere else. Would he be able to find me? That was very important. So when one of the mothers came close to me I raised my hand and tried to grab her sleeve.

"Ou est Monsieur L'Ange?" I asked. My voice felt rusty, and she didn't seem to have heard me, so I said it again, trying hard to talk louder. She turned and bent over me.

"She isn't a mother at all," I thought. "She's too young." I could see smooth brown hair under the veil she wore. "So she's a nun," I thought. Then, "What's a nun?" Her eyes were light brown, with little green flecks.

"Oh, you can speak now," she said. "That's good. I'll tell Major West. He specially asked us to tell him when you started to talk."

Of course she spoke in English, and even though I could understand her, I couldn't answer in English, only in French. *"Qui est Major West?"* I asked. But she was gone.

When he came, he spoke French to me. At first I couldn't understand him, because of his strange accent. Plus I had just woken up from a long sleep, so I was feeling stupid. I asked him the first thing that popped into my fuzzy head.

"Is your name Raphael?"

He smiled. "No. My name is Herbert West. I'm your doctor. And you, it seems, are Andre Boudreau, from Grassadoo, New Brunswick."

He tripped over "Grassadoo," just enough to make me smile too and nearly forget that the name Andre Boudreau didn't mean a thing to me. He might have been introducing a stranger.

"If you say so," I said. "I don't know who I am. Or where I am. Or anything."

"It's all right, Andre," he said. "You're perfectly safe with me. I'll help you get better. So don't worry." He touched my shoulder and smiled. And I stopped being scared and went back to sleep.

That was the first time I had this dream: a rutted country road, curving around the side of a hill, and a girl running along it, crying. The girl is my sister, Marguerite, carrying a bundle of food from our mother. "*Maman* said that no child of hers would ever leave her house hungry." So sad, her little face was, so sad.

****

Notes from the Case Book

August 28, 1917
Subject #17.8.5R (Andre Boudreau)

Subject appears to be a complete amnesiac. Cognitive abilities may be normal. Speaks English and French (New Brunswick dialect? Odd pronunciation). Short term memory good. Retains knowledge of concepts – hospital, war, army, etc. – but no specifics about himself.

Physical condition improving rapidly. All wounds nearly healed.

Must find reason to keep him here. Amnesia might preclude return to action – verify. Is he a tabula rasa? Experiments with his mental development might prove interesting.

Are you eager to proceed? Go to: http://audreydriscoll.com/the-herbert-west-trilogy/